ONE

E ven on a good day I don't enjoy being shot at. Been there, done that, and it bloody hurts.

I wasn't kidding myself this was going to be a good day.

Maybe that had something to do with the fact that my gun hand—my right —was securely handcuffed to a reinforced briefcase weighing probably twenty-five pounds.

That in itself wouldn't have been so bad. I'd put in enough time on the range to be proficient with either hand. My left wrist, however, was just as firmly handcuffed to Sean Meyer's right. Neither of us was exactly overjoyed by this state of affairs.

Especially when everything was about to go to shit around us.

We were on a quiet street of generic storefronts, parked cars dotted along either side. There were people nearby but nobody gave us a second glance.

And then, just when the tension began to give me heartburn, a dozen rapid shots cracked out further down the street. I was half expecting them, but still they startled me. I forced out a strangled yelp, even though I knew they were scare shots, fired from a single weapon rather than part of an exchange, designed purely to start a stampede.

They got the job done.

Sean wheeled and I had to swing fast to stay with him. His eyes were everywhere. He'd already drawn the Glock 17 semiautomatic, hefted it in his left hand, but he stayed on his feet, upright, alert.

Next to him, useless as a stuffed lemon chained to that damn case, I felt helplessly exposed. I willed myself calm, knowing I *had* to rely on Sean to protect me—to protect both of us.

1

People started to stream past us. Some screaming, some shouting—unintelligible words filled with a contagious panic. I tugged deliberately at his arm.

"Sean! We need to get out of here—"

"Shut up."

It was the vicious tone more than the words that shocked me into silence. As we turned, I caught a glimpse of figures crossing between the buildings. They were dressed in jeans and loose shirts like the rest of the crowd. Unlike everybody else, though, they moved with direction and purpose, and they were armed.

I didn't speak, didn't distract Sean, but by the way he tensed I knew he'd seen them, too.

His brows were drawn down flat in concentration, making his harsh face seem colder than usual. Cold enough to make me shiver.

He muscled me sideways effortlessly, snatching roughly at the cuffs so that it jarred my whole arm. I should have been protesting at this point, but I said nothing. It took willpower to remain passive.

Sean went down on one knee, pulled me into a crouch alongside him, using an old parked Chevy for cover. We stayed up by the front wheel where the engine block provided more of a shield.

More people sprinted by. A man tripped and went sprawling right behind us. Sean ignored him. He had the gun up in front of him, head tilted to best utilise his dominant eye.

A target broke cover, dodging through the remnants of the fleeing people. Sean fired on him without hesitation, four fast shots that somehow threaded through the crowd, tracked and hit. He went down.

Before the first man finished falling another had appeared, jinking between parked cars on the opposite side of the street. He had a machine pistol held at waist-level, and he strafed us as he ran. Sean held his nerve, his position and his aim, taking only two rounds to drop him.

The third and fourth assailants came in together from oblique angles, taking advantage of any tunnelling in Sean's focus. Sean twisted, forgetting about my dead weight on the end of his right arm. He growled in frustration as his first shots went wide, taking an extra fraction of a second he barely had time for.

2

His breath hissed out as he swung his arm over the top of me and fired again, so close I felt the gases blast past my cheek, heard the brutal snap of the report clatter in my ears. The hot dead brass spun out and scattered around me. One casing hit the side of my neck, burning the skin. Instinct told me to stay on my feet. Instead I dropped flat, trying to get my hands over my head. Not easy with unwieldy objects attached to both arms.

Then I heard the Glock's action lock back empty.

I hadn't been counting the rounds, but I couldn't believe Sean let the gun run dry in these circumstances.

I raised my head, my locked-together fingers hampering his reload. Sean hit the release to drop the magazine and shoved the Glock, butt upwards, into the vee at the back of his bent leg. He snatched the spare mag out of his belt and slapped it home with the palm of his hand, then pulled the gun free and flicked the slide release awkwardly to snap the first round up into the chamber.

The whole operation had taken maybe a couple of seconds, left-handed, smooth and without a slip, but he was staring at me as if I'd just tried to get him killed.

As if I wanted him dead ...

"Come on—up!" he commanded, almost wrenching my arm out of its socket as he dragged me upright. The briefcase dangled painfully from the short cuff chain, gouging at my right wrist. I groped for the case's handle, stumbling as we fell back into the mouth of an alley.

The expanding slap of a long gun rebounded between the brick buildings, and then they came at us thick and fast, half a dozen armed men, experienced pros, motivated, confident.

It was always going to be a no-win situation.

Sean went to the wall that allowed him to keep his left hand free, facing outwards, elbowing me round behind him. He fired at anything that showed itself past the edge of the scarred brickwork, dialled in now, emotions buttoned down tight.

And this time he dropped the magazine out before the last round was fired, keeping the Glock's working parts in play. He shoved the gun into his belt to reach for a reload.

I stayed close up behind him—I had no other choice. But I had my face slightly turned towards the back of the alley, and for this reason I saw a door open halfway back, a man emerge with a

3

gun in his right fist. He was tall, rangy, his arms already raised to firing position, and he was smiling.

I sucked in an audible breath. Sean heard it, head snapping round. For the merest fraction of a second he hesitated, then tried to hurry the magazine into the pistol grip and fumbled it.

The man's smile became broader. He fired.

Not at Sean, but at me.

I felt the punch of the impact in my chest, high on the right, where he knew the round would drill diagonally through ribs, lungs and heart. Where he knew it would do the most harm.

Bastard.

I gasped but couldn't get my breath, started to slide down the rough wall as my legs folded under me. Sean turned into my body as if to stop me falling. His face was an inch from mine. I stared into eyes dark as mourning and saw nothing reflected back at me.

That hurt worse than the shot.

His left hand was empty. It snaked under the tails of my shirt. I felt his fingers close around the SIG Sauer I wore just behind my right hip, pulling it free.

He knew I carried the gun ready, with a round jacked up into the chamber. There was no safety.

He fired as soon as the weapon cleared my torso, four rounds straight into the centre of the smiling man's body mass.

As the guy went down I just had time to note that he wasn't smiling any more.

TWO

C'mon, Charlie, it was just an exercise," Parker Armstrong said. "The whole point was for you to make things as difficult for Sean as possible, really test the guy out."

I remembered my faked mini-hysteria, the deliberate inaction that had stuck in my craw to maintain. I looked down at the coffee cup clasped between my tense fingers. "Well, I did that all right."

My boss's smile was dust dry. "I'll bet. But Sean passed the course—top ten per cent."

I remembered the shots that had threaded through the crowd. That they'd been accurate was not the point. Collateral damage was not supposed to figure in our line of work.

"Yeah, but—before—we both know Sean would have been in the top *two* per cent, easy."

Before.

It was how we'd taken to referring to Sean's near-fatal shooting and the resultant coma that had locked him down for nearly four months. Before he'd nearly died and then come back to us changed not just physically and mentally but emotionally, too.

Before the part of him I knew—the part that really knew me—*had* died, in a way.

"It's only been five months since he woke up and he still passed fit, Charlie. That's impressive, by anyone's standards."

I hunched my shoulders. "You didn't see him, Parker—the way he looked at me ..."

And the way he didn't.

Parker leaned forwards on my sofa, elbows resting on his knees, and pinned me with a level gaze. "There's no point in taking a Stress Under Fire course unless it lives up to its name.

Your job was to drive him hard, to look for the cracks." His voice softened sympathetically. "Nobody escapes unscathed, Charlie— that's the point of it. Sure, it was never going to be a cakewalk for either of you, but I knew no one else would push him harder. You're the one who knows him best."

"I *knew* him best," I corrected. "But that's not true any more."

We sat there in the high-ceilinged living room of the New York City apartment. Parker looked at home there, but his family owned the building so I suppose he had every right.

He'd offered it to us at a ridiculously subsidised rent as part of the relocation package that had tempted Sean and me away from the UK in the first place. Otherwise there was no way we could afford to rent within sight of Central Park, even if you did practically have to stand on a chair to see the greenery.

I glanced up, found him still watching me. There was something both soothing and unnerving about Parker's calm silence. "The old Sean would never have let them shoot me in the chest," I said at last. It sounded almost plaintive.

Parker smiled more fully then. It transformed his rather sombre face, took half a decade off his age. "C'mon, Charlie, Tony's been waiting to get his own back ever since you shot him in the balls last year."

I felt a sheepish grin of my own rise up. "Hey, that was just his bad luck. I was aiming for low-centre-body mass, just like he advocates—the most static part of a moving target. He should just be thankful we weren't using live rounds."

"As should you," he said. "How're the ribs?"

"Black and blue, thanks."

"Yeah, those sims sting like a bastard, don't they?"

The Simunitions training rounds used on the SUF course were designed to give participants a nasty and painful reminder of the consequences faced in the field. Heavy or protective clothing was disallowed by the instructors, so there was nothing to lessen the impact. As with the real thing, nobody wanted to take a hit.

The sims had the advantage that they could be fired from a replacement barrel in the shooter's own weapon. They were the most realistic training round I'd encountered short of live ammunition.

Getting shot in the chest had been an experience that left me bruised and aching, but it had only been a day or so ago. In a

6

week the visible marks would have faded like they never were. Only the implanted reflex would remain.

I drained my coffee, rose stiffly and reached for Parker's empty cup too. He'd come straight from the office and was wearing his usual formal dark suit. It was well-cut without being flashy. I could have used the same words to describe Parker himself—everything about him capable of blending into the background. Unless you looked closely at his eyes. Then you realised he'd seen and done more than you ever wanted to know about.

Sean had eyes like those.

I took the cups into the apartment's kitchen area, dumped them in the sink. When I came back, I found my boss standing by the tall windows looking out across the Upper East Side. His hands were in his pockets, but I knew from the angle of his shoulders that he wasn't anywhere near as relaxed as the pose suggested.

Parker wasn't only my employer and, I suppose, my landlord—over the course of Sean's incapacity he'd become a friend. He could have become much more than that, if we'd let it happen.

He turned around. "So, how are things between the two of you?"

I shoved my own hands into the back pockets of my jeans, wished I hadn't when I saw Parker divine the defensiveness of the gesture. "OK-ish," I said. "Intellectually, Sean accepts I'm not the girl he remembers from the army—the one he thinks betrayed him. He accepts that we moved on, found each other again, came over here together and are sharing this place, working for you."

"But?"

"*Intellectually*, he accepts it, but emotionally?" I shrugged, shook my head. "That's another thing altogether."

Parker stepped in suddenly, reached out and took my upper arms. His grasp was light, but sufficient to stop me getting my hands free without a struggle. I didn't try.

"Look, Charlie, if things have gotten too … difficult here, you can always move out. I know the two of you are not sleeping together—"

I did wrench free then. "Sean told you that?"

7

"He didn't have to," he said gently. "This is a two-bedroom apartment, and you've moved your gear into the second bedroom."

For a second I thought about telling Parker that Sean had become a violently restless sleeper, racked by desperate nightmares as if back in the coma's grip. Besides, he'd shown no inclination for intimacy—not with me anyway.

How can I share a bed with someone who not only doesn't love me, but doesn't really even like me any more?

I shrugged. "He snores."

Parker placed his hands back on my shoulders, not calling me on the lie. "Hey, Charlie, I know it's tough," he said softly. "But if the both of you need some space, some time, I have room at my place. You're welcome to stay as long as you need."

My throat tightened. "Parker—"

Off to my left, the apartment front door slammed. I jerked back automatically, but was aware of the shocked guilt plastered across my face when Sean appeared in the living room doorway.

He was dressed in his running gear and dripping with sweat. No longer as wasted as when he'd woken, Sean had worked hard to rebuild his muscle bulk. But his right leg was dragging a little as it did when he pushed himself to the point of exhaustion. He'd done a lot of that.

The gunshot wound to his left temple had disrupted his brain's control over his right side. Remastering simple coordination was just one of the battles still raging.

Sean saw the pair of us, standing together like that and his eyes flicked over us with unreadable intensity. I thought I caught just a flicker of contempt.

"Hi, Sean," Parker said with remarkable composure. "Charlie and I were just discussing your Stress Under Fire course. Sounds like you aced it. Tony says it's the first time he's ever been taken down by someone using a New York reload."

A New York reload was simply to pull a second loaded gun when the first was out of action. Simple, but effective.

"It wasn't against the letter of the rules," Sean said shortly. "The spirit, maybe, but it got the job done and that's what counts, right?"

"Right," Parker echoed, wary of his tone. He nodded towards Sean's clothing. "How's it going?"

"Fine," Sean said, straightening as if in the presence of a senior officer. "Just done a quick five miles. No problem."

I frowned, but Sean nailed me with a single, deadly glance which Parker deliberately ignored.

"That's great, Sean. You're looking good."

He started for the door, stopped after only a few strides, as if changing his mind about something.

"Ah, Charlie, I need for you to come in early tomorrow. We've been tasked with security for a client who's attending a big fundraiser down in New Orleans next week. Some of the areas worst hit by Hurricane Katrina are still derelict and it seems the glitterati finally decided to do something about it. They've organised some big charity gala, plenty of feel-good largesse and displays of ostentatious wealth—including high-profile security. Nothing too taxing."

"So why the need to contract out?" I asked. "Don't they have their own people?"

"Not necessarily," Parker said. "And you were specially requested—an old client. He reckons you saved his ass once before, and he wants you assigned this time around."

In the periphery of my vision I was aware of Sean shifting impatiently.

"OK," I said quickly, curiosity curbed. I checked my watch automatically. "I'll start putting together the usual security inventory first thing. Be a nice chance to see if that new comms gear is all it's cracked up to be."

"How many on the team?" It was Sean who asked the question, but my eyes flew to Parker's.

"That's up to Charlie," he said, impassive.

He's not ready!

If not now, then when?

Sean watched the silent exchange with narrowed eyes, his body tense. For a long extended moment, nobody spoke.

I swallowed. "Can we ... talk about this when I've had a chance to look over the logistics?" I said then, keeping my voice as neutral as possible. "See how many people we actually need?"

Parker considered for a moment, then turned to Sean. "You feel ready to come back?"

I failed to hide my dismay at Parker's question. A mistake on my part.

Sean turned on me. "What?" he demanded roughly. "With respect, Charlie, wind your bloody neck in." Those dark eyes fenced with mine, filled with an impotent fury and something else, too—fear.

I held my tongue. I'd been injured in the past and faced the sheer frustration of needing to get back on the job—long before anyone else believed I was fit to do so.

"Yeah, I'm ready," he said. "Especially for a job that's 'nothing too taxing', eh?" He might have got me with that argument, had he not added, "Besides, if *she's* up to it, then so am I."

I swear I saw Parker flinch. I know I did.

"Whatever personal issues you have with Charlie, keep them outside the office," he said, pleasant but icy at the same time. "Charlie's a first-class close-protection operative, as she's proved on more occasions than I care to number."

Sean's nod was fractional at best, and aimed solely at Parker.

"Looks like I'll see the both of you in the office tomorrow morning," Parker said. He smiled. "Good to have you back, Sean."

Sean didn't say anything after he'd gone, just headed for the shower.

I was left standing by the window, looking down onto the afternoon traffic, with a sense of foreboding deep in my chest that had nothing to do with being shot, even by a bullet filled only with paint.

Parker had taken Sean on as a partner. As far as many people were concerned, I'd just hitched along for the ride. Armstrong-Meyer held the enviable position of being regarded as one of the best close-protection agencies in the States—if not worldwide. Sean was a vital, visible, part of that. Parker would, I recognised, always take his side. He had no choice.

But I did.

And if things didn't improve between Sean and me—maybe not back to the way things were, but at least to the point of easy civility—then one of us was going to have to quit.

Didn't take a genius to work out who.

THREE

A week later, I stood leaning against the front end of a GMC Yukon on the tarmac at Lakefront Airport in New Orleans, watching a Citation X executive jet taxi in from the main runway.

The temperature was in the low seventies and not too humid, which was apparently about average for this part of Louisiana in late September. If it hadn't been for the squadrons of little flying thingies surfing the air currents coming in off Lake Pontchartrain, it would have been no hardship to wait out there in the sunshine.

I'd chosen a gunmetal grey trouser suit cut so I could move without restriction, but smart enough to look inconspicuous among the kind of people who travelled by private plane. I'd had the jacket tailored, with a row of tiny weights sewn into the hem so it draped well over the gun behind my right hip. The collar of the white shirt I wore under the suit was crisp enough to conceal scars both old and new at my neck.

Sean Meyer stood—somewhat pointedly, I thought—on the other side of the SUV. He refused to lean, but had the relaxed slouch any former soldier would recognise. He was wearing a dark suit that fitted him a touch more loosely than it once had, with a narrow black tie and Aviator sunglasses. What I could see of his expression was stony, despite his minor victory.

I'd tried in vain to talk Parker out of sending Sean on this job. My arguments were sound. Sean wasn't fully fit, wasn't fully ready—mentally prepared—for the role of executive-protection officer. It was a miracle that his brain had reforged many of the shattered connections while he was unconscious, but he still had a long way to go.

There were holes in his memory that didn't only concern our relationship. He thought like the Special Forces sergeant he'd once been, not the bodyguard he'd since become.

"Then it will be your job to retrain him," Parker said when I'd tackled him about it the day after he'd come to the apartment.

I let my eyebrows rise. "With a live client in play?"

"You've done the security inventory yourself on this one, Charlie. You know it's a minimum-risk assignment. We've had no threat intel, nothing to suggest this is anything other than a weekend of good-natured excess in the name of a worthy cause."

But I knew him well enough to recognise when he was being cagey. "And?"

He sighed, the corner of his mouth twitching. "There will be a lot of VIPs there. And that means industry people alongside them—*our* industry. It will be good for Sean, and the company, to have him *seen* to be back on his feet."

I frowned. *But he's not—not completely.*

I didn't have to say it. Parker simply held up his hand and moved back behind his desk. The way he took his seat spelled an end to the discussion.

"He can stay in the background, handle logistics—no heavy lifting, OK?"

"And if by any chance there *is* some heavy lifting to be done?"

"You'll cope." Parker's eyes flicked over my face and he sighed. "One way or another, you two are going to have to learn to get along," he said. "Give it your best shot."

Give it your best shot.

I'd thought about those words a lot over the past few days, ever since Sean and I had flown down to New Orleans and begun double-checking the advance arrangements for the After Katrina Foundation event.

I'd tried very hard to keep things matter-of-fact between us as we ran over the routes we'd need to take from airport to hotel, and hotel to various functions. We noted traffic bottlenecks and areas where we'd be most vulnerable to hijack. We knew which police departments had jurisdiction and their average response time to call-out. We knew locations of the nearest ambulance station and fire department, the best trauma centre, the nearest emergency dentist and late-night pharmacy.

We'd spent an entire day going over the hotel in detail, paying particular attention to where the bad guys could get in as well as where we could hustle our principal out of there if the need arose. Just because we weren't expecting trouble didn't mean we had to be lax about it.

We also introduced ourselves to the in-house security guys both there and at the main venues. They were mostly ex-cop or ex-military, big guys with quiet voices and watchful eyes.

They all naturally assumed that Sean was in charge and he let them do so, which pissed me off royally even if he did constantly refer to my opinion. I recognised he was still readjusting, and by the end of it reluctantly had to admit that at least he was treating me as an equal rather than a subordinate.

I supposed it was uneasy progress, of a sort.

I'd discovered when Sean came out of his coma the bullet that had so nearly killed him had stripped his memory of the past four years. He didn't remember us getting together after our disastrous time in the army. He didn't remember finding out that I wasn't to blame for ruining both our careers, that I'd nearly died for him.

He certainly didn't know that I'd killed for him.

Or that I'd brought him to the brink of fatherhood. I hadn't exactly been overjoyed to discover my unexpected pregnancy, but miscarrying the baby before I'd found a way to break the news to Sean had been a numbing blow. He'd found out, of course. It had never been my intention to keep it from him indefinitely, but the circumstances had been less than ideal. We might have struggled to overcome that, even without our current state of ... alienation.

I didn't even know if he recalled anything about the child we'd lost. He'd never mentioned it, and I—coward that I was—had clung gratefully to that omission. It might have emphasised the ties between us, but at the same time it might have driven him further away. After all, he had woken with a false picture of me as a calculating schemer, something this would not help to address.

I lived in a world of constant risk assessment. This was not a risk I wanted to take.

On the Lakefront tarmac, the Citation powered down and the door cracked open. I straightened away from the car, but Sean snapped almost to attention as a slim well-preserved man with silver hair and an expensive tan came bounding down the steps.

Blake Dyer had been born into money and married into it deeper still. His only ambition, apart from living the good life,

13

had been to keep the family fortune intact enough to pass on to his own offspring. This, I gathered, he'd already achieved some years previously through a network of offshore bank accounts and trust funds, so that he now considered himself in well-earned retirement.

He was the sort of guy I would have loved to hate, or at least quietly despise, but it was hard not to like Blake Dyer. He had charm and wit, and he was unfailingly courteous to other people's staff.

Now, he made a point of speaking briefly to the plane's crew who were decanting his luggage from the hold to the rear of the Yukon. Then he came forwards to greet us with all the energy of a man who plays tennis or golf four days a week.

"Charlie!" he said, pumping my proffered hand with both his own, then impulsively pulling me close enough to air-kiss either cheek. "It's good to see you again, young lady, and looking as cool, calm and collected as ever."

"And you, sir. Thank you for requesting me for this."

He smiled, flirty as always. "How could I ask for anyone else?" He turned to Sean. "Charlie saved my life," he said. "A hell of a woman."

Sean allowed himself a small smile as I introduced them, adding. "Sean is Parker Armstrong's partner."

Dyer's eyebrows quirked. "Sending out the big guns, huh?" he said. "Well, I'm honoured to make your acquaintance, Sean."

"Thank you, sir. We'll do our best to keep you safe."

Dyer's smile broadened. "Ah, you don't need to flatter my ego," he said. "We both know this is something of a dick-waving contest—if you'll pardon my language, Charlie."

I hid a smile as I opened the rear door and ushered our principal inside, following him in. Sean got behind the wheel. The muted rush of the air-conditioning was louder than the engine.

We rolled across the airport land, a man-made peninsula stretching out into the lake, and pulled out past the restored art deco terminal into traffic. Despite the US Marine Corps T-45 Goshawks and the sleek modern aircraft, the airport itself still had the feel of the pre-war years to it. I half expected to see gleaming old DC-3 Dakotas and gangster cars with running boards.

Maybe it was just that New Orleans had a mixed-up vibe between the historic and the modern, as if it couldn't quite decide what to let go of and what to hold onto.

"'Dick-waving'?" I queried. "If there's going to be much of that, I want hazard pay."

Dyer laughed again, batted a hand. "You know what I mean—all posturing and posing," he said. "These days, you're not a big shot unless you have a half-dozen bodyguards shadowing you everywhere—even to the john."

I nodded, muffling a mild exasperation. I'd lost count of the number of times I'd been hired as a status symbol or executive toy. It never failed to put my back up. While the idle rich were showing off, I could have been looking after someone who really needed it.

"If I'd known," I said dryly, "I would have brought a bigger team."

"I'm happy to go for quality rather than quantity," Dyer said. "And my wife insisted I have some protection before she let me out on my own."

We chatted on the drive in. Mrs Dyer, I discovered, had stayed in Miami to be on hand for the imminent arrival of their first grandchild. By the time Dyer had finished telling me all about it, we were swinging into the hotel entrance. Sean pulled up under the portico and we debussed without drama. Dyer's luggage was handed off to a hovering bellboy—a college kid we'd screened well enough to know he was about to flunk history and had a dog named Blue.

The hotel, located in the historic French Quarter, was swanky by anyone's standards. Dyer's suite had a private balcony overlooking the Mississippi. We'd already cleared it and checked him in prior to his arrival. As we crossed the lobby I gave him his key. All he had to do was walk straight to the elevators and ride on up.

If only things were so simple.

"Hey, Blake, you son of a gun!" called a booming voice. "Damn, I'm glad to see you here."

We turned as a single unit. A tall, almost gaunt man in a handmade cream suit was striding towards us, a linebacker bodyguard keeping pace at his shoulder. The tall man's smile engaged his whole face and his hand was outstretched in greeting, but I still stepped in front of Dyer before either of them could intercept us.

"Relax, Charlie, he's not going to bite," Dyer murmured, moving out past me. And louder, clasping the man's hand, "Tom. Good to see you."

But I'd placed the newcomer even before Dyer spoke his name. Tom O'Day, electronics billionaire. Probably gazillionaire, if the fawning of the financial press was anything to go by. In a volatile economy, it seemed he could do no wrong. You certainly saw his company's stylised dragon logo just about everywhere.

Maybe his wealth and power was the attraction to the model-thin blonde who followed him across the lobby. She was almost as tall as O'Day, most of it leg, although there was a generous dollop of chest thrown in for good measure. On a figure so slender it looked out of proportion, like her airbag had gone off.

The bodyguard's name was Hobson, I recalled. He was an ex-Marine who'd been with O'Day for a decade. No doubt this familiarity explained why O'Day ignored his presence, but introduced the blonde to Dyer simply as "Autumn".

I caught Sean's eye out of habit, expecting to see a cynical glint. Instead, I saw just a glimmer of calculated interest.

I looked away, aware of a certain hollow feeling just below my ribs. Where once Sean and I had been in tune, now I found myself surprised and occasionally disappointed by his actions. Whoever he'd become, I didn't really know him any more.

I let my eyes roam the lobby. O'Day talked like a man who thought a lot of what he had to say. But as he was the driving force behind this fundraiser I was prepared to give him the benefit of the doubt—for now.

Dyer's face had taken on the look of polite concentration that people get when they're being lectured by an evangelist. From the way O'Day poured himself into his subject, his self-made fortune was not hard to understand. He gave everything to it. The force of his will was almost tangible.

I mentally turned down the volume, listening for keywords without giving the rest of it chance to swamp me. I did another visual sweep.

Outside the main doors another limo had pulled up—a stretch Cadillac Escalade with gold trim just about everywhere it was possible to have it.

16

A young guy with the loose square frame of an athlete climbed out. He was early twenties, with stylised facial hair around his mouth, oversize designer shades, and trendy clothing about two sizes too big. His gold jewellery rivalled the Escalade for gaudiness. A white kid who desperately wanted to be black.

If Blake Dyer had inherited most of his wealth and O'Day had built his up over decades, I judged this young man had come into a lot of money very fast and was still experimenting wildly on the best way to spend it.

Photographers appeared out of nowhere, snapping furiously around him like a pack of starving dogs around a butcher's cart. He ignored them with the blasé air of someone for whom this was such a regular occurrence he didn't even see them any more.

His security guys were large and obvious. The leader elbowed a path to the door and ushered him inside. The youngster paused just inside the entrance, making the most of it.

The commotion finally penetrated O'Day's focused spiel. He turned and caught sight of the newcomer and his whole body reacted like he'd just seen the *Mona Lisa* for the first time.

"Gabe, my boy!" he cried. "Glad you could make it. Come and meet one of our benefactors—a very dear friend of mine, Blake Dyer."

Gabe came ambling over, an odd way of walking that moved his shoulders but not his head. He hooked one arm of his shades into the neck of his shirt and smiled at Dyer.

"Blake, I'm sure this young superstar needs no introduction. This is Gabe Baptiste." He did not seem to get the irony of his words. "Finest baseball player of his generation—the next Tom Seaver."

Dyer held out his hand, but Gabe Baptiste had suddenly frozen in mid-stretch. I was close enough to see his pupils dilate, the hairs riffle along his forearms. I recognised it as pure, instinctive flight-response.

I glanced at Dyer. He was staring in bemusement at the guy and clearly had absolutely no idea what should have caused this kind of reaction.

My eyes flicked back, but this time I tracked Baptiste's sightline and realised he wasn't looking at my principal. His gaze had slid past Dyer's right shoulder and was locked, firm and terrified, on Sean.

17

FOUR

Baptiste is a last-minute substitution," Parker said. "Trust me, I had no prior knowledge of his involvement or I would have warned you."

"Warned me about what, Parker?" I demanded. "All I know is, as soon as Baptiste clapped eyes on Sean he panicked like someone had stuck a cattle prod up his backside. I'm amazed his goons didn't draw on us."

I was in my room at the hotel, which adjoined Blake Dyer's. Sean had the room directly across the hall. He was currently conferring with our client about his schedule for the next few days, in case there were any other surprises. I'd left Sean to go through the details—tried to make it seem that I had absolute confidence in him. It was not an easy façade to maintain.

"O'Day had the reigning NASCAR champion, Lyle Junior, all lined up as his star attraction," Parker said. "Then Junior hit the wall on turn three in California doing about one-ninety-five last weekend and rolled a half-dozen times. Won't be out of traction for a month. They had to find a big-name draw to take his place in a hurry. Just so happens that Gabe Baptiste was born right there in New Orleans—in St Bernard Parish—before he got out and made good. I can see why he was considered the ideal choice."

"I realise this Baptiste guy is some kind of hot-shot ball player, but what's his connection to Sean?"

Parker's dry chuckle came clearly down the phone line from New York. "You're never going to pass for American if you don't understand our national obsession with baseball, Charlie."

"Why? It's exactly like the game they foisted on the girls at school who weren't tough enough for hockey, only we called it rounders. This is just played by guys in old men's underwear, with frequent ad breaks and more spitting."

I thought back to my schooldays. *Well, OK, maybe not* more *spitting …*

He laughed out loud. "Don't let anyone hear you say that or they'll practically throw your ass in jail."

"Well, it won't be the first time," I said dryly. "And I know I can rely on you to post bail, can't I?"

"You can rely on me for anything, Charlie," he said, and the sudden intensity in his voice made the blood drop out of my face. "There isn't much I wouldn't do for you—you must know that."

"Parker …" My voice caught. I swallowed. "Please, this is hard enough without—"

"I know, I know." I heard him sigh. "I'm sorry. I promise I'll try to keep things strictly professional—most of the time, anyhow. Good enough?"

"Good enough," I agreed. I cleared my throat. "So, what's the story on Baptiste and Sean?"

A pause. "What's Sean got to say about it?"

The strings of my patience stretched and frayed. "What do you *think* he's got to say? He has no idea."

No idea of the UK close-protection agency he'd founded more than five years before, or even the principals he'd guarded twelve months ago. Almost his entire career since leaving the army was one giant void. The occasional fractured flashes of recall confused more than they enlightened.

At the other end of the line, Parker gave another sigh. It was late afternoon in New Orleans, an hour ahead of New York. Standing by the long window I leaned my forehead against the glass. Outside, the sky over the Gulf of Mexico was washed with pinks and pale blues and flittered with seabirds. A poetic dying fall towards evening.

Parker would still be at work in his corner office with a stunning view of a different kind—out over Midtown Manhattan. His desk was positioned facing inwards with his back to the vee of the corner. When we first moved over to the States it took me a while to figure out why he ignored the view, until I realised Parker was a New Yorker born and bred. I still wasn't quite that nonchalant about the cityscape that had become my adopted home.

But I wouldn't have sat with my back to a window, either.

19

"OK, Charlie," he said at last. "When Sean and I went into business together—when I offered him the partnership—we agreed on full disclosure. I read him in on the clients *I'd* never work with again. He did the same from his end. The name Gabe Baptiste was top of his list."

"Why? What did he do?"

"I don't know."

"So when you say 'full disclosure' it was something of an oxymoron—like 'military intelligence'?"

"At the time, I admired his discretion." I heard the suggestion of a smile in his voice. "Just telling me the guy's name was enough. I blacklisted him. Cost me, too. When Baptiste made the play offs earlier this year and had that crazy fan stalking him, we were asked by his manager to provide a protection detail. I turned him down."

Earlier this year ...

"That was when Sean was ... in his coma," I said slowly.

I almost heard Parker shrug. "What difference does that make?"

None at all, I realised. His sense of honour was one of the things I admired most about Parker. He was the dictionary definition of a straight arrow. And if we'd come close to nudging a personal line, the two of us, we had not actually crossed over it. Even if the temptation had been tantalisingly strong.

The Sean I'd known had not possessed the same kind of scruples, was not above bending the rules if it got the job done. Between them, he and Parker had been two halves of a whole, dark and light. Where Parker went around, Sean went straight through. Conscience and muscle. It made them a good team. I'd once thought the same about Sean and me.

Even if my conscience probably wasn't quite as pristine as it once was.

"So you've no idea what Baptiste might have done that was bad enough to get himself on the shit-list?" I pressed.

"Soon as I heard his name today, I got Bill onto it," Parker said. Bill Rendelson was Parker's electronic surveillance and security expert and all-round major-domo, an embittered former operative who'd lost his right arm on a close-protection job some years previously. If his attitude was anything to go by, he missed both it and the action every single day.

"And?"

"We only know the rough date of when Sean was last in New Orleans—I checked with his old agency in London. They tell me he was the only one who had the full details, and he didn't share."

I murmured, "Now why doesn't that surprise me?" But if Parker heard, he didn't respond to the jibe.

"All we know is that Baptiste was a local kid, grew up in a rough neighbourhood. Had an attitude and the talent to back it up. The scouts were all over him from when he was a teen, but it was like he was playing with them, not taking it all seriously. Then not long after Katrina he suddenly leaves town, signs with the Boston Red Sox and starts working his ass off."

"Something made him grow up fast," I said. "Sean can have that effect on people."

I recalled the first time I'd met him, back when he was a sergeant on the Special Forces training course I'd begun with such hopes. His grim warnings of what we could expect and how many of us would wash out before the finish had not shaken my determination. Maybe it should have done.

"Well, whatever it was, it worked," Parker said now. "Last season Baptiste had a two-nine ERA. They're saying he's the next Tom Seaver."

"So I hear—and I'm impressed," I said. "Or I would be if I had any idea what you're talking about."

"I'm telling you, Charlie, you go on like this and the federal government will be knocking at your door asking for your green card back."

"They'll have to fight me for it," I said.

"Well, that's one bout I wouldn't put money on," Parker said. He paused again, as if feeling his way. "How do you want to play this—with Sean and Baptiste."

"Well, at the moment Sean's as puzzled by the guy's reaction as the rest of us. I'd take a guess that as long as he stays that way, we should be OK."

"And if he doesn't?"

I smiled faintly into the gathering dusk. "Then Gabe Baptiste should have brought a lot more goons."

FIVE

Blake Dyer stood in front of the full-length mirror in the bedroom of his suite, struggling with his tie.

The tie was a proper self-assembly silk bow. It went with the immaculate tuxedo and the crisp white dress shirt with pearl studs down the front. I reckoned, at a cynical guess, he was wearing more than the cost of my last motorcycle. And possibly the one before that.

I wondered briefly if he'd ever owned anything that wasn't brand new or made-to-measure.

He fumbled for another few seconds, made a frustrated noise in the back of his throat. "My wife always takes care of these for me," he complained, turning. "Never could quite get the hang of it myself."

He'd been getting ready for more than half an hour. Back in my room it had taken me eight minutes to pull on my all-purpose black evening dress, add a quick gloss of lipstick and swap boots for lowish heels.

A quick check in the mirror showed I was done. My hair never seemed quite sure if it wanted to be blond or red. Not long after I'd moved to New York I'd opted for having it cut into an all-purpose bob. At least it survived being under a bike helmet reasonably well and—like tonight—was presentable with little more than a quick brushing.

The dress was stylish enough to be presentable anywhere but fell mercifully short of actual trendiness. Mostly, however, I favoured it because I'd discovered the fine-knit fabric had enough natural elasticity not to restrict movement and it hid blood-spatter remarkably well.

Now, I stepped away from the bedroom door frame where I'd leaned my shoulder while I'd been waiting for my principal to finish primping. "May I?"

Dyer gave me a relieved smile. "See? I knew I was right to hire you again, Charlie. I've been in town less than a day and already you're coming to my rescue."

I patted the back of an upright chair just behind him. "Sit."

"Yes, ma'am."

As he took his seat he automatically hitched the legs of his trousers so they wouldn't bag at the knee. A man brought up to respect the finer things. To expect them, too.

I leaned in close behind him, reached around his neck and threaded the ends of the tie over and through, smoothing the folds so they lay neatly. He watched my hands, then smiled at me in the mirror. The smile went all the way up to his eyes.

"Perfect," he said. "Ah, if I wasn't a happily married man ..."

"... you'd be a miserable divorced one," I finished for him.

Dyer laughed, but as I straightened something riffled at the hairs on the back of my neck. I half-stepped in front of my principal, body starting to twist, before I realised it was Sean. He'd taken my place in the bedroom doorway and was watching us with narrowed eyes.

"Ready to go down whenever you are, sir," he said with a studied blandness.

I scanned his face and saw only a taut disapproval there. He had not, it seemed, lost his knack of creeping up on people like a bloody ghost.

Dyer frowned at the pair of us, took a breath as if to speak but didn't quite know what to say. He got awkwardly to his feet.

"Shall we?"

I threw Sean a daggered look that he parried without concern, and let him lead us out of the suite.

He went ahead, a couple of paces in front. I stayed at my principal's shoulder covering side and rear. I don't like admitting that only half my brain was on the job in hand, even though experience had taught me to remain alert to possible threat on an almost subliminal level, like a muscle memory.

The other half of my mind was thinking about Sean. About who he'd been when we first met and who, apparently, he'd now become.

Back then we were both in the army. Sean was my sergeant and my instructor. He'd known from the outset that allowing himself to get involved with me—one of his trainees—on any kind of personal, intimate level was to risk career suicide.

He'd been tough and cynical where I'd been idealistically determined. When we eventually came together we tore down the barriers between us—even ones that should perhaps have stayed firmly raised. It had made us both targets in different but equally disastrous ways.

The vast majority of my fellow trainees were almost entirely male and viewed the few women who'd made it through Selection as freaks—or potential prey. I suppose I shouldn't have been surprised when a group of them asserted their machismo in an age-old act of group brutality that cost me everything I had—my sense of self, of self-worth, my confidence and my pride. It had very nearly cost my life.

Donalson, Hackett, Morton and Clay.

Lately I'd found myself thinking a good deal about the four men who had raped me. Years might have passed, but sometimes it felt very present.

Back then—with a scandal already raging about the brutal hazing of trainees at another military training camp—the High-Ups were never going to allow transparency in their enquiries. And when the details of my affair with Sean surfaced it presented the perfect opportunity to shift responsibility squarely onto my shoulders. I'd spent several years after my dishonourable discharge blaming Sean for his unwitting part in my downfall. Without realising he'd been told I was to blame for his own.

And that time in between—those wilderness years—was the only thing Sean now remembered about our relationship. It didn't matter what anyone said. It was what he *felt* that coloured his thoughts, his actions, his view of me.

We didn't speak as we travelled down in the lift to the lobby. We'd already called ahead to the parking valet. The rented GMC Yukon was waiting outside with the engine running and the air-con cranked up high. Sean tipped the valet handsomely and took the driver's seat. As we followed him out Dyer glanced at me again. This time he wasn't smiling.

"Is everything OK with you, Charlie?" he murmured.

No, of course not.

"Thanks, but it's nothing I can't handle."

"Oh, *that* I do not doubt," he said. "But at what cost?"

SIX

The opening night reception was held at the home of a local politician called Ysabeau van Zant. She was New Orleans old money, who'd married an off-comer with even more in the bank than she had. With a name like that I half-expected crinoline gowns and long white gloves for the ladies, white linen suits and big cigars for the men. I wasn't far off the mark.

The van Zant family home was in Old Metarie in Jefferson Parish. It was an area of country clubs and exclusive golf courses. No two houses were alike, each with total privacy from its neighbours and at least one tennis court or pool in the grounds.

The van Zant place had the look of an old Deep South plantation house. A sprawling mansion with French doors opening out onto wide verandas right the way around both upper and lower floors.

In fact, when Sean and I had done our security inventory prior to Blake Dyer's arrival, we'd learned that it had been wiped to the foundations when Katrina came through. What little remained had been knocked flat and rebuilt less than five years ago. A modern contrivance aping the glory of times past.

I wondered what it was, exactly, that the van Zants were trying to achieve.

Gridlock, it seemed. Sean weaved our rented GMC Yukon through the jam of vehicles already half blocking the driveway. He managed to squeeze through a gap that brought us within about six or seven metres of the steps leading to the main entrance.

"You take Mr Dyer in, Charlie, I'll find us a parking space."

I hesitated just a fraction before nodding. It was a sensible suggestion but that didn't alter the fact it should have been my call.

25

I hopped down, made a visual scan as I rounded the tailgate to open the other rear door. Dyer emerged buttoning his tux jacket, and stuck one hand in his trouser pocket like he was striking a pose.

Just before I shut the Yukon's door behind him, he leaned back inside and said to Sean, "If all else fails, leave it on the front lawn with one wheel in the fountain."

It was hard to tell from his voice if he was being entirely flippant or not.

House security had already checked us off the guest list at the main gate, but even so I was surprised to be allowed to walk straight in unrestricted through open front doors.

Inside, the oval hallway was two storeys high and straight out of *Gone With The Wind*. Marble tiled floor, sweeping staircase wide enough for a chorus line, and a crystal chandelier suspended above half an acre of exotic hothouse flora. The flowers were arranged in a huge vase on a table hewn from yet more marble.

Blake Dyer paused inside the doorway, eyes tracking up the chain from which the chandelier dangled ominously, like a Poe pendulum. A slight smile played across his lips, as if he'd made some kind of private bet with himself about the decor, and had just won.

From further inside the house came the full-bodied timbre of a string quartet—live, I reckoned, rather than a recording. Above the music I caught the tap of approaching heels early enough to be watching the far doors before the woman wearing them actually came through.

I recognised the owner of the house, Ysabeau van Zant, from the briefing pictures rather than our previous visit. The lady herself had not been At Home to anyone as lowly as other people's staff.

Mrs van Zant was a tall angular woman who dressed to intimidate and impress rather than to enhance her physique.

She was wearing a narrow sleeveless sheath of blue silk with a modest split to the knee so she could actually walk in the thing. I would have ripped the side seam wide open the first time I tried to get out of a car. Some attempt had been made to soften the outfit with a gauzy scarf that floated around her shoulders. It wasn't altogether successful. I wouldn't have wanted to arm-wrestle her.

If I hadn't been watching her entrance, I might not have spotted the momentary hesitation when she saw Dyer, then she put on a professional big smile and moved forwards, hands outstretched.

"My dear Blake, how *good* of you to come." She had the whole double-handed shake, the air-kiss and the fake sincerity down pat. And if she noticed Dyer's stiff response, she gave no indication of it. A real pro. "How *wonderful* that you could make it. We're all *so* grateful."

"Ysabeau," Dyer murmured, as good manners forced the greeting out almost against his will. "The After Katrina Foundation is a worthy cause. Important enough to override any … personal considerations."

Oh-oh …

"Of course," Mrs van Zant agreed equably, but her face registered the hit in the sudden tightening around her eyes. Quite a feat, if the amount of cosmetic work she'd had done was anything to go by. Just for a second I thought she might lash out, verbally or physically, then the moment passed like it had never been. She flicked her eyes sideways, weighing up my possible importance as a witness to this exchange. Not much, if her instant dismissal was anything to go by.

She linked her arm through Dyer's and steered him towards the interior of the house, back the way she'd come, with her head bent towards his. They were of a similar height. I fell into step close enough behind to eavesdrop shamelessly.

"As you say, this is an important event," Mrs van Zant muttered through clenched teeth. "And if I can damn well put aside our … differences for a couple days in the name of such a good cause, my dear Blake, then so can you. Suck it up."

"The fact I'm here at all should tell you that I have 'sucked it up' as you so charmingly put it," he said. "That doesn't mean I haven't taken certain … precautions." His gaze slid pointedly to me.

Mrs van Zant shot me another quick glance, just as narrowed but slightly more venomous this time. I threw her a guileless smile in return—it always confuses them.

Footsteps on the tiles had all of us turning, just as Sean Meyer circled the colossal flower arrangement and moved to join us. Presumably so they wouldn't be mistaken for anybody important, all security personnel had been instructed to wear dark lounge suits rather than full evening dress.

Even without that distinction, nobody could mistake Sean for a member of the idle rich. It was something in the way he moved, the way he carried himself. The veneer of polish he'd cultivated had worn thin enough to see through. Not necessarily a good thing in our line of work.

And even if Mrs van Zant did not recognise the underlying grit, the way he stopped a respectful distance from the client and stood easy should have told her all she needed to know.

She ignored him after the briefest stare, but the interruption gave Blake Dyer the opportunity to extricate himself from her taloned grasp. He stepped neatly away to prevent her re-engaging, heading towards the gathering inside. It was clearly not the first time he'd had to diplomatically escape a woman's clutches.

"Blake—" she began in a low voice, more urgently, but that was as far as she got before they reached the doorway to the next room, where the strings were louder, battling for supremacy over the hum of conversation.

"Blake! 'Bout time you showed," came the buoyant tones of Tom O'Day. Here was someone who had no difficulty making himself heard.

He came striding through the crowd trailing little eddies of excess energy in his wake. O'Day was wearing a black suit that looked almost funereal on his tall frame. As he moved, the light picked out a pair of dragons woven into the fabric of the lapels in silky thread. Maybe not so traditional, then. The bodyguard, Hobson, was his constant shadow.

He clapped a solid arm around Blake Dyer's shoulder, making him wince. For maybe half a second I wondered if breaking the event organiser's fingers would count against me.

My eyes flicked to Hobson's face. He was watching me as if he could read my thoughts. *Hmm, probably.*

"Ysabeau, you'll forgive me for stealing a few words with an old friend, I hope?" Tom O'Day said. And without waiting for an answer he whisked Dyer away.

Sean and I were swept along with him, me taking the lead this time. I'd already argued that it made more sense for me to stay close to our principal, leaving Sean to stay further out as an early warning system. Dyer had requested discreet protection and I looked a lot less like a bodyguard, for one thing. As he was not with his wife for this trip I could hover around him under the guise of companion—read into that what you will. It seemed that Sean had already read plenty.

Tom O'Day towed us across to a space beside an oil-black grand piano, halting beneath a gloomy life-size portrait of some bloke in Civil War-era garb. If the subject's scowl was anything to go by he had not enjoyed the experience of being immortalised on canvas. Perhaps that was why the artist had gone heavy on ugly sludge tones by way of retribution.

A member of the wait-staff appeared almost immediately, bearing a tray of champagne flutes. Dyer courteously offered me a glass before taking his own. I had no intention of drinking on the job, but I accepted as camouflage, holding the stem in my left hand to leave my right free. The SIG was within easy reach in a small-of-the-back rig hidden beneath the weighted hem of my evening jacket.

"Tom—" he began.

Tom O'Day held up a silencing hand. "You don't need to say it, Blake. I know what's on your mind."

Dyer took a minute sip of his champagne, was obviously pleasantly surprised by quality he hadn't expected. "I doubt that, old friend."

Tom O'Day sighed, let his gaze roam the assembled guests. We were in a ballroom, with high ceilings and a proper suspended wooden dance floor. The paintings of more ancestors, real or imaginary, glowered their disapproval from all around the walls.

"You've been away a while," he said. "Things change—"

"And the more they do, the more they seem to stay the same," Blake Dyer finished for him.

Tom O'Day smiled a touch ruefully. "Well, you may not like the look of the horse with the best form, but if it's a sure thing to win a man would be a fool not to back it. Makes no sense to do otherwise."

Blake Dyer, taking another sip, snorted into his glass. "And Ysabeau van Zant was that fast mare, was she?"

The rueful smile broadened momentarily before being manfully smothered. "You know as well as I do that nothing gets done around here without greasing the right palms. Way of the world."

"This part of the world, certainly."

Tom O'Day's eyes skimmed over me in much the same way Ysabeau van Zant's had done, but this time I put on my best part-of-the-furniture face. He nodded acknowledgement and I let my eyes drift around the room as if slightly bored, lifted the champagne glass to my lips without actually taking a swallow.

"We needed her," Tom O'Day told my principal quietly. He waited an artful beat. "Didn't have to *like* it overmuch, though."

I glanced back. Blake Dyer finally allowed his face to relax for the first time since he'd entered the house. He rolled his shoulders a little inside that fitted jacket, opened his mouth.

A commotion by the doors from the hallway distracted him. Everybody twisted to look, necks craning. Even the ladies of the string quartet petered into silence, but since they were playing the live equivalent of lift muzak they might simply have reached the end of a piece.

Through the crowd I caught a glimpse of a tall young man with a lanky build and a distinctive gait.

I heard someone nearby say, "It's Gabe Baptiste!" with something approaching awe in their voice.

Tom O'Day heard it, too. He nudged Blake Dyer's arm, leaned in close. "Ysabeau was the one who sweet-talked the prodigal son into returning home. When young Lyle put himself in the hospital, she was the one who came up with a suitable replacement. Gabe Baptiste—hell, he would have been my first choice if I'da thought we stood a cat in hell's chance of getting him to agree." He shook his head. "Boy didn't even come home for his papa's burial. But Ysabeau makes the call and here he is. Don't have the faintest idea how she did it."

"Oh, I think you have more of an idea than that." Blake Dyer flashed him a cynical look. "You just don't *want* to know for sure."

Across the room, Baptiste emerged from the knot of admirers who'd engulfed him, smiling, shaking hands. There was no sign of the outright fear he'd shown back in the hotel lobby when he'd come face-to-face with Sean Meyer. He was back in control, confident and cocky, a sporting superstar heading for legend status.

Maybe that confidence was the reason Baptiste was allowing his hands to wander more than they should over the tall cool blonde on his arm. I was surprised to recognise her as the young

30

woman O'Day had introduced earlier—Autumn. She was currently managing a much more convincing impression of boredom than I had, a tolerant smile on her face at all the fuss. And yet, underneath it, I sensed something more than the surface illusion.

After our earlier meeting I'd checked over the guest list again. It merely said "O'Day, T—plus one" which hadn't been overly helpful.

Now, I passed a dispassionate eye over the expensive silvered gown that fitted her like a second skin and speculated over several possible roles she might have been asked to play in the proceedings. It crossed my mind that she might be some kind of "professional" O'Day had brought along to keep the talent happy. I daresay she would not have been flattered by any of my other guesses, either.

Out of habit, I made a quick pass over the rest of the crowd, watching eyes and hands for anyone whose attention seemed oddly focused or who was using the new arrival as a distraction. It's a routine I've been through a thousand times before, in all kinds of situations, with all kinds of principals.

On this type of low-level assignment, with a client against whom there have been no specific threats, it very rarely—if ever—came up positive.

This time was different.

SEVEN

The man who tripped my internal alarm system was dressed in a lounge suit rather than the tux of an invited guest, but was clearly not a member of the security contingent either. He was too lightly built to be a heavy, too hesitant to be someone who relied on speed rather than weight for the kill.

But he was almost incoherently angry and that made him just as dangerous.

I could see it in the tension of his upper body, the white-knuckle fists. He shouldered his way around the piano heading towards my principal—and if there wasn't actually steam coming out of his ears it was a close-run thing.

"Sean," I said quietly. I stepped around Dyer, closed on my target, checking his angle of intent. Definitely heading straight for us.

One more step, sunshine, and you've crossed the line ...

The man kept coming.

I moved in, one long stride, and thrust my empty right hand between his arm and body as he took a mirror-image stride towards me. From there it was easy to use own momentum to swing his arm back and round, locking it up hard behind him.

He turned into me automatically with a yelp of hurt surprise. I stuck out my foot and tangled it between his ankles. He went crashing to his knees. I followed him down, keeping the armlock in place, and reinforced it with a knee in the small of his back once he was there. I didn't even slop any liquid out of the champagne flute I still held in my left hand.

I looked up, aware of a sudden buzzing silence. Blake Dyer was frozen, white-faced, but I guessed that this was an unpleasant reminder of the last time I'd worked for him. I'd taken out a potential threat at another high society gathering. Hell, at least I didn't shoot this one.

Tom O'Day was staring down at me with a look of total bemusement on his face. His bodyguard, Hobson, might have just been told an off-colour joke in mixed company. He'd allowed a tiny smile to crack his stony face. Hard to tell if he was suppressing something bigger or simply didn't find it funny.

Sean, I was gratified to see, had at least got himself in close to our principal, even if he was showing no emotion at all. I hoped people would read that reaction as calm rather than inertia.

And then, into that shocked hush, came the sound of a semiautomatic hammer going back. I slid my eyes sideways without moving my head, saw the muzzle and front sight of what was probably a Beretta, just visible in my peripheral vision.

"Let him up," said a man's voice. A British accent, north London, gruff with anger.

I released the lock and rose in one movement, moving back quickly. It's been my experience that men who've been taken down by a woman often try to get their retaliation in really promptly. In which case it's always wise to be out of range.

In this case the young man groaned a few times, flopping around until he managed to get his loose arm back under control. Conversation started up again, a little too loudly in the way it does when people are more excited than shocked by what they've just seen.

To my surprise, it was Tom O'Day who came forwards and scooped a hand under the young man's elbow. It was only as he came to his feet and the two of them stood next to each other that I realised the startling family resemblance.

Oh ... shit.

"I think you should apologise," O'Day said.

"Of course," I said at once, contrite. "I didn't—"

"Not you—him," O'Day interrupted, eyes twinkling. "Jimmy?"

"Dad!" The young man's voice emerged as a squawk. He had his father's facial structure without his confidence, height or breadth. "*She's* the one who attacked *me!*"

"You came charging over here with a face like thunder, boy. In a room full of bodyguards, you're lucky she didn't break your arm."

"Well, how was I supposed to know that's what she was?" Jimmy O'Day threw me a sullen look. There was a long pause, during which time he tried for defiance and his father beat him down with age and experience. I got the feeling their clashes usually ended the same way .

Eventually, Jimmy muttered, "Sorry." His gaze shifted across to where the star guest had barely paused during the interruption to his grand entrance. The only change was that the blonde, Autumn, had disentangled herself and was heading over, concern on her lovely face. Baptiste was self-absorbed enough to have hardly noticed her departure.

"Jimmy, what happened?" she asked. "Did you fall?"

Tom O'Day harrumphed. "Boy's a damned fool," he said.

His son made an effort not to appear sulky in front of her. So, he still had male pride. "No, I was pushed."

"Lucky she didn't break his arm," Tom O'Day repeated, ducking his chin in my direction. Whatever dignity Jimmy had regained, O'Day had just taken it away from him again.

Jimmy's eyes flashed, then slid to the man who'd shoved a Beretta in my face. "No, *she's* lucky Vic didn't shoot her."

It was only then I glanced at the man who was clearly Jimmy O'Day's bodyguard. The man with the north London accent who'd been too slow on the uptake to prevent his principal putting himself in harm's way. Up 'til then, I'd dismissed him for that reason alone. Now I finally gave him my attention.

And as soon as I looked at him full on, I realised he wasn't a stranger to me.

But I wished to hell that he was.

EIGHT

The last time I saw Vic Morton I'd wanted to kill the bastard. If I'd had the means, the opportunity, and the faintest chance of getting away with it, he would be an integral part of a concrete motorway bridge support by now.

Even years later I still felt my fingers contract in a reflexive grip, desperate for the feel of his windpipe beneath them.

There was a buzzing in my ears, a flash of adrenaline-fuelled rage coursing through my system. The SIG was suddenly an almost irresistible weight at my back. If the Beretta hadn't been still in his hand, held loosely at his side, maybe I would have considered it.

As it was, I saw him eyeing me with some apprehension and realised that he hadn't kept his gun out by accident. He knew me all right, and was wary—maybe even scared—of my reaction.

So you bloody well should be.

At least he had the sense to hand off cover for Jimmy O'Day to another of the O'Days' team. They shifted their young principal just out of my reach. He was still protesting about the treatment he'd received at my hands.

"The kid's hot-headed, what can I say?" Morton said with a smile. "Sometimes it's easier to let him make a few easy mistakes and save him from the really stupid ones rather than nursemaid him all the time."

"He was heading straight for us," I said. "I could have hurt him. Where the hell were you?"

Morton gave a shrug. "Oh, I didn't think you were going to do him any serious harm."

It was Sean who stepped forwards, brows down like a big dog coming in for the kill. Unutterably heartened, I put out a hand, almost said his name. I didn't get the chance.

35

"I know you, don't I?" Sean said, and for the first time since we'd landed in New Orleans, there was some animation in his face, his voice. "I recognise you."

Morton braced. "That's right," he said, clipped. "Been a long time, Sergeant."

"Vic ... Vic"—he clicked his fingers—"Morton, yeah?"

For a moment, Morton didn't answer, but I could hear his brain turning over, even from a metre or more away. He must have heard all about Sean's head injury—everyone in the industry had by now. The rumours I'd come across ran the whole gamut from having him walking round with the bullet still lodged inside his skull to being a drooling vegetable on life support in some private asylum. Another reason why Parker had been so keen to have him back out in the field. Especially on such a visible assignment.

"That's right," Morton said again now. "We trained together, you might say."

"Right," Sean said. "Right. Good to see you again, Vic." I knew that the warmth in his voice was not for the man, but the memory—for the fact that he remembered him at all. But even so it was a bitter blow that Sean should show such apparent pleasure to be faced with one of the men directly responsible for my ruin.

One of the men who had raped me.

Donalson, Hackett, Morton and Clay.

I didn't think I'd ever forget them. I'd tried my damnedest but now fate had conspired against me.

"You weren't on the original staff list for this job," I said, aware of the brusque note in my voice, the taste of acid in my mouth. "What happened?"

Morton, buoyed by the lack of aggression in Sean's welcome, looked almost jubilant. "Last-minute replacement," he said. "I'm normally assigned to another member of the O'Day family, but one of Jimmy's regular team fell ill—must have been something he ate. So they called me in."

He made it sound like they'd sent a private jet. Instead, I suspected he'd been the only one standing around with his hands in his pockets when the extra duty came up.

"Relax, Charlie," Sean said, a little too sharp for my taste. His eyes went to the baseball star, Gabe Baptiste. Now the initial adulation had died away, Baptiste was moodily swigging

36

champagne with the look of a man waiting for his first chance to leave. "It's not like it's the first substitution, is it?"

"Gotta expect the unexpected in this job, Charlie," Morton said with a quick insincere grin that didn't go anywhere near his eyes. "First thing you learn, eh, Sean?"

Any number of vicious retorts hovered on my tongue. I swallowed them back down. He was treating me like a first-time rookie but I wouldn't—couldn't—let him see he'd got to me. To anyone who mattered, the fact I'd just taken down his woefully under-protected principal one-handed should speak for itself.

Wasn't much consolation for not twisting his head off his shoulders, though.

"You're looking good, Sean," Morton said now, injecting a matey note into his voice. "I heard about ... what happened. Musta been tough. Still, here you are, eh? Good as new." His eyes swapped between the pair of us, caught on the tension we couldn't hide. "And still with a soft spot for the lumpy jumpers, I see."

As a sideways swipe at the fairer sex, being referred to as a "lumpy jumper" was not the worst I'd had by any means. But having it said by a man I'd happily watch die, to another I'd killed for, was as much as I could bear.

I turned away, stepped in closer to Blake Dyer, who was still standing next to Tom O'Day and his son. From the look of it, whatever had been eating at O'Day junior was still very much on his mind now.

"Apologies for the interruption, sir," I said.

Dyer waved a dismissive hand. "Always a pleasure to see you in action, Charlie."

I turned to Jimmy O'Day. "I'm sorry if I overreacted, sir," I said. One thing I'd learned early on in the army was that it never does any harm to call everyone "sir" until told otherwise. "You were looking somewhat dangerous."

From the look on his face, nobody had told Jimmy O'Day he looked anything close to dangerous for a long time—if ever. He actually forgot to scowl for several seconds before his face closed up again. "Yeah, well, damn near broke my arm," he muttered.

"Kid was all bent out of shape because Autumn came in with young Gabe," Tom O'Day said, making it sound like a bad case of playground scuffle.

37

"You're practically pimping her out, Dad—" Jimmy protested, and although he spoke through his teeth, it was still loud enough to turn a ripple of nearby heads.

Tom O'Day looked around before responding. His manner was calm, apparently relaxed, but when he'd finished none of those who'd been staring before were still staring afterwards. Some people can do that with just a look.

"I asked her to escort our star guest while he's in town, keep him happy—nothing else. I have absolute respect for that lady, Jimmy, and by God you better show her the same courtesy, or you'll be on the next flight out of here—hold baggage—d'you hear me?"

For a moment Jimmy dug his heels in. He wasn't a bad-looking kid when he had on a determined face. It gave him a little much-needed fire and colour. But he caved before his father's stern disapproval, of course he did.

From what I'd read of Jimmy O'Day, he still lived at home—albeit in a spacious apartment within the family ranch—and held an Executive Vice President post in some obscure department of his father's company. It sounded like a sinecure.

Hard to be brave when one false move could find you homeless, jobless, and disinherited.

"Oh, I hear you, Dad," he muttered. "Don't worry, I hear you." And with a disgruntled twitch of his shoulders, like a cat with ruffled fur, he stalked away. Morton shot me a forefinger salute and sauntered after him.

"I'm sorry you felt you needed to make a move on the boy," Tom O'Day said. "Jimmy tends to shoot from the lip. Not a bad trait, I guess ... if only he knew when to use it."

"Oh come now, Tom, he was just being a little over-protective," said the blonde, Autumn. Her voice was more breathy than a short walk across the room should have warranted, even in the pair of perilous heels she was wearing. I couldn't have gone more than a couple of metres in them without a tightrope balance pole and a safety net.

"I guess you're right," O'Day said, beaming at her. In that voice she could have just told him the moon was made of cheese and would likely have received the same reply. Some women just have that effect on men.

Now, she turned to bestow a beautiful smile on Blake Dyer and I watched him glow in its reflection.

"Tom's told me so much about you," she said.

"None of it good, I'm sure," Dyer said modestly.

She laughed, breathy again, like a lover's gasp and put her hand on his arm. "On the contrary."

Dyer smiled at her with more warmth than he'd shown when Ysabeau van Zant had tried the same move earlier.

"Well, in that case, I feel it's my duty to share some scandal about my old friend," Dyer said. His eyes flicked across the rest of us, amused. "Would you care to dance?"

He and Autumn took to the floor as the string quartet launched into something that required coordinated dignity to master. I moved in closer to Sean, who was watching the pair of them intently—well, maybe he was watching her just a little more than him.

I glanced around as I did so. Jimmy was across the other side of the room. He was trying to engage in casual conversation with an elderly, smartly dressed couple—all of whom were trying to pretend his earlier scuffle with me had not happened. It wasn't working out well for them.

Vic Morton was by his shoulder, but his eyes were on Sean and on me.

"Sean," I murmured, urgent, "that guy Morton—he's trouble—"

Sean turned abruptly. "Oh?"

I took a breath. "Back in the army, he ..."

My voice trailed away, the words sticking in my throat. How could I begin to go into any of it here? Besides, Morton's story that I'd led them on was backed by the official verdicts. My word against his—my word against the four of them—had not been good enough.

What could I say now that wasn't going to make things worse?

I caught a glimpse of Sean's expression, hard and tight, and realised that just by saying anything at all, I probably already *had* made things worse. Still, I had to try.

"He might tell you—"

"Tell me what?" Sean demanded, his voice low. "What is it you think he might tell me about you, Charlie, that you don't want me to know?"

39

NINE

Our principal did not have the stomach for making a late night of it, which was a good thing. To be honest, neither did I.

It was barely after midnight when Blake Dyer indicated we should bring the car round to the front entrance. I was the one sent out to retrieve the Yukon, while Sean stayed with Dyer in the ornate mausoleum of a front hallway. The more I thought about it, the more that enormous vase of flowers on the marble table resembled something you'd see on a grave.

Maybe it was just the way I was feeling.

As I pulled the Yukon up at the front steps, I could see the two of them standing in the lit hallway. I gritted my teeth about the security breach such a move represented, then saw they were not alone.

I recognised the slouched figure of Jimmy O'Day standing close by Blake Dyer's elbow. The older man was talking to him intently, using his hands for emphasis. Whatever he was saying didn't look like something Jimmy particularly wanted to hear. Not if the way he was staring at the floor was anything to go by.

Jimmy had managed not to disgrace himself again during the remainder of the evening. He'd chatted with apparent calm while Gabe Baptiste danced a slow one with Autumn. Or rather, Autumn danced and Baptiste held her close and shuffled awkwardly. For a man with such physical dexterity on the playing field, away from it he was not adept at the social niceties. It didn't surprise me that he made his excuses and left before we did.

Autumn had danced with Jimmy, too, and with his father. For all the expression of enjoyment she showed for either of them, she might as well have been playing chess against a computer.

I allowed the Yukon to creep forwards a little further, covering the brake. Sean came into view. At least he was watching for my arrival. I saw his head come up and he caught Dyer's attention to move him out. But just before he left, Sean turned to shake hands with another man who'd been standing outside my immediate field of view. *Deliberately?*

Vic Morton.

The thought of what Morton might have been saying to Sean during that brief exchange made my stomach bunch up tight under my ribcage as if expecting a sudden blow.

The urge to punch something—hard, and keep punching—was difficult to resist.

Sean had a memory of our time in the military and it was a true one—but only as far as it went. A lot had happened since then, for both of us. For one thing, Sean discovered about the rape that was the reason for my ignominious ejection from the British Army.

I'd never told him the names of the men responsible. Talking about it was still hard even now. Part of me wanted him find out some other way, knowing what action he would have taken. But now I had proof positive that he'd never uncovered their identities.

Because Morton was still alive, living here in the States and working in the same field I myself had gone into after the army.

Of course, there was no real surprise about that. There are only so many employment options open to ex-Special Forces soldiers returning to civilian life. If you don't go down the dark path and become a gun for hire, the legit avenues are limited. You tend to join the circus that is the private military contractors' circuit—mercenaries, more plainly put—or you go into security of another type.

You become a bodyguard.

That was the path Sean had chosen and, some time after leaving the army myself, I reluctantly joined him.

Reluctance was only my initial response. Sean had asked me to go to a close-protection training school in Germany to find out what had happened to one of his former trainees there. For various reasons, I didn't even finish the course.

I suppose you could say there was a pattern forming with that one.

But the more I learned the intricacies of the job, the more I'd realised it was right for me. It wasn't just a good career move for someone of my mindset and skillset.

It was the *only* career move.

The only one that would allow me to live with myself, at any rate.

And coming to the States with Sean, accepting this job with Parker Armstrong's elite outfit, seemed like the reward for a lifetime of being a round peg trying to hammer myself into a square hole and wondering why there were gaps and voids around the edges of my existence.

And I was not going to let a fucking bastard like Vic Morton take that away from me.

Not again.

I tapped the heel of my hand against the horn press, just a short toot. Sean's head came up quickly in a gesture that could have been part impatience, part warning. Either way, I did not sound the horn again.

After a few moments they both emerged, Sean moving alongside Blake Dyer, opening and closing the rear door for him, then coming round to climb into the front passenger seat.

I took my foot off the brake and we moved forwards, down the long straight drive lined with magnolia trees and out past the gate guards onto the roadway.

Sean twisted in his seat. "So, you want to tell us what that was all about?"

I glanced across at him quickly, a surprised retort on my lips. Then I realised he wasn't looking at me. Instead, his focus was on the man in the rear seat.

"OK, I'm not going to play around, Sean, and ask dumb questions like, 'What was what all about?'" Blake Dyer said, which was an evasive technique in itself.

He seemed to realise that without being told, because he gave a heavy sigh I heard even over the hum of the engine, the tyres on the road surface, and the air-conditioning system.

"Let's just say Ysabeau van Zant and I go back a long ways, and both of us probably wish that wasn't so."

"If you had history with Mrs van Zant—something that might affect your relationship with her now—we should have been told," Sean said, sounding far more like his old self.

I saw Dyer's eyes flick to mine in the rear-view mirror. "Yeah, I guess you should," he agreed. Another evasion.

"And?" Sean demanded.

This time he *didn't* sound like his old self. The Sean who had built up a successful close-protection agency of his own would not have been so blunt, so combative. This was the training sergeant I'd known in the army, who brooked no arguments and accepted no excuses.

Only trouble was, Blake Dyer was a rich client not a failing recruit.

I took another glance in the mirror, saw Dyer's face tighten just a fraction and knew Sean had lost his cooperation with that single brusque word.

"That is a private matter between me and Mrs van Zant," Dyer said. "And has no bearing on current events."

"That's not your call to make."

"Oh, on the contrary," Dyer said, and his voice had turned uncharacteristically steely, "as the man paying the bills here, I believe you'll find that it is."

The silence for the remainder of the drive back to New Orleans was not a comfortable one. I held my tongue. They were both in the wrong, but pointing that out right now would just end up with me being snapped at by the pair of them. Not quite the end to the evening I had in mind.

Sod's law, then, that of course things were not destined to go smoothly at the hotel. When we turned into the entrance we discovered there had been a minor fender bender in the line for valet parking.

Two men in evening dress were having what appeared to be a redneck slanging match over a dented wheel arch on a Bentley Continental and a broken headlight on a Porsche Panamera. It did not look like something that was going to be over any time soon with a philosophical shrug and an exchange of insurance details.

I kept my eyes on the mirrors, just in case this was little more than an expensive diversionary tactic.

"Just take us right around into the garage, Charlie," Dyer said when we'd sat for maybe a couple of minutes watching the drama unfold. "These idiots are going to be here all night."

"That's not a good idea," Sean said immediately. If you were going by the book, it wasn't. But sometimes you have to recognise

43

when you can stick to the letter of the rules and when you can't. And I would have said this was one of the latter occasions.

"Frankly," Dyer said, sounding weary. "I don't much care. I'm tired and I'd like to call it a night without waiting for one of these clowns to call triple-A."

Alongside me, I saw Sean's jaw tense to the point where I feared for the enamel on his teeth. "Yes, sir," he said, and jerked his head.

"Walk Mr Dyer in from here," I suggested. "I'll park the car and meet you up in the suite."

"Soon as I get upstairs I'm hitting the sack," Dyer said bluntly. "Besides, it's late and although I'm only too aware of how capable you are, Charlie—and you proved it again this evening—my mother would turn in her grave if I left a young lady to walk through a darkened parking garage alone at this time of night."

"Trust me, sir, you don't have to worry about me. I can—"

"For God's sake, don't *you* start arguing with me as well," Blake Dyer said and although there was a smile hovering around his mouth I heard the warning snap in his tone.

I opened my mouth to protest, then shut it again. Sometimes it's just easier to give in gracefully. "Well, for the sake of your mother's continued eternal rest ... thank you," I said.

I glanced at Sean but he just gave a shrug of assent as if not trusting himself to speak.

I manoeuvred through the jam of other cars waiting in line and swung the Yukon round into the parking garage structure, which stood next to the hotel but detached from it. The garage was well-lit and reasonably secure, but the most convenient spaces were all reserved for the valet service, on the grounds that a quick turnaround means a bigger gratuity.

The hotel was packed with guests for the fundraiser, and for this reason we had to go up five levels to find a space. Even then, there was nothing close to the stairwells or elevators.

As we climbed out of the Yukon's air-conditioned interior, the muggy heat of the night closed around us like a wet fist. From this height, the sounds of the city bounced up across concrete, glass and steel, amplified with a slightly artificial sheen. Shouts, horns, sirens, and the drone of traffic. I didn't like the fact the interior of the garage was lit and open on all sides to other

44

buildings. While we couldn't see out past the glare, anyone could see in. I didn't like it at all.

But the trouble didn't come from outside.

TEN

Sean was on point again, walking a couple of paces ahead of
Blake Dyer. I was back and to the right of him. My evening
bag was across my shoulder. I flicked it open and made
sure my cellphone was within easy reach. Maybe it was instinct,
maybe it was premonition.

We heard the trouble before we saw it. Raised voices that
echoed off the bare concrete walls, too close and too loud to be
coming from the street below.

I stopped, put a hand on Blake Dyer's arm. Sean took another
two paces before he, too, realised we were walking into a
situation.

Too slow.

The voices were between us and the nearest exit on this level.
Harsh, raised, an argument just about to boil over into a fight.

"Back up," I whispered in Dyer's ear. "*Now.*"

He nodded, catching on right away without making a fuss
about wanting to take the shortest route to his bed. But as he
turned the leather sole of his dress shoe caught on a piece of grit,
grinding loudly in the reflective space.

The shout of alarm came immediately. The words were too
heavily accented to decipher the words but I gleaned their intent.
The floors of the parking garage sloped so they gradually
spiralled upwards at one side, down at the other. I had only a
partial view up onto the next level, but it was clear they had
spotted Sean out in front.

The sound of a semiautomatic slide being racked back to
chamber the first round was instantly recognisable. Two more
followed in quick succession. I didn't need to hear it more than
once.

I grabbed the back of Dyer's neck, bending him into a crouch as we swung round, putting my body between him and the potential threat.

As I forced him back the way we'd come, I heard one of the men below us shout, "*Sortie!*" It took me a moment to realise it was French.

Exit.

It could have been an instruction for them to get the hell out of there, but I didn't think we were so lucky. Whoever was in charge had just ordered one of his foot soldiers to cover the stairwell, preventing us getting out of the parking structure that way. No doubt, if he had any sense, he'd call and hold the elevator, too. And if they got to the lower floor before us, we were cut off.

Shit.

Our only logical recourse was to hole up and call in local law enforcement. We already knew how long it would take them to get here—soon enough for us to stay out of trouble in the meantime.

The SIG was already out in my hand and I levelled it, one-handed, keeping a tight grip on my principal with the other. Sean had reached for his Glock and was backing after us, covering our withdrawal.

The first shot was an echoing crack. It went wide, gouging a strake out of the concrete ceiling way to our left. I increased my pace.

Sean stopped.

What the ...?

Before I could speak, he'd gone into a stance and fired a three-round burst towards the source of the gunfire. The shouting grew in intensity and volume. We took more incoming fire. I was used to the unprotected sound of gunfire, but in that environment it was percussive enough to make me wince. The shots twanged and hissed from every surface. They were still going wide, but the concrete everywhere made the dangers of ricochet very real and very nasty.

I stuffed Blake Dyer down between the front wheels of two parked SUVs, grabbed for my phone and stabbed at the 9-1-1 keys. I gave the female operator the bare details fast—what, where, who—and ended the call, knowing they would have it recorded anyway.

No doubt the recording would also pick up the signature of another couple of gunshots aimed in our direction while I was on the line.

Sean came skidding into cover and loosed two more rounds before ducking down. I caught a glimpse of his face—set but strangely alive, eyes glittering.

He remembers this, I realised. And suddenly wished that he did not.

I shoved Dyer down onto his side with his back hard against the concrete wall and flattened myself in front of him, covering as much of his body as I could. From down there I had a clear line of sight beneath the vehicle's underbody.

Past the tyres, I saw a man's legs approaching. He'd been using all the noise as cover to get closer to us. I could tell by the way he put the balls of his feet down first, the slightly sideways shuffle, that he was armed and intent.

I rolled onto my stomach and shot him very carefully, just once, through the right calf, which I knew would hamper his getaway even in a car with automatic transmission.

The man gave a yell of pain and fury. He let go of his gun. It landed with a clatter on the concrete and because of the incline spun away downhill before coming to rest somewhere under the far line of parked cars.

And at the same time I heard the first distant sirens approaching on the street below.

The effect was electric. Our attackers fell back. I counted four, including the man I'd shot. An old 'eighties saloon car—when the American car industry was going through its big-and-ugly-with-it period—appeared up the ramp from the floor below and slewed to a stop. As it moved, I caught the flare off metal-flake paint that gleamed and shimmered under the lights. The car was on huge chrome wheels that must have been nearly two feet in diameter, lifting the body an exaggerated amount off the ground.

Not ideal for outrunning a police cruiser, I wouldn't have thought.

The man with the newly acquired limp dragged himself across and bundled inside. The car took off with a chirrup of smoking rubber, leaving two black streaks until the tyres gripped.

Ah, maybe with that much power available it wasn't such a bad choice after all.

Sean dived out and took another two shots at the disappearing vehicle. I hoped he was also getting the licence plate while he was at it, otherwise it was just self-indulgence on his part.

Behind me, Blake Dyer sat up and shook his head as if to clear his ringing ears. He let out a low whistle.

"Wow, Charlie, life around you is never dull."

"I could say the same about you," I said. I tucked the SIG away again, not wanting to have it on show when the police arrived to a "shots fired" call. I flipped open Dyer's jacket and started to run my hands around his torso.

"Hey, you can quit that," he said. "I'm fine."

"When someone tried to assassinate President Reagan back in the 'eighties, initially he had no idea he'd been shot," I said. "Shock can do funny things to you."

"I remember," Dyer said, and when I glanced at him he added dryly, "I was there."

"Everyone OK?" Sean asked, dropping back between the SUVs.

"We're fine," Dyer repeated. "I was just—"

A slither on the upper level of the parking structure had Sean taking a firm grip on the Glock again.

"Sean, the police will be here any minute—" I began.

He didn't listen.

I stayed with Dyer as Sean crossed to the far rail and peered through it cautiously.

"Show yourself!" he shouted. "Let me see your hands. LET ME SEE YOUR HANDS."

"OK, OK, man, don't shoot! For the love of Jesus, man, don't shoot."

I rose in time to see a figure move slowly into view, a little shaky, one hand clutching a bloodied rag to his head. He brought the other hand up as he began to turn.

Alongside me, Dyer gave a shocked exclamation and hurried forwards. I stuck with him, but it took me a moment longer to realise the reason for it.

The injured man was the baseball player—the star guest for this whole performance. Gabe Baptiste.

ELEVEN

The police took their time with us, thorough but respectful. Clearly the mention of Ysabeau van Zant's name had a ripple effect further up the chain of command. Within thirty minutes, two uniforms had become a bevy of detectives and forensics people.

They'd started combing the area, rapidly finding the dropped gun from the man I'd shot. Now they were painstakingly marking and photographing all the ejected brass. It all meant that Blake Dyer wouldn't get to his bed any time soon.

A couple of paramedics finished patching up Gabe Baptiste. The blood turned out to be little more than a scuff to the side of his head. Scalp wounds always bleed worse than they are.

But I could still remember seeing the blood spray outwards from the gunshot injury to Sean's temple. Seeing the way his head had snapped round in response to the hit. The way his body instantly dropped.

Now, watching him give a lucid and reasoned statement to the cops, he rubbed at the site of the scar almost absently. Unless you knew what you were looking for you'd hardly notice it was there.

Our principal had been given a blanket and a cup of something sweet to combat the shock. He sat on the steps of the ambulance next to Baptiste, looking tired. Baptiste, no longer needing treatment, was signing autographs for a couple of the younger cops.

"Meat and drink to a guy like that, ain't it?" said the older plainclothes man alongside me.

There was something dismissive in his voice that caught my attention. "Not a baseball fan, detective?"

"Oh, I like the sport well enough," the detective said. He was a black guy in his late fifties, heavy with the passing of time, in a

50

shirt that was not on its first day of wear and a suit not on its first decade. "Just don't agree with some guys being allowed a free pass, that's all."

"A free pass?"

His eyes flicked over me, considering, and for a moment I thought he regretted having said anything at all. Then he sighed, "I remember Gabe Baptiste when he was just a mouthy kid from the wrong side of town," he said. "Got himself into some trouble back then. Would have thought it'd count against him when one of these fancy teams wanted to sign him up." He shrugged. "Funny how they kinda forgot all about that when they wanted to."

"What kind of trouble?" I asked, but one of the other cops approached him then, and he seemed glad of the opportunity to end that line of questioning. He snapped his notebook shut. "Thank you, ma'am. We need any more, we know where to find you."

Sean's cop had left him alone, too. Looked like they were winding up. I crossed to join him. "What's the story from Baptiste?"

Sean shrugged. "Reckons we interrupted a robbery gone wrong."

I glanced over at the ball player, noted the ornate Rolex still on his wrist, the gold chain around his neck that was heavy-gauge enough to anchor a battleship. "Pretty shonky robbers if four of them didn't even manage to get the bling off him before we came along," I said.

Sean just smiled. He was still buzzed, I saw, skin clammy and pale, hands just a little shaky. I opened my mouth to ask if he was OK but he headed me off.

"If the cops are all done, we need to get the boss man upstairs, Charlie. Get him squared away for the night, yeah?"

"Yeah," I agreed. I watched him stride away from me.

I hope you don't expect me to square away what happened here tonight as easy, Sean, because this isn't over yet. Not by a long way.

TWELVE

We got Blake Dyer upstairs, gave him a brandy and let him talk himself down out of the worst of it. By the time he finally called it a night the sky was starting to lighten over the Gulf of Mexico.

I walked the few paces up the hallway to my own room and took the paddle-rig holster out of the small of my back, keyed in the code for the in-room safe and topped off the magazine from one of the boxes of ammo I'd stored there.

I'd recently changed up from my usual 9mm SIG to the .40 cal P229. Sean carried a Glock 27 in the same calibre. It made sense for us both to use common ammunition.

He'd certainly used enough of it tonight.

And suddenly I couldn't wait for morning. I couldn't leave things there.

Reluctant to go anywhere without it when I was still officially on the clock, I shoved the SIG back under my jacket, grabbed my room keys and crossed the corridor.

I knocked on the door to Sean's room, but when there was no movement behind the Judas glass I let myself in anyway. We both had three keys—to each other's and Dyer's room, just in case of emergency.

I reckoned this counted.

"Sean?"

After a moment he emerged from the bathroom, drying his hands on a towel. His jacket and tie were gone and his shirt hung loose and open. I swallowed at the sliver of bare chest on show.

"Something you need, Charlie?"

Oh yes. Hell, yes ...

I needed a sign that the man I'd fallen for was still living inside the body in front of me. That there was still a reason to prolong this awkward, constant, painful contact. I was a slave to hope. It kept me alongside him when sense and pride dictated retreat long ago.

It took me a moment to realise that for once his words were said without undertone. He just sounded weary with the post-contact fatigue that hits like a truck when the adrenaline is gone.

"What happened back there?" I tried to match my tone to his, matter of fact. I almost succeeded.

"Does it matter?" He threw the towel over the back of a chair. "We got the job done. No sweat."

"No, Sean, *I* got the job done. The job we're being paid to do. *I* got the principal to safety, kept his head down, kept him covered, while you went in there all guns blazing."

Sean's jaw clenched. "Didn't stop you getting a shot off, though, did it?"

"*One* shot," I said. "At a clear target presenting a viable threat. What did you think you were doing?"

"Keeping them away from the principal," he said, but there was something defensive in his voice now. "I knew you had his back—mine too, eh?"

I sighed. "That's not the point, Sean. You reacted with maximum speed and aggression—in other words, like a squaddie, not a bodyguard. What were you thinking?"

"There wasn't time to think, Charlie. You know that. You just have to go with your instinct."

"There bloody well *should* be time to think," I said. "That parking garage was the worst place for a stand-off. No decent cover, no decent exits, and concrete everywhere just waiting to cause ricochets."

Sean started to turn away. "You're exaggerating the risks, Charlie—"

I lunged forwards, spun him to face me. As I did so, I let my grip slide into his shirt, peeling it back from his body. Just below the point of his left shoulder was the puckered scar of an old bullet wound. I could still remember what it had looked like fresh and raw, bright and raging.

"Remember *that*, Sean? No, I don't expect you do, but trust me when I tell you it came from a wild shot that ricocheted off a bare concrete wall."

He looked down at the scar as if noticing it for the first time, a deep frown creasing his face. I could see the turmoil in him, see him battling and failing to recall.

"What ... happened?" he asked quietly.

I let go and stepped back. It wasn't up to me to fill in the blanks more than I had done. Petty, but it felt like cheating. Besides, I didn't think he'd appreciate hearing about my part in it. Even so ...

"I got you out," I said, blunt, heading for the door. "And my father, for his sins, rolled out to patch you up." I waited a beat. "Despite the fact the police were after you at the time." I should have known that last bit didn't come as the biggest surprise to him. He touched a hand to the scar as if that might bring it all back.

"Your *father*? But ... your old man can't stand me."

So, he remembered *some* things, at least. I paused.

"Times change, Sean."

Yeah, and not always for the better.

THIRTEEN

I was too wired to sleep. Instead, I changed into a T-shirt, jeans and a hoodie. I clipped the SIG out of sight on my belt, slid my phone and room key into a pocket, and jogged down the deserted stairwell. Then I crossed the lobby and slipped out through the glass doors into the quiet dawn of another day.

It was already warm rather than overpowering—about the level of an English summer day. Or the summers we used to get when I was a kid, but don't seem to any more.

Outside, the front of the hotel was quiet. The valet parking station was unoccupied except for a single sleepy attendant, trying to hide a cigarette cupped in the palm of his hand. I smiled to let him know I wasn't going to tell tales. He grinned back, sheepish.

The weight of the phone in my pocket was a temptation. After a moment I dragged it out, stared at the display for a long time, then gave in and dialled.

Parker answered on the second ring like he'd been waiting for my call.

"Hi, Charlie," he said. "I hear you had a little excitement down there last night. When were you planning to let me know you were safe?"

There was a note of censure in his voice, and it wasn't quite as casual as I knew he would have liked.

"You're well informed," I said mildly. "You mean you wanted to know that our *client* was safe."

He never did like us using names on an open line if we could help it.

"Ah ... of course."

"Well, the local cops kept us talking for three hours and then our client kept us talking for another two. We've only just put him to bed."

55

"The news agencies have already picked up on the player's involvement," he said. "They're calling it a robbery gone wrong. What's your take?"

"Could have been, but if so they didn't manage to rob him very successfully—he wasn't missing anything but a patch of skin and a few mil of blood."

"They cut him?"

"More like a cuff to the head from what I saw," I said.

"But you're OK?" he insisted.

"We're *both* fine—well, no. Not exactly."

"Tell me."

I took a breath. "You know before we left New York I told you I didn't think Sean was ready?"

"Uh-huh."

"Well, he's *not* ready," I said flatly. "Now I can tell you that for a fact."

I heard him sigh. "What happened?"

I sat on a concrete planter, kicking my heels against the stucco while I explained, watching a weird shiny black insect about the size of a mouse climbing up the trunk of a potted tree. I gave him my report, clear and concise, not offering any opinions one way or another.

"He really has reverted back to military mode," Parker said at once when I was done.

"That's my take on it, yes."

"Well, you're going to have to snap him out of it—and do it fast, before he lands the pair of you in deep trouble."

"Would you like me to find a workable solution to the Middle East situation while I'm at it?" I demanded, allowing a hint of snark. "How about the energy crisis? Climate change?"

"When you put it like that, I guess you may as well," Parker said gravely, "although I'm not convinced climate change isn't just the Arctic oscillation in play."

I knew he was trying to lighten the situation, but this time it didn't seem to help. "And our client is not being straight with us either," I said. "He's got some history with a local politico called Ysabeau van Zant. Bad history at a guess, but he clammed up tighter than a fish's armpit when we pressed him on it. That's another thing—Sean seems to have had a diplomacy bypass at the same time as—"

I was suddenly aware of a feeling of being watched. I let the phone drop into my lap and hopped down from the edge of the planter, twisting as soon as my feet hit the ground.

Across by the entrance to the hotel, exchanging a cigarette for a light from the valet, was my old nemesis, Vic Morton.

The sight of him, so unexpected, brought a repeat of the raw urge to reach for my weapon, point and shoot. For a second I daren't move for fear I'd follow through on it.

He was still wearing the suit I'd seen him in at the van Zant mansion. I assumed he'd only just delivered Jimmy O'Day safely back to the hotel after an all-nighter. Never my favourite detail. Still, he looked lively enough on it.

Morton wasn't a big guy but he had always been quick on his feet. Quick to grease himself out of danger if there was blame to be apportioned, too, I seemed to remember.

It pleased me to note, in a purely bitchy kind of way, that he looked older than he should have done considering the time that had passed. I hoped the weight of carrying round a guilty conscience was responsible for the premature ageing. Certainly, his once high forehead was now a definite full-blown receding hairline.

What guilty conscience?

I pushed aside the hint of bile that had risen at the back of my throat and checked the distance between us, reassuring myself he was too far away to possibly overhear. But I took one look at that knowing smirk and the suspicion he'd somehow been listening to my entire conversation wouldn't be shaken. I slowly brought the phone back up to my ear.

"Charlie! Are you OK?"

"Fine," I murmured. "Look, I've got to go, but I think you need to check out the connection to the politician for me—soon as you can, if you wouldn't mind? The big shindig on the paddle steamer is tomorrow night and I've no desire to have things turn into a remake of that old disaster movie *The Poseidon Adventure*."

Parker laughed. "The *Miss Francis* is an ex-floating casino and party boat," he said. "I doubt if she will even untie from the dock. But I'll get Bill right on it."

"One last thing," I said, casually shifting my grip on the phone so my mouth was obscured by my hand. "There's a guy subbing on Jimmy O'Day's security detail—name of Vic Morton.

57

Get Bill to do a run on him as well while he's at it. If there's dirt, I want to know it."

As I spoke, I was watching Morton shoot the breeze with the valet. And the more I watched him, the more convinced I became that he'd been eavesdropping.

"Vic Morton ... why do I know that name?" Parker asked slowly. "Wait a moment, wasn't he—?"

"Just get Bill to dig up something—anything—that will get that sneaky bastard packed back to the UK in the hold of the first cargo plane heading east, will you?" I said, my voice rough. "I've had quite enough nasty surprises for one trip."

FOURTEEN

The surprises weren't over yet.

As I ended the call and walked back towards the hotel entrance, Morton gave the valet a sideways flick of his eyes that was an obvious signal for the guy to make himself scarce.

The valet threw me a slightly panicked look, as if he'd been happy enough to take whatever gratuity Morton had palmed him to leave the two of us alone together, but now it came down to it he was having second thoughts. Didn't stop him leaving, though.

I braced unconsciously, tried hard to keep the stress out of my frame as I approached. Knees soft, shoulders open, hands ready. In my left I still carried my cellphone, carefully gripped so I could weight a punch with it if I needed to. Or use the hard plastic corners on any one of the strategic strike points. The list of exposed areas scrolled through my head as I moved.

Better than shooting him, however much satisfaction that might bring.

Because I knew I didn't trust myself not to simply keep firing long after the target went down. If I had a second magazine on me I would probably empty that into him as well.

About half a dozen strides away, I stopped. There was no point in letting him get too close. Better for him to telegraph his first move—if he was planning on making one—to give me time to consider.

To consider just how much damage I might possibly get away with doing him.

I let my awareness expand outwards but he'd picked his time and place well. Apart from the single security camera, which we both knew provided only rotating views with four other fixed-position cameras relayed to the monitor behind the reception desk, we had the space to ourselves.

He took a drag on his cigarette, deep enough to hollow his cheeks, then regarded me with narrowed eyes through a long exhale of smoke. I assumed it was supposed to make him look dangerous. All it did was give him a slight squint.

I almost laughed. I'd once been terrorised by this man, woken in abject sweats in the night from the memory of what he and the others had done to me.

Of what I had allowed them to do.

I felt the pressure begin to build inside my head, my body, until I vibrated with the force required to keep it contained.

The urge to kill—the *need* to kill—was a chant in my head, a buzz in my ears, an acrid taste in the back of my mouth like smoke from a chemical fire. And now I knew just how small a step I needed to take to satisfy that urge.

A stark image flashed into my head. A figure lying on a darkened walkway, blood oozing from the single bullet wound that had killed him, the gun still warm in my hand. And most of all, the fierce gladness in my heart.

I shook my head a fraction and the vision folded, blinked out. But while it was there it had been sharp and vivid. The realisation of what I had allowed myself to become scared me far more than I'd been prepared for. Far more than I liked to admit.

I had to clear my throat before I could speak, found I could do so only with effort.

"There something on your mind, Morton?"

He noted my reaction and misinterpreted it badly enough for a tiny smirk to form at the corner of his lips.

"Never thought I'd come up against you again, Foxcroft. Or should I call you *Miss Fox* now, eh? Heard you changed your name. Trying to escape your past sins, were you?" He paused. "Didn't think you had the balls for this kind of work, though."

I took my time about replying, let my eyes do a slow survey with my face blank as if what I saw had no meaning. As if I was staring at nothing. Through nothing.

"Sometimes not having balls has its advantages," I said coolly. "At least I don't have to think with them all the time."

He kept the hit out of his face but couldn't prevent the reflexive twitch of his fingers around the cigarette. As if realising the betrayal he dropped the half-finished butt on the concrete and ground it out. He stepped forwards, aiming to get in my face with a sneer.

"Did you think you'd be any safer here, Fox? Did you think anybody was going to stand up for you when they never did before?"

Instead of backing off I stepped up too, got in *his* face toe-to-toe. He didn't have much on me in height anyway.

"You haven't changed a bit, have you, Morton?" I murmured. "And that's a pity—for you. Because I *have* changed—a lot." It felt like the mother of all understatements.

My eyes dropped to his mouth, lingered, then I lunged forwards a fraction, as if either to kiss him or bite out his tongue. He jerked away automatically, annoyance ticking at his jaw.

"You really think I give a flying fuck if anyone's prepared to stand up for me?" I said, keeping my voice entirely conversational. I dialled down both the volume and the temperature. "Well, you might like to keep in mind that this time you haven't got three other cowards backing you up, and I don't *need* anyone backing *me* up. Not any more. You try to mess with me, sunshine, and *this time* I will fucking *bury* you."

I stepped back, arranged my face into a smile that did little to reassure him. "Have a nice day."

FIFTEEN

Blake Dyer was up bright and early for his room-service breakfast, despite the disturbed night. Bearing in mind my own lack of sleep I'd been quietly hoping he'd opt for a lie-in that would allow the rest of us to do the same.

"Today it all begins, huh?" he said, shaking out the starched linen napkin and laying it across his knees. He lifted the domed lid covering his breakfast, scooped up a forkful of crispy bacon and scrambled eggs with a sigh of pleasure. From the evident enthusiasm I guessed his wife kept a watchful eye on his cholesterol intake at home and he was determined to make the most of being unsupervised.

"It does indeed, sir."

I sat opposite at the small table. I was cradling a coffee I'd poured from one of the insulated jugs that had arrived a few minutes earlier. It was delivered by a waiter called Jerold whose background check revealed he still lived at home with his mother and had a liking for tropical fighting fish.

Sean helped himself to his own cup. He'd made an effort to overcome last night's awkwardness on the journey back with Dyer. I reckoned he was largely succeeding.

And if he'd been quieter than usual I didn't find anything too odd about that. After all, I'd dealt him a couple of hefty blows which he'd apparently absorbed without obvious mental trauma.

So far, so good.

Dyer chewed and swallowed. "I understand Tom's organised a little sightseeing for us this morning," he said. "I guess he plans to show us the ongoing effects of Katrina first-hand before he hits us for the big bucks tomorrow night."

"It's what I'd do," I agreed.

Dyer grinned at me as he fed in a mouthful of toasted bagel slathered with full-fat cream cheese.

Oh yeah, he was definitely off the nutritional leash.

"Mr O'Day's people have sent through a revised schedule for the helicopter tour," Sean said. "There've been one or two drop-outs after last night's bash."

News to me. I sent Sean a brief questioning glance, which he pointedly ignored.

"Well, I guess not everyone wants a bumpy flight over an environmental war zone with a hell of a hangover," Dyer said. "And there'll be a few of those this morning." He sounded gleeful not to be among their number. "I hear young Jimmy O'Day didn't make it in before dawn."

I glanced at him sharply but didn't detect more to his words than their face value.

"You've known the O'Days a long time?" Sean asked. He moved over to the window and leaned his shoulder against the wall alongside it, where he could survey the street without presenting an easy target. Some habits were too deeply ingrained ever to change.

"He and my father met in Korea," Dyer said. "Tom was a young cryptographer in the navy back then—one of the best. Fluent in Russian, Korean, Chinese." He paused reflectively. "In fact, I do believe it was my father who introduced Tom to his wife. They moved in the same circles." He gave a small chuckle. "Made Dad *persona non grata* for a while there, I can tell you."

"Oh?"

Dyer gave me an assessing glance. "Back in those days Tom didn't have two cents to his name, but Marie's people were big into mining. Lost most of it in the late 'seventies. Seemed like their star was falling as Tom's was rising. I'm proud to know him." He paused. "Jimmy was a late gift, you might say—I think they'd given up hope of having children. My wife and I are godparents."

I felt a damning flush steal up into my face. So I hadn't just knocked his host's son on his arse at the party last night, but my principal's godson as well. *Nice going, Fox.*

"Sir, I—"

He chuckled, mopping his mouth on the napkin. "Forget it, Charlie. I was there, remember? Hell, young Jimmy had a face like thunder. Never seen him look so riled." He leaned across and gave my arm a reassuring pat. "If I hadn't known the boy I probably would have taken a swing at him myself."

63

Relief invested my answering smile with a touch more warmth than it might otherwise have had.

Sean made a tiny noise in the back of his throat that could have been a growl. He levered away from the wall and strode across the suite.

"I'll check the ETA on the helo," he said brusquely as he went. "Charlie will escort you down when you're ready to go, sir."

There it was again. Just the faintest emphasis on the word "escort" giving it a whole host of different meanings. None of them especially flattering.

I glanced at Blake Dyer. He merely raised an eyebrow and made the slightest duck of his head in Sean's direction. *Go after him.*

I pushed back my chair, murmured, "Excuse me a moment, would you?" and hurried out after Sean without waiting for a reply.

"Sean!" By dint of jogging along the corridor, I caught up with him near the door to the stairwell. He was still conscious enough of his reduced fitness levels to automatically go for stairs rather than take the easy option.

"What do you want, Charlie?"

Another double-edged question.

"I want to know what's making you behave like—"

"—a bear with a *sore head?*" he shot back, face bone white.

I took a breath. "I was going to say 'like an amateur thug', if you must know, but I expect there are similarities," I said, my voice mild. "I know you have a problem with me, Sean, but if we're going to do this job you're going to have to put it aside—for the next couple of days, at least, or—"

"Or what?" he demanded. "Or you'll phone New York and ask Parker to recall me, is that it?"

What the …?

He squared up to me and his eyes went flat, his voice deadly soft. "When were you planning to tell me you'd already made that call, eh?"

I said nothing. There was nothing I could say that wasn't a lie, at least in part.

He knows.

And I could take a pretty good guess how he'd found out.

That *bastard* Morton. I knew he'd been too far away to overhear naturally, but maybe not if he'd been using some kind of electronic amplifier. Morton always had liked his gadgets.

"It was a judgement call," I said with as much calm as I could manage.

He scoffed. "It was an emotional call, certainly."

I flinched, hit by a sudden flashback to the last time I'd tried that argument on him. An argument to explain away why I hadn't acted with more aggression against a perceived threat.

His response had been the same.

Exactly the same.

Jesus ...

The argument hadn't worked for me back then, either. In fact, Sean had actually pulled a knife to goad me into what he'd considered was a proper reflex reaction to danger. Of my own volition, my eyes flicked to his hands.

They were empty.

I let my breath out nice and slow, tried to roll some of the tension out of my shoulders before they cracked. "Sean, you went over the top last night—way over the top. You're not a soldier any more, and if you need extra time—extra training time—to get yourself back into the right mindset for this job, then you *need* to take it. It's Parker's name above the door of the agency as much if not more than yours, so he had a right to know. You have to realise that it only takes one mistake in this business to get a reputation you just can't shake."

"Oh, and you'd know all about *getting a reputation* for yourself, wouldn't you?"

My core temperature dropped so suddenly I had to suppress a shiver. Even then, I couldn't resist the urge to wrap my arms around my upper body. An utterly stupid defensive gesture. I brought my chin up to counter it.

"Get it out, Sean," I said, my voice hollow now. "Say what you have to."

"The way you've been behaving with Dyer since we got here— half the time I'm not sure if you're trying to be bodyguard or a bloody hooker."

It was the "trying" that stung hardest.

"So, what was I last night, Sean, while you were playing Rambo? I got the client down into cover and put my body in front of his. What—you think I somehow got off on it?"

65

He took a deep breath in, let it out through his nose like a bull faced with a platoon of Household Cavalry in full ceremonial scarlet dress.

"Dyer's a flirt—always has been," I said. "Last time I worked for him he was exactly the same even when his wife was there. It's just a—a mannerism. There's nothing *meant* about it. He's like a dog chasing cars. If he caught one he wouldn't know what to do with it—it would scare him half to death."

I stepped in, tried a smile, reached for his arm as if actual physical contact might help convince him. Instead, he jerked away.

"So it's just flirting, is it? That what you've been doing with Parker, too, eh?" His eyes flicked over me again and there was nothing flattering in the look. "Is that how you got your job with the agency?"

I felt my face close up. "I'm not going to dignify that one with an answer," I said, turning. "We'll talk again when you've calmed down enough to see reason."

But he only let me get half a stride away.

"Tell me the truth, Charlie—I wasn't the only one you were fucking back in the army, was I?"

It came out fast and vicious, but under his anger I thought I detected shades of pain.

As if what we'd shared really had meant something to him.

As if facing the idea he'd been just another notch on my bedpost—that he'd risked everything he'd made of himself for somebody so unworthy—hurt him more than he could bear.

That, more than the slur, almost undid me. I turned back.

"I bet I know who filled your ear with that delightful little titbit of information. Wouldn't have been Vic Morton who couldn't wait to drip that bit of poison would it, by any chance?"

I could hear the brittle quality in my voice now, my accent smoothing out to reveal my parents' upper-middle-class origins. I'd done so much to blunt down and hide my background from Sean in the beginning, fearing he might despise me for it. If only it had been that simple.

He didn't answer, but I looked him in the eye and didn't need him to.

So, it seemed we were neither of us prepared to lie to the other.

Well that was progress of a sort.

"As a matter of fact you weren't the only one, Sean," I said, cold and clear. "Did Vic happen to mention he was also a lucky recipient of my oh-so-indiscriminate sexual favours?"

He didn't answer that one either.

Nearby, the lift pinged as it reached our floor and the doors opened. Despite everything, we both altered our stance, turned a fraction to meet the new arrivals. I ID'd them instantly as two guys from another team. They nodded to us, acknowledging rather than friendly, but didn't stop to check in.

It was a worrying omission, as if they were making a point of not getting too close, just in case. Or maybe they simply picked up on the atmosphere between us.

Not so much intense as frozen solid.

We watched in silence as they retreated along the corridor. Even so, I moved in closer again and lowered my voice.

"I don't suppose Vic Morton also happened to mention that—to get me to lie still enough for long enough to allow him to fuck me—he had to beat the shit out of me first and then had three of his mates holding me down waiting their turn?"

Sean's head reared back as if I'd slapped him. Just for a second I thought the shock tactics had worked, had finally penetrated, but when he spoke again his voice held only a cynical detachment, and any trace of sympathy had vanished from his features.

"Yeah," he said coldly. "He told me you'd probably say something like that."

My turn to reel as if from a sudden blow. I clamped my jaw shut, fought not to let the emotion cloud my voice for one last superhuman effort.

"Did he really?" I asked. "Well you might want to keep it in mind, Sean, that the last time you said that—the last time you believed someone else's word over mine—you ended up getting shot in the head and left to die ..."

SIXTEEN

The helicopter Tom O'Day had hired for the sightseeing tours of New Orleans was a six-seat Bell 429 corporate model, dressed in the discreet livery of a local oil company. I say "hired" but in fact he probably talked them into lending it for nothing. All in aid of a good cause.

The flights were taking around thirty minutes, taking off from the open top floor of the parking structure next to the hotel, beating north over the city towards Lake Pontchartrain and then circling back over the network of canals and levees that protected the city's eastern side.

I'd heard the rapid thrum of the rotor blades as the helo came and went all morning, starting around nine-thirty and running straight through like continuous flight ops from a carrier deck. The only break was a short one to refuel, then it was back on station.

The pilot was laid-back about the whole thing. Sean and I had already met him. The guy was a former US Army captain called Andrew Neal, who spoke little and missed less. Although he never mentioned it, we knew from the standard background checks that Capt Neal had actually been at the controls of a Sikorsky Black Hawk that fateful day in 1993 over the Somali capital, Mogadishu.

I assumed his reluctance to discuss his experiences was very much like the members of the SAS assault team who stormed the Iranian Embassy in London many years previously. There are a thousand pretenders to that particular crown. Those who really *were* there rarely talk about it.

Blake Dyer was booked for the last flight before lunch. We took the elevator up to the roof where O'Day's Foundation people had set up white marquees to keep potential donors from letting the sun go to their heads. Uniformed wait-staff circulated with trays of canapés and yet more champagne. I wondered if O'Day had bought up an entire vintage to give away over the course of the weekend.

News teams and reporters were among the guests, mingling and interviewing. Must have been one of the few times everybody was happy to see them.

Dyer had a few words with the front man from the local news channel, a bouffanted guy whose expanding waistline was mostly concealed by careful tailoring. He was in full make-up that was wilting slightly even out of direct sunlight. Despite the electric fans blowing from every corner, the marquee was coming up to a midday high temp.

Sean and I stayed out of the way and let Blake Dyer circulate unmolested. He seemed to be enjoying himself, chatting to Tom O'Day himself like the old friend he professed to be, as well as taking Jimmy aside in a godfatherly kind of way. I don't know what he said to his godson, but Jimmy didn't look any happier afterwards.

Not that he looked happy before. Maybe he'd finally got wise to that snake Vic Morton, who was constantly by his elbow. I wondered if the bodyguard had been told to stick close and make sure the kid didn't screw anything up.

Or it might have had more to do with the state of Jimmy's hangover battling against the smell of jet fuel and the constant noise of the Bell cycling through its turnaround routine. Land, unload, reload, take off again. Efficient and neat. No fuss.

It was apparently left to Jimmy to keep things running to schedule on the ground. He swung by to collect Blake Dyer about ten minutes before our designated flight-time, took him over to gather with Ysabeau van Zant as if unaware of the tension between them. Mrs van Zant was coldly immaculate in a pale blue dress suit that reminded me vaguely of the former UK Prime Minister, Margaret Thatcher. Mrs van Zant was alone, apparently confident that her status would protect her. She and Dyer studiously ignored each other. I stayed nominally between them, just in case.

Behind Jimmy O'Day's shoulder, Vic Morton's eyes volleyed back and forth between me and Sean as if trying to spot the cracks he'd undoubtedly caused. I reckoned I had them pretty well plastered over by that point.

You know exactly what you're trying to do, don't you, you little bastard?

Sean and I were filling two of the available seats on the Bell. The remaining pair had been earmarked for an old-money banking couple from Boston, but when I looked round I couldn't see them on the roof.

"Where are the others?" I asked Jimmy O'Day. "They're cutting it fine."

Jimmy kept throwing me little sideways glances without turning his head to look at me directly, as if afraid I'd turn him instantly to stone if he did so.

"Um, they're not coming—heat's too much for them I guess," he said, but he sounded as if he was taking no-shows as a personal affront. "Looks like you guys will be able to really stretch out."

I should have known it wouldn't be that easy.

Because at that moment I felt a ripple through the crowd. I turned. The young baseball star Gabe Baptiste had just stepped out of the elevator. The stunning blonde, Autumn, was on his arm again. I wondered how Tom O'Day felt about their sudden palliness. She was wearing a white dress covered with a huge red poppy motif that should have looked gauche amid the sophistication, but came across as fresh and simple.

Maybe she was part of the reason the newsman abandoned another guest in mid-sentence and swam for the pair of them like a shark aiming to keep ahead of the pack.

Baptiste sidestepped the newsman with practised agility. Instead, he headed in our direction. His bodyguard stuck to his shoulder like a conjoined twin. The guy was built like a gun emplacement in a pinstripe suit.

And where were you last night, hmm?

"Mr Dyer," Baptiste greeted our principal, a little hesitant. "How you doin'?"

"Good, Gabe, thanks. And please, it's Blake."

Baptiste ducked his head in acknowledgement, but his gaze had shifted over to me, and to Sean.

"Just wanted to say thanks, you know?" he said. "For saving my ass last night up here."

He still had a small dressing just above one ear. I let my gaze drift to his bodyguard. "You're welcome," I said, keeping my voice neutral.

Sean didn't respond. He was frowning as if the inside of his skull was being tickled by a memory he couldn't quite grasp. After a few moments he shook his head, let it go.

"Been a long time, Sean," Baptiste said, voice sober. "Didn't think we'd ever see each other again, huh?"

"I'm afraid I don't … remember you," Sean said stiffly. "I'm sorry."

"No shit—that for real?" Baptiste checked our faces like we were all in on some massive joke at his expense.

"Sean's recall of names and faces is the only thing affected by his recent injury," I put in, filling an awkward silence. I added a tight smile. "But, as I'm sure you realised from the … incident last night, he's as effective an operator as he ever was."

It might have been stretching the facts a little, but there was no way I was going to admit to anything less in front of a client— past or present.

Baptiste continued to eye Sean for a moment longer, then grinned. "Sure," he said. "That's cool. So, we good?" He offered a hand bearing more gold and diamond rings than most of the women present—and that was saying something considering the company.

"Looks that way." Sean answered the smile with a cooler version of his own—but a smile nevertheless—and gave the ball player's hand a perfunctory shake.

"Well, shit, that *is* cool. In that case, I am *so* riding with you guys." He glanced at the stoic bodyguard. "That cool with you, Frankie?"

John Franks—the gun emplacement—gave a fractional twitch of one massive shoulder. It might have been a shrug, or he could simply have been troubled by insects. It was hard to tell from his blank expression. I guessed Franks had been employed more for his size than his skillset.

Well, you can't have everything—where would you put it?

"It OK with you if we take the next ride?" Baptiste asked Jimmy O'Day. And just before Jimmy could answer, Baptiste added casually, "Oh, and Autumn's coming with me, of course."

If Jimmy O'Day didn't like Autumn dancing with Baptiste at the van Zant reception, he liked the prospect of her taking a pleasure flight with the ball player even less. He frowned, almost a scowl. It took a brief look from the blonde, almost too fast to register, to have him backing off, flustered.

71

He muttered an excuse about needing to redo some calculations—probably the fuel load taking Franks's sheer bulk into account—and scurried off. Baptiste ignored him with the air of someone who takes it for granted that whatever he wants will miraculously happen.

It made me wonder again about Autumn's role in the proceedings, though.

Meanwhile, Ysabeau van Zant had been sizing up Autumn with zealous intensity. I could almost see the calculations forming inside her head. If it came to photo opportunities, she knew she would be better to stand as far away from the younger, taller, thinner woman as she could manage.

Baptiste's face when he realised that Ysabeau van Zant might be on the same aircraft with him was a picture of consternation. I watched him weighing up how much offence was likely to be caused if he backed out now because of it. Too much, clearly.

Ysabeau van Zant came to the rescue of both of them. She showed her teeth briefly to Autumn. "My dear, you must take my place. I'll go this afternoon. I insist."

Autumn flashed a sunny smile and thanked her with grave politeness that, in someone with more apparent depth, might have been mocking.

Jimmy O'Day fussed around us, making furious notes on his crumpled list, the deeply scarred pencil notations a visible sign of his inner frustration. I put my hand in my pocket and found a strip of paracetamol still lurking there. With a sudden burst of sympathy, I handed the painkillers to Jimmy. He glanced at them for a moment, frowning, then gave me a fleeting, weary smile.

Overhead came the sudden fast chop of rotor blades as the Bell circled the rooftop and dropped down for another centimetre-perfect landing. After the last round of passengers had been disgorged, the group of us walked out onto the sun-baked concrete towards the waiting helo sitting with its main rotor still turning lazily. We ducked instinctively below the blades as we approached.

"Mind your heads," Jimmy shouted over the whine from the twin turbines. "And please don't go aft of the doors when you're boarding. Wouldn't want to lose anybody in that tail rotor before you've had a chance to let my father talk you out of all your money tomorrow night, huh?"

It sounded forced, like he'd been making the same joke every time, all morning. Dyer and Baptiste gave dutiful laughs the rest of us didn't feel the need to emulate.

I looked at the mixed emotions on the faces surrounding me. This was not, I realised, going to be quite the fact-finding pleasure flight it was meant to be.

Inside the rear cabin the plush leather seats were laid out in rows of three, facing each other. There was a slightly undignified rush for the honour of helping Autumn up into the cabin. The poppy dress only reached about halfway down her thighs and all the guys in the party jostled for the best view.

I climbed up unassisted and took the centre of the rear seats between Autumn and Blake Dyer. There was a noise-cancelling headset on a hook by the headrest. I put the cans on, adjusting the flexi-boom mic so I wouldn't heavy-breathe into everyone's ears.

Alongside me, Autumn strapped herself in. She looked less than thrilled at the prospect of messing up both her hair and her dress in one hit, but managed to don both the harness and headset without anyone needing to push her chest in and out while she thought about it.

Then she settled back and crossed those spectacular legs. The move was followed in minute detail by three pairs of male eyes on the other side of the cabin.

Gabe Baptiste had slumped into the seat by the far window, while his bodyguard, Franks, had folded himself awkwardly into the middle seat directly opposite me, probably because he recognised that his bulk might make us fly round in circles if he sat to one side. He was too big for the harness to fasten around him, even in the land of six-XL clothing as a standard size. He left the thing unfastened and fiddled with his headset.

Sean climbed in last. Jimmy O'Day gave Autumn one last worried look and slammed the door behind us. He looked terrible, but maybe that had something to do with the fact he'd been performing this duty all morning with the mother of all headaches and no ear defenders. He'd know better next time.

Once the door was closed I buckled my harness like a good little airline passenger, pulling the lap-belt tight and low across my hips.

The pilot twisted in the left-hand seat. "Morning folks," he said. "We good to go?"

It was clearly a rhetorical question. Even as he spoke the Bell was lifting off as if of its own accord, rotating effortlessly onto a new heading as it rose.

Show-off.

Just before we cleared the edge of the rooftop I glanced out of the door window and saw Jimmy O'Day still standing on the concrete below. There was something a little mournful in his rounded shoulders—the big man's son reduced to playing the kind of role that normally netted minimum wage and a uniform with a name-tag attached.

By Jimmy's shoulder stood his bodyguard, Vic Morton, who was staring up at the departing helo with his hand shading his eyes, almost in a parody of a final salute.

I shivered and looked away, meeting Sean's eyes across the cabin. They were cold and distant.

What further damage was Morton going to do to the pair of us, I wondered, before the day was out?

SEVENTEEN

This is the Lower Ninth Ward," Capt Neal said, half over his shoulder. "Katrina hit the whole city hard, but I'd say she hit here hardest of all. West of here, the parishes of Jefferson and St Tammany got away pretty lightly. But they reckon that here in St Bernard parish, only three houses were left standing."

He brought us in low over an area to the east of the Industrial Canal, which he'd been using for his own personal equivalent of a Dambusters run south from Lake Ponchartrain.

"If you stick to the tourist areas—the French Quarter and the Garden District—you don't get a true picture of how bad things were," Capt Neal went on. "And how bad they still are."

As we overflew industrial buildings I thought I could make out water marks still remaining on some of the exterior walls, like a badge of honour.

"It's the kids who get the worst of it. Hardly any place safe to play. There's only one school remaining for the whole parish, and fewer buses running means they can't get to schools further out."

With our forward speed slowed to a crawl, we craned to look down out of the cabin windows. Seeing the place from the air was effective in a way no ground-based trip would ever have been. In a city where housing tended to be packed in close, here there were only empty concrete slabs to show where houses had once stood. They were surrounded by overgrown lots as nature clawed back what was rightfully hers.

"They're rebuilding slowly now. But in some cases the insurance companies paid out a fraction of what the houses were worth, and then only after the work's been done. Not many folks can afford to pay up front. Pretty much the whole of this neighbourhood—everything north of Claiborne—has been derelict since."

I thought of Ysabeau van Zant's reconstructed mansion. Charity, it seemed, did not begin at home.

"Why was this area so badly affected?" Blake Dyer asked, leaning forwards in his seat.

"Poverty," Capt Neal said bluntly. "Most of the folk here didn't own a car, couldn't afford a bus or train ticket. Katrina hit at the end of the month—a time when money's always thin on the ground. So a whole bunch of them decided to stay put and ride it out, like they'd done before. Only, ground level round here can be as much as four feet below the level of the Gulf, and the houses were mostly single-storey homes. Then the storm surge came in, and the flooding, and when the levees broke they were under water. People drowned in their attics."

He lowered the Bell towards an abandoned house, its front façade delicately adorned with wrought-iron railings. Weeds choked the approach to the gaping front door. Only darkness showed inside, like a mouth opened to scream.

Keeping a wary eye out for overhead power wires, Capt Neal inched the Bell forwards and the engine note rose in pitch and volume. In plaintive harmony I heard the cries of an underclass betrayed, of victims brushed aside and forgotten. It seemed to resonate with the beat of the engines, flung back from the few remaining derelict houses that were still standing. As we gazed down from our air-conditioned, cushioned luxury it wrapped itself around us like a taunt.

"With half the police force gone, New Orleans has one of the highest crime rates in the country," Capt Neal said. He did not sound proud of the achievement. "We got half the police force and a population down by two-thirds, but there's still the same number of arrests. Times like these, seems only the lowlifes prosper."

I skimmed the other faces. Their expressions were largely turned inward, sombre.

"This was a tragedy," Gabe Baptiste said, as if a news crew was there to record his concern for posterity.

If you care so much, why haven't you been back before now?

Blake Dyer leaned forwards to catch Baptiste's eye. "Son, look around you," he said. "It still is."

Capt Neal started to take us up, guiding the helo onto a new course.

"I'll take you out over what's known as the funnel," he said. "The storm surge came up the Mississippi about fifteen feet high, as well as into the Mississippi River Gulf Outlet and through Lake Borgne, and it all converged in the funnel. Then as the eye passed over, it pushed colossal storm surge down Industrial Canal from Lake Ponchartrain as well." He shook his head. "This area got hit every which way."

I peered out of the far window. Below I could see the wide canal, just beyond what looked like the world's largest scrapyard.

And just as we started to pass over it, Sean—sitting by the near window—went rigid and let out a yell.

Just one word—possibly the word nobody in a low-flying helo ever wants to hear. I certainly didn't.

"INCOMING!"

You can't shout something like that to a pilot with combat experience and not expect an instant, visceral response. Capt Neal was a decorated veteran who had lost none of his instincts when he'd returned to civilian aviation. He jinked, almost a nervous twitch of hands and feet on the controls. The cabin tilted wildly and lashed sideways.

I looked left. The view through the side window was almost straight down into the street below. I was just in time to see the streaking exhaust of the shoulder-launched missile heading straight for us.

EIGHTEEN

Time slowed, the way it does for me at moments of high-intensity stress. The rocket-propelled grenade seemed to hang in the air, climbing so slowly I was almost certain the pilot's split-second reaction would get us clear.

It didn't, of course.

Shoulder-fired RPGs have a relatively low muzzle velocity—around three hundred metres per second. Half the speed of an average rifle bullet.

Still much too fast to miss a large, near-static target less than a hundred metres away—barely a quarter of the weapon's maximum effective range.

Capt Neal's manoeuvre saved us a direct hit, but didn't turn it into a miss.

There was an explosive impact somewhere aft of the cabin. The whole airframe shuddered like a harpooned whale, staggered to the side and went into a violently uneven lateral spin.

This close to the ground there wasn't much anyone could do, least of all the pilot. He fought gravity and physics all the way down, yanking up on the collective just before contact to bring us in as gently as he could. It was a losing battle.

We made a rough landing—worse than any bike crash I've ever had. And I've had one or two.

I'd already jammed my head back against the rest to protect my neck, and wrapped my arms tight across my body, but even so we impacted with an almighty buckling whumph that jolted the breath right out of me. I was aware of screaming, male and female, and unsecured limbs jerking around in my peripheral vision.

The Bell continued to spin viciously, ripping the skids loose. The sheer rotational force of the main rotor dragged us round in a horrendous graunching scream of tearing metal on the stony surface. The aircraft kept turning even after we hit, as if trying to screw the wreckage right into the earth. Dead and buried all in one move.

The Bell was wrenched across the ground. It lurched onto its right-hand side. As the rotor blades hammered into the earth and debris they shattered in all directions like flashing daggers in a psycho circus act. One piece sliced through the skin of the cabin right in front of my face. I swear I felt the swish of hot displaced air as it hissed past.

For a second after impact nobody moved. It took that long to recognise we might just have made it down alive, if not exactly unscathed.

The cabin was at almost ninety degrees to vertical, canted over onto its starboard side. I was hanging suspended from my seatbelt and I stretched out my feet onto the cabin wall before releasing the buckle. The turbines were still shrieking and the slop-slop of spilling jet fuel was an acid chemical burn on the back of my tongue. The potential for fire reared up in my mind with nightmare intensity, a visceral response to a primal fear.

I ripped the useless cans from my head and twisted up towards Dyer, still hanging half-above me. I hit the release for his belt and half-caught, half-slid him onto his feet next to me, then ran fast hands over him looking for obvious injuries. There weren't any. He was shaken but basically unhurt.

"Blake, you with me? Blake! We need to get you out, sir, right now!"

He baulked. "But, the others—"

"Sir, with respect, they can go fu—"

"We'll get everyone out." It was Sean who cut harsh across the pair of us. "Nobody gets left behind."

He'd cut himself loose. Before I could argue, he'd gripped the interior grab handles and jacked his body, using both feet to punch the upward door open like a giant flip-top sunroof.

The action drew instant automatic weapons fire from outside. He ducked back immediately and swore under his breath.

From what little I could see of the outside world, we'd come down in the middle of the giant scrapyard I'd seen just before we crashed. Ahead of us was a small mountain of crushed cars and twisted trucks. There were even a couple of old yellow school buses.

79

At a rough guess, the direction of fire was away to our left, which put the helo's floor between us and our attackers. The 429 model's corporate spec included a lot of bells and whistles, but I very much doubted battle-hardening the under-shell was one of them. We were sitting ducks.

"Hey, guys—a little help here?"

It took me a moment to realise the calm voice came from the blonde, Autumn. I glanced down, found her crouched against the far door, which was now the lowest part of the cabin. She was leaning over the inert form of Baptiste's bodyguard, John Franks. He was crumpled against the frame, pale and unconscious, lying half on top of Baptiste. I'd known he was loose in the cabin during the crash, but my responsibility was to my principal, so I'd blanked him out.

Baptiste himself was pale and silent, eyes closed. There was a little blood trickling from a cut above his eyebrow, though, so I judged he was unconscious rather than dead.

But Franks had been the only one not wearing his seatbelt at the time of the crash and had been thrown around the cabin like a medicine ball as we went in hot. The rest of us were lucky he hadn't crushed us to death in the process.

As it was, to begin with I thought Autumn's poppy-covered dress had acquired a few more flowers than I remembered. Then I saw the belt she was heaving tight around Franks's thigh just above the knee, both hands wrapped in the leather, tanned arms taut.

As she shifted position I saw he'd clearly suffered a double compound-fracture of his tib and fib, the jagged ends of the bone jutting out from the lacerated flesh of his lower leg. Even with Autumn's makeshift tourniquet, he was losing blood fast—too much of it. The broken bones must have severed an artery. He had minutes—if he was lucky.

I met Sean's eyes. Franks must have weighed a good two-hundred-and-fifty pounds. We didn't have the sheer muscle available to move him, but— if we wanted to survive—we couldn't stay put either.

"You're going to have to leave him," Sean told her roughly.

"He'll die."

"So will we all if we don't get us the hell out of here," said Capt Neal. He was still dangling half sideways from his harness in the pilot's seat. "I don't suppose one of you boys has a spare pistol, do you? Only, I left mine in my other pants and we got hostiles a'coming in."

I reached down and took Franks's gun off his hip. He wasn't in any state to use it. The gun was a Glock nine. I couldn't see a pro carrying it empty or safe, but as I handed it past the forward row of seats I checked the weight and slid a finger across the loaded-chamber indicator just to make sure.

"There's one up the spout all ready to go," I told the pilot.

"Much obliged," Neal said, like I'd just passed him the salt. "Might want to cover your ears, folks."

With that, he swung the gun towards one of the plexiglas windows in what had been the floor of the cockpit beneath his feet and kept pulling the trigger until the action locked back empty—standard US military operating procedure. The Glock held seventeen rounds and one in the chamber. Even with the warning, it was horribly loud inside the tin can cabin.

"That should keep their heads down a little longer," Neal said with a tired smile. "I'd appreciate an assist with debussing, though. I think I busted both my ankles when we set down."

NINETEEN

John Franks didn't make it. Even with Blake Dyer lending his weight to put pressure above the gaping hole caused by the sheared bones, the wounded man continued to bleed out at a ferocious rate. By the time Sean and I had heaved Capt Neal out of the pilot's seat, it was clear the big bodyguard had already passed desaturation point.

"He's gone," Dyer said quietly, putting one bloodied hand on Autumn's shoulder as she knelt by Franks's side.

She hesitated long enough that I thought she was going to raise objections about leaving his body behind, but she simply nodded tiredly.

"What about Gabe?" Dyer asked. The baseball player had remained with his eyes closed, still and quiet throughout, even while the pilot got his gun off.

Before anyone could stop her, Autumn reached across and slapped Baptiste across the face a couple of times, not lightly. He began to groan instantly, eyelids fluttering.

"He's fine," she said. "He fainted when he saw the blood, is all."

Sean was supporting Capt Neal, one arm under his shoulder to keep just about all the man's weight off his broken legs. No strain showed on Sean's face, only that narrowed down focus I'd seen so often before.

"Charlie, you're going to have to take point."

I nodded, reached for my discarded headset and poked it carefully up through the open door, just a fraction, skylining it.

A single shot pinged off the door frame about half a metre from my hand. I yanked it back down again.

"Well, that's encouraging, I suppose," I said dryly. "Not only do they not have an unlimited supply of ammo, but they're also shit shots."

82

"Why we trying to get out?" Baptiste demanded. He'd come round enough to scrabble his way greenly out from under his bodyguard's corpse and was now trying very hard to keep his gaze anywhere else.

"You smell anything over that cologne you wearing?" Capt Neal demanded. "That's jet fuel, son. Those cowboys want rid of us, all they have to do is toss a cigarette in that growing pond out there, and we're toastier than hell on a *real* hot day."

For a moment I thought Baptiste was going to make a dive for the open hatch regardless of the dangers. Autumn must have thought the same, because she put a hand on his arm that was both reassuring and restraining.

"Best way out is probably through the canopy—unless they got the nose covered, too," Capt Neal said. "There's an axe clipped just under the front of my seat."

"You carry an *axe* on a helicopter?" I asked. "Did your horoscope this morning warn you to expect a bad day at work?"

"Hell no, or I'd've called in sick."

Carefully, leaning past the edge of the passenger seating, I worked my arm around the base of the pilot's seat and found a blunted handle of what felt like a short fireman's axe. It was held on quick-release spring clips. One wrench had it free.

Without a pause I swung the axe backhanded into what had been the upper part of the canopy above the co-pilot's seat. The clear plastic dome cracked without breaking. I hit it again in the same place, and a third time. A fourth.

I'd always assumed the plexiglas canopies on aircraft were designed to withstand bird strikes at a hundred-and-fifty miles an hour, so there was no way it was going to give in gracefully to a small Brit with an axe—even one as pissed off as me. In reality, I was surprised how easily it all gave way after half a dozen decent swings.

Our attackers couldn't fail to miss what we were doing, and they didn't like it much. More shots poured in, striking sparks off the road surface around us and pummelling into the body of the stricken Bell. I widened the hole in the plexiglas along the edge of the frame until it finally crumpled outwards. Incoming rounds punctuated every beat.

"OK, people," Sean shouted above the gunfire. "Get ready to move."

"They'll just pick us off as we go out," Baptiste objected.

I don't care how talented he was at throwing a ball, I was getting kind of tired of this guy.

"Maybe, maybe not," I told him. "But if we stay where we are they'll pick us off for sure."

I scrambled out of the cockpit first, the SIG in my hands, and took the luxury of maybe half a second to orientate. The landscape was bizarre and alien, a mass of twisted metal from industrial and domestic machinery, all mixed in together. In front of me I could see old truck rims, chain-link fencing, and fancy wrought-ironwork like the front of the derelict house we'd been looking at only minutes before.

We'd come down at the base of the mountain of half-crushed cars, leaving no safe escape route that way. Climbing up would have been too slow and too exposed. I already felt like I had a target pinned to my chest. What was left of the rotor head was jammed up close into the side of a pickup truck. Given enough time and the right tools we probably could have built ourselves an armoured car out of the bits lying around. Shame we didn't have either.

To one side of us was a storage shed, surrounded by long grass, twisted weeds, and huge lumps of rusted metal. They were so big it took me a moment to realise they were engine blocks. Some of them were bigger than a family car.

Could be worse, could be better. We'll just have to make the most of it.

Autumn climbed out next. I pushed her down into a crouch next to the collapsed pickup while I pulled first Baptiste then Dyer out of the downed helo, then helped Sean haul Capt Neal through the jagged aperture.

All the time, intermittent shots thunked into the underside of the Bell. It was almost inevitable that eventually something would spark hard enough to ignite the spilled jet fuel. It had pooled into the muddy ground around us like snow-melt from a mountain in spring.

"We got fire!" Autumn called, sounding remarkably calm.

I looked in the direction of her flung arm, saw the first of the flames licking around the back of the cabin, stealing up on us around what was left of the tail section.

"We head for the shed over there," Sean said. "Charlie's on point. Autumn, stick with her." He looked at the two men. "You'll have to carry our pilot."

84

"Sure," said Dyer.

"What?" said Baptiste. "Who *you* carrying?"

"The rest of you," Sean told him shortly. "I stop anyone shooting you in the arse while we're getting to safety. Now move it!"

I didn't stop to see if Baptiste obeyed, just ran in a sideways crouch, keeping the SIG up. Autumn had slipped out of her high-heeled strappy sandals and was holding them as she ran with me, those long legs effortlessly keeping stride. No fuss and no complaining. I looked at the wicked debris lying around and hoped her anti-tetanus booster was up to date.

As soon as we cleared the flames licking around the tail, the gunfire switched target from the Bell to us. I took a bearing and returned fire in two-round bursts, enough to suppress their aim rather than with serious intent.

The fire was now giving off heavy smoke, which would work in our favour on all kinds of levels as far as both rescue and evasion was concerned.

I thought of Franks, whose body still lay in the burning wreckage, then let it go. There'd be time for the dead later. Right now my mind was focused on how to keep the rest of us from joining him.

TWENTY

Behind us, I could hear Baptiste and Dyer running awkwardly with Capt Neal slung between them. As his feet occasionally tagged the rubble underfoot, the pilot let out a roar of rage, using the pain, turning it into a battle-cry that urged them on.

Then Sean cleared the Bell's tail and took up fire.

The door to the storage shed was studded metal and half open. I caught a flash of dirty rust before I hit it hard with my shoulder. I expected resistance but it crashed inwards and I went stumbling through much faster than I'd intended, almost splintering the rotten timber of the frame in best Hollywood style. Still, better that than bouncing off for a second try.

Inside the shed were a couple of giant earth movers, no doubt used for shovelling the scrap into manageable piles. They loomed above us like mechanical monsters. I ducked between the two of them and got everybody down on the ground where the cover was best. The shed had no windows and although the walls were only corrugated iron sheeting at least they'd be shooting blind.

Dyer was panting with the effort. His regular visits to the tennis club and the golf course had not prepared him for this kind of effort, I realised—certainly not under this kind of pressure. Baptiste was used to pressure of a different kind—big game outcomes rested on his physical prowess and he was fit enough to cope, but he was also shit-scared and not hiding it well.

Autumn, on the other hand, was taking all this with a simple acceptance that was raising all kinds of nasty suspicions in my mind. She had not been on the original guest list, and although superficial checks had come up clear, I made a mental note to ask Parker to dig deeper, first chance I got.

Either that or it was a bastardisation of the old Kipling poem. Something about those who keep their heads when all about them are in panic being too stupid to fully appreciate the true seriousness of the situation.

Sean backed into the shed with his Glock still up and level, aimed for the door aperture. The first person to stick their head through would lose it.

"I called it in before we evac'd the helo, so all we've got to do is sit tight and repel incomers until the good guys get to us—they reckon ETA nine minutes," he said to me, not shifting his gaze from the hallway except a brief flick towards the injured pilot. "How you doing, Captain?"

"Better than I would've been, if you hadn't gotten me out," Capt Neal said. "Much obliged to you all for that, too."

"Hey, your part of the deal was getting us down in one piece."

Capt Neal gave him a wry look. "Yeah, that one didn't work out too well, now did it?"

He glanced at Baptiste as he said it, but the younger man had not shed any tears for his dead bodyguard. I just felt a great sadness for Franks. In this business we were all of us prepared to die if the job demanded it, but to go down so uselessly seemed a waste of his courage and his intent, like a soldier dying in a training accident instead of on the battlefield, or a racing driver getting knocked down crossing the road.

Still, dead was dead, whichever way you squared it.

"What happens now?" Blake Dyer asked, getting his breath back.

"I hit the emergency distress beacon, so they know to look for us," Capt Neal said. "I guess the smoke'll guide 'em in easy enough."

"You had time to do all that as we crashed?" Autumn asked, eyebrows climbing.

"Afterward," he said. "I kinda had my hands full up to that point, ma'am."

"I expected more warning buzzers and sirens as we went down," I commented, keeping my voice low. I was watching the light patterns outside the cracks in the shed wall as I spoke, checking for anybody approaching from the rear. I suppose we should have been keeping silent, but what with the crash and the exchange of gunfire my ears were in temporary shock. The bad guys could have stomped around out there with steel segs on their boots and I would barely have heard them coming. I preferred to trust my eyes.

Besides, most of the little group were shocky. Better to let them talk it out.

"All you get's a low-rotor-speed warning. Not much call for anything else," Capt Neal was saying. "Once you lose the anti-torque rotor and you start to plummet and spin like some whirling dervish, you kinda know it's all going to shit—pardon my language, ma'am."

I smiled. "Ever have anything like that happen to you before?"

He shrugged. His face was pale and clammy. The ankles must have been giving him hell, but I knew taking his boots off at this stage would be a mistake. Better to leave them holding everything together until we could get him professional help.

"Had a couple of engine failures and had to auto-rotate down. And I knocked a dead branch out of a tree once in Africa. Damn thing fell down through the rotor blades and snapped one of 'em clean off. We were three hours' flight time from nearest civilisation at the time."

Autumn asked, "So how did you get back?"

He gave her a pain-hazed smile. "Carefully, ma'am. Damn carefully."

Half a dozen shots suddenly crackled through the walls of the shed high above the earthmovers and disappeared straight out through the far side. New little beams of light appeared to mark their passage. Everybody ducked instinctively. At the same time, we took fire from the front, the rounds zipping through the doorway. A couple pinged off the front of the earthmover behind me. I was pleased to note they didn't have much effect.

I lifted the SIG up past the massive front tyre and loosed two shots in reply through the open doorway. No point in more.

Then we waited. There was maybe ten seconds of silence before a voice called out loudly from outside.

"Hey, *mes chers*, you know we got you pinned down in there." There was a certain rhythm to the voice I'd noticed down here, the softening of "there" almost into "dere". So, these were local boys. "You wanna give yourselves up and come out, maybe we don't shoot you. You fight well—full of courage, huh? But fight on and you die."

"You think you can kill us?" I called back. "How's that working out for you so far?"

88

That earned me a vicious stare from Baptiste. "What the hell you doing?" he hissed. "*Trying* to get these guys mad?"

It was Sean who threw him a brief silencing look. "They already brought down a helicopter and shot the shit out of us," he murmured. "You think they're not fairly pissed off already?"

"You one of the bodyguards, huh?" shouted the voice from outside. "You prepared risking those people in there to find out? *Quoi faire?*" The voice was neither young nor old, but there was a lazy arrogance to it, and a cold winding thread. He would kill us if he got the chance and would maybe even enjoy it. "We only want one of you. The rest can go free."

"Yeah, but which one?"

There came a harsh bark of laughter. "They know who they are."

I glanced between Blake Dyer, Autumn and Baptiste. "You want to draw lots?"

Baptiste's mouth gaped. Autumn leaned across to him. "For God's sake, Gabe, she's kidding."

Damn, but I was actually beginning to like this woman.

"I know that!" He scowled, voice sulky. "But her timing sucks."

I raised my voice. "Are you going to tell us who it is you're after, or do we play twenty questions?"

He laughed again. It was not a happy sound. "So you want to play games with me, *chérie*? Only, that will just make me crazy, and you wouldn't like me when I'm crazy." He paused. I could almost see him posturing with his gang outside. "You ask me I think I can kill you all? Want to see me try?"

"Do, or do not," I shouted back. "There is no 'try'."

"What's that from—Sun Tzu's *The Art of War*?" Blake Dyer asked.

I grinned at him. "I think it was Yoda in *Star Wars: Return of the Jedi*, actually."

Even Sean allowed himself a small smile, a nod that might even have been approval. Past a clenched jaw he muttered, "Just stall him 'til the cavalry gets here."

"Hey, *friend*," I called outside. "How many men do you have with you?"

"Enough, I think."

"Really—more than we have bullets? I only ask because I'm guessing your guys are all gangbangers and wannabes and hangers-on, yeah?"

"I said 'stall', not provoke him into something stupid," Sean added.

There was a long offended pause. "Is there a point to these insults? Only, if you're right, and I am surrounded by lowlifes and outlaws, *chérie*, what's to stop me letting them have some ... fun with you and the other *beb* after we kill the rest?"

"Training and experience, friend. We're trained for one shot one kill and we've done it plenty of times before. And we have more than enough ammo to take out your crew with a few to spare to *have some fun* with you before we're done. Still want to play?"

Sean rolled his eyes. I winked at him. Baptiste was staring open-mouthed again.

And then, in the distance, we heard the first of the sirens, the fast chop of an incoming helo. Never more welcome. I heard shouts from outside, angry instructions and not a little swearing.

"Looks like you have friends in high places, *chérie*," the man outside said, sounding rueful rather than angry. "So ... until next time. And there *will be* a next time. On that you have my word."

You and whose army?

But I said nothing. There was nothing to say. I reckoned the growing sounds of incoming law enforcement—police and SWAT—pretty much said it for me.

TWENTY-ONE

I woke in the dark, sweating, and fearful that I was not alone.
It had been another late night, another delayed turn-in.
First there'd been the local law enforcement agencies to deal
with, then the paramedics who'd carted Capt Neal off to hospital.
They'd insisted on checking us all over with irritatingly slow and
methodical thoroughness.

Up until that point, I thought I'd escaped uninjured from the
crash. It was only when the paramedics began examining me
that I realised just how bruised and battered I was.

Fortunately the bruises were nowhere that showed, although
I had purplish discolouration spreading from elbow to shoulder
that resembled a scale map of New Zealand. It looked like it was
planning to reach actual size.

Now, I had to suppress a groan for the effort it took to roll
over fast and grab the SIG from under a folded towel on the
nightstand. In the past I'd tried sleeping with the gun under my
pillow but if I had a restless night there was no telling where it
could end up by morning.

I'd foreseen a restless night, but not because of this.

"If there's anything in your hands," I said, my voice a sleep-
laden growl, "throw it away now or I'll make you drop it."

A shadow detached itself from the wall by the three-pace
hallway leading to the bathroom and outer door. I felt my right
index finger begin to tauten, but a moment later there was a
click as the bathroom light flicked on. I flinched from the sudden
brightness but saw enough to recognise Sean in the shaft of light.

There was something about the way he stood, the tension in
his body, that kept the SIG in my hands and the fear in my
throat.

I swallowed, forced my shoulders down as I sat upright,
letting the gun relax into my lap, finger resting outside the

trigger guard. If Sean noticed that I didn't lay the weapon aside completely, he didn't comment.

"Hello, Charlie," he said softly. "I s'pose it's stupid to ask if you're awake."

"I'm bloody *wide* awake now," I said, and saw for the first time he was carrying a bottle of Glenfiddich single malt in one hand and a pair of cut-glass tumblers in the other.

"I'm guessing you don't really want me to throw this away?" he said, lifting the whisky.

I hesitated. I was dog tired, but this was the first time since coming out of the coma that Sean had sought me out. The first time he'd reached out to me. I sensed his need for reassurance and craved my own.

"And I'm guessing you can't sleep," I said.

I always wore shorts and a T-shirt to bed when I was working, just in case I had to jump up in the dark. No point in having to take on an unexpected midnight threat wearing nothing but a smile. Besides, ejected brass spits out plenty hot enough to burn unprotected skin.

But for all the protection my clothing seemed to be offering me right now I might as well have been naked.

I sat up, pulling the sheets more tightly around my body and wrapping them under my arms.

"I get the feeling I never used to like drinking alone," Sean said. "Join me?"

How can I say no to that, Sean? Even if I wanted to ...

"OK."

He didn't move right away, just stayed by the edge of the hallway with the light behind him and his face in shadow. I half turned, reached behind me and switched on the bedside lamp just for my own defence.

He was fully dressed, I saw. Not the ruined suit from earlier but jeans and a plain black T-shirt that sat flat and broad across his chest. My heart kicked like a long-distance runner entering the final bend before the home straight.

"If you're staying, take a seat," I said. I cleared my throat. "Glenfiddich always was one of my favourites."

"I know," Sean said quietly.

My heart lurched. "Oh?"

"You drank it at the little pub we went to—that first weekend we spent away together. Remember?"

92

Oh Christ, did I remember ...

I'd never forgotten a moment of that time-out-of-time. It had seemed somehow surreal back then, as if it wasn't meant to be and couldn't last. But it had been perfect, too. Even what came after had failed to eclipse it totally from my mind.

It was an illicit assignation—the first time Sean and I had been away together, the first time we'd slept together. Neither of us got much sleep. Having only a forty-eight-hour pass from camp tends to concentrate the mind. We'd crammed as much sheer experience of each other as we'd been able to into that limited time together.

"... Remember?"

In one explosive instant I remembered it all. A bombardment of sensation, of touch and feel and sight and smell and taste. I'd absorbed Sean on a cellular level, in every way I could possibly imagine. I'd given him all of myself, poured myself into him. I'd held nothing back.

I'd thought he'd done the same.

A whisper: "I remember ..."

He moved further into the room with that easy stride, but instead of heading for the armchair near the window he sat on the end of the bed. He set the glasses down on the mattress and unscrewed the cap of the distinctive triangular bottle with those long clever fingers, pouring generous measures for both of us.

I took the glass he offered, careful not to let our hands touch, chinked the rim to his.

"*Sláinte,*" I said, and let the liquid courage run down my throat, light my veins.

"*Na zdoravye,*" Sean replied, took a long swallow of his own.

The silence lay between us, crouched and vibrating gently, almost a shiver. I stretched round to put the SIG back under the towel on the bedside table. When I turned back I found Sean's eyes on the scar around the base of my neck. He was frowning again, the same way he'd frowned when Gabe Baptiste had pushed him to recall the last time they'd met. I struggled not to put a hand up to the fading line, to cover it from his gaze.

Occasionally I'd claimed the scar was surgical, but anyone with knowledge could see it was from an attack. You don't have to add the words "near fatal" when somebody tries to cut your throat. Not when they've done it before and were looking forward to doing it again.

93

That scar, a fading four-inch ragged line, served as a permanent visible reminder of what people were prepared to do to me, if I let them.

And triggered the memory of what I was prepared to do in return.

"I should know how you got that, shouldn't I?" Sean said, almost under his breath. He dropped his nose into the glass again. "I should ... but I don't."

"You weren't around when it happened," I said, "if that helps."

He paused as if considering. "No. No it doesn't. All I get is a feeling—a feeling that I ... let you down somehow. Did I?" He shook his head before I could answer. "I mean, was I supposed to have your back and I ... didn't, is that what happened?"

I heard the tension in his voice, the intensity. This mattered to him, but I didn't allow myself to wonder why, or how much.

"No," I said softly. "That's not what happened. You weren't there, Sean. It wasn't your fault. It was nothing to do with you."

We sipped again in silence. The room began to buzz. I told myself that was the whisky. I'd been too tired to face dinner, so perhaps the effect of the alcohol was amplified and accelerated by an empty stomach.

Or perhaps the buzzing was just inside my head.

"Was it anything to do with ... Vic Morton? With what you told me—about ... you and him? I don't remember that, either. Nothing. It's all just one big void—kind of grey-black, like a TV set picking up a dead channel."

For just a moment a kind of warmth flooded me. Sean admitting he didn't remember something was so much better than him denying it had ever happened.

Progress, of a sort.

He shifted, leaned his forearms on his knees with the glass cradled in his hands, suddenly fascinated by the way the whisky swirled around inside it. "It's like, occasionally the picture flickers and just for a second I get an image I can hardly catch, never mind know what it means. Subliminal, you know?"

"I know," I said. The doctors had told us what to expect. They'd explained it in complicated terms, full of jargon that meant as little as Sean's disjointed memories.

I'd even swallowed my pride and called upon my father's medical expertise to cut through the excess terminology and give me the bottom line.

94

He'd come back with a bagful of maybes. *Maybe* Sean would reforge the neural pathways that connected him to his past, and his past to mine. *Maybe* he would remember fully or even partially what we had.

Or maybe he would never remember "us" at all.

There were only so many times I could rephrase the same question before it finally hit home that I was not going to get an answer I liked. An answer I could live with.

I stopped asking.

"You weren't there, Sean," I said again. "There was nothing you could have done."

"I'm not sure if that makes me feel better or worse," he said, rubbing at the side of his temple in that unconscious gesture. It made me want to gather him close, to hold his head to my breast and rock him to the beat of my heart, a strong and steady proof of life beneath his ear. To stroke my own fingers across the scar as if by doing so I could smooth it all away. I took a knuckle-whitening grip on the whisky instead.

"You didn't come over to my place to discuss old news," I said, aware of the uptight tone in my own voice but unable to let go. If I did I might never get a hold of myself again. "So, why don't you tell me what's on your mind?"

TWENTY-TWO

Sean took a long pull on his Glenfiddich, watching my face above the rim of the glass as if he knew what I'd really been asking. He had the darkest eyes and right then, in the subdued cross-flow of light from the bedside lamp and the bathroom, they looked totally black from iris to pupil.

The eyes of someone not entirely human.

I suppressed a shudder. There had been a lot of times when Sean had frightened me on an instinctive, visceral level, as if I was trying to domesticate something wild. Every so often I got the feeling I really shouldn't turn my back to him.

Now was one of those times.

So I waited, glass cradled in my hands, letting my body heat warm the spirit and the spirit warm me in its turn. It took Sean a few moments to answer my question, but I would have taken anything faster as a sign of glib evasion.

"You were good out there today," he said at last, his tone dispassionate. "Cool, deliberate, focused."

I shrugged, awkward. Whatever I'd been expecting, that had not been it.

"Yeah, well, I've had some good training."

He watched me for a moment longer. "So that's your Achilles' heel," he murmured. "Throw accusations and insults at you, you come out fighting. Try a compliment and you crumble."

"Not so," I denied, my voice dry. "Sometimes I take a swing at people who are nice to me as well."

"Doesn't come naturally to you, though, does it, Charlie? Accepting praise, I mean." He paused, as if uncertain. "Did I never ... praise you?"

I swallowed, mouth suddenly dry, but resisted the urge to gulp down more whisky. That way untold danger lay.

96

"It has been known," I said carefully. "But you pushed hard, too."

He nodded like that made sense to him. "Because I wanted you to be the best," he said, and it was Sean the training instructor talking, not the close-protection expert. *Not the lover.* "Ever thought that might have been because I didn't want you to get yourself killed on your first covert op?"

"I never made it into active service with any kind of black ops unit," I said. "I was out on my ear well before any postings like that were handed out."

They made sure of it.

I so nearly added, "Your mate Morton knows all about that one. Ask him if you don't believe me," but I held my tongue.

"You worked for me as a bodyguard before we came over here to work for Parker," Sean said, almost to himself. Something about his voice told me he was only repeating what he'd been told. External information rather than internal knowledge.

He looked at me again, gaze switching from my eyes to my mouth. "How could I let you do that kind of work if we were...?"

"... in a relationship, you mean?" I finished for him.

You think you had that kind of say over what I did with my life?

Perhaps not the most diplomatic of possible answers. Instead, I gave another shrug that had the sheets threatening to desert me. I pulled them more firmly into place. "You pushed me all the harder." My turn to pause, then a little reproach: "And you trusted me."

"Yeah, I can believe that," he said slowly. "Like I said, you were good out there today, Charlie. Bloody good, if you must know. It makes me wonder ..."

His voice trailed off and I was the one left wondering where he'd been heading with that thought.

Wonder what, Sean? You wonder if Vic Morton's been filling your head with lies about me? About how I only managed any kind of advancement on my back? About how I used "crying rape" as an excuse because I wasn't good enough to make it and couldn't face the ignominy of walking away of my own volition? Why don't you ask that kind of question out loud, Sean? Oh boy, then you'll see me come out fighting ...

But some battles you know from the outset you can't win.

He looked up, straight into and through my eyes, into my mind—just like he always could. All I could see in return was my own face reflected back at me.

"It makes me wonder if you were right to call Parker about me. To tell him you didn't think I was ready," he said, stark—and so out of left field it came from another field altogether. "After today *I* don't think I'm ready either."

A part of me wanted to agree with him and reach for the phone, but another part knew what that would do to him—to any chance of us. Instead I found myself saying, "It's a skill like any other, Sean. You acquired it once. You can do it again."

"How do *you* do it?"

I stared at him blankly. "Do what?"

"All ... this." He gestured with both hands, glass still in one but almost empty now. "The job. The life. I mean, Christ Jesus—getting shot at while you're walking down the street—or parking your car, or taking a sightseeing flight. All of it."

I went very still inside. *My God, it ... scared you*, I realised. *Today actually bone-deep-and-shaken scared you.*

But the very fact that I'd finally found something—anything—that put the wind up Sean Meyer did not give me any satisfaction. In fact, it put the wind up me to a far greater degree.

Sean had always been my rock, my anchor point and my centre. When I feared I might have crossed the lines of violence into a no-man's land from which there was no safe return, he'd been the one whose calm voice of reason had talked me back in. The one who convinced me I might still be a viable member of the human race after all.

Without him I'd already come dangerously close to losing that grip on my humanity. I'd killed a man—not for self-defence or to defend another—but to extract a form of justice that was as primitive as it was extreme.

An eye for an eye.

And my most fervent hope, when I learned Sean had woken from his coma, was that one day I'd be able to tell him what I'd done. That one day I'd maybe even get his blessing, or at least his forgiveness.

The old Sean would have approved. Hell, he would have fought me for the privilege. But the new Sean ... that was a different matter.

98

Now, I shrugged, hunted for words I didn't have and suspected probably did not exist.

"I do it because … it's who I am," I said at last, and saw a frustrated gesture forming at what he assumed was a throwaway answer. "No, let me finish, Sean. You told me once that I was perfect for Special Forces—that Colonel Parris was a fool to let me go. But he *did* let me go—with a boot up my backside to help me on my way." I still remembered that conversation with Sean, every word of it. OK, so I'd had to pull a gun to get him to sit still long enough to listen. But listen he did—in the end.

Looking at his face now I knew he had absolutely no recall of it.

I sighed. "Close protection is about the nearest I can get to that life and still live with myself." I tried a smile. "The nearest I can get without ending up in prison, that is."

I remembered, too, a lecture from my father some time ago. After Sean and I had reunited, after I'd headed down the road which led me here. Up to that point, the deaths on my hands had all been judged justified. But what would happen, he wanted to know, when it all became so easy—so second nature—that I took a life I *couldn't* justify?

"If you stay involved with Sean Meyer you will *end up killing again,"* my father said. *"And next time, Charlotte, you might not get away with it."*

"Out there today, pinned down in that crashed helo with the fuel pouring out of it and taking fire"—Sean shook his head as if to clear it—"I was fucking terrified, if I'm honest."

"And you think I wasn't?"

"If you were, you hid it bloody well."

"Just because you couldn't see it, doesn't mean it wasn't there," I said. "Fear helps keep you alive—if you use it rather than let it use you. It's what tempers recklessness, makes you think through an action, however briefly, before you do it."

"I was close to losing control," he admitted abruptly, unconvinced.

I reached out then, tentative, put a hand on his bare forearm and tried to ignore the fizz of contact through every nerve. Hairs riffled along my own arms, but the touch also set off a more basic chain-reaction that pooled in my belly. I tried to ignore it.

"Everybody with half a brain is scared under fire," I told him. "What matters is how you deal with it."

99

His gaze was locked on my fingers where they rested on his arm. "Simple as that?" he murmured dryly. "And who dispensed that little pearl of wisdom?"

I knew his reaction was an instinctive denial of something he must have known, deep down, was true. Even so, the edge of derision to his voice stung enough for me to remove my hand. I washed down the last of my whisky and held the empty glass out towards him.

"You did," I said.

TWENTY-THREE

Excuse me," Sean said, "but that's bullshit—and you know it."

Tom O'Day looked vaguely shocked by the blunt declaration. He glanced at me but I kept my face professionally blank. The old Sean—the polished version who'd run his own highly successful close-protection agency for five years after the army—would not have been so forthright in tone, even if he might have echoed the sentiment.

It was the morning after the helo crash. We were in Blake Dyer's suite with the remnants of his belated breakfast still on the table. In view of the events of yesterday, though, the table was no longer quite so close to the window as it had been.

Tom O'Day had arrived while our principal was still eating, and studiously ignored the packed suitcases standing in the suite's hallway. We'd already persuaded Dyer to recall his pilot. A flight plan was filed for later that morning to take him straight back to Florida as soon as a slot opened up. I confess that he hadn't taken much persuading. If anything he seemed relieved to have the decision forced on him.

The memory of the missile striking the tail rotor, the brief but terrifying plummet, the shock of impact. It was all still very fresh in Blake Dyer's mind and was likely to remain so.

As well as the ubiquitous and silent Hobson, O'Day had Autumn in tow. He and the cool blonde chatted with Dyer inconsequentially over coffee and croissants for maybe half an hour. After he'd expressed admiration for my principal's courage and iron constitution, O'Day got down to business.

"Need you to do something for me, Blake," he'd said, looking his old friend straight in the eye. "Need you to put yesterday's excitement down to some random act of violence and stay on. Can you do that for me?"

101

It was at that point Sean made his interjection. It ran so close to the immediate thoughts passing through my head that for a second I wasn't sure which of us had actually spoken.

Tom O'Day might have looked shocked, but Blake Dyer put his coffee cup down slowly. His eyes met those of Autumn, sitting opposite. She was wearing a designer trouser-suit today with a long-sleeved jacket, probably to hide the bruises from the crash. But from her bored expression she may as well have spent yesterday morning at some mid-town gallery, gazing at mildly inferior works of art.

"There was nothing random about it, Tom—as I'm sure the young lady here will tell you," Dyer said at last, nodding towards Autumn. "They were after somebody most particularly—no doubt about that. And the death toll could easily have been seven instead of one if it wasn't for this fine pair of professionals from Armstrong-Meyer." He indicated Sean and me, keeping station on opposite sides of the room. "And the casualties could well have included two people sitting at this very table right now."

Tom O'Day cleared his throat. "Aw hell, Blake, you think I don't know that?" he demanded. The animation went out of him for a few moments and he suddenly looked a decade older. "But I've spent best part of two years putting together this whole dog-and-pony show. If one of my oldest friends turns tail at the first sign of a little trouble, how's that gonna look?"

"If you call firing some kind of ground-to-air missile at us 'a little trouble' then I'd hate to know what you think of as a major disaster," Blake Dyer said.

O'Day leaned forwards in his chair. "Hurricane Katrina was a major disaster, Blake," he said quietly. "And the tragedy is still ongoing—folk down here have been abandoned and ignored by their own government. Kicked to the kerb like so much garbage. We have a chance to make a real difference to these people. You really going to let a small minority ruin all the good work we're trying to do here?"

Blake Dyer dabbed his lips with his linen serviette, put it down very deliberately. "Hard to play the poverty card when they're toting military hardware."

Tom O'Day gave a dismissive shrug. "We're shipping so much out to the Gulf and Afghanistan that stuff like that goes missing all the time," he said. "RPGs are a dime a dozen at just about any surplus store."

Blake Dyer raised an eyebrow but didn't contradict his assertion. "You'll still get my cheque, Tom," he said, "but it will be in the mail—*after* I get home to the sunshine state."

O'Day sighed, as if he really hadn't wanted to bring out the big guns, but had been given no option. "You're godfather to my son," he said flatly. "Apart from me and his mother, the boy has no other family. He's taken on a big role in all this—finally shouldering some responsibility. How's it gonna look to Jimmy if you don't stick around to see it?"

"That's a low blow, Tom," Dyer said, but his mouth quirked just a little. "Even from you."

"Yes, it surely is," O'Day agreed cheerfully. "You feeling guilty yet?"

There was a pause and then both men were smiling. And Sean and I were not.

I stepped forward. "Sir—"

"No, Charlie. I'm afraid Tom's right," Blake Dyer said without taking his eyes away from his old friend. "Cancel the plane, would you? I think I'm going to stay 'til the fat lady sings."

It was casually phrased, but there was no doubt in my mind that if we tried to change his mind again we'd run headlong into a steel plate wall.

Tom O'Day sat back in his chair looking thoroughly satisfied. Well, I hadn't thought he'd got a sale-or-return deal on all that champagne.

That didn't mean I had to like or approve the situation, though.

O'Day allowed himself a deep chuckle. "I knew you'd come around, Blake," he said. And just when that made me bristle he added candidly, "Leastways, I hoped to hell you would. 'Sides anything else, if I come right out and announce that some of the very folk we're trying to help most just tried to kill a bunch of us with a damned bazooka, what effect d'you think that's gonna have on potential benefactors?"

He had a point. If the locals had cash for that kind of ordnance, they had money for reconstruction without any outside help.

Blake Dyer sat back in his chair, unconsciously mirroring his friend. "Are you asking me to lie for you, Tom?"

"If that's what it takes to keep this show on the road? Damn right I am."

Dyer paused, considering, then took a breath. But to my complete surprise, it was to Tom O'Day's companion that his attention switched. "What about you, Autumn?" he asked. "You think that will work?"

TWENTY-FOUR

The blonde pursed her lips. "The news networks were slow to get wind of the crash, by which time SWAT had cleared the scene and only local law enforcement personnel were visible on the ground," she said calmly. "The damage to the helicopter was disguised by the crash and the fire, and was not obviously caused by an attack, so putting it out that it was some kind of mechanical failure might just hold up." She gave O'Day a faint smile. "It's an oil company helicopter, after all. They're notoriously hard-ridden. After Capt Neal's valiant efforts, I'm afraid I'd be reluctant to go along with any kind of 'pilot error' claim."

I felt a guilty astonishment wash down over me. My eyes flicked to Sean, leaning with folded arms against the far wall. His raised eyebrow mirrored my own.

What was that about never judging a book by its cover …?

Tom O'Day beamed. "Bright as well as beautiful, huh?" He was proud as a parent showing off a precocious child.

Autumn favoured him with a faint answering smile of her own, then her gaze veered and met mine. I saw a certain conspiratorial glimmer there.

You get underestimated based solely on the way you look, too, don't you?

I hoped she'd never guess that I'd made the same false assumptions about her as everybody else, but I had a feeling she already knew.

Shit.

Blake Dyer spread his hands in capitulation. "Who am I to argue with the experts," he said, reaching across the table. "OK, Tom, you have my word. It was a terrible accident and nothing more." They shook on it with knuckle-cracking gusto. "I assume you've also had a chat with young Gabe Baptiste. This whole thing really had him shook up."

"Oh, I don't think you need to worry about him. Whatever negatives darlin' Ysabeau is holding on the kid, they're keeping him pretty much in line," Tom O'Day said, uncoiling his lean frame from the chair. "By the time I got there this morning, she'd already put the squeeze on him to stay."

Autumn rose gracefully, turning to me.

"Would you mind showing me to the bathroom?" she asked.

I bit back the comment that I was sure someone of her evident intelligence could find their own way unaided, and inclined my head politely.

Just outside the door she paused. "I'll save you the trouble of investigating me, Charlie," she said, "although I have no doubt that someone with your level of professionalism will have already set that ball in motion."

"I rang New York as soon as we got back yesterday to ask Parker Armstrong to put together a packet on you," I admitted. I checked my watch. "I'm expecting a call back from him any time."

She smiled, genuine and infectious, engaging her whole face. "How about I give you the highlights now?" she said. "Yes, I did some modelling while I was at Harvard, but only because it was fun for a while, and easy, and helped buy my first Mercedes-Benz. I have an IQ in the one-seventies and was a partner in one of the largest PR companies on the East Coast before Tom head-hunted me to shake up his corporate PR division last month. Will that keep you happy for a while?"

"For a while," I agreed gravely. "But Parker will also tell me what you like for breakfast, and what you wear to sleep in."

She laughed out loud, a husky wisp of sound. "An oat-based smoothie before my personal trainer arrives at six every day," she answered in turn. "And—like Marilyn Monroe—I wear nothing in bed but Chanel Number Five."

I laughed with her. Hard not to. "You were terrific yesterday, by the way," I said. "Not many civilians can keep it together under fire so well. I wondered if you might be a spook."

"I'll take that as a compliment," she said. "And right back atcha'. I've worked with a lot of rich and famous people, been around a lot of security personnel. You're right up there with the best of them, and I'd take a guess that the only reason you're not

106

running your own outfit right now, honey, is because you're just a little woman in a big man's world."

"That's not an assumption most people make more than once," I said dryly.

The smile widened again. She opened her small clutch bag, magicked a card out of the interior without having to dig for it. "I could have you perceived as the leading close-protection expert in the country inside twelve months," she said. "If you ever decide to hang out your own shingle, give me a call. What you have—what you are—trust me, it's marketing gold."

I smoothed my thumb across the embossed lettering. A.D. SINCLAIR—PUBLIC RELATIONS was all it said across the centre, with a discreet phone number in the bottom right-hand corner.

"I thought you worked for Tom O'Day," I said.

"Honey, I can do that job before I have my morning coffee every day. I only agreed to Tom's proposal on the basis that I had carte blanche to take on certain ... side projects occasionally. Ones that interest me. And you interest me, Charlie." She nodded to the business card. "Put that somewhere safe. I hope you'll realise that you need it."

She closed the clutch, slung the strap back onto her shoulder, started to head back along the hallway.

"Haven't you forgotten something?"

Autumn stopped, turned, and I nodded towards the bathroom, standing open and unused.

"No, thanks," she said easily. "I believe I've done everything I needed to."

TWENTY-FIVE

We let Blake Dyer finish his breakfast in relative peace before we ganged up on him.

All I needed to do was exchange a single brief glance with Sean, and suddenly we were tuned in to the same wavelength again, like discovering a favourite radio station bursting through after travelling for miles with nothing but static.

How long it would last was anybody's guess, but for now ...

I took the seat Tom O'Day had so recently vacated. Sean moved up to stand behind Dyer's shoulder, not quite looming.

Our principal saw the expression on my face and glanced between us, beginning to frown.

"Why is it I get the distinct feeling I'm not going to like what you have to say?" Dyer murmured. "Look, guys, I'm sorry. I know what we talked about, but Tom's right—I can't leave now."

"Why?"

He sighed, took his time about replying. "Before she hit New Orleans, Katrina hit Florida," he said. "I was in Miami and let me tell you, we took a beating." He glanced at us. "She was only a Cat One at that point, but she seemed to last for ever. The damage ... More than a dozen people were killed. I guess we thought we had enough troubles of our own without helping others."

I saw the regret in his face. "I remember the initial reports on New Orleans played down the problems here."

He nodded. "They did, but that doesn't excuse it," Dyer said. "We heard the weather reports. We knew that by the time Katrina hit the Gulf coast she was a Cat Five. We, of all people, should have known what that was going to mean. But we were slow responding—*I* was slow responding. And twelve hundred people died. Thousands more lost everything they had." He

108

looked up, fixed me with a determined eye. "I need to make up for that. I won't turn my back on these people again."

"And that's commendable," I said. "But it's not the issue here. The real issue is why would anyone want to kill you?"

His eyebrows climbed in genuine surprise. "Who says they do?"

"An RPG aimed at the aircraft you were travelling in pretty much says it for you," Sean put in.

Blake Dyer didn't like the tone. He particularly didn't like it from a man like Sean who was standing behind him at the time. He twisted in his chair. "You think that thing was aimed at me?"

"If not you, then who else?" I said, swinging his focus back. "If anyone had Sean or me on their shit-list, we wouldn't have come. Our job is to protect you, not turn you into collateral damage."

Blake Dyer picked up his coffee, a reflexive stalling gesture. He realised the cup was empty and set it down again. I could almost hear the tumult of his thoughts.

"What about young Gabe Baptiste?" he said. "He was born and raised here. Got himself in a lot of trouble here as a kid, too. Why else would he leave and never come back, even to lord it over those who never believed he had it in him?"

"Baptiste was a last-minute substitute on that flight," I pointed out. "Up until a few minutes before take-off he wasn't supposed to be on board at all—nor was Autumn Sinclair."

"Or John Franks," Sean put in, voice quiet but no less harsh for that. "And now he's going home in a box."

"I really don't think I care for the way this conversation is going," Dyer said, keeping his own voice even.

"And I really don't care for being shot at without at least knowing the reason why," I said. "But the thing is, if you disregard our advice after a threat of this type, the terms of the agreement you signed with Armstrong-Meyer mean we can walk away."

I rose, deliberately smoothed the hem of my jacket over the SIG on my hip and knew he'd seen the gesture.

"What Charlie's saying, *sir*," Sean said over Dyer's shoulder, "is that if this threat *is* directed against you, you'll be leaving yourself wide open."

Dyer's face hardened. Finally too uncomfortable with being the filling in a bodyguard sandwich, he stood up, stepped back so he could glance at both of us.

"No," he said. "I think you'll find that it's *you* who'll be leaving *me* wide open, and I'll see to it that everyone is aware of that fact."

"You ignore us, we walk," Sean insisted. "Nobody would call us on that decision."

"Maybe not—*if* it was known that helicopter was brought down deliberately. But Tom is determined to put it out that this was nothing more than an unfortunate accident. How do things look for you then?"

For a second neither of us moved or spoke.

Much as I hated to admit it, he had a point. Either we left without further explanation and looked like total scaredy-cats to the whole industry, or we spilled the beans about what really happened to that helo, with all the shit-storm that would entail.

I'd learned enough about Tom O'Day's business empire to realise a couple of things about him. One was that he had a very high-powered PR division, headed by a ferociously bright ex-Harvard graduate with a stratospheric IQ, who could spin things whichever way she wanted just for the hell of it.

Autumn Sinclair was not someone I wanted to piss off—for all kinds of reasons.

Of course, getting on the wrong side of a man as powerful as Tom O'Day would undoubtedly prove a very bad move as far as Parker's professional reputation was concerned. Big as Parker was, Tom O'Day was a corporate giant. If we put the mockers on his pet project, O'Day could crush the whole lot of us without a second's thought. Hell, he'd been prepared to emotionally blackmail his son's godfather to keep him on side. What would he do to total strangers who crossed him?

We were over a barrel and Dyer knew it.

He nodded, just once, and began to turn away.

The reality of the situation hit both Sean and me at almost the same moment, but our reactions were very different.

I let my breath out fast through my nose. A gesture of annoyance and compliance, both at the same time.

But Sean lunged for Blake Dyer, grabbed his shoulder and spun him round, piling him backwards at the same time until they were both hard up against the nearest wall. Dyer's head bumped against one of the room's original canvases, almost dislodging it. Sean got a forearm across the older man's throat and wedged it there, holding him effortlessly pinned.

110

TWENTY-SIX

I shot my chair back, snapped, "Sean, for God's sake let him go."

"He's lying to us," Sean said tightly over his shoulder. "Does he think we're stupid or something?"

"Of course he's lying to us—clients never tell *the whole truth and nothing but*," I said calmly. "The question is only ever how much we're prepared to let them get away with. Let him go," I repeated. "I'm sure we can talk about this almost like grown-ups if we make the effort."

"Talk's cheap," Sean said, and something in his voice, his whole stance, chilled me.

"He's reverted back to military mode," Parker had said only yesterday. And it struck me that back in Special Forces Sean had not just been a first-class soldier, training instructor, lethal with a weapon or with an empty hand.

He'd been a bloody good interrogator as well.

Ruthless, tenacious, cold.

"Sean, let him go," I said again, and this time there was an edge to my voice that had not been there before. I reached out and touched his shoulder lightly, careful not to get too close. Sean's right elbow was halfway back towards my face before he curbed the instinctive response. I'd already made sure I was beyond his reach but it shook me, even so.

"Stand down, Sergeant," I said, putting some bite into it now.

"When he starts levelling with us."

"And what are you planning to do in the meantime— waterboard him in the bathtub until he starts babbling?" I demanded acidly. "You know as well as I do that confessions extracted using extreme methods are worthless."

I met Blake Dyer's eyes, keeping my face relaxed, trying to silently reassure him that I would not let anything happen to

111

him, regardless of what words passed between me and Sean. He stood quiet, not struggling against the chokehold, which probably explained why he was still breathing.

Help me.

I will. I am.

Sean was not going to be talked down from this. So I'd have to take him down instead. I took a quiet breath, let it out.

Sean was braced with his left leg forwards, putting his bodyweight into the hold. I stepped in and stamped down onto the back of his right knee so the leg folded under him. As it buckled I grabbed for his right arm, digging my nails into the tender skin under his bicep.

With my left hand I reached over the top of his head to grab his face with clawed fingers, locating the delicate septum and the points of his cheekbones, pushing down and back. By the time he realised what I was doing and tried to duck forwards to evade me it was too late, I'd already taken control of his head.

My initial attack might have taken Sean by surprise in both direction and severity, but his training kicked in almost instantaneously. He let go of Blake Dyer and wrenched out from under my grip, twisting to launch a vicious left as he did so.

As I'd hoped he might.

Sean had always been lightning fast but now I knew I was faster. I watched the blow coming, side-stepped at the last possible moment and caught his hand and arm, using his own momentum to swing him further away from our principal, locking his elbow out straight to control his shoulder. Then I swept his legs from under him again.

Sean went down hard on his stomach. If he hadn't turned his head just before he hit, he probably would have bust his nose in the process.

Still controlling his arm locked out straight across my bent knee, I went in heavy on the side of his neck, aiming for a point high behind the jaw that I knew would totally immobilise him.

There was no need to worry about what he might try to do with his free hand. The nerve point I was applying pressure to made it impossible for him to form any useful counter-measure. His left foot had begun to jitter uncontrollably.

"When I said 'stand down', I really did mean it," I said. "Now, I can kneel here all morning, but the longer I do the longer you're going to need to get any feeling back. Are we clear?"

"Yes, sir," Sean said through his teeth.

I took the male address as the ultimate show of respect. Right at that moment Sean's brain simply could not compute that he'd just been put down so hard and so fast by a woman.

I eased back on my heels, then stood and stepped back all in one move, just in case. Sean wisely did not attempt to get up right away.

I glanced at Blake Dyer, still leaning slumped against the wall. He was staring open-mouthed at the pair of us.

"You OK?" I asked.

"Holy crap, Charlie," he said in a strangled voice that was not entirely caused by the chokehold Sean had put on him. "If I hadn't just seen that for myself I would never have believed it. You are indeed a hell of a woman."

I shrugged. "Maybe, but I'm also a hell of a pissed-off woman," I said. "Because although I may not agree with my colleague's methods, I do agree with the sentiment. You have not been truthful with us, Blake and it's time you started."

He flicked his gaze to Sean, who'd just managed to flop over onto his back and was trying to persuade his arms to coordinate long enough to make it to the next stage. It was taking a while and he didn't meet my eye while he was doing it.

"Or you'll kneel on my head, too?"

"I do have two knees," I pointed out. "Now—talk."

Blake Dyer sighed, pushed himself away from the wall and straightened the canvas before moving back to the breakfast table. He was careful to make sure his route did not take him too close to Sean, who had now managed to reach a sitting position. He was rubbing the feeling back into his arms and legs and rolling the kinks out of his neck.

"There's another possibility about the attack on that helicopter you don't seem to have considered," Dyer said, hitching his trousers slightly as he retook his seat.

"You mean the one person who was *supposed* to be on board, but who changed her mind right before take-off?" I asked. "Right after she realised you were going to be on the same flight, as I seem to recall? Oh yeah, we considered Ysabeau van Zant all right, but I was hoping *you* might be able to tell us more about her role in all this."

TWENTY-SEVEN

There was a time when I would have counted Ysabeau van Zant as—if not a friend exactly—then at least a ... close colleague," Blake Dyer said.

"But?"

"Oh yeah, there was a big 'but' all right." He gave a wry smile. "And I'm not talking the kind that goes away if you spend an hour a day on a Stairmaster."

I pointedly raised my eyebrows and waited for him to continue. Sean had made it to the nearest sofa by this time and was perched on the edge of it, leaning forwards with his forearms supported on his knees. Dyer and I were sitting opposite each other at the breakfast table, as we had been.

Dyer sighed, and said with great reluctance, "There were some rumours that Mrs van Zant's political ... backers, shall we say, were not chosen as wisely as they might have been."

"So, she was taking dirty money," Sean said flatly. He'd got his legs back beneath him again and to a stranger he might have seemed as if nothing had happened. It was only because I knew him better than that I could see how just shaken he was.

Well ... good.

Dyer, meanwhile, gave an uncomfortable twitch of his shoulder, halfway between acceptance and denial.

"Maybe," he said. "And not all of it, by any means." He paused again, as if considering how much to tell us. "I was one of those bankrolling her, too," he said then. "Back when she was first on the campaign trail. My God, but she was a sight to behold in those days." His voice had grown almost wistful. "We had no doubts she was destined for great things—the White House, even. It didn't seem too much to hope for."

"I hear that big 'but' again," Sean put in.

Dyer nodded. "Turned out one of her other major backers had certain ... connections, shall we say, with a local family who were reputed to be involved in the drug supply business. They're known as the Bayou Mafia, pretty notorious around these parts."

Why not just come right out with it and say she was taking drug money?

"What connections?" I demanded. "These days most people tend to accept that every banknote in circulation has a little white powder on it somewhere. Metaphorically if not literally."

"Maybe I'm not most people," Dyer said, his face a little stony now. "You may think I'm a member of the idle rich, Charlie, and that I am, but I do a little more toward managing my money than calling my broker every six months. I take an active role choosing ethical investment opportunities." Dignity made his tone a little pompous. "I decided that Mrs van Zant's possible ties with a money launderer made her no longer suitable for my portfolio."

"Based on rumours?" Sean asked.

Dyer flashed him a dark glance. "That and a little more," he said. "Just before Mrs van Zant was elected here the city was having one of its periodic anti-drug campaigns. A feel-good show for the voters rather than a serious attempt, I think, but it gave most of those running for office a chance to puff out their chests and talk the talk about how they were going to clean up this dirty old town."

I heard the slight emphasis. "When you say 'most of those running for office' why is it I get the feeling Mrs van Zant was not among their number?"

"She was strangely ... muted in her response," he agreed. "And those rumours suddenly carried a whole lot more weight. The media started to ask difficult questions, and then a man was murdered and everything changed."

"Murdered?" Sean repeated flatly. I flicked him a quick look, but there was nothing in his face. "Who?"

"A member of the Bayou Mafia. Guy called Leon Castille. He was found shot to death in a derelict house. The police reckoned it was some kind of drug deal gone wrong, as I recall. No need to guess that he was selling rather than buying."

I shrugged. "I hate to use the old cliché 'no humans involved', but he doesn't sound like an upstanding member of the community. Why did that make a difference?"

Blake Dyer sat back in his chair, crossed his legs and brushed a piece of lint from his trousers. "There you have me," he said, "but after Castille was dead Mrs van Zant joined the crusade with something approaching fervour. Enough to see her swept into office anyways."

"If she's so dodgy, why the hell has Mr O'Day involved her so much in the festivities—that party at her place, for example."

Dyer gave a slight smile. "You're forgetting the whole politics of the situation, Charlie. That murder took place years ago. Hurricane Katrina came along and everything that went before seems to have been forgotten. And since then Ysabeau van Zant has gone about systematically increasing her power-base in this state. Nothing—and I mean *nothing*—gets done around here now without her say-so."

TWENTY-EIGHT

Blake Dyer shook his head a little. "Truth be told, Tom O'Day didn't want her within a thousand miles of this whole thing, but if you need anything done in this town you've got to have that lady's blessing or you're doomed from the get-go."

"She's on the take?" I said, surprised. It didn't quite square with the sophisticated image she presented. But hadn't I learned already this trip that appearances should not be taken at ... face value?

"Nothing so crude as cold hard cash," Dyer said. "Mrs van Zant trades favours like baseball cards. Lord alone knows what kind of a future marker she's going to call in from Tom for giving him free rein with the Foundation here."

"You would have thought that it would be *her* owing *him* favours for bringing in the money to regenerate some of the worst-affected areas of this godforsaken city."

Dyer laughed, not an entirely happy sound. "Ah, but that's not the way her mind works, Charlie. If she's not getting something out of it, then she'd pretty much rather nobody was."

"Sounds like the kind of woman who'd hold a grudge," Sean said, and if something in his tone scratched across my skin, I ignored it—for now.

Dyer paused, frowning, as if he'd never had cause to give it much thought. "I guess she would," he agreed at last. "It's never come up—our paths haven't crossed in years."

"Well now they have, you *might* want to give it some thought," I said. "She obviously isn't about to put you on her Christmas card list. But how far will she go to even the score?" I got to my feet and buttoned my jacket. "Bringing down a helicopter she'd decided not to get on, for instance—?"

117

How Blake Dyer chose to answer that question might have been very illuminating, but we never received his answer. At that moment there was a knock on the suite door that sent both Sean and me into instant high alert, weapons in our hands like a synchronised display.

Our agreement with the hotel was that no room numbers were to be given out. Visitors for our principal were to be greeted at the front desk, who would call ahead to announce them. The management had provided additional security to keep autograph hunters and paparazzi away from the more famous faces, and that meant nobody got past up to the bedroom levels unless they were invited, or another resident of the hotel. It was a good system, but not foolproof.

As somebody had just proved.

"Please stay here, sir," I murmured. "Out of sight of the door, if you don't mind."

Sean and I were already moving across the suite to the main hallway. I jerked my head towards the bathroom doorway, just off to the left. The door out in the corridor hinged at the right-hand side, so opened up directly into his field of fire. And if the worst happened the bathtub was enamelled cast iron, ornate and solid—and plenty thick enough to act as a shield to the heaviest calibre our unexpected visitors were likely to be carrying.

I holstered the SIG, stood to the side of the door and put a hand over the Judas glass before sliding the cover aside and peering through, so the change in light was not so obvious from the other side.

What the ...?

The face of the person waiting anxiously outside the door to Blake Dyer's suite was one I recognised only from the briefing photos Bill Rendelson had prepared. Not someone I'd been expecting to see here now—for a whole raft of reasons.

118

TWENTY-NINE

I opened the door to a small grey-haired woman who looked as surprised to see me as I'd been to see her. Behind her, hovering discreetly, was a youngish guy in a suit, thickset and wary.

The woman was dressed with immaculate smartness as if for a formal occasion. That particular style I've dubbed Mother-of-the-Bride because you see it in wedding photos just about anywhere. Pastel suits in long slimming lines, with pearls and matching accessories. All she needed was a hat.

"Oh, excuse me," she said, a little flustered, looking past me to Sean, showing half an eye from the bathroom doorway. "Am I in the right place? I was looking for Blake."

Despite my instructions, our principal stepped into view behind us. I really was going to have to talk to him about that.

"Marie! My dear—you look wonderful," he said, holding out his arms in welcome. "But what the heck are you doing here?"

Much as I also wanted to know what Tom O'Day's wife was doing outside their home in Virginia, I couldn't agree with his first statement. The lady did not look wonderful. She had an almost translucent paleness and frailty, as if a strong wind would blow her tumbling across the street. We'd been told that her health had been a recent issue—a big issue—which was her reason for not travelling with her husband for this occasion. I'd wondered if his head of PR might have had more to do with that, but now I wasn't so sure.

Marie gave us an absent smile and hurried forwards to greet Blake Dyer. The bodyguard ventured just far enough into the suite to see all the corners, then stood with his back to the wall near the hallway, watchful.

Dyer, meanwhile, folded Marie into a big but gentle hug and kissed her on both cheeks. She had to stand on tiptoe to let him

119

do it. Then she stepped back, still holding his arms, and took a good look at him like an anxious parent.

"Blake," she said. "I came as soon as I heard about what happened yesterday. I couldn't believe it when Jimmy called to tell me. How awful—and that poor man who died. Are *you* all right?"

"I'm fine, Marie, but you didn't need to come. I'm real sorry I didn't call you myself. I guess I just didn't want to worry you."

"Hmm, like I wasn't going to be worried when I heard you'd been shot out of the skies over the very city my husband's doing his best to save?" she said with spirit. "Why aren't you on your way home to Patti and the children this very moment? She must be worried sick."

But without waiting for an answer she stepped back and turned to glance at me and Sean. "Don't tell me," she said. "He wouldn't go, huh? Always the stubborn fool, our Blake." So, despite the butter-wouldn't-melt looks, she knew exactly who we were and why we were there.

Shrewd.

"Now, Marie, you know I couldn't let Tom down—not when he's put so much into this," Dyer protested smoothly. "How would that look to everybody?"

"You mean he blackmailed you into staying on, didn't he? The cunning old devil," she said, adding with brisk affection, "I'll have his guts for garters—isn't that how the English put it? Such a *lovely* expression."

Marie smiled. In someone less dignified it might almost have been a grin. As it was, the smile lit up her face and crinkled the corners of her eyes. It set up a twinkle in their depths that hinted at a robust sense of self, even if she might be physically frail. In some ways she reminded me of my mother.

Seeing her together with Tom O'Day would be interesting. After all, she could have reassured herself about Blake Dyer's condition with a phone call. I wondered if she knew about her husband's apparently close relationship with Autumn Sinclair. Was that why she had really come?

"Will you be at the gala dinner tonight?" Dyer asked, deflecting. "In which case, can I claim the first dance?"

Marie patted his arm with affection. "Bless you, no. I never was much good at the glad-handing—that's far more Tom's specialty than mine. A nice room-service tray and a night of old weepy movies on the TV is far more my style. Jimmy can tell me all about it when it's over." She paused, and the anxious look was back in her face. "How do you feel he's doing?"

"He's doing good—a real chip off the old block," Dyer lied gallantly. His eyes flickered in my direction, no doubt remembering Jimmy O'Day's abortive lunge during the opening night reception, and my interception of it. How to voice that? Eventually he settled for, "He's got some spark, that boy."

Even his mother looked doubtful. "Well, as long as he's not allowing it to get him into any trouble," she said. She turned and seemed to look right at me as she went on, "I don't quite trust young Vic Morton to keep Jimmy out of hot water while he's down here—he's more likely to hold Jimmy's coat for him." She slid her eyes across to the silent bodyguard near the hallway and gave what might have been a sniff. "Thad here would have kept him on a tighter rein, had he not gotten sick."

The bodyguard shuffled his feet, felt compelled to announce in a slightly aggrieved tone, "Everybody knows I have nut allergies, Mrs O'Day, and I'm real careful. I tell you, somebody tampered with my food."

"Yes, dear, so you said." Marie O'Day turned to me. "I don't suppose you know where I can find that damn fool Vic Morton, by any chance?"

I shook my head. I knew I should stay entirely neutral, but couldn't help asking, "Isn't Morton *your* security man?"

"Just because he works for me doesn't mean I'm blind to his faults," she said briskly. "Heaven knows, I see them more clearly than most in my husband. And my son, too, for that matter—however much the proud mother I may sound. Knowing and understanding are two entirely different things, though, as I'm sure you'll find out as you get older, my dear." She smiled again, a little wistfully this time, I thought. "Besides, I'm not sure how much longer I'll be needing my own security."

Dyer took a half-step forwards, alarm and distress in his face. "Marie—"

"Oh, not like *that*, Blake. Don't go all over-dramatic on me. No, I simply mean I plan to stay home a lot more. Take things quietly. I have my art and my books, so I'm content." The twinkle was back again. "And I confess that I've found mention of the O'Day name is very useful when it comes to persuading dealers and so on that if they really want to make a sale, they should

121

travel out to Virginia to show me what they have. May as well take advantage of that pull, hmm?"

Even with the breezy reassurance, Dyer was silent as he digested the possible meaning of her words. There were a few directions you could take with them—none of them exactly optimistic.

He gave her an odd glance, said, "Tom *does* know you're here, doesn't he?"

Marie beamed. "I thought I'd surprise him," she said, and wagged a warning finger. "So don't you go calling him the minute I'm out the door, Blake. I know he'll be up to no good without me, but catching him in the act is so much more satisfying, don't you think?"

THIRTY

Blake Dyer shuffled his feet closer to the tee, lined up the face of a driver to the ball, and unwound his whole body in one fluid, practised motion.

The little white dimpled ball catapulted away into the distance almost too fast for the human eye to track. Dyer followed its progress with a hand shading his eyes from the afternoon sun, his expression clearing as he realised the scope and accuracy of the shot.

"Not bad, Blake, not bad at all," Tom O'Day said. "Shall we say a thousand bucks a hole?"

Blake Dyer gave him a wry smile. "Does it matter?" he asked. "If I lose you'll tell me to donate the money to the Foundation."

"True enough."

"And if I win?"

"I'll *ask* you, most politely, to do the same thing," Tom O'Day agreed comfortably.

Dyer paused as if considering his options. Then he nodded. "Sounds like a fair deal to me," he said amicably, as if they were discussing playing for loose change one of them had found down the back of his sofa.

"Just as long as you don't expect me to contribute, Tom," Autumn warned as she stepped up to tee off. "That's a little rich for my blood—not to mention my present handicap."

Tom O'Day laughed and nudged Blake Dyer's arm. "Don't believe a word of it, old friend. This lady is a shark, on or off the golf course."

Jimmy O'Day, partnering his godfather, scowled furiously and fumbled getting his club out of his bag, rattling the shafts together in his frustration. O'Day turned to glance at him, frowning. I think he was more concerned that Autumn not be put off her opening shot rather than that he might have offended his son.

I was no golf expert beyond knowing which club carried the most weight and which make was least likely to break if you hit someone with it—a Callaway putter for preference. Autumn's initial swing looked fast and smooth, and her ball seemed to travel almost as far as Blake Dyer's had done.

Jimmy sliced his dangerously close to the rough grass at the edge of the fairway. Morton, who'd selected the club for him like a bloody caddy instead of a bodyguard, did not trouble to hide a smirk. How the hell that guy had survived for so long in an industry which is such a fine balance of subservience and authority, I had no idea.

Tom O'Day, by comparison with his son, uncoiled a big lazy drive off the tee that went further than anyone else's by a country mile.

"Shall we?" Autumn asked, slotting her club back into the bag on her electric cart. They'd commandeered a small fleet of the things back at the clubhouse.

Maybe it was a power play, but Sean had drawn himself driving duty. My immediate role ended once they trundled away towards the first hole. I watched them go for a while, just to keep an eye on who was coming up behind.

Tom O'Day had supplemented his usual bodyguard, Hobson, with a second man today, an ex-navy SEAL. Both were obviously determined to provide a visible deterrent, making no effort to blend. The group of them had formed a presidential-style cavalcade. Even in an upmarket place like this it was attracting more attention than I would have liked.

Sean did not look back. After our earlier confrontation, I hardly expected him to. Still, it grieved me. Just when I thought we might be making progress on a personal level, I'd been forced to take us right back to square one.

I felt more alone now, I realised, than I had done during Sean's coma. At least then I'd believe that if he woke up—when he woke up—we would be together again. I'd never imagined that he would come back indifferent to me.

I stepped back to allow the next group to prepare themselves. It was a mixed double of husbands playing a round with either their wives or mistresses. Or it could just as easily have been a pair of wives with their boyfriends, for that matter.

Morton, in one of the carts with Tom O'Day's other bodyguard, turned in his seat to give me a mocking salute as they trundled away. As if he knew exactly what doubts and fears were running around inside my head, and revelled in them. I ignored him, relying on my dignity to take the moral high ground. It was a strangely unsatisfying victory.

As I moved away my cellphone buzzed in my pocket. One of the women players had just been handed a club and she shot me a sharp glance as I pulled it out and checked the number. I nodded to her and walked farther away before I answered the call.

"Hi," I said, brusque. "What have you got?"

"And it's good to speak with you, too," Parker Armstrong said dryly. "You OK?"

I'd called him to report on the crash and its immediate aftermath, if not Sean's delayed reaction to it later the same night.

"I'm fine," I said. "But I'm really hoping you've called with something on that bastard Vic Morton, because he's starting to piss me off no end."

Parker saw past the flippancy at once. "Look, Charlie," he said, his voice suddenly very focused, "I know you have history with this guy and you must hate his guts. Jesus, no one on earth could blame you for that after what he did to you—" He shut off abruptly, as if not trusting what he might have been about to say.

"It's OK," I said, softening. "Whatever I might be capable of, Parker, I'll do my best not to embarrass you or the agency."

"You think that *matters* compared with—?"

"Please," I said, twisting in the face of words that should remain unsaid. I forced my tone to lighten. "I'll behave, which is a shame really, because that man has a face I'd never get tired of kicking."

"Go buy yourself a voodoo doll from the French Quarter and stick pins in it instead," he said, determinedly matching his tone to mine. "And let me know how that works out for you."

"Damn," I said. "I assume that means you haven't found anything I can use to get that little waster punted?"

"Uh-uh," Parker said. "He moves around quite a bit—never out of work for long, but never *in* work for long either."

125

"Hired for his professional qualifications and fired for his personal failings," I said, trying to keep the satisfaction out of my voice. "Sounds like he's using whatever he can get to keep his record nice and shiny."

Close protection was a very fine line, a difficult tightrope act. Safeguarding a principal meant keeping them away from dangerous situations and locations, but that did not mean we could prevent them going somewhere they wanted to go, or from doing something they wanted to do. Not if we wanted to stay in work.

The pressure to procure for them—alcohol, drugs, sex—was constantly applied. It was a line both Sean and Parker had been adamant was never crossed. Not for anybody. Doing so would have been a firing offence—for operative and client.

I recalled a low point when Sean and I had been arrested during a police raid on a brothel in Bushwick with our supposed client and a barely legal hooker. Only the fact that nobody was there from choice had saved us.

But for someone whose moral compass was skewed to start with, it would be an all-too easy step. And once you've got that reputation you get all the wrong kind of offers—from people who then don't really want to see a self-righteous, smirking face in the cold light of day the following morning.

So they find an excuse to let you go—with a great reference, of course. To do otherwise would be to assure a kind of mutual destruction.

"I think you got that one nailed," Parker said now. He paused, almost a hesitation, before launching into one last try. "Look, I know how you feel about this guy, Charlie. If you want me to make some calls, get him blacklisted, just say the word."

"Thank you, Parker," I said, genuinely touched. "But it sounds like he'll crash and burn sooner or later without my help."

And I can't go there—won't *go there*—*not again ...*

Or where would I stop?

It was my turn to hesitate. "I think you should ... convey your suspicions to the husband's chief of security, though," I said carefully. "I rather like the wife, and Morton is not the kind of guy anyone should want looking after their loved ones."

THIRTY-ONE

Tom O'Day and his head of PR won their mini golf tournament by a convincing margin. Blake Dyer took losing in good heart but Jimmy O'Day sulked for most of the return journey into New Orleans.

On the way back to the hotel the four of them decided to detour into the heart of the French Quarter for afternoon coffee and *beignets* at the Café du Monde. I'd heard of the place but never been there. It turned out to be more laid-back than I was expecting, with the tables crowded together under a green and white striped awning, open to the street.

This made things awkward from a security point of view, particularly in light of yesterday's attack on the Bell. I wondered if the choice was a kind of provocation. And if so, who was it aimed at?

The café was full, the nearby streets bustling with the city's distinctive, slightly exotic energy. Tourists strolled and gawked, or rode in the elegant four-wheel horse-drawn carriages along Decatur Street, their white knees pinking in the sun.

I stood at the front of the café with Sean. Tom O'Day's security guys took a table inside, near to our principals without overcrowding them.

Given a choice, I would have positioned Morton solo by the entrance to the kitchens, but I was not given that choice. Left to his own devices Morton chose to cluster with Tom O'Day's bodyguards instead.

I was initially thankful. Then I saw the way he was talking to the two men, leaning forwards conspiratorially with his head bent—and the dubious looks they flicked in our direction—and I wished I'd kept him close enough to strangle whatever rumours he was spreading.

I pointedly kept my attention spread between our principal and the street. Across from the café were tall brick buildings adorned with verandas and balconies in the typical New Orleans style, delicate wrought-iron tumbled with greenery. It made for a lot of access points to cover. The only consolation was that the elevation made it harder to pinpoint a target under cover.

I remembered the RPG and was not reassured.

"Parker's not happy," I said to Sean, sipping the ice coffee I'd ordered.

He gave me a sharp glance. "Been running to the boss man again, Charlie?"

"Hey, *he* rang *me*," I said, keeping it as neutral as I could. It seemed whenever Sean had been in close contact with Morton he was prickly with me afterwards, his mood changeable. Something else I'd have to damn well watch.

"And what did Parker say, exactly?"

"That he doesn't like the incident rate so far on this job—not when we haven't even got to the main event yet."

"One car park ambush and one mid-air ambush," Sean said lightly, still trying to shrug off his assumption and not quite managing it. "What's not to like?"

"Where do I start?" I murmured. "If it had been up to me we'd have hauled Dyer back onto his executive jet, in a straitjacket if necessary, and he'd be safely tucked up in bed back home in Florida by now."

"You offering to tuck him in, are you?" Sean said, and just when I began to think he'd turned into a total jerk, he added, "Besides, it's nowhere close to bedtime in Miami."

I half smiled, put a hand out to touch Sean's arm, in solidarity, friendship, but I caught Vic Morton's lascivious gaze out of the corner of my eye. I could see him almost willing me to touch Sean in some way that could be used against me in the eyes of his companions. I redirected my hand to my paper cup, turning it in my hands before I took another sip. An old saying fell into my head:

Fool me once; shame on you. Fool me twice; shame on me.
Fool me three times; shame on the both of us.

I'd once thought Morton was an OK kind of bloke. Not quite the kind I wanted to turn my back on, maybe, but not one who'd stab me in it either. Turned out that should have been the least of my worries about him.

He was not as silently malevolent as big Clay, or as easily egged-on as Donalson. He wasn't as intrinsically nasty as Hackett, either—he'd been the one leading from the front there. Leading by example.

I tried and failed to stop my skin shimmying at the memory.

"You going to tell me the rest of it?" Sean asked.

For a second my mind rushed headlong down a completely different track, back to a cold dark night, a hint of mist, a hint of frost, danger lurking like a sleeved blade. I had not seen it coming.

I would have done so now.

Sean sighed, not altogether patiently. "What else did Parker say, Charlie?"

Reality nudged me back into step. The darkness receded, replaced by the bright busy street, the chatter of people, and a muggy heat only lazily dispelled by the overhead fans.

Along with their coffees our group had ordered the café's famous *beignet* pastries. These appeared to be squared-off doughnuts covered with enough icing sugar to make my teeth itch at the sight of them. Even the floor inside the café was dusted with it. Blake Dyer was tucking into his *beignet* with evident enjoyment. I flicked my eyes back to Sean.

"Parker strongly suggests that we keep a very close eye on Ysabeau van Zant," I said.

"So the rumours Dyer told us about are solid."

"What worries Parker more, I think, are the rumours that she might have contracted out a hit on that dealer who got himself shot, Leon Castille. One way to show them she meant business— especially when he wasn't exactly an upstanding pillar of society."

"Did it smell like a pro hit?"

I shrugged. "One round in the back to put him down, then finished off with one to the head, according to the reports. First round was a through-and-through—never found the bullet. Second round stayed inside the skull but was too mangled to try for a match. The shooter policed his brass. And all this went down in a part of town where there were never going to be any witnesses prepared to come forward. Nothing to go on and nobody to care. Case closed."

Sean nodded, took a sip of his coffee. I lifted my own drink just for something to do with my hands, and debated on how much of the rest to tell him.

Because, Parker had also been in touch with Madeleine Rimmington back in the UK. Madeleine had assumed control of Sean's close-protection agency when he and I moved over to the States to take up Parker's offer. She was an information expert who'd since specialised in data protection and counter-espionage for all things electronic. But to protect stuff like that, you had to first know how to steal it. If it was stored on a computer and made up of pixels or binary code, Madeleine seemed to be able to access it.

In this case, though, all she'd found were the dates of Sean's last visit to New Orleans, back when he'd been assigned to a fledgling young baseball player called Gabe Baptiste. A babysitting job he'd been reluctant to take on in the first place, but had done so anyway because it was a chance to work in America, the land of opportunity. A chance to gain a reputation, to make a name.

A job he'd canned early and come home, with Baptiste's name firmly removed from the list of possible future clients. It would seem he'd expunged any other record of the job.

But the dates of his trip just happened to coincide with the death of Ysabeau van Zant's troublesome drug connection.

A killing with no apparent witnesses.

But what if there *had* been a witness? What if Gabe Baptiste had seen what happened and had chosen not to come forward, not to speak out? I already knew he'd got himself sorted afterwards, mentally and financially. Did Mrs van Zant pay him off and tell him to get out of New Orleans and stay out, no matter what?

Did she, in effect, pave the way for his glittering career?

If so, perhaps that was the marker he owed her—the one she'd now called in. Not to keep him away from New Orleans, but to force him back here. It would also explain his response to Sean when he saw him again.

Because the man Sean had been before he was shot would not have liked letting someone get away with murder. Not when it was straightforward assassination anyway. I still hoped he might not see it quite that way in my case—if it ever came to that.

I had a vision of the old Sean—the Sean who'd come before—disagreeing vigorously with Baptiste's decision to allow himself to be bought off.

Sean had a strong sense of justice that did not always conform to legal niceties. In the right circumstances he would have done the job himself, but not to take the heat off some unknown politico—they were never his favourite breed at the best of times.

Besides, I reassured myself, if that had been the case then surely Ysabeau van Zant would have reacted to Sean in the same way that Baptiste had when they were first introduced. Instead there was not a flicker of recognition from her—even allowing for the fact that she was, by definition, a professional-grade liar.

But the only person who really knew the answers to these questions was Sean himself.

And the way things stood at the moment, he was the only person who would not—*could* not—provide them.

THIRTY-TWO

Sunset brought with it a hazy low cloud that crept in from the Gulf and threatened to solidify into fog. It also brought another surprise we hadn't planned for and didn't like much.

It was early evening—less than an hour before we were due to leave for the glitzy main event on the paddlewheel floating casino—when they sent Jimmy O'Day up to break the bad news.

He stood in the middle of Blake Dyer's suite at the hotel, with Vic Morton slouching near the wall by the hallway, and faced us down with weary defiance.

"I'm real sorry," he said for about the dozenth time since he'd entered the suite, "but the captain of the *Miss Francis* is adamant. He will not, under any circumstances, have firearms carried aboard his vessel. No exceptions."

"If there was going to be a problem with this, we should have been told days ago when we did the recce," Sean put in sharply. "What's he so worried about?"

Jimmy gave him an exasperated look. "Well, we had to let him know about what happened with the helicopter getting shot down—couldn't let him go into the situation blind," he said. "I guess he just feels you guys may be a little ... trigger-happy at the moment."

"I prefer 'alert' if you don't mind," I said. "And it's not like we're a bunch of cowboys—most of us anyway." I studiously ignored the way Morton scowled at me from across the room.

"If we hadn't been armed aboard that helo, you'd have a much higher body-count on your hands right now," Sean added. "It's not like we're using them to *start* a bloody fight—just to finish it."

Jimmy held up his hands in a gesture that indicated both surrender and command, his face doleful. "I know, guys, trust

132

me, but the whole evening hinges on getting everybody's cooperation on this. I've spoken to most of the security teams so far and they've agreed to go along with the captain's ruling, just so long as it's the same for everyone. Level playing field."

I caught Sean's eye. My instinct was once again either to pull Dyer out of there and bundle him back onto his private jet bound for the sunshine state, or to pack ourselves onto the first flight back to New York without him.

But what would Tom O'Day's reaction be if we did that, and what rumours would he instruct Autumn Sinclair's PR minions to circulate about Armstrong-Meyer's unreliable, flighty personnel?

Not something I wanted to find out.

It was perhaps fortunate that our principal was at that moment engaged in a long shower before his evening out. Arguing our case in front of him would have been that much harder. No doubt that was why Jimmy had chosen to come to each room in turn rather than call us together for any kind of group meeting. Maybe something of his parents' shrewdness had filtered down through the genes after all.

Although it was a formal evening event, I'd decided not to wear a frock myself, despite the fact it all sounded very glamorous. Sean's comments about the way Blake Dyer was behaving towards me had stung just enough that I was determined to be all business tonight. I'd chosen loose black silk trousers and a matching embroidered jacket that would have hidden the SIG very nicely—had I been allowed to carry it. And bearing in mind that we would be on a boat I'd chosen soft-soled low shoes rather than heels. If the skipper was throwing a fit about firearms on board he would no doubt be equally picky about stiletto marks all over his decking.

Eventually, Sean let his breath out short and fast down his nose. "Rock and a bloody hard place, this, isn't it?" he demanded. "If we say 'yes', you tell the next lot we're happy to agree—even when we're not. And if we dig our heels in about it, we're the villains of the piece."

Jimmy allowed a small smile to brave its way past his lips. In that moment he looked very much his father's son. "I guess so," he admitted. "So ... you prepared to give it a shot? Um, no pun intended there."

"Do we have a choice?"

Jimmy gave a fractional shake of his head. "Not if you want to get onto the boat tonight, no," he agreed. "Since nine-eleven they installed those metal detectors like they have before you get on an airplane, just to be sure. I guess they thought a riverboat casino might be some kind of target."

"For some disgruntled gambler, maybe," I said. I caught Sean's eye. He gave me a shrug. I sighed, too. "I already know what our client is going to say, so I suppose we have no choice but to agree. Make a note that we're sodding unhappy about it though, will you?"

"You and everybody else," Jimmy muttered, scribbling hastily on the clipboard that seemed to be permanently attached to the end of his arm. "Thanks anyhow, I appreciate it. And apparently there will be a couple of Zodiac inflatable boats acting as outriders while the *Miss Francis* is taking us on our river cruise, just in case of trouble. I'm told the guys in them will have some pretty heavy artillery. Um, not that we're expecting any more trouble, of course," he added hastily.

But I remembered the vehemence and determination in the voice of the man who'd shot down the Bell and pursued us into the giant scrapyard near the Lower Ninth Ward, and I wasn't so convinced.

It was only after he and the for-once silent Morton had departed that the bathroom door opened and Blake Dyer stepped out, still flushed from his shower. He was wearing one of the thick bathrobes the hotel provided, and towelling dry his hair.

"Did I hear visitors?" he asked with apparent innocence.

"Just your godson," I said, "letting us know about some last-minute ... adjustments to security on the boat trip tonight."

"Ah," Dyer said. He heard the tightness in my jaw, eyes flicking between Sean and me questioningly. "What 'adjustments'?"

Why do I get the feeling you already know ...?

"We're being asked to all go in our birthday suits," Sean said heavily. "As far as weapons are concerned, anyway. They want us unarmed."

Dyer was silent for a moment, still rubbing at his damp hair. "Well," he said slowly at last. "From what I've seen of young Charlie here, she doesn't need to carry a weapon." He smiled. "Hell, Sean, she *is* a weapon ..."

Of course, what we didn't reckon on was the first hostage being taken before we even stepped on board.

THIRTY-THREE

As it turned out, getting on board the *Miss Francis* took more than simply leaving our guns behind in the hotel's main vault. It seemed that Jimmy had not quite given us the full story about the eccentricities of the paddleboat's skipper.

Not only was the old fruit bat in charge determined to prevent anybody stepping aboard his floating bit of Vegas with a piece on their hip, he didn't want anybody talking about him behind his back, either. As we found out as soon as we reached the waterfront and were ushered into a striped marquee off to one side.

"No comms gear," Hobson announced. "Sorry, people—it causes too much electrical interference with the ship's nav systems." The apology was perfunctory. He had a surprisingly high-pitched voice for someone so wide across the shoulder.

"I didn't think we were going far enough for navigation to be any kind of an issue," I said. "Don't these old riverboat guys do it all by landmarks and whose dog's barking on shore?"

Hobson didn't even glower, just did his best to stare me down. I stood my ground with a look of polite enquiry.

"OK," he said at last. "The skipper's on a cut of the casino take, and there's no way he's going to allow anybody onto the casino deck who might stand a chance of beating the house through ... unfair advantage, shall we say."

"That's more like it," I muttered, but I could see his point—even if I didn't like it much.

Hobson nodded. "Bags will be provided and you can collect all your gear again when you disembark. Oh, and you will be swept so don't even think about trying to hang onto anything. The old guy in charge of the *Francis* is a law unto himself—still thinks he can make you walk the plank if you cross him."

He can try.

There was a long pause while everyone waited, I'm sure, for Hobson to admit with a laugh that he was joking. He did not do so, just stood and waited with the patience of a crocodile, muscular arms loose by his sides.

Then, with much muttering, the line broke. Close-protection personnel—more worried about facing their irate principals than a threat—began unbuttoning their jackets. I watched them stripping out wires that disappeared inside shirt collars and sleeves to transceivers in inside pockets or clipped onto belts.

As they did so, it was interesting to note how many had chosen to wear covert body armour under their clothing, even though there were supposed to be no firearms on board.

I put a hand on Sean's arm when he would have started to pick out the ultra-slim wireless earpiece that sat deep inside his ear canal. "Leave it," I murmured. "I have."

Sean frowned at the hand. "If they throw us out now," he said after a moment, keeping his voice an undertone, "do you really think—at this point—our principal is going to let us take him with us?"

"Probably not," I agreed, hardly moving my lips just in case. "But don't forget the comms gear Parker provided for this job is the latest top-grade military spec. It's so new it's not even on the market yet. The manufacturers claim in standby mode it's impossible to detect and in use it's impervious to any kind of scanning. Might be a nice opportunity to find out if it lives up to the hype, don't you think?"

For a moment Sean frowned, considering. "If you'd had as much supposedly top-spec gear as I have go down in the field, maybe you wouldn't be so keen," he said. But he let his hand drop away, gave me a brief nod. "All right then. Let's hope this stuff's up to the job, eh?"

I risked a smile. "If it's not, I'll tell them it was all your idea."

If I'd hoped for a smile in return I was disappointed there, too.

Sure enough, Hobson ran a scanner over each of us in turn, which came up empty. *So far, so good.* He glanced at the sullen faces in front of him.

"Now, I don't believe for a second that you've all been good little boys—and girls," he said, giving me and the one other female bodyguard a mocking little bow. "So now we get you to prove it."

He lifted a small transceiver off the table behind him and flicked it on, then hovered his thumb over a button. "If I hit this, anybody who's trying to pull a fast one and keep hold of their comms gear is going to get a burst of static that will probably burst an eardrum," he said with grim satisfaction. "Not to mention the fact it will get them kicked off this old tub with my boot so far up their ass they'll have to swallow boot polish just to get a shine." He surveyed us slowly with small pale eyes. "So, any of you got anything they 'forgot' to take out?"

A couple of the other guys shuffled their feet and sheepishly removed their earpieces. From the little snatch I saw, it was high-quality hardware that blended so well with their natural skin-tone I hadn't spotted it—even though I'd been looking.

Hobson took a last long look around us, then raised his eyebrows. "Don't say I didn't warn you," he said cheerfully.

I tried not to meet Sean's eyes, not to look guilty. Most of all I tried not to tense in expectation.

Hobson hit the button.

THIRTY-FOUR

The burst of static was as loud and as painful as Hobson had predicted.

But it wasn't in my ears—or Sean's, come to that. I had time for a brief prayer of thanks that, for once, a piece of untried kit had lived up to the hype.

Instead, the static hit the guy next to us, who I knew was assigned to an oil millionaire from Texas. The errant bodyguard jumped back with a yell as one ear exploded into white noise I could hear from where I stood.

Hobson kept his thumb on the transmit button, face impassive, until the pain of it had driven the bodyguard almost to his knees.

I would have had more sympathy, but I happened to know the guy's principal had a rep as a fanatical poker player, so I could guess that his motives for wanting comms up and running were not entirely motivated by concern for the Texan's safety.

I was aware I was holding my breath as the bodyguard scrabbled at his own head, trying to escape from the noise. Eventually, it was Sean who stepped forwards, his gazed locked on Hobson, looking very much like the old Sean.

"OK, he's had enough," he said coldly. "You've made your point. Shut it off."

Hobson stared for a moment, clearly tempted to face him down. But Sean still had a rep himself, as a man who would go straight through you and not notice the bump if you gave him cause. Despite a gunshot wound which should have killed him, and all that followed—the coma, the memory loss, the long road back to some kind of physical and mental fitness—Sean still carried weight in this industry. It was nice to see that he had regained enough confidence to throw a little of it around.

Hobson released his thumb with a casually exaggerated motion. Like he was trying to pretend he'd been about to let the guy off the hook anyway. I'm not sure who was convinced about that, but the others threw Sean respectful glances as he stepped back.

I recognised that if it had been me who'd spoken out, the action would have been seen as typical feminine weakness, but in Sean it was a sign of strength. I'd long since given up trying to work out the logic—never mind the fairness—of that kind of attitude. Still, mounting a crusade would be a waste of time and energy. Some things were never going to change.

Now, we were finally allowed to readjust our clothing and join our waiting clients in yet another marquee. This one had been set up on the wooden jetty area that extended out into the Mississippi itself and formed the paddle steamer's berth. I saw Hobson cross to have a quiet word with the Texas millionaire. He did not look happy.

I assumed the sudden loss of his electronic advantage meant he was probably going to end up making a somewhat more substantial contribution to Tom O'Day's worthy cause than he'd planned.

He wasn't the only one to be disappointed at the outset. The *Miss Francis* might have had the appearance of a classic old stern-wheel paddle steamer from the turn of the twentieth century but it turned out she was a totally modern fabrication. Her two hundred and fifty foot hull was steel plate, and her ornate superstructure was steel and glass fibre dressed with enough wood trim to look the part until you got a nose-length away from it. By then the realisation that you'd been somehow fooled, however briefly, made the disenchantment all the more profound.

We had been given the precise specs on the *Miss Francis* as soon as the job came through, so I already knew the rough layout. The paddlewheel steamer had three separate deck levels with the wheelhouse perched on top. Below that were cabins, bars and the main restaurant, leading down to the casino in the main part of the shallow-draught hull. Where, presumably, nobody needed—or was interested in—the view.

Tom O'Day was almost hopping in his excitement to get all his guests up the red-carpeted gangway and on board. There were probably a hundred and fifty people by the time you'd counted all

140

the security personnel. I'd been to charity events in New York and LA where the invites went out in their thousands, but looking at the display of wealth around the necks and wrists of the people here, I reckoned O'Day would not have any problem raising a substantial amount of money for the After Katrina Foundation.

He was also clearly a devotee of stern-wheeler paddleboats. I gathered that his naval background might have had something to do with his interest and knowledge. Certainly, he spouted history and statistics of their association with the Mississippi to anyone who'd listen. I gathered from the slightly weary expression on Hobson's face that he'd heard it all before—probably more than once.

Ysabeau van Zant managed to maintain an apparently fascinated face while he was speaking. I suspected that as a long-term resident she knew more about the area than O'Day ever would learn as an occasional visitor. She was wearing dignified silver, a long-line jacket over a matching floor-length dress.

The mist that had been gently rolling in from the river solidified into fog by the time darkness thickened out. The *Miss Francis*'s running lights would have made Las Vegas seem refined, and cut down night vision out over the water until it was almost non-existent. I hoped our eccentric skipper knew how to read the river even in these conditions or we would all end up wedged on a sandbank by the time this escapade was over.

As for the armed chase boats Jimmy O'Day had promised us, I couldn't hear or see anything out there on the grainy black waters. I would have hoped for a glimpse of them in the reflected lights from New Orleans glowing through the fog, or the buzz of a high-power outboard motor. Over the throb of the paddle steamer's own engines I could hear nothing.

"I don't like it," I murmured to Sean. He'd just done another circuit of the bar area where the partygoers were being served an array of complimentary cocktails to get them into a generous frame of mind. I reckoned that was probably going to be their last freebie of the evening.

"Hmm, that's weird," Sean said, "because I don't like it much either."

I glanced across at him. He was looking tight and wired, something tense about the set of his shoulders, the tilt of his head.

141

"What is it?"

He shook his head, frustrated, rubbed distractedly at the scar on his temple. "Damned if I know."

Blake Dyer was engaged in conversation with the banker from Boston and his stick-thin wife—the ones who'd decided to pass on the helicopter ride where Gabe Baptiste's bodyguard has lost his life. They did not look sorry to have missed out on the excitement.

Baptiste himself, meanwhile, was taking centre stage near the O'Day party. He was being fawned over by a number of young women. I assumed their ego-stroking was sufficient for his boredom threshold to remain unbreached so far.

O'Day's PR guru, Autumn, left Baptiste to cope unaided tonight. She was staying close to O'Day himself, with Jimmy in attendance. And bloody Morton, of course. He caught my eye and gave another of those mocking salutes. I kept my face deliberately stony, let my gaze drift away as though there was absolutely nothing of interest to hold it there.

But watching the dynamics of that little group several things finally struck me. The fact that Morton was quietly contemptuous of his charge and didn't mind who gleaned that from his face or his body language. That Jimmy O'Day both admired and resented his father in equal measure. And that regardless of Tom O'Day's relationship with Autumn—professional or personal—Jimmy was ever so slightly in love—or at least in lust—with on her.

The lady herself was such a consummate professional in the way she schooled her face into polite attentiveness towards anybody who was speaking to her that it was hard to tell *what* she was thinking. It wasn't so hard to tell what all the guys in the room were thinking when they looked at her, though.

Autumn was wearing a sparkly gold floor-length dress that moulded itself to her hourglass figure and flared out from her knees like a mermaid's tail. I wouldn't have dared wear something that covered and revealed so much both at the same time. Besides, there was nowhere to conceal a weapon.

Sadly, tonight that was not an issue for any of us. The only things I carried in the small bag hanging from my shoulder were my mobile phone, an emergency field dressing, painkillers and a couple of usual standbys—two tampons and some safety pins. You never know when something like that would come in handy,

142

and I'd previously been asked for both at one time or another by clients who'd suddenly developed an urgent need for them in the middle of a job.

Not that I thought Blake Dyer was going to have any cause to ask for sanitary protection during the course of an evening, but you never knew.

THIRTY-FIVE

"**M**onday, August twenty-ninth two-thousand-five, at six-ten in the morning, Hurricane Katrina came ashore in Plaquemines Parish, Louisiana, about sixty miles south-east of New Orleans," Tom O'Day announced.

He was speaking to the assembled guests down in the main casino area on the lower deck, his voice slow and solemn. They might all be standing around in their finery, clutching glasses of champagne, but he was not about to allow them to forget why they were here.

"By the time she hit land the weather people reckon the wind speed was between a hundred-thirty and a hundred-fifty-five miles an hour. That's right on the nose of a full-blown Cat Five. At those kinds of levels the official Saffir-Simpson Hurricane Scale summary states that 'catastrophic damage will occur'. Well, my friends, it surely did. If you'll forgive me quoting statistics, more than ninety thousand square miles of the Gulf Coast was affected."

He paused, not embellishing the story. Everybody had seen the news reports at the time. This was little more than a gentle reminder.

"But what has happened in the months—the *years*—since Katrina is a tragedy and a disgrace," he continued. "Eighteen hundred and thirty-six people lost their lives during the hurricane itself. Seven hundred and five are still missing. Two hundred and fifteen thousand homes were devastated and today the population of New Orleans has fallen by more than half. Over fifty thousand souls are *still* living in trailers provided by the FEMA emergency management folk because less than forty thousand homes have been approved for renovation. Almost a hundred thousand derelict cars are still waiting to be towed. There is a genuine feeling here that the rest of America has

144

abandoned this city. With your help, I aim to show these people that we have not forgotten Hurricane Katrina and we have not forgotten New Orleans."

A smattering of applause broke out, was taken up. It grew in volume and vigour. Like everyone else, I found it hard not to be affected by Tom O'Day's passion for the city and its people, but I tuned out the words, let my gaze trail over the crowd.

The only ones with their eyes not on O'Day were the security people and the wait-staff weaving among the guests with refilled champagne flutes. A cluster of empty bottles already stood on a table near the doorway. I did a quick count and reckoned it was probably best that the speeches were made now, before the consumption rose much higher.

O'Day had moved on to the subject of the *Miss Francis*, how she'd survived the hurricane unscathed by steaming up the Mississippi River as fast as her paddlewheel would propel her, her decks loaded with evacuees. And then how she'd returned at similar speed a few days later, this time carrying medical supplies, clothing, and bottled water.

When the rest of the speeches started I took another turn around one of the upper decks while Sean stayed with Blake Dyer in the main casino area. The visibility had not improved. In the distance, the lights of New Orleans faded to an orange blur off the starboard side.

I peered into the gloom, looking for the Zodiacs that were supposed to be shadowing us. If they didn't stay close in this weather, they would lose us. Having said that, losing several hundred feet of brightly lit paddle steamer would be pretty hard, even in these conditions.

But however much I shaded my eyes and leaned out into the night, I couldn't see anyone escorting us. I climbed to the top deck, looked again. Nothing.

I jogged towards the wheelhouse and put out my hand to knock on the door. I don't know what made me hesitate, what made me stop and check through the reinforced glass porthole set into it before I announced my presence.

The rotund skipper was sitting slumped in his captain's chair. His hands were bound through the frame at the back and he was obviously not happy about it. I could take a pretty good guess at the cursing, even without being able to hear the words.

One of the crew members was at the wheel. Behind him was a man dressed in SWAT black, including webbing and gloves. A balaclava covered his features. In his arms was cradled a stubby Heckler & Koch MP5K submachine gun. The man's trigger finger rested casually inside the guard. He looked both willing to use it and able to keep order without. I had no illusions that he was there in any kind of official capacity.

Shit!

I slipped away from the porthole and flattened against the wall of the wheelhouse. My heart rate stepped up, bounding, and my senses suddenly went into overload, stiffening the hairs on my arms and neck.

Almost in reflex my hand reached for the SIG, only to remember that my sidearm, still in its Kramer paddle-rig holster, was tucked away in the hotel safe. Never had I wanted it more.

The realisation that I'd been had—we'd all been had—flipped through my mind. Either that or this was the unluckiest of unlucky coincidences. And I didn't believe that for a moment.

I blinked, saw again the *Miss Francis*'s skipper, wrists bound tight enough to bleed through the cuffs of his shirt. I'd found that the Americans were not big on irony, but I wondered if it had gone through his mind that here he was in the middle of a situation on a boat filled with hard-cases whose hands, in a way, were now just as firmly tied behind their backs. At his instigation.

I retraced my steps, moving fast. No point in creeping when the whole of the superstructure was lit up like a fireworks party and it was pretty obvious I didn't have an invite.

Shouting somewhere below made me dodge to the railing and lean out cautiously. From there I could see one of the Zodiac chase boats coming alongside, the four men aboard bristling with armament—M16 assault rifles, mainly, one with a Mossberg pump-action shotgun for close-quarter work. All had holstered sidearms, too. *Thank Christ for that.* I could only assume that the skipper must have managed to put a call out before they grabbed him.

I leaned out a little further, preparing to shout down to them, let them know I was a friendly and, if necessary, guide them in. Timing was crucial. But just as I opened my mouth, one of the guys in the bow of the Zodiac stood up, legs braced against the backwash slapping into the rigid-hulled inflatable from the *Miss Francis*, and threw a line up towards the deck.

A black-clad figure leaned out from the lower deck a little further forward of my position. He was dressed exactly the same as the man holding the skipper hostage in the wheelhouse. As I watched, he stretched out and the rope was caught, held, made fast.

It took me a moment to realise the full implications. The men I'd thought were coming to rescue us were, it seemed, here for very different reasons.

A bad situation had just got a hell of a lot worse.

I slid back out of sight, took a breath. Coordinating an attack on a moving target, at night, in fog, took planning and manpower. There was money behind this, and with it came determination to pull the job off—whatever that might be. I thought of the casino deck full of multimillionaires. Robbery seemed highest on the list.

I put a hand into my pocket and pressed the transmit button on my comms gear.

"Sean, do you read me?"

Nothing.

"Sean! Are you there, over?"

This time, all I received in reply was a double-click through my earpiece. He could hear me but clearly did not want to respond, which meant he must be with people he didn't want to alert to the fact he was wired. I reached for the transmit button and nearly pressed it so I could give him a bit of a mouthful about how we had bigger problems right now. Then I bit back my anger. He didn't have all the facts, and staying covert might well prove to be our best course of action.

"Sean, we are being boarded by a shitload of armed hostiles. Control of the ship's been lost. I repeat—armed hostiles have taken control of the ship," I said in an urgent whisper. "Get Dyer—right now. And if he's not with you, find him and get him out of there. Move, Sergeant!"

There was a pause, then another double-click through my earpiece. I just had to hope it wasn't some glitch on the network giving me a false positive.

I checked around me, stepped around the corner of a bulkhead and flattened against the superstructure again. The way it was vibrating suggested that the *Miss Francis* was

147

moving fast, picking up speed. Her shallow draught made her seem to skip over the darkened water rather than punch through it.

I pulled out my cellphone, started to dial a number.

No service.

The phones Parker issued to all his personnel were top of the line with the latest bandwidth technology. They'd been chosen specifically because they could pick up a signal where other, older models wouldn't get a sniff of a line out.

Not this time.

I held the phone up, stepped a little further out from the superstructure as if that might be shielding it in some way.

Nothing.

Of course there isn't, said a cynical voice inside my head. *You think they would have left you with your cellphones if they hadn't already jammed them?*

The small handheld jammers only had an operating radius of around eight or nine metres—not big enough to cover the entire ship. The more simple devices blocked either incoming or outgoing signals, which were on different frequencies. But to combat sophisticated cellphones—the ones that hopped networks looking for an open line—they'd have to be blocking all cell frequencies at once.

The cops used jammers powerful enough to blank out everything within a one-mile radius. The Mississippi was wide enough so that if a unit of that type was on board somewhere it would cover us as we moved but not black out great chunks of New Orleans as well. That would attract entirely the wrong kind of attention.

I set the volume control down to vibrate only, just in case, and shoved the useless cellphone back in my pocket.

OK, time to improvise.

THIRTY-SIX

Getting back to the casino deck meant dodging armed figures on the way there. I ran on the balls of my feet, grateful I'd worn soft-soled shoes. I'd thought I'd be protecting the deck, not my own life.

Half of me was convinced they would have secured the crowd already. But the other half knew that wasn't what I would have done. Making sure the rest of the boat was fully under control would have been my priority, rounding up the crew and any stragglers first, and leaving the bulk of my would-be hostages contained and unaware in the casino. Why bother guarding them when they could be left to their own devices until I was ready to take them down?

Shit—why did you have to go thinking in those terms, Fox?

The most straightforward route to the casino deck was down the main stairwell, but as I headed for that I heard voices, booted feet. It seemed that not everyone was bothered about damaging the *Miss Francis*'s plank decking.

I dived for the nearest doorway and grabbed at the handle. It turned. I shoved through, found myself in what looked like a crew cabin, a tiny space with a bunk and a one-place table, and hanging space between them. A spatter of photographs was tacked to the bulkhead above the table—a woman and a couple of small children, a long-legged shaggy dog who seemed keener than any of them to be in front of the camera.

I heard the boots approaching, moved back away from the windows as they slowed outside. Some people just had the hunter instinct, were able to sense prey on an almost subconscious level. I stepped back again, silently, and burrowed my way into the clothes hanging between table and bunk. If he took a cursory glance he would miss me. Anything more I'd deal with when I had to.

Inside my head I was still cursing the fact I didn't have a weapon. It had become so second-nature to carry the SIG that I realised the lack of it was distracting me. My reliance had become a handicap instead of a freedom.

I shook it off, tried to concentrate instead on what I *did* have. On the table was a pen and pad with an almost unintelligible To Do list scrawled across it. I reached out, plucked the pen off the pad.

The cabin door opened—a crack that widened very slowly. I shifted my grip on the pen, readying it so that it both reinforced my fist and protruded from my clenched fingers as a kubotan. I found that although my body was revving, my mind was suddenly cold and calm.

Come on, I found myself willing him. *Come on in. Come closer.*

Close enough for me to strike.

Close enough to kill.

The man took a step forwards. I had one foot braced against the base of the wall behind me as a springboard now, poised, tense. I could feel his wariness, his caution. Could almost smell it. As if his own instincts were warning him of danger but he could not quite identify the source.

Through a gap between a pair of old jeans and a work shirt, I could see the man standing just inside the cabin door, one hand still on the open handle and the other wrapped around his MP5K. His head was tilted as if he tasted the air for trace of me. But like the man in the wheelhouse he wore a balaclava which prevented me gauging anything from his features.

For maybe ten seconds we stayed like that, frozen. Then the man took another step and reached to nudge aside the clothing on the rack in front of my face with the muzzle of the gun. He let go of the door handle and the door began to swing shut behind him.

As soon as it closes, you're mine ...

The door never closed.

A moment before it would have latched, a booted foot was stuck inside the frame.

"You looking to lie down on the job, huh, Sullivan?" demanded the newcomer. "Get on with it for Chrissakes, or we'll be running behind schedule."

"Hey, I was told to be thorough," said the man named Sullivan, his voice leaning towards whiny. "He should make up his goddamn mind."

"You want to tell him that yourself?" asked the second man.

There was a short pause while Sullivan tried to work out exactly how sorely tempted he might be, considering the undoubted payback. Then he turned, shoving his way out without a word.

The second man made a harrumph of sound as he started to close the cabin door. Then he stopped, as if he too had sensed me watching in the shadows.

Hell, he only had to look down to notice a disconnected pair of legs behind the hanging clothing.

But he didn't notice. A moment later he'd yanked the cabin door shut behind him and I was left listening to the thump of their combined bootsteps fading along the deck outside.

I slumped back against the bulkhead, the adrenaline hangover hitting hard and fast. It scared me how close I'd come to killing him. How disappointed I was to be denied.

No! That isn't true.

I told myself I was disappointed only to be robbed of the chance to interrogate one of the other side and extract vital intel from him—numbers, aims, and their line of retreat once they'd done whatever it was they'd hijacked the *Miss Francis* to achieve.

Right now, I was back to guessing.

I straightened gradually, no sudden moves or I was likely to keel over. And that, I was sure, would bring Sullivan and his mate running.

Instead, I waited until my system had climbed down from screaming high alert to just your everyday normal hijacked-riverboat kind of levels.

I pushed through the unknown crew member's clothing and reached for the door handle myself. I confess that I opened it with extreme caution, skylining my head as little as possible past the aperture.

But of Sullivan and his cheery friend, I saw no sign.

THIRTY-SEVEN

I don't know what Sean told Blake Dyer about leaving before the impending threat. I could only guess he must have phrased it as an order rather than a request. By the time I arrived on the casino deck, identified my principal and hurried across, they were involved in a quiet but vehement argument.

Now, I considered, was not the bloody time for either man to get stubborn.

It didn't help that he was only a few metres from Tom O'Day himself, who watched the exchange with undisguised curiosity, even if they were keeping their voices down. The body language spoke volumes.

"Sir," I cut in as soon as I reached them. "We need to leave. Right now."

"So Sean here has been informing me," Dyer said with a certain coldness. He indicated the crowded room with a flick of his hand. "And what about everybody else?"

"They have their own protection," I dismissed. I stepped in close. "Sir, if you don't walk with us, *right now*, then if I have to I will punch your lights out and *carry* you out of here."

His head reared back in shock, checking between our grim faces as if—after all that had happened so far—he still thought we might possibly be joking. I saw him waver as he realised there was a distinct chance we were not.

Then Sean made a guttural noise of impatience in the back of his throat and took hold of Blake Dyer's arm.

Mistake.

Dyer twisted out from under his grasp, face closing down. He turned towards Tom O'Day, who was now staring with frank fascination at the unfolding scene.

"Tom," he said, loudly enough to be awkward, "they're telling me your guys have apparently lost control of this old tub to some kind of river pirates—is that so?"

Shit!

My turn to grab Dyer. I did so with both hands—one at the back of his wrist and the other pinching in hard to pressure points just behind his elbow. He went rigid but allowed me to turn him. Unless he wanted it to really hurt, he didn't have much of a choice.

Tom O'Day moved forwards as if to intervene. Or maybe he couldn't quite believe the question Blake Dyer had just asked. "Now, wait just one moment—"

I ignored him and began to hustle our principal towards the nearest exit. "We don't have time for this."

Tom O'Day came after us. Of his own bodyguard, Hobson, there was no sign—and that worried me. It worried me a lot.

I glanced around, took a mental snapshot of the casino as it stood at that second. I'd been half expecting Morton to be among the missing, too, but there he was near one of the blackjack tables, staring over at the commotion we were causing. There was something akin to amusement on his features.

Jimmy O'Day, on the other hand, was goggling at us in horror. I made a mental note to ask him some tough questions about the reason for it—when all this was over. It was as if he knew something bad was about to happen, if it wasn't doing so already. The look he threw Morton contained total panic. He received no obvious reassurance by way of response.

Even Gabe Baptiste showed the beginnings of concern, but after a supposed mugging and a missile attack on the helicopter he was riding in, I guessed he had every right to a little paranoia. Interestingly, though, the person he edged nearer to was not his replacement bodyguard, but Ysabeau van Zant. As though she had got him into this mess and he was relying on her to get him out of it.

Sean and I almost had Blake Dyer as far as the service entrance when the double doors leading out of the casino were rammed open so hard they bounced back from the frame on both sides.

Armed men poured in through the gap, a mix of MP5Ks and M16s pulled up hard into their shoulders. I swung Dyer round behind me, almost onto my back, to keep my body in front of him.

153

I half expected Sean to step up, step in, but realised in shock that he'd let go of the pair of us and was already moving away.

I could only watch as he shifted sideways. I took a look at his face and knew he was not in escape-and-evade mode—he was on the attack.

For a second my mind faltered as the prospect of Sean killing himself at the hands of our attackers burst into it, overwhelming any logical thought processes taking place there.

But as I watched—still shuffling backwards towards our exit and dragging Blake Dyer with me—I saw Sean casually reach out and pluck a couple of the heavy champagne bottles from the table where they'd been stacked up.

He threw the first of them overhand towards the nearest attacker. The bottle flashed outwards, tumbling in flight like a circus performer's flying dagger, catching one black-dressed figure full in the face and dropping him like a stringless marionette.

Sean wielded the second like a club, smashing it down into another man just at the juncture between his neck and the front of his shoulder. There was too much noise to hear the crack, but I saw his arm suddenly droop, letting the stubby machine pistol dangle from its strap, and knew Sean's blow had smashed his collarbone.

"Get Dyer out of here," he yelled at me over his shoulder, then waded in with another bottle.

I didn't hesitate—couldn't allow myself to hesitate. I piled Blake Dyer back towards the doorway. We almost knocked Tom O'Day flying in the process. He stumbled. Dyer grabbed him and, as the casino deck erupted into panic and confusion, the three of us half crashed, half staggered out of the door into the stairwell beyond.

The last thing I saw before the doors punched shut behind us was Sean going down amid a flurry of black-clad figures with fists and boots swinging wildly.

THIRTY-EIGHT

I took them back to the crewman's cabin on the upper deck where I'd so nearly had my run-in with the man called Sullivan.

The logic of that decision was simple. They'd already searched the cabin and found it empty. There were plenty of nooks and crannies aboard the *Miss Francis* left still unexamined. Why would our attackers go back over ground they'd already covered until there was nowhere else left to look?

The two of them followed my lead in compliant silence—for once. Blake Dyer must have been only too aware that his own stupid stubbornness had just cost Sean dearly. If he'd done as he was bloody well told at first time of asking, he and Sean would have slipped quietly away before the trouble even started. Now, they knew to look for us.

As for Tom O'Day, I suspected he might well be in shock. His face was bagged with disbelief, eyes dazed in denial. But more than that I sensed a bitter, overwhelming disillusionment. I thought back to his speech earlier. This was something he'd fought for with a passion, more than just a project or a hobby. This had been a crusade. And now his dream lay in tatters around him.

It was hard not to feel sorry for the man.

When we reached the tiny cabin I shoved them inside and took a moment with the door ajar, listening for signs of pursuit. None came. I closed the bolt as quietly as I could and twisted the Venetian blinds so they were almost closed, slanting upwards so I could see the legs of anyone passing but they could not easily see in.

All the time I was aware of the sweat sticking my shirt to my back but also of a terrible anger fizzing coldly at the base of my brain. I had come so close to losing Sean at the beginning of the

155

year, in more ways than one. We'd had a breakdown in communication that had nearly damaged our relationship beyond repair. And just when I thought things were all over for us, that we'd never come back from that precipice, Sean had been shot. The whole edge of my world had collapsed underneath me. I'd been falling ever since.

I pushed it aside, locked it away, keening, into a dark recess of my mind. If Sean had sacrificed his life for our principal, at least he'd done it willingly this time—knowingly ...

"Charlie, I am so sorry," Blake Dyer said at last, his voice shaky. "You have to believe me—I had no idea there was any real danger—"

"You were supposed to be paying us to have those kinds of ideas," I said roughly, then bit down on it. If I'd let the rest of it spill out I might never be able to stop.

I turned away, keyed the mic on my comms unit, two clicks.

There was no response from Sean.

Tom O'Day had slumped onto the crewman's narrow bunk and was sitting with his hands dangling slackly in his lap. I didn't like the vacantly inward look in his eye.

"Where's Hobson?" I demanded.

O'Day barely seemed to register. "Hmm?"

Give me strength!

"Hobson—your bodyguard," I repeated with more patience than I thought I possessed. "Where the hell is he?"

Tom O'Day made a concentrated effort to pull himself together. "He, um ... went out. Got a message. Some guy came with a message for him. He said the skipper needed him to handle some kinda problem or something topside." He thought for a moment, nodded with slow sadness. "I guess they ... got him, huh? No way would he have willingly let this happen to us."

Unless he's on the payroll. No way could they have done this without an inside man.

I said nothing. I didn't see any point in making Tom O'Day feel worse. I pulled out my cellphone and checked it again. Still no service. Whatever jammer they were using, it was damned effective.

Blake Dyer was pacing restlessly. Not easy in a cabin that wasn't big enough to pace even if he'd been on his own.

"So, what do we do now?"

"Do?" I queried. "We're already doing it. Get away, find a place of safety, lie low until rescue."

Blake Dyer stopped pacing and stared at me incredulously. "That's *it?*"

"That's it," I said firmly, and just when his face began to twist in disgust I added, "It's textbook procedure for close protection—keep the principal out of danger. And, if that fails, get him away from danger as fast as possible and then keep him as far away from it as possible. That's my remit and I've followed it to the letter." And if my voice was harsher than it should have been, maybe there was a healthy understanding of his incredulity mixed in with it.

Tom O'Day looked up, caught the hunch of his old friend's shoulders. "She's right, Blake," he said, aiming for reasonable but actually coming out weary to his bones. "Don't give the lady a hard time. She's just doing her job."

"Yeah, and a lousy job it must be at a time like this," Dyer said. He shook his head. "You're playing God with people's lives, Charlie. I don't envy you those kinds of choices."

Did you have to remind me?

I would have said the words out loud, but I knew if I did there would be a shake in my voice that I couldn't disguise. I would *not* show that weakness. Instead, I aimed for a calm stare, said: "I knew what I was signing on for."

"What about all those other poor people—including Sean?" Blake Dyer persisted. "Are you really going to leave him to the mercies of those thugs?"

I tried not to remind myself of the last mental snapshot I had of Sean, going down before a beating, outnumbered and definitely outgunned. That he would undoubtedly have taken a few of them with him was suddenly of little consolation.

"He knew what he signed on for, too," I said, stony.

"Yes, but—" Dyer broke off, took a breath. "I thought you and he were ... connected on more than merely a professional level."

We were. We are, dammit!

"Look, I can't ... think about what might be happening to Sean." I took a breath of my own, deep and shaken. "I cannot allow myself to be concerned about his safety when my first duty is to ensure the safety of my principal—you."

Dyer fell silent. It was left to Tom O'Day to say quietly, "The young lady I brought on board with me, Autumn, is still down there, Charlie. And my son. I will not hide under a bunk like a coward while they're suffering God knows what at the hands of those goddamn pirates."

"I sympathise," I said. "Believe me, I do, but my hands are tied. There's nothing I can do."

Blake Dyer straightened suddenly. "No, but there's something *I* can do," he said. He looked me straight in the face and gave me a tight little smile. "Sorry, Charlie but ... you're fired."

THIRTY-NINE

I leaned my hip against the small table at one side of the cabin, glad of its support, and folded my arms.

"Are you seriously trying to tell me that you want to dispense with my services? Right now?" I said with remarkable calm. "I have to say, sir, your timing stinks."

Blake Dyer shot a cuff, straightened the sterling silver link that fastened it. "On the contrary," he said, sounding irritatingly cheerful. "I very much doubt that my timing has ever been better."

"How do you work that one out?"

The smile appeared again, brief and grim. "Because you make a damn fine bodyguard, Charlie, as I've cause to know on more than one occasion now. But the way you dealt with Sean this morning showed me your skills are not confined to defence. You're a pretty formidable offensive tackle, too. I'd back you to make any play."

I shrugged, expelled a long breath and tried to let my anger go with it. "With all due respect, sir," I said, "this is not a bloody game."

"Damn right it's not," Blake Dyer agreed. "Doesn't stop me wanting to win, though. In fact, it makes it a whole heck of a lot more important that we do."

I noticed the "we" and was not reassured by it.

"We're on a boat in the middle of the Mississippi River, at night, in fog, with no means of communication with the outside world, an unknown number of armed men on board, and no weapons between us except what we can scavenge, improvise, or steal," I said. "What exactly are you proposing that we do?"

"We do what we in this country have always done best when the odds are stacked against us, ma'am," Tom O'Day said, breaking his silence. His voice sounded slow and rusty, as if it cost him to use it. "We fight." He nodded as if to himself, as if to confirm that his train of thought was logical and valid.

Then he looked up, and the old man of a few minutes ago had been replaced by the mogul he'd made of himself. "I had the honour to serve my country in Korea," he said, "and while that may be many years ago the experiences I had there are not something I simply put aside and forgot afterward. It kinda lingers." He pushed down on his thighs and stood up, the action emphatic. "So, either you're with us, Charlie, or I would advise you to stay the heck out of our way."

"Wait a moment," I said. "There's no way I'm going to let you go gallivanting off on some kind of"—the word "geriatric" so nearly popped out but I managed to suppress it in time—"of crusade. Besides anything else, nobody should go into any kind of fight without a plan. You have one?"

The two men exchanged glances as if each hoped the other had already thought of that. Neither of them, it seemed, had done so.

"Well, I kinda thought trying to regain control of the ship might be a good place to start," Tom O'Day said cautiously.

I shook my head. "I've already been up to take a look at the bridge," I said. "The skipper's tied to his chair and they have a guy with a gun to the helmsman's head. Without a weapon there's no way you're going to get a foot inside the door before somebody gets killed—probably one of us."

Damn. I meant to say "you". Not "us"—"you"...

I saw by the glint in Tom O'Day's eye that the slip had not gone unnoticed.

"So, ma'am, what do you suggest?" he asked.

I shook my head again. "Oh, no," I said. "You're not putting me in charge. I was never an officer back in the army and I don't intend to become one now."

"Would you settle for a non-commissioned rank?" Tom O'Day asked. "I seem to recall a Marine Gunnery Sergeant who had your kind of attitude. He was pretty good at not letting a certain wet-behind-the-ears young lieutenant trip over his own bootlaces too often."

He was good, I'd give him that. But then he'd made a fortune in business by recognising when to push, when to plead, and when to downright flatter someone into getting what he wanted. I just didn't like being manipulated in any direction.

But how could I leave them to their own devices? Two men who might be in good shape but were still not in the first flush of youth. And both who'd had things go their own way for far longer than was good for them.

This is a bad idea, Fox. Quite possibly the worst you've had in a long time. But still …

After all, what else was *I* going to do? Hide behind someone else's skirts in the corner of a cabin while two old men went out and fought my battles for me?

No way.

Was I going to go my own path, try to find out what had happened to Sean, to the others, and possibly have those same two old men get in my way while I was doing so?

Again, not happening.

I exhaled, long and slow.

"Are you happy to accept that this is an extremely risky enterprise, however you go about it?" I demanded.

"Yes ma'am," Tom O'Day said.

"Of course," Blake Dyer said at the same time.

"Good. In that case you won't mind putting it in writing for me. I reached for the pad of paper on the tabletop, and the pen I'd picked up previously to use as a weapon against Sullivan, offered it to Blake Dyer.

He took it slightly dumbly. "What do you want me to write?"

"For a start you can make my dismissal as your bodyguard official," I said. *Just in case you don't make it.* I didn't say the words out loud but from the hollow look on Dyer's face I didn't need to.

He wrote in a beautifully legible hand, a few quick sentences that were brief and to the point. He even added that my dismissal was nothing to do with my competence and that professionally he held me in the highest esteem. It was more like a eulogy than a legal document. He ended it with a note that I was in no way responsible for anything that might happen to him, then signed and dated it with a flourish.

Tom O'Day had been reading over his shoulder as he wrote. He took the pad from Blake Dyer when he was done and added his own signature, then handed it back to me.

"What now?" he asked.

I read through the note, folded it carefully into an inside pocket.

"We arm ourselves," I said, "and then we go and see how much trouble two old geezers and a girl can cause these bastards."

FORTY

At first I thought the clicking through my comms earpiece was random static—maybe some kind of interference from the jamming signal that still rendered my cellphone a useless lump of pretty plastic. It took a moment before I realised there was a rhythm to the fast-and-slow staccato beat that I recognised.

Morse code.

Sean!

I jerked upright, startling the two men.

"Charlie, what—?"

"Shush." I cocked my head, concentrating. It was a short repeating pattern, and gradually I was able to make out two letters, over and over:

— ·— · —— ·—

C.Q.

Not a message as such, nor a military call sign, but two letters sent out over the airwaves by amateur radio enthusiasts around the world, a question expressed in the most economical terms.

It meant not simply the letters C and Q, but phonetically *Seek You.*

I seek you.

I keyed my own mic. "Sean? Can you hear me?"

Y.E.S.

"He's OK?" Blake Dyer demanded. I silenced him again with a quick hand swipe, then turned it into a "maybe/maybe not" gesture.

I thought furiously for a moment. During the time we'd been working for Parker Armstrong, we had developed plenty of code-words and test phrases. Words to check the presence of threat, of stress or duress. Besides anything else, Sean and I had once had

163

no problem communicating without words. He'd always seemed to have very little difficulty reading my mind.

Before.

The problem was that I had no idea which—if any—Sean would remember. And without knowing who we could trust, I couldn't ask him questions about before—about our time in the army together—and expect an answer that would tell me anything one way or another.

Supposing Vic Morton was the inside man? Supposing he was standing over Sean right now, with a gun to his head, to get him to talk us into an ambush? If I asked him the name of our commanding officer back then, for example, Morton would know if Sean tried to twist the truth. And anything that had happened since—since we got back together four years after my court martial—was hit-and-miss hazy in his mind.

Shit! Have to be much more recent then.

"Sean. You came to my room last night," I said, ignoring the way Tom O'Day's bushy eyebrows shot up, crinkling his forehead. "What did we do?"

There was a long pause. I tried not to hold my breath, felt the beat of my own pulse in my ears.

D.R.A.N.K. W.H.I.S.K.Y. came the reply, slow enough for me to translate it even with my rusty Morse.

Clever, too. He could have added an "e" into whisky without arousing suspicion from an American eavesdropper. The very fact that he did not suggested he was a free agent—for the moment anyway.

"Wait one," I murmured into the mic, and closed the channel. "Sean at least is alive," I told the two men, trying to keep my voice calm and matter-of-fact but unable to keep the relief out of it entirely.

"That's good news, Charlie," Blake Dyer said, putting a hand on my shoulder. The smile I gave him in return was more weary than I'd intended.

"Is he OK?" Tom O'Day wanted to know, galloping on before I could answer. "And what about the others?"

I relayed the questions, to which I received the answers Y.E.S. and O.K.

"Thank the Lord," Tom O'Day said when I told them, and somehow I knew he was thinking of Autumn rather than his son. "Can he get them out of there?"

164

That was one question I didn't need to pass on. "If it was possible, he would have done it by now," I said. "You'll just have to settle for him being our eyes and ears on the inside."

Tom O'Day nodded, then started frowning. "'Eyes and ears ...?' I thought Hobson said everyone had agreed not to come aboard wired?" He glanced at his old friend. "You were planning on cheating me at the casino tables, huh?"

"Whatever Charlie and Sean were planning, I wasn't in on it," he said, rather more quickly than I would have liked.

"There was nothing sinister, I assure you," I said with a touch of bite. "We held onto our comms because we're trained to plan for every eventuality—like a hijacking for instance."

"You make a fine point," Blake Dyer agreed at last.

"So, let's use it to our best advantage," I said, and keyed my mic again. "Sean, have these people said what they want? Is it ransom? Or robbery?"

I got two clicks to the second suggestion. The jewellery alone must have amounted to a decent haul. Still something didn't gel for me. Was it really worth all this effort?

"How many attackers do you see?"

He came back with an answer of four.

With machine pistols against an unarmed crowd. I swore under my breath. Plus the man holding the skipper hostage and a couple of roving two-man patrols that made nine or ten minimum. A lot—especially when the only troops we could muster against them were contained in this very small cabin, without a weapon between us. If you didn't count the pen I had slipped into my pocket.

"Have they kept everyone together or split you up?" I asked. Again Tom O'Day made an anxious gesture.

S.P.L.I.T. came the response from Sean.

Damn. "Split how?"

B.G. C.I.V.

OK, I could work out that one. The hijackers had split the group up into bodyguards and their civilian principals. On the face of it, not a bad idea to cut the possible troublemakers out from the herd so they could be watched more closely.

In reality it was both a sensible move and a bad one. Putting a group of highly trained professionals into a tight knot might have made them easier to cover, but it also gave them a chance to plan, to subtly shift into positions of maximum effectiveness.

Four men covering the whole room was cutting it fine. At least one had to be watching the guests, which left only three on the bodyguards.

If they had any sense the hijackers would mostly stay at a distance to give themselves the greatest response time to any threat. That also meant they'd miss minor communications, plans being formed, signs of readiness. Most of these guys were ex-military. They all thought along the same lines.

It was almost a certainty that, sooner or later the captive close-protection personnel were going to try something. They had to—their reputations were at stake.

But if they did, this was going to turn into a bloodbath.

FORTY-ONE

Communication by Morse code when neither party has used it for real since the army does not make for free-flowing conversation. I knew Sean wasn't trying to be cryptic, just as I wasn't trying to be slow on the uptake.

"Is Morton in with them?" I asked him.

N.O. came the immediate reply.

I frowned. "They must have had an inside man or they would never have managed to get aboard in the first place," I pointed out. "Somebody had to nobble—or turn—the outriders in the Z-boats."

H.O.B.S.O.N. G.O.N.E.

I pondered on that one for a moment—"gone" as in "not here"? Or "gone" as in "dead"?

Not dead, I realised, *or Sean would have said so—same number of letters.* So, "gone" simply meant not among the hostages, nor among the hostage-takers either. Hobson was simply not there.

"Well," I muttered, "*that* would make sense, I suppose."

"What would?" Tom O'Day wanted to know.

"Hobson's disappeared," I said. "If he was their inside man, either he's taken his money and run, or he's making sure nobody sees him colluding with the bad guys."

Tom O'Day shook his head firmly. "Rick Hobson's been with me for ten years," he said. "I can't believe he'd ... do something like this."

I didn't say anything to that. Nobody ever expected someone they trusted to betray them. That had always been our advantage, coming in as outsiders. We didn't trust anybody.

"Sean, when—?"

W.A.I.T. 1.

167

The interruption was messy, sharp. I could hear the tension in his fingers on the mic key.

"What—what is it?"

Nothing.

I swore quietly under my breath. Not quietly enough if the raised eyebrow Tom O'Day gave me was anything to go by. The guy had the most expressive eyebrows I've seen in a long time.

"How clever is your equipment, Charlie?" Tom O'Day demanded.

"State-of-the-art," I said shortly, still trying to listen for the faintest click of Sean's mic through my earpiece. "Good enough to escape your guy's scanner anyway."

He looked only slightly pained at that. "And where's the mic?"

There was something focused enough about the question to be more than idle curiosity. I flipped down my shirt collar to reveal the mic on a thin neck loop underneath. With a little more work they could have disguised it as a piece of jewellery, although considering ninety per cent of the users were male, it probably wasn't worth the company's effort.

"It's all wireless," I said. "The mic's either voice-operated or works from a pocket key—it looks like a key ring." I fished my wallet out of my back pocket and opened it up. The main transmitter was the thickness of two credit cards and sat neatly inside.

Blake Dyer glanced at his old friend. "And here was me thinking your specialty was cryptography—codes and such," he said.

Tom O'Day smiled. "Still had to know how to get a hold of the intel before we could set about decoding it," he said. He peered at the device. "Things have come on a pace since my day," he admitted, "but I would guess that thing has some kind of volume or sensitivity setting, if Sean can wind his mic up full you should be able to hear what's going on at his end, save him having to translate everything for us."

"If we leave the channel open, there's more chance of it being picked up," I argued. "And it will whack through the battery. You get about eight hours of talk time, but up to a hundred-and-fifty on standby." I gave a twitch of my shoulders, tried to work out why I was being awkward and added grudgingly, "Still, I don't expect these guys are in for the long haul."

Tom O'Day nodded, accepting my acquiescence. "He only has to open the mic when there's something you need to hear," he pointed out reasonably. "At which moment in time I'd guess those people will have other things on their mind."

My turn to nod. I forwarded the information to Sean, aware that he'd already caused the men holding him trouble. If they had any sense, they would have bound his hands, but they had not—or if they had, they'd done so in such a position he could still reach his mic key. Getting his wallet out of his pocket to fiddle with the sensitivity settings on the transmitter, however, was a whole different ball game. One that was likely to get him shot.

Maybe it was a good thing the hijackers were likely to be standing well back after all.

G.O.T. I.T. he sent back when I was done. W.A.I.T.

There was silence for a few long, agonising minutes, then suddenly Sean keyed his mic and held it open. Everything that was happening inside the *Miss Francis*'s casino came flooding through my earpiece and directly into my head.

FORTY-TWO

"Leave him alone, you bastards. Leave him alone!"
The voice that came buzzing through my earpiece had a Brit accent and, to my utter surprise, I recognised it as belonging to Vic Morton. I'd never heard him so intense.

Who the hell was he talking about?

The shouts were quickly followed by the thud of blows landing, someone hitting the deck hard. Then more scuffling terminated with groans and muttered swearing.

"There's no point in fighting them, Vic, mate," came Sean's voice with a taut calm, but so loud it was distorted from being closest to the mic. "Trust me, cowards like this lot never play fair."

"You can shut up, too. What is it about you fucking limeys— you just love to hear the sound of your own voices, huh?" A new voice, American, from somewhere like New Jersey if my ear for the accent was correct.

"Yeah, it must be a real novelty for you to hear someone not talking out their arse," Sean shot back.

I sucked in a breath. Sean was letting his temper get the better of him. Not his usual reaction—whatever that was now. Either way it was unwise.

"You don't shut up, you can take his place next time," warned the man from New Jersey. And louder, to someone else off in a slightly different direction, he added, "Get him out of here."

Did he mean Sean? I held my breath, listening to sounds of a renewed scuffle. Then Sean said, "What's the matter? You don't have the guts to kill him in front of witnesses? He's the kid's bodyguard—he's just doing his job."

Was Morton really getting himself worked over for Jimmy?

170

"Unless you want to join him, can it." The threatening voice suddenly grew louder, lowered to a growl. Was that what Sean was doing—tempting the guy in close for the kill?

I held my breath again. With three other armed men in the room it was suicide to try anything solo. I was amazed they hadn't slotted Morton as soon as he'd kicked off. Slimy little sod always did have Teflon-coated shoulders for sliding out of trouble.

But where were they taking him—and Jimmy?

More to the point—*why?*

Inside my head I could picture the layout, the large deck area with the gaming tables dotted around the place. If they'd any sense, they would have all the hostages sitting on the floor. Easier to keep an eye on them, and harder for anybody to launch any kind of surprise attack.

Sean had said there were four of them holding a roomful of people. Any of the bodyguards would earn themselves a massive bonus if they managed to disarm one of the attackers.

More, no doubt, if they managed to kill any of them. Or all of them.

It all made isolating and separating out any possible troublemakers even more important for the hostage-takers. Whoever got brave would almost certainly also get very dead. But once someone took a chance and led the initial charge, the rest would be quick to take advantage of the situation. A few wouldn't make it, but with their military background they were used to the concept of acceptable losses.

"You're wasting your time," came another voice that was both shaken and shaking. I heard fear there, and pain, all being manfully hidden. His voice was quite distant. It wasn't hard to identify the new speaker as Jimmy O'Day. *"I hate to disappoint you, but there's no way my father is ever going to make any sweeping sacrifices on my account,"* Jimmy said. *"You can take that to the bank."*

I found my eyes straying to Tom O'Day as his son's words came into my ear. O'Day senior certainly didn't strike me as filled with paternal pride.

"Well, let's hope you're wrong about your old man, because otherwise things are gonna get very nasty for you, Jimmy boy," said the man from New Jersey with a certain grim relish to his tone. *"Very nasty indeed."*

171

"This is pointless. There's no point to this," Jimmy protested, sounding close to tears. There were jerks in his voice, too, as if he was still struggling against being restrained. *"Why are you doing this? You think you can get away with holding us hostage? You think you can get away afterwards?"*

"Thanks for your concern, but we got that part under control. You got other things to worry about right now." New Jersey man's voice turned from almost cheerful to coldly precise like flicking a switch. *"So, let me ask you one more time. Where. Is. Your. Fucking. Father?"*

There was a moment's pause while the room as a whole held its collective breath.

Then Jimmy O'Day spoke again, and this time the only thing I could hear in his voice was raw defiance. *"Where is he? How the hell should I know? The old bastard wouldn't tell me if he was going to the john, never mind anything important, OK?"*

I heard two quick steps before another blow landed. There was the gasp of expelled air, a muffled groan. Further off came more scuffling and cursing. Tuned in now, I put that down to Morton again. The guy had a lot more guts than I'd given him credit for.

A lot more than I remembered.

Then a new voice joined the fray. *"I can hardly believe this is what you came for, is it?"* Autumn said, her voice as cool and clear as I'd come to expect. *"If you wanted to beat up on the defenceless, you could have picked a fight on a street corner. So, are you simply here to rob us, or are you really here for something else? Something to do with Tom?"*

Jimmy shouted, *"Autumn! No—"*

"Ahh, yes," said the man from New Jersey, satisfaction in his tone now. *"Miss Sinclair. I was just getting around to you."* He let out a low whistle. I could almost feel him stripping her with his eyes. *"Well, I'm guessing it's O'Day's money keeps you by his side, sweetheart, rather than his youthful good looks. Still, let's hope he's a little more fond of you than he is of his own flesh and blood, huh?"* He paused. *"You may as well take her away, too."*

FORTY-THREE

I reported the gist of what had gone on down in the casino, trying not to add my own spin on things. Not altogether successful if Tom O'Day's reaction was anything to go by.

"First you blamed my son's bodyguard for this, Charlie, then my own guy, and now it's *my* fault all this is happening?" He shook his head. "Maybe these guys just want me because I put this whole deal together, so they kinda think I'm the icing on the cake."

"I'm not saying it's anybody's fault—just that they want you and seem determined to get you."

"We can sit around here arguing who's to blame 'til Doomsday," Blake Dyer said. "How about a little action?"

Tom O'Day smiled at him. "Sounds good to me, my friend." He glanced at me again. "So, Charlie, you with us?"

"OK, OK," I said sourly. "First we need weapons—or anything we can use for weapons. Any ideas where to look?"

Tom O'Day pursed his lips. "Boat like this will carry distress flares, just in case of emergency, but they'll be most likely on the bridge," he said, considering. "The skipper's cabin might be the best place. These old guys sometimes have a shotgun or some such. Never know what we might find there."

It sounded reasonable to me. "I'll go alone, see what I can find, and come back for you. Less risk of exposure." *And in a fight I don't have two civilians to worry about.* "The captain's cabin is right at the stern, isn't it?"

O'Day's smile broadened. "You know, I'm kinda hazy when it comes to giving directions, ma'am. Better that I show you the way, don't you reckon?"

"And left on my own I might fall asleep. My wife says my snoring would waken the dead, so we'd best not risk leaving me alone, just in case," Blake Dyer said, deadpan. "I'll come along, too."

I took in a lungful of air, let it out slowly. "You two," I said, "will be the death of me."

As it was, getting there was no mean feat.

The *Miss Francis*'s skipper had his personal quarters on the uppermost deck, just behind the wheelhouse. In some ways the positioning made perfect sense. He could be quickly summoned from his bunk if there was a problem.

Or at least it *would* have made sense had this been an ocean-going liner. But for a riverboat that was never out of sight of land, it seemed an irrelevance. Maybe the eccentric skipper just liked to cling to past glories.

Either way, being at almost the highest point of a shallow-draught boat did not seem conducive to a good night's rest. Any inherent motion would be exaggerated the further above the waterline you got. Maybe the skipper liked being rocked to sleep, too.

The cabin occupied the greater part of the stern area of the very top deck, separated from the public areas by a low gate with a No Admittance sign firmly attached.

Unfortunately, getting to that area involved going past the wheelhouse itself, with the armed guard in residence. Not only that, but the deck lighting meant there were no shadows to hide in. The area at the top of the stairs leading up to the bridge deck seemed like half a football field of empty, illuminated space.

At least the proximity to the rear-mounted paddlewheel, threshing the water behind us into white-foamed chop, meant noise was not a significant factor. Beneath the decking I could feel the thrum of the diesel engines, smell the sluggish river mingling with salt water coming in from the Gulf. The air was thick and clammy in the darkness, weighting my lungs with every breath.

I led the two men up the stairs and made sure they kept their heads down as we crawled past the bridge. Light from every window spilled onto us. If anyone inside had looked down instead of outward we would have been dead ducks, but for once our luck held.

The low gate was obviously well-used enough to operate freely and without undue noise —always a bonus. The three of us slunk through and I latched it again, then we scuttled for the unlit doorway and bundled inside.

I dropped the blinds on all the windows and flipped on the light. The way the *Miss Francis* was lit up anyway, it was unlikely to draw more attention. And it was better than leaving the lights off and blundering around in the dark.

The cabin was surprisingly spacious, completely lined with glossy wood panels. I had to remind myself that they were all decorative—that they were just window-dressing on a glass fibre shell. The rear had fold-back doors that opened out onto a short deck overlooking the giant stern-mounted paddlewheel. When I looked out I saw what appeared to be artificial grass lining the deck, as if the skipper had built himself a little garden out there. Well, we knew he was a character ...

"Ah, looks like the captain of our vessel is a sensible guy," said Blake Dyer when he looked out, too.

"How do you work that out?" I asked, but he was already pulling open doors to built-in cupboards and storage, peering inside. He was also making more noise about it than I was happy with considering the occupied wheelhouse was only a bulkhead away in front of us. There were limits to what the paddlewheel would cover up.

Tom O'Day peered out, just as mystified, then he too seemed to have a eureka moment and joined Blake Dyer in his search. I shrugged and concentrated on the small built-in bedside drawer and the desk, which seemed the most likely places to hide a gun. Sadly, if the skipper had one, he didn't keep it any place I could immediately find. There wasn't even a lock-box or safe.

Shit.

"Ah-ha!" said Blake Dyer at last. I turned in time to see him pulling a bag of golf clubs out of a narrow cupboard on the other side of the bunk. He slid a long wood out of the bag, hefted the shaft in his hand to get a feel for the weight. "Just what the doctor ordered."

Tom O'Day joined him, picked out a seven iron. "Ping, too," he commented, impressed. "Not used on the Pro tour so much now, but still a decent make. I knew that any guy who puts down Astroturf to practise his putting is serious enough not to skimp on his clubs."

I remembered O'Day's long effortless drive off the first tee at the golf course and suddenly realised he could be a formidable

175

opponent with one of those things—and not just on the greens and fairways.

Still, a golf club might be a fine weapon above decks, but in a confined space, below them, that was another matter.

"You know your golf clubs for playing, but if you're going to use them as a weapon, you need something shorter than a wood," I said. "I'd go for a five or six iron if I were you."

Blake Dyer grinned at me and selected a six iron.

For myself I wanted something shorter still and easier to handle. I scanned the cabin again and my eye landed on a large Maglite near the spacious bunk. The flashlight was a five-cell in black—no flashy reds or silvers for our skipper. I was liking this guy more by the minute.

And there, sitting on a shelf above the desktop was a roll of heavy-duty duct tape. The kind of thing you'd use for running repairs on just about anything. Or for securing a captive. I picked up the roll.

"We all set?"

"I just need to use the bathroom," Blake Dyer said.

"Make it fast," I said. "And whatever you do, don't flush it." I'd been on some yachts supposedly a lot more luxurious than this where the marine toilets clanked like an old mine pumping engine when they flushed. There was no way I wanted to call that kind of attention onto us.

Dyer nodded, laid down his club and pushed through a louvred door near the far side of the bunk. To my surprise he was back a moment later.

"I know I said 'make it fast', but you can't have had time to—"

"I didn't have time," said my former principal, face pale and voice sober. "It was ... already occupied."

I pushed past him, went into the small en suite. Inside was a toilet so close to the sink that it would have been impossible to sit straight on it. The sink also overhung the cramped bathtub on the other side. In fact, the mixer for the shower came directly from the sink taps. It was an ingenious use of space, but I daresay this element of the design—however clever—was not appreciated by the dead man who lay in a crumpled pile of limbs in the bottom of the bathtub.

FORTY-FOUR

The image of the dead man sparked a memory—of the last time I'd faced a corpse in a bathroom. Must be the proximity of a drain and running water that made killers choose them as ideal storage places for bodies.

The last time, I'd been in California, in a cheap motel just off Sunset Boulevard. The dead man had been someone I'd known only slightly but his death had hit me hard. I felt responsible for it.

I knew this man, too, but felt nothing. His mistakes were all his own.

"What is it—?" Tom O'Day demanded, peering over my shoulder. He saw the body and made a choking sound in his throat. "Oh my Lord," he murmured, "that's Hobson."

"Yes," I said. I looked at his hands, the cuts and scuffs across his knuckles. "If it makes you feel any better I'd say he didn't go down without a fight."

O'Day cleared his throat. "To be honest, ma'am, no it doesn't," he said slowly. "Knowing that makes me feel no better at all."

I knelt by the side of the bathtub and leaned in over the body, laid my fingers against the pulse point in the dead man's neck as a formality, not expecting the faintest flutter. I didn't find one. Hobson was still warm to the touch like he was sleeping or in a coma.

The feel of him brought back another painful memory, of Sean lying inanimate in his hospital bed for more than three months after he was shot. His skin had taken on this same loose quality. As if the essence of him—the element that made him truly human—had gone elsewhere. As if he were trapped somewhere between the living and the dead.

In Rick Hobson's case, though, there was no possibility he was ever coming back.

Tom O'Day waited until I'd confirmed life extinct, then backed out of the bathroom without a word. Through the open doorway I could see Blake Dyer sitting on the bunk, eyes fixed on nothing. If the two men had ever truly thought this was a game, they'd just realised it was not.

In an ideal world I knew I should disturb the body as little as possible, but this was not an ideal world. I flipped open the dead man's jacket and ran my hands down both sides of his torso, finding no wounds. No weapons either, more's the pity. It seemed that Hobson had obeyed his own orders not to bring a firearm onto the *Miss Francis.*

"Bloody hell, Hobson. Why couldn't you of all people have broken the rules?"

He was a big guy and he fitted snugly into the bath, so moving him took real effort. I bunched a fist in the front of his clothing and heaved, leaning my bodyweight into it. His upper body rose slowly and gradually folded so he was slumped forwards. And as his head lolled down I found out what had killed him.

The back of his skull had been smashed flat, either from a high fall or a fast-moving blunt instrument. Not being a pathologist, it was hard to tell which. Either way, he wouldn't have stood much of a chance. Nor would he have lasted long afterwards.

I checked the back of his jacket, his rear trouser pockets. Nothing.

Cursing under my breath, I stood up, sluiced the blood off my hands and went out, closing the door behind me. Blake Dyer was still sitting on the bunk, Tom O'Day in a chair across the other side of the cabin. Both men looked shocked and thoughtful.

"Somebody caved his head in," I said bluntly.

Blake Dyer closed his eyes briefly, looked away. "Poor guy," he murmured.

"Still think he was their inside man?" Tom O'Day asked with a little edge to his voice.

I shrugged. "No reason why he couldn't have been," I said. "Maybe they decided to cut their costs and kill him once his role was over. It's not like he could sue them for breach of contract."

"Or maybe he saw them coming aboard and single-handedly put up a fight," O'Day said stubbornly.

"Maybe," I agreed. "Or he could have played his part and then been taken by surprise by someone he had reason to trust."

He glanced at me sharply. "You have anyone in mind?"

I shook my head. There was no way I was going to get into that kind of argument—they'd already had enough to send them reeling.

Maybe one day we might even discover which of those scenarios was closest to the truth. Now was not that day.

"We need to move—we've been here too long already." I hefted the Maglite, holding it just behind the bulb where I could use the tail end as a club and still be able to see what I'd hit afterwards. I handed the roll of duct tape to Dyer and gestured to the open golf bag. "Choose your weapons."

They stuck with their original choices—a couple of medium irons. I couldn't comment on that one way or another. But from the way they gripped the clubs determinedly I'd say the image of Hobson's body was painted large and fresh in their minds. If it came to it, they wouldn't hesitate to lash out like they meant it. I couldn't ask for more than that.

We switched off the lights and I checked we had no company before we slipped out of the skipper's cabin onto the deck. The fog made it impossible to tell what part of the river we were passing along now. I made a note, when we reached a place of safety, to ask Tom O'Day if he knew where we were. He seemed to know this area better than most. How would his fervour for the After Katrina Foundation survive this episode, I wondered. Would it survive at all?

Although O'Day was the one with expert knowledge of the *Miss Francis* I recalled enough of the layout to lead from the front. Every time we reached a corner, a doorway or a stairwell, I braced myself, ran through a rapid subliminal list of actions, moves, alternatives.

The bad guys were armed with automatic weapons. I had a flashlight. Not exactly a fair fight, but not a hopeless one either. I was expecting them and if they were expecting anybody, they were most likely not expecting me.

Not many blokes, whatever their training, can shoot a woman without a moment's hesitation. I'd learned that statistic a long time ago. Now I was banking my life on it being true.

If Hobson was indeed the inside man on this job, he would have briefed our attackers about the personnel coming aboard.

Whether they would have worked out I was missing or not was another matter. Clearly, they knew Tom O'Day and Blake Dyer had made it out of the casino in the confusion, but could well have assumed that Sean was Blake's man and discounted me altogether. I could only hope so.

After all, everyone had assumed Sean was in charge and I was merely ... what—window dressing?

We headed back towards the crewman's cabin where I'd first hidden away. It still looked as undisturbed as it had been when we'd left it. I riffled through the clothing on the hanging rail, just to be sure nobody hid where I had hidden. Nobody.

"So, do we have a plan?" Blake Dyer asked, sitting down on the edge of the bunk. He sounded exhausted, as though the adrenaline that had been firing him had leached away, leaving him old and tired and just a little bit wishing he'd never got involved with this damn stupid stunt in the first place.

"We need to get to those people in the casino—get them out of there," Tom O'Day said promptly. So much for him needing a rest—even a nap—before we could go any further.

"The casino deck is three down and slightly aft of here, isn't it?" I asked.

O'Day stood, turning a little to get his bearings, then said, "You nailed it, Charlie." He sounded confident but I made a mental note never to play poker against this man. And definitely never for money.

I flipped a slat of the blinds aside and peered into the darkness outside. "Where are we in relation to the land, any ideas?"

Tom O'Day joined me at the window, pursed his lips as he squinted out much as I had done.

"Damned if I know," he admitted at last.

"I thought you knew this whole area?"

"Hey, it's kinda dark out there, ma'am, in case it escaped your notice. And foggy. All I know is we've been heading up river."

Considering upstream was the direction we'd taken when we set off, that wasn't much help. I refrained from pointing that out and wondered instead where the *hell* we were going. And—more importantly—why were we going there?

I shook my head, stepped back from the window. There was a reason it was called "intelligence gathering". Right now, we needed to go out and gather some.

FORTY-FIVE

As we left the cabin, Tom O'Day indicated we should turn left, heading aft. I shook my head and jerked it in the opposite direction.

I put my lips close to his ear and whispered, "Roundabout route—safer."

When I pulled back it was to find him frowning, but here was not the place to argue. That was why I'd picked it. If he realised that he gave no sign.

But both of us knew my choice had nothing to do with safety. I was setting myself up both as hunted and hunter.

Finding suitable prey took maybe a couple of minutes. So far, we'd been purposely avoiding any roving patrols, diving out of sight whenever we heard bootsteps or caught the suggestion of movement ahead.

Now I headed for the source of the noise, with O'Day and Dyer creeping along behind me. Their only job, I'd told them, was to watch my back. So far they seemed to be taking the task seriously.

But I was gambling and I knew it. I needed to find a man alone to stand a chance of taking him down, quick and clean. I'd seen what I was about to attempt done in training but never tried it for real—when the stakes were higher than a mere technical defeat.

If I got this wrong I would end up seriously injured or dead.

And who will mourn for you? Sean?

The way things stood, that wasn't a certainty.

Parker?

In private, maybe. No, that was unfair – and demeaning to the depth of feeling I knew he had for me. But in public he would show only the same sadness as for any employee. My mother might weep with decorum, clutching a lace handkerchief. My father would not allow himself to weep at all.

I shook myself roughly. *Better concentrate on staying alive then, Fox.*

And then, halfway down one of the side decks a man stepped into view around the corner of a bulkhead. His gaze was slanted towards the railing and the darkened river, bored and dulled by a route he'd tramped a dozen times already. Repetition with no variation.

Until now.

It took me a fraction of a second to register that he was alone. By that time I had already launched myself towards him. I put everything into an explosive burst of energy and movement, using my arms to drive up instant speed.

The man had been about five metres away. Even as his focus finally snapped onto me I'd closed that distance by half, arms still pumping furiously. Maximum speed, maximum aggression. The watchwords Sean had drummed into us back in the army filled my head like a roar.

I should have been yelling, a battle cry designed to disorientate and paralyse the enemy, but I couldn't afford to make so much noise. I settled for opening my mouth and eyes wide as I charged and hoped that the man's mind would fill in the rest.

It did.

For maybe another half a second he was locked motionless, then he grabbed for the H&K machine pistol hanging by its strap from his right shoulder. He fumbled it.

That was all it took and I was on him like a lioness taking down a wildebeest on the African savannah.

I didn't aim *for* the man, I aimed *through* him. I hit him midstride, punching my knee upwards dangerously low into his belly, followed up fast with the Maglite straight to the throat.

He was bowled over by the attack, crashing backwards and skidding along the deck with me on top of him, adding knees and elbows as he hit. The breath was blasted out of him along with any warning cry he might have been about to make.

He dropped the MP5K. It went clattering away. I ignored it for now. As long as it wasn't actively in his hands I didn't care.

I hit him again, in the face this time, just to get his attention and give him something to think about other than fighting me. I used the end of the Maglite to break his nose with one sideways sweep. By the looks of him he'd never had it broken before. The shock and surprise would be all the greater.

It certainly took the wind out of him. He arched away from me, gasping and moaning, offered no resistance when I rolled off him and dragged him by the collar of his jacket towards the nearest cabin. As I did so I glanced up, found Blake Dyer and Tom O'Day staring down at the pair of us.

"Where's the gun?" I demanded.

"It went over the side when you tackled him," Tom O'Day said.

Shit.

"Erm, a little help here?"

Blake Dyer jerked out of it and grabbed for the door handle. Tom O'Day got a grip of the downed man's arm. He slid much faster with two of us. We bundled him inside. I checked we'd left no trace behind, aroused no pursuit, then shut the door firmly behind us and flicked on the light.

I quickly checked the man over, hoping he was carrying a back-up piece, a handgun of some description. Sadly, he was not.

I ripped out his radio mic and the curly-cord that led to his earpiece. The transceiver for his comms system was hooked to his belt. I took that away, too, made sure it wasn't set for voice-activation. I fitted the earpiece into my own ear, adjusting the volume. If they started calling for him, it was best to be forewarned.

I looked up. The men were still clutching their golf clubs ready to take a swing if our prisoner showed signs of resistance.

"I wish I'd managed to grab the gun before it went over."

"Don't beat yourself up about it," Tom O'Day said. "It was a *damned* fine tackle, ma'am."

"Yeah, well, I always wanted to play rugby at school but they wouldn't let me."

"You played too rough for the boys, huh?"

"Something like that, yeah," I murmured.

Over the side ... Double shit. All that risk for nothing.

I slumped back against the bunk. The cabin was another crew quarters, although I hadn't seen enough crew to warrant the number of cabins the *Miss Francis* seemed to have prepared for them. Maybe the sternwheeler doubled as a floating brothel. I glanced at the narrow single mattress. *Hmm, maybe not.*

I stared down at the man moving dazedly on the cabin floor between us. If he couldn't provide us with a weapon, at least he could give us intel.

Or he'd follow his bloody gun into the river.

FORTY-SIX

L et's start with an easy one," I said. "What's your name?"

The man with the broken nose glared at me resentfully but I couldn't blame him for that. When he opened his mouth it was only to breathe, not to speak.

I said conversationally, "Just because I've broken your nose once doesn't mean I can't break it again. And trust me, it will hurt more the second time."

I'd taken the roll of duct tape back from Dyer and had used a good measure of it to secure our prisoner to the upright chair in the cabin, hands behind him and ankles attached to the front legs. I knew enough about the technicalities of it to make his bonds uncomfortable as well as secure.

"OK, so maybe the nose doesn't bother you," I said. "What about your kneecaps?" I let my eyes slide to my companions, standing awkwardly near the door. There wasn't much room for four of us in there. "Any room to put some decent power behind that club, Tom?"

He held my gaze, playing his part. "It's a bit tight, but I'm sure I can get the job done," he said easily.

Blake Dyer made a kind of muted gagging noise and looked away.

"OK, OK, it's Lu-Lukas," the man with the broken nose said quickly. "My name's Lukas."

"No it's not." I shook my head, regretful. "Your name's Sullivan—isn't it?

The fear leapt in his eyes then. He swallowed, coughing as the blood trickled down the back of his throat. Then he let his head hang, gave a brief nod.

Unseen over the top of him, Tom O'Day and Blake Dyer passed me astonished looks. I shook my head. Now was not the time to explain that as soon as he'd spoken I recognised the man.

185

He was the same one who'd searched the cabin where I'd been hiding when the hijackers first came aboard. I wondered if he would have treated me any better, had our positions been reversed. Then I thought of Hobson lying dead in the bathtub.

No, probably not.

I sighed. "Look, Sullivan, you're going to talk to me eventually. Why drag this out and make it more painful for yourself?"

"You're not going to torture me," he said, half bravado, half hope.

I shook my head. "No, I'm not," I said patiently. I pointed to Tom O'Day and hoped he'd play along. "But you killed this guy's personal bodyguard—his friend. And, trust me on this, he's the wrong man to upset."

"What?" Sullivan managed. "Hey, I didn't kill nobody—"

"Guilty by association, my friend. That's how the courts see it, that's how I see it." I gestured to Tom O'Day again. "And that's certainly how he sees it."

Sullivan squinted at O'Day as if trying to remember where he'd seen the face before. It didn't take him long to work it out. "But that's—"

"Tom O'Day, yes," I agreed. "The millionaire—"

O'Day cleared his throat.

"—Make that *multi*millionaire," I corrected. "But what most people don't know about him is that during his time in Korea he was considered something of an expert at … extracting information—usually from people who did not want to reveal it. They never thought he could break them, but he did."

O'Day's eyebrows shot up again but he played along and didn't contradict me. After all, I'd spoken the exact truth … in a way. What else did a cryptologist do but interrogate codes and ciphers until they spilled their guilty secrets?

"I guess I'm a little rusty," O'Day said easily, linking his fingers together and cracking his knuckles out straight, "but they're the kinda skills you don't forget in a hurry." He favoured Sullivan with his best hostile-takeover boardroom stare. "Especially for the man who had a hand in murdering Rick Hobson."

"For God's sake, man, I didn't have nothing to do with that. We just needed to know what he'd done with you. He should never have—"

Sullivan broke off, gulping down his words as he realised he'd said too much. But once he'd started it was hard to stop.

"He should never have done what?" I prompted. "Run? Fought back? Told you he didn't know anything?"

Sullivan didn't have an answer to that one, wouldn't meet my gaze.

"If you were hoping he'd tell you where his boss was hiding, he couldn't," I said roughly. "I got O'Day out when it all kicked off in the casino. Hobson didn't have anything to do with it." I paused, let that one sink in. "So you killed him for nothing."

Well, that answers another question. Hobson was not the inside man.

Sullivan's eyes fluttered closed for a moment, as if he were praying.

"Talk to me," I said softly. "Before it's too late. Before anyone else dies." I didn't need to be psychic to know Sullivan had automatically included himself in that group.

I'd intended that he should.

"Look, I hired on to do a straightforward job," he said then, speaking low and fast, like he might not get another chance. "Come aboard, round up the rich folks, take whatever they had. That was all."

But there was something evasive in the way he spoke that told me he was holding back.

"Hired by who?"

"You think they told me that?" he threw back. "Lady, I'm not far enough up the food chain to know that kinda thing."

"OK, who else was hired—guys you knew? Guys you'd worked with before?"

He gave a shrug, as if trying to sideslip the question. "Some," he admitted. "Guys I'd seen around—contractors, y'know?"

"Mercenaries."

"Like you're any different."

I raised an eyebrow. "Who else—local talent?"

"Local guys, sure," he said. "Fucking gangbangers. Can't turn your back on 'em."

"Yeah, 'cause the rest of you are *so* trustworthy," I murmured. "What else? And don't tell me there wasn't anything, Sullivan. That will only piss me off. Why did you need to know where O'Day was?"

He threw me a quick glance that was almost fearful. "Because we were supposed to grab him, hand him over."

"Hand him over to who?"

"I don't know, I swear! All I know is, we were promised a big bonus if it all went off as planned."

"The robbery?" I queried. "Or the snatch?"

"Both, I guess," Sullivan said dully. The fear was receding, I saw. Before too long he was going to start feeling ashamed of his cowardice, and then he was going to either start lying to us, or clam up completely.

I kicked the front edge of the chair between his knees, rocking it back dangerously and giving him another jolt. "Why O'Day? Why here? Why now?"

Sullivan stared at us. "Smokescreen," he said, like it was obvious and by asking we were just trying some kind of trick. He ducked his head towards O'Day. "So his wife could have him killed before the divorce."

FORTY-SEVEN

Wwhat goddamn divorce?"
Tom O'Day's voice was harsh but with an underlying thread of bewilderment that had to be real. If there really was a divorce in the offing, then it was clear he was not the instigator.

But I remembered Marie O'Day's words, back when she'd visited Blake Dyer in his suite, the morning after the helo crash. She had made some reference to wanting to catch her husband in the act.

In the act of doing what?

O'Day loomed over Sullivan. He had big hands and they gripped tight round the shaft of the golf club. Sullivan tried not to cringe away.

"Hey, don't blame me. That's what I heard," he gabbled. "That's what they told me."

I stepped in front of Tom O'Day just in case. "Why?"

Sullivan tore his eyes away from the other man with difficulty. "W-what?"

I spelled it out. "Why would Marie O'Day want to have her husband murdered before the divorce?"

"Now just wait one minute," O'Day blustered. "There *is* no goddamn divorce—"

"Say there is," I interrupted gently. "Just hypothetically speaking. You're a rich man. Surely there's enough to go around if you and your wife split up?"

From the other side of the cabin Blake Dyer cleared his throat, said, "They made him sign a pre-nup."

My turn for confusion. "Who?"

"Marie's family," Blake Dyer said. "They mistook Tom's natural ambition for gold-digging. They had no idea how successful he'd become so they made him sign a pre-nup—to

189

protect her inheritance." He gave a dry smile. "Of course, they also had no idea how cruel a hand fate and time would deal them. If Marie were to divorce Tom now all she'd end up with would be her family's debts."

Tom O'Day shrugged. "She always refused to have the damn thing annulled," he said with a fond little smile of his own. "Sticking it to her daddy right to his last breath and beyond."

"And there's no chance she's decided to cancel that pre-nup now—permanently?"

Tom O'Day shook his head, but I caught the fractional hesitation even he couldn't entirely prevent. He gave an open shrug. "Why the heck would she?"

I suppressed a sigh. "Well, maybe she's taken exception to the amount of time you spend with your very attractive young PR consultant."

He looked genuinely surprised. "*Autumn?* My goodness, you got that wrong, ma'am. I can assure you there is *nothing* like that going on between us." A little colour bled across his cheekbones. "If she were a six-XL with a face like a prospector's mule nobody would question the fact it's her brains I most admire," he added with a little more spirit. "But a woman's beauty can be a curse as much as a blessing. People automatically assume she must be my mistress, not my protégée."

I said nothing, vaguely ashamed that I too had fallen into the same trap.

"Besides," Tom O'Day said with dignity, "I'm old enough to be her father."

I privately considered that he was actually old enough to be her grandfather. But that's when I really got it—from the words, the tone.

Regret.

Autumn Sinclair was everything, I realised, that Jimmy O'Day was not. She was bright, ambitious, ruthless and driven. Qualities that Tom O'Day appreciated fully because he possessed them himself in spades.

Qualities his only child quite simply did not have.

Jimmy O'Day might have been a nice kid once, probably right up to the point when he recognised he was never going to grow into the man his father desired to succeed him.

190

I wondered if that was when the bitterness had kicked in. A part of Jimmy O'Day must have known that to gain his father's respect he needed to get out from under and make his own way. And another part knew he couldn't hack it in the big wide world. So he kept his sinecure and was thus reminded on a regular basis of his own inadequacies and cowardice.

From such daily belittlings resentment could grow into a monster.

Maybe it already had ...

I thought back to what I'd overheard down in the casino over Sean's open comms link. Besides the murder of the bodyguard, Rick Hobson, there were those taken away from the others—Autumn Sinclair and Jimmy O'Day.

Of all the guests, the hostages, those were the people connected most closely with Tom O'Day. They were the ones most intertwined with his life and that of his wife.

"We need to find Jimmy and Autumn," I said. I glanced up at Sullivan. "Where were they taken?"

"I don't know," he said, sullen now. Then—as Tom O'Day took a step towards him—with more fervour, "I don't!"

"Well use your imagination," I said coolly. "If not to think where your colleagues might have stashed them, then to imagine what we're going to do to you if you don't come up with something convincing."

"I don't—" he began again, almost a squawk.

"The meat locker," Tom O'Day said calmly, cutting Sullivan off in mid-protest. "Well-insulated, big lock on the outside of the door—it's secure as any brig."

I couldn't tell from the crushed look on the other man's disfigured face if the guess disappointed him for being correct, or because he didn't come up with it himself.

"They cater enough dinner parties on the *Miss Francis* to have a well-equipped galley aboard," O'Day said. "Climate like this, you need a full-size meat locker or half your clientele would go down with food poisoning."

"Do you know where it is?"

He hesitated a moment, then nodded. "I took a tour of the ship when we selected her for this ..." His voice tailed off as if he wasn't quite sure how to describe what had been designed as a celebration of renewal and had turned into an orgy of destruction instead.

"Good—you can lead the way," I said. I picked up the Maglite, weighed it in my hand, paused. "What do we do with him?"

Sullivan's eyes bulged. "Now, wait, please—"

"Well, we damn well gag him, for sure," Tom O'Day said. His eyes drifted around the narrow cabin. "No telling how much noise he might still make, though."

To my surprise, it was Blake Dyer who stepped forwards. "I think I can help with that," he said. He drew out a pen from his inside jacket pocket, found a sheet of dusty paper and wrote across it in neat capitals:

MR SULLIVAN TOLD US EVERYTHING

Tom O'Day looked at the paper uncomprehendingly, a frown pulling those bushy eyebrows together into a single furry line.

I taped the paper to Sullivan's chest with enough duct tape that he wouldn't easily dislodge it, then used another strip to clamp his lips shut. Above the makeshift gag his eyes were wild.

"You do get it, don't you?" I murmured. "If your mates come in here and see that note, do you think they'll bother to untie you to get your side of it? Or do you think they'll just chuck you, chair and all, straight into the river?"

FORTY-EIGHT

The galley aboard the *Miss Francis* was down in the bilges, adjacent to the casino where the majority of the hostages were being held.

Of course. It would be.

Tom O'Day led us along the upper deck away from the cabin where we'd left Sullivan still tied to his chair. I hoped having that note on his chest would dissuade him from trying to attract anyone's attention. It was a fiendishly neat and simple device. I wished I'd thought of it myself.

I waited until we were out of Sullivan's earshot, then gave Sean a brief rundown on events via the comms. Sullivan's team might yet find and release him. No point in him being able to tell them we had a man on the inside. Sean responded with a brief double-click but no other comment.

I would have felt a lot better about the expedition if I'd managed to secure Sullivan's weapon, but once his H&K had gone over the side the only thing he'd been carrying were spare magazines. Heavy enough to throw at someone but not otherwise useful—unless I got lucky with the next hijacker we encountered.

I didn't want to count on that.

We found a stairwell, dropped a deck to the main restaurant area and crept inside. The restaurant was largely arranged in booths around the outer walls with a few loose tables dotted across the centre space. No doubt the fixed seating came in useful in rough weather—not that I could imagine the *Miss Francis* casting off in anything other than calm conditions. The skipper was probably on a cut of all the tips handed out. Violent seasickness would not make for a generous gratuity—or *lagniappe* I'd heard it called here.

There was a small bar in one corner near the door to the service entrance. We crossed to that and ducked behind it just in case of a cursory sweep.

"From here the galley is straight beneath us, another deck down," Tom O'Day reported quietly. He nodded to the service doors. "Through there are the dumb waiters they use to bring the food up, and stairs in case the staff need to go fetch anything."

I made a "wait here" gesture and inched across to nudge one door open, shifting around to peer carefully through the gap. Beyond were two large dumb waiter lifts, as he'd described. There was also a small prep area with a sink and a line of stainless steel tables where the food could be loaded onto serving trays and carried out to the waiting guests. It was bare and utilitarian, no frills, no fuss. I checked for cutlery, knowing I could make a useful weapon out of a table knife or a fork, but the drawers were empty.

To one side were more double doors with small windows in them. The doors had finger plates that were scratched and discoloured from the careless shove of numerous wait-staff hands. Always in a hurry, always against the clock. I guessed that those doors led to the service stairwell that went down directly to the galley itself.

I moved across to them, careful how I put down my feet on the hard decking. The doors both had clear panels at head height— wire mesh embedded in safety glass. I peered through. At an angle I could see straight down into the stairwell. As I watched, a shadow moved slowly and steadily across the area below.

I eased back, rejoined the two men behind the bar.

"Is it clear?" Blake Dyer asked, strain in his voice.

I shook my head. "Looks like there's a sentry at the bottom."

"Just one man?"

I looked at him. "That's all they need."

Especially with no weapon of my own.

I looked at the bottles of spirits hanging from their optics above me. Any number of highly flammable liquids here—the makings of any number of improvised explosive devices that would clear a stairwell faster than just about anything. I thought of the hostages in the bowels of the boat. Fire was my last—and worst—option.

We crossed to the opposite side of the boat and moved out of the restaurant. Tom O'Day guided us to another stairwell. Alert

194

for more guards, we slipped down it onto the next deck level and tried to keep out of sight.

Eventually, O'Day came alongside me and murmured, "If we go out and round we should be able to come at the galley from the dock loading entrance. Keeps us away from the bow area."

The casino was in the bow. The galley was further back, where the only view to be enjoyed was the murky river rushing past at close proximity. The galley staff must have been able to hear little beyond the thud of the engines right behind them.

I nodded and we slipped out onto the side deck. We were low enough to hear the water slopping against the hull as we cleaved through it. The air was thick, damp, heavy.

I gazed out across the slide of the river, expecting to see nothing but distant lights glinting against the surface through the fog. Hoping that's all I'd see, anyhow.

It was not.

I nudged Blake Dyer's arm, waited until he'd nudged his friend's. "We've got company coming up on our starboard side."

Tom O'Day craned his neck. We could just make out the darkened shapes of inflatables closing rapidly on the *Miss Francis*. "Who in hell's name is *that*? They called in reinforcements you think?"

"There you got me," I said. "But I don't think it would be wise to be caught out in the open when they get here, do you?"

We scuttled back the way we'd come, careful not to silhouette ourselves against the boat's own lights. Fortunately, coming out of the misty blackness and reaching such a bright-lit beacon must have played havoc with the new arrivals' night vision. There were no sudden shouts of alarm or recognition as we retreated.

Of course, that could simply mean they didn't want to alert the existing crew to their presence. Just because we had one hostile party on board didn't mean the newcomers were in cahoots with them.

One thing was for certain, though. Whichever scenario I plumped for I somehow doubted our lives were about to become any easier.

FORTY-NINE

W hat are you doing here, Castille?"
The voice belonged to the man with the New Jersey accent I'd heard on the casino deck. In person his voice was fuller and more rounded, all the upper and lower frequencies intact. It was still instantly recognisable.

It took me a moment to place the name he spoke, though. The drug dealer who'd been killed when Sean had been last in New Orleans—his name had been Leon Castille.

"Keep a hand through my belt," I whispered to Dyer and Tom O'Day, handing over the Maglite. "If you hear anyone coming, haul me up and out of there, OK?"

They nodded. I crept across the side deck and lowered myself over the edge so I could hang down and see onto the deck below. I was almost instantly blinded by the deck lighting strung there. I shaded my eyes with my hand. At least nobody was likely to stare up straight into the bare bulbs and spot me. All I had to do was keep still, no matter what.

Below me, further along the lower deck, I could see a group of men. From the way they stood it was difficult to work out who was part of the original raiding party and who were the new arrivals. But something, I realised, was just about to come unstuck.

Not good—for anybody.

"This wasn't part of the plan," New Jersey said. He was a tall, spare-framed man, wide across the shoulder the way mercenaries tended to be—the good ones, anyway. Their lives depended on their level of fitness and they worked hard at it if they wanted to survive for long.

He had ripped off his balaclava leaving slightly long pale hair sticking up at sweated angles from his head. It did not add to his air of command.

196

By contrast, Castille—the man at the centre of the newcomers—was altogether too sleek, too smooth. His complexion was olive, almost Latin, his hair slicked back with enough gel to gleam in the lights like the coat of a wet seal. Despite climbing off an inflatable in the middle of a foggy river he was wearing a black suit complete with a waistcoat. It might have been expensive but there was some kind of glittery thread woven into the fabric that made it look cheap. Despite tooled boots with a heel, he was still shorter than the man from New Jersey, a little softer around the middle, but no less dangerous for all that.

"On the contrary, *cher*," he said. "This was always part of *my* plan."

As soon as I heard his voice, the whole of my body tingled in reaction producing instant goosebumps.

It was the man from the scrapyard near the Lower Ninth Ward. The one who'd brought down the Bell. He'd wanted one of us then and hadn't succeeded.

I put it together—the name, the determination. Only one name popped: Baptiste. He'd tried for the ball player once already—maybe twice. I was pretty sure now it must have been Castille's men in the parking structure next to the hotel, as well as downing the helicopter.

Baptiste. And there was nothing I could do about it.

"C'mon, Castille," New Jersey said now, sounding tired. "We had a deal—"

"And I intend to keep my side of it, but with certain ... alterations."

New Jersey let out a snort of breath. "And if I say no?"

From where I lay, looking down, I saw Castille smile and spread his hands. He had small hands, the fingers slim and delicate.

"Come now, *cher*, let us not fall out over this. After all, I have allowed you use of my men for this enterprise, no?"

New Jersey glanced around him as if realising for the first time that he was surrounded by more unfamiliar faces than trusted ones. Just for a second his hands strayed towards the MP5K. It dangled from its shoulder-strap like Sullivan's had done. The men around him tensed in automatic response. His hand stilled.

"What do you want?"

Castille smiled again. It was not a pleasant smile.

"I can see you are a reasonable man," he said. "I want simply for you to bring her to me."

New Jersey hesitated. Clearly he did not need to ask who the other man meant. He knew. So his hesitation was caused by ... what? I ran through half a dozen different emotions before I came to it.

Dread.

New Jersey was a mercenary. He was prepared to kill if he had to or he would not have survived long in that profession. On occasion he might even have been prepared to act as an executioner—if Sullivan had been telling us the truth, they had come aboard intending to kill Tom O'Day as part of the deal.

But some of the toughest mercs I've ever known can suddenly develop a squeamish side when it comes to killing women and children. And by bringing this unknown woman to Castille, I realised, he knew he was condemning her.

He closed his eyes just for a moment as if in brief prayer. Maybe he was just considering his options and coming to the conclusion he didn't have any. Then he jerked his head. A couple of the men behind him turned and hurried away.

My mind flitted to the hostages. To the only woman they'd separated out from the others—Autumn Sinclair.

I could not for the life of me imagine what connection Castille might have with Tom O'Day's protégée. We'd hardly spoken, but nothing she'd told me had set any alarm bells ringing. *No*, said a cynical internal voice, *you were too busy being flattered by her attention ...*

For maybe a minute, the men below me stood in silence. Occasionally, as the *Miss Francis* hit some kind of cross swell, they swayed slightly to keep their balance. Castille looked faintly bored.

We were turning, I realised, feeling the boat cant slightly, the buffeting of the river alter in character. We had reached the extent of our outward journey and were slowly coming about. Somehow, the thought did not reassure me.

I lay quiet on the deck above, my head and the tops of my shoulders exposed beneath the railing to get the best view. If there had been a moon, a clear night sky, I would have been plainly visible. But out beyond me the darkness of the river merged into the fog that surrounded us. The atmosphere closed around me like a clammy fist, comforting and suffocating in equal measure.

I felt the reassuring hand through the back of my belt, not knowing if it was Blake Dyer or Tom O'Day who had a grip on me. I realised it didn't matter. I trusted them equally.

Eventually, I heard the click of heels on the deck beneath. They approached New Jersey from behind. He did not turn to watch the woman approach.

As the footsteps neared the group they faltered, just for a stride, as she caught sight of who awaited her, then came on with renewed purpose. So, she knew Castille and had decided either that she was not afraid of him or that she would not allow herself to be afraid.

I saw legs first—not in gold but in a silver floor-length dress. I slithered forwards another inch, just as the woman stepped forwards and I saw her face for the first time.

FIFTY

Ysabeau van Zant faced Castille with her head arrogantly tilted and a small smile flickering around her narrow mouth. If she had found her ordeal this evening harrowing in any way, it did not show.

Ysabeau van Zant. Parker's report had hinted that she was behind the hit on the drug dealer, Leon Castille. He had to be the son or brother of the man standing in front of her now.

If it was revenge he was after, why had he waited so long to take it?

"What do you want?" van Zant demanded, her manner haughty.

Castille spread those delicate hands. "As if you have to ask, *chérie.*"

"Do not forget that it was *I* who came to you. Of my own free will. To make amends."

"And you thought that would be all—that your debt to me would be cancelled because you issued a simple invitation?"

"Hardly simple. The boy had to be forced to return."

"But how could he refuse a command from his patron?" Castille said. "I'm sure you were very ... persuasive."

"I was never his patron," van Zant said, snap to her voice. "The boy had talent. I merely ... took an interest in his career."

"You covered up for him because it suited your own purposes, *chérie.* You did not want Leon's murderer brought to trial for fear of what else might be uncovered. So you attempted to bury your own sins along with his."

"And now they have risen," van Zant said, her tone fatalistic. She shrugged, as if unconcerned. "I played my part."

Castille shook his head. "You should have been the one to tell me about the helicopter, the change of plan. Instead, I had to find out another way."

"There wasn't time. It was a last-minute rearrangement."

"But clearly there *was* time, *chérie*. I made the time."

"And you failed," she said, her voice cool. "Perhaps it's fate, Castille. A sign that you should let this go. Leon is dead. Nothing you can do will bring him back. It was a long time ago."

"To me it was yesterday."

"So this is how you remember your brother and forget your sorrow?" she scoffed, encompassing the men surrounding her with a flick of her hand. "By robbery?"

"Who said anything about robbery?" Castille said calmly. He looked around him. "All this—it's a distraction. I am here for you."

For the first time the fear showed in Ysabeau van Zant's face. She took an almost involuntary step backwards, started to bring her hands up. The man from New Jersey shifted slightly behind her. She sensed him and stopped. Castille recognised the man's move for what it was—capitulation.

He smiled, stepped in close to van Zant. Of the two of them he was the shorter but he still dominated. He reached up, stroked her face with those soft-looking hands. She flinched at his first touch, forced herself to remain impassive at his second. I could almost see her quivering with the effort it took not to break and run.

An echo of remembered panic shivered through my belly.

Do it anyway, I willed her, filled with foreboding. *Run. Go over. Even a cold river at night has to offer a better chance than this ...*

Castille's hand drifted down the side of her long white neck, his eyes on her skin as if enthralled. His men stood and watched. I could almost feel them holding their breath.

It reminded me suddenly of another group of men watching violence about to be done to another woman—to me. Their faces were professionally blank, but even so I expected to see a faint feral excitement come off them like a heat haze in the hot damp air. Instead I caught a hint of shame.

Ysabeau van Zant let Castille caress her, as if she thought humiliation might be her only punishment.

"Such a pity," he murmured at last.

The realisation jumped in her eyes. She sucked in a breath either to beg or to scream. I never found out which. At last, she started to turn, to run. As she did so, Castille's hand snaked

201

around her windpipe and tightened into a claw. The illusion that his hands were soft and delicate evaporated in that moment. He brought up his other hand, grasped her as if he wanted nothing better than to squeeze her head off her body. I saw his knuckles tighten, whiten. One of his men shuffled his feet. Castille turned his head slightly and stared. The man stilled.

For a moment I considered levering myself over the edge of the railing and dropping down to the deck below. The thought did not last more than a moment. It would have been a useless, futile effort. There were half a dozen armed men down there. Any one of them could slot me before I got both feet flat on the deck. I cursed again that Sullivan's weapon went over the side when I tackled him.

But the fact remained that I was unarmed and Ysabeau van Zant was going to die as a result.

There was nothing I could do for her now except be a witness, however much that sickened me.

And that meant staying alive.

Ysabeau van Zant began to choke, her eyes bulging as her face engorged. She staggered, tried to pull backwards, her fingers clutching at his hands, but could not break his grip. She stretched for his face, but could do no more than grab at the empty air in front of his chin. He didn't even bother to lean back away from her, knowing he was out of reach.

Stupid. Going for the hands was stupid. The elbows were far more vulnerable. A downward blow would have unlocked his arms, bringing his body within striking distance. If there was too much sheer muscle to overcome, her next option should have been an upward punch to the back of the elbow joint. Break the arm and the hand is useless.

Legs are longer than arms. She should have been kicking out, aiming for the instep, shin, kneecap or groin. Twisting sideways to bring her knees into play, or those spike heels.

I shifted restlessly against the deck, my own hands and feet twitching in automatic response. Silently, I raged against the woman allowing herself to die so easily in front of me, for so little effort. For so little trouble to her attacker. I knew it was unfair, but I couldn't help it.

Ysabeau van Zant's breath was a desperate gurgle now, body sagging as her legs gave out. She no longer clawed at Castille's

202

hands but was almost petting him as her own muscles slackened and her struggles grew weaker.

It takes very little time to be strangled. Back when I taught self-defence, escaping from strangleholds had been one of the most important lessons—and the most basic. By allowing herself to be killed so pointlessly, so easily, all I felt for Ysabeau van Zant was a dark abiding anger. My fists were clenched so tight I was sure I'd drawn my own blood.

Under my breath I murmured, "Damn the pair of you."

It took a few moments longer before her body ceased to support its own weight and went limp. Castille gave her neck a final shake like a dog with a dead toy. He let go and was already turning to the man from New Jersey even as her body hit the deck.

From behind me I felt a tug on my belt, a low warning: "Charlie."

Castille stilled, head turning in my direction. I froze. He began to walk in my direction, his Cuban heels making a precise click as he approached. His head was cocked to the side, listening above the tap of his own footsteps.

New Jersey was staring after him as if he'd lost his mind. "What the hell is it?"

Castille held up a peremptory hand, fingers in a careless twist to silence him. I was sharply reminded of what I'd just seen that hand do, of what this man was capable of.

Another tug on my belt, more insistent this time, the whisper more urgent: "Charlie!"

Castille's head jerked as if in direct response. He moved a little further, a little faster, sliding his feet now to muffle the sound.

I daren't make a noise. Instead I reached behind me and dug my fingers hard into the hand that held onto me, aiming for two pressure points to release the grip. I couldn't tell if it was Blake Dyer or Tom O'Day, but I hoped they'd get the message that moving was far more dangerous than staying precisely where I was. For a moment I thought he was going to be stubborn, then the hand released abruptly and pulled back.

Below me, the man called Castille was less than a couple of metres away. He looked around him, eyes narrowed. He even stared up at the row of deck lights that obscured me from view. I held my breath as he squinted directly into the beam, sure he must be able to see me clearly.

"Castille!" New Jersey said sharply. "What the fuck is going on with you?"

Castille didn't answer right away. He continued to stare at the light for another long few seconds. On the other side of it, I continued to stare back at him. Eventually, he turned away, strolled back to where the men were clustered around Ysabeau van Zant's body. Castille pulled out a white linen handkerchief, fastidiously wiped his hands on it.

"See that she is weighted down before you put her over the side," he said.

New Jersey glanced at the crumpled form on the deck. "Is that the end of it?"

Castille paused. "No, but it is a start."

They moved away. I let my breath out slow and shaky.

A hand latched onto my belt again, yanked me back through the railing and flipped me over. The move was rough, careless. I was expecting to see Blake Dyer or Tom O'Day looming over me, annoyed with my pinch-grip and getting their revenge.

Instead I found myself staring straight up the barrel of an assault rifle.

FIFTY-ONE

U p!"
     The man on the other end of the M16 was dressed like the other hijackers, in black from boots to balaclava. He pressed the muzzle of the gun into the centre of my chest, grating against my sternum, and gave it a jerk.

"Come on, move," he ordered.

I let my eyes widen, my peripheral vision reaching out. Dyer and O'Day were nowhere to be seen. *Good.* No point in them hanging around when I refused to listen to their warnings of approaching danger. I was glad to see they possessed a little survival instinct.

Playing for time, I let my face screw up in a show of fear. "OK, OK. Please, don't hurt me!" At the same time I brought both hands up with my fingers spread as if in surrender.

The man shifted his stance a little, relaxed. He lifted the muzzle out of my chest and didn't seem to notice that my hands were now within a few inches of the weapon.

Even so, I knew trying anything was going to be incredibly chancy.

Until two things happened. The first was that he reached for his radio mic with his left hand. The action made him alter his grip on the M16 to account for the change in balance.

The second was that the cabin door directly behind him opened and Blake Dyer stepped out, his golf club raised at shoulder height like a samurai sword.

The masked man's reflexes were excellent. He caught the movement and began to twist instantly, ducking his knees as he did so.

I don't know where Dyer had intended to strike him—or even if he'd thought it that far through. But as the man turned the total power of the golf club hit him full across the throat. Dyer was at maximum extension, unwinding his best drive.

The club face met the man's neck with almost perfect precision. Had it landed across the top of his spine it probably would have broken his neck. As it was, I heard his larynx collapse with an audible soft pop.

The man started to collapse forward onto me, gasping. I twisted sideways as the muzzle of the M16 rammed down into the deck, just avoiding being skewered, and levered my feet up into his pelvis as his body flopped. From there it was a straightforward judo manoeuvre. A swift upward jerk of my legs and he was flipped out over the railing. I tried to keep a grip on the M16 as he went but his arm was wrapped up in the strap and it tore from my grasp.

He dropped soundlessly into the water two decks below. By the time he landed there was nobody to hear the splash.

I rolled over and stared down into the dark water that slipped past the hull of the *Miss Francis*. If the body surfaced I didn't see it.

I looked up again to find Blake Dyer trying to wrestle a lifebelt free from its rack on the cabin wall.

"Leave it," I said.

"We can't just let him drown," Dyer said, still struggling to untangle the line that was wrapped around the belt.

I opened my mouth to tell him that drowning was the least of the guy's worries, but Tom O'Day stepped in, put a staying hand on Dyer's arm. "He's gone, Blake," he said quietly. "Let him go."

For a moment it was like Dyer hadn't heard, then he slumped against the rack.

"Oh God, I never meant ..."

"I know, old friend," O'Day said. "You did what you had to do."

Dyer glanced at me, his face pale with anguish. "You wouldn't move," he muttered. "You told us to warn you, but you wouldn't move. If you had—"

"Then the guys on the deck below would have shot all of us," I said. "There was nothing I could do about that."

Dyer shook his head like he didn't believe me, or didn't want to. I got to my feet. O'Day handed me the Maglite he'd been safeguarding. I picked up the golf club Blake Dyer had abandoned, offered it back to him.

206

Dyer shook his head again, more vehemently this time. "No," he said. "I don't think I can ... not again. Not after ..."

"It's OK, Blake," Tom O'Day said. "You've done enough."

"I—"

"They just killed Ysabeau van Zant," I said baldly, hoping to shock him out of it. His eyes jerked to mine, a little wild. The information did not bring him any comfort.

"How ...? We didn't hear anything," Dyer said, his voice faltering. "I mean, are you sure?"

"Yes, I'm sure," I said grimly. "A man called Castille—he strangled her."

Tom O'Day looked saddened rather than shocked. "Why?"

"It goes back to some guy who was killed a few years ago—Castille's brother. I think Mrs van Zant was part of the cover-up."

Tom O'Day shrugged helplessly. "But why wait until now to—?"

I grabbed his arm, cutting him off. I still had Sullivan's earpiece in one ear and through it I'd just heard the sudden muted stutter of radio traffic, but there seemed to be an echo. I yanked the earpiece out. The noise came again, ahead of us and just around the next corner.

I turned, piled into Blake Dyer and heaved him through the doorway back into the cabin, hoping Tom O'Day would get the message. He did.

The three of us disappeared through the open doorway just as a black-clad figure appeared around the edge of the superstructure further along the deck.

He plodded past, gun held slack. There was a cigarette dangling from the mouth-hole of his ski-mask. Stupid. Stupid and amateur.

The burning end of the cigarette would not only negate what little night vision he had, but also give a sniper the perfect aiming point in the uncertain light.

Shame I didn't manage to grab that damned M16 when I had the chance.

Tom O'Day put his lips close to my ear. "What do we do now?" he demanded in a loud whisper.

I restrained myself from snapping back at him that we kept our mouths shut. At least until our armed opponents were far enough away not to turn around and come back if they heard that kind of a stage whisper.

Fortunately, the sentry's cigarette seemed to be blocking his ears as well as his arteries. He didn't show any signs of disturbance as he walked on. I let out a long quiet breath of relief, felt rather than saw or heard Tom O'Day and Blake Dyer do the same.

And then, in the quietness that followed, I heard another soft exhalation. I widened my eyes, as if doing so would help them see better in the gloom.

Nothing.

As my vision reached out I could tell we were in another small cabin. It was not much more than a storage locker, cluttered with deck chairs and old lifebelts. I made a mental note of the latter. We might need them.

But right now I was more concerned by the fact that there were supposed to be three of us hiding in that narrow space.

And there seemed to be four.

FIFTY-TWO

It's very difficult to convey to two comparative strangers that there's someone else in the room, without causing panic. Especially hard when you're restricted to sign-language in the dark.

I closed my mind to the fact that Parker or Sean—Sean *before*—would have cottoned on in a heartbeat. Instead, I tried all the inventive puppetry I could think of. All that did was confuse them more.

Eventually I gave a suppressed sigh, rose and launched myself into a stack of deck chairs behind me. It made more noise than I was happy with but there wasn't much I could do about that.

It was also effective.

When I emerged I had a man with my arm around his throat and his arm locked up his back at the wrist. He was trying not to squeal.

"Where's that damn Maglite?" I demanded.

I heard fumbling, then the flashlight clicked on.

"My God," said Tom O'Day. "What the—?*Jimmy?*"

Aw, shit—not again.

I downgraded the wrist lock from damaging to merely painful, unclamped my forearm slightly from across the kid's throat. He began to cough and wheeze. Genuine lack of air, not an act. I let go of him completely. He went to his hands and knees and stayed like that for a minute or so while he got his breath back. In my opinion, he was playing up that part of it.

But it was a mark of his distress—real or exaggerated—that his father and godfather did not ply him with questions until they thought he could speak again.

I crouched on my haunches and flicked on the Maglite so it lit his face. He flinched away from the bulb.

209

"Jimmy," I said. "What the hell are you doing here?"

"What the fu— heck does it look like?" he rasped, mindful of the company. "Hiding."

"O–K," I said slowly, "but last we knew you were being dragged out of the casino kicking and screaming. How did you get from there to here?"

"How did you …?" He took a moment, swallowed. "They were looking for my father," he said. "Thought I either knew where he'd be, or they could use me to tempt him out somehow." His gaze flicked to Tom O'Day with a hint of reproach. "I told them nothing doing—told them he wouldn't fall for that. So they tied me up and just … left me."

"They left you," I repeated flatly. "Where?"

He shrugged. "I don't know. Somewhere below decks, I guess," he said vaguely. "By the time I got loose I didn't much care. I just wanted out of there." He tried a smile that faltered when it didn't get a response.

I remembered the sounds of struggle we'd heard before Jimmy had been removed from the casino. I tried to add nothing to my voice when I asked, "What about Morton?"

"What about him?" Jimmy O'Day said dully. "Guy did his best to stop them taking me away—got beat up for his trouble, too."

I remembered that brief image of Sean going down under a barrage of black, of fists and feet. The fact he'd been able to communicate proved only that they'd left him one hand undamaged.

And his head—don't forget that.

I set the flashlight down. The pool of light from the bulb spilled across the floor, illuminating his hands. They were smeared with blood. I began running my hands over Jimmy's body. He tried to bat me away but wasn't up to it yet. "Hey."

"Don't get your hopes up," I told him. "I'm just checking for injury."

"Well, you don't need to," Jimmy said, sounding offended. "I'm good."

I gripped his collar and forced him to meet my eyes—not an easy task.

"So, whose is the blood?"

He glanced down at his hands as if only noticing it for the first time. "They gave Vic a pretty nasty beating," he said at last. "Even handcuffed the guy—and still he tried to stand up for me."

"But none of it's yours?"

"No."

"OK, let me get this straight," I said mildly. "They drag you out of the casino—thrashing your bodyguard in order to do so—because they think they can force you to tell them the whereabouts of your father, which you can't. But they don't lay a finger on you."

He flushed, Adam's apple bouncing in time with his unease, gave a nervous laugh. "When you put it like that it does sound a little ... unlikely, I guess."

I thought back to Ysabeau van Zant's final conversation with the man called Castille. He had been disappointed because she had not told him about the switch in helicopter flights—so who had? Who was in a position to communicate that change as soon as it happened? I couldn't ignore Jimmy as a possibility. Just as I couldn't ignore the possibility that they'd safeguarded his role by taking him out to make it look good, then told him to lie low and wait until it was all over.

"Not as unlikely as them simply letting you go wandering the decks."

"But that's not what happened. They tied me to a chair. See." He indicated an almost invisible mark at his wrist. He could have got it from wearing his watch too tight. I was not exactly convinced.

It was interesting to note that Jimmy's father did not leap to his defence. It was left to his godfather to be the voice of reason.

"Come on, now—who knows how these damn people think," Blake Dyer said. "And why wouldn't they turn him loose? It's not like there was anywhere he could go."

But it wasn't where he *could* go that bothered me. It was where he might already have been.

FIFTY-THREE

I stared at Jimmy O'Day and thought back. To that bitterness I'd sensed in him. To his discontent at the way his father thrust Autumn into the limelight in his stead.

I thought back to the stricken expression on his face when the raiders had burst into the casino, right before I'd piled his father and Blake Dyer out of the room.

And to the night of the reception at Ysabeau van Zant's place, when he'd been so angry I'd taken him for a genuine threat.

What might that long-term, festering resentment make him do?

"We need to get back to the upper deck," I said abruptly, getting to my feet. Tom O'Day and Blake Dyer followed suit more slowly. I could see they'd been hoping for a break, a rest, but they voiced no complaint.

Plenty of time to rest when you were dead.

I realised something else, too. That I'd become, by dint of battlefield promotion, their commander. By dint of being the most willing to commit acts of violence on the enemy. Leading from the front was always dangerous. It tended to get you killed.

"You can't be serious about going out there?" Jimmy O'Day demanded. "These people are *armed*, for God's sake." He gestured dismissively to the Maglite. "What are you going to do—frighten them away with shadow puppets?"

Before I could speak, Blake Dyer put a gentle hand on his arm. "Trust me, Jimmy," he said. "You don't want to see the kind of damage this woman can do to a man with just a flashlight."

Jimmy shot me a dubious glance but stopped protesting, so at least I didn't have to prove it. Probably for the best.

"We're not going out," I said. "We're going back in."

He frowned in silence. They all did. That was probably for the best, too.

I led my increasing band of misfits out of our place of comparative safety and into relative danger again. We had two golf clubs and a flashlight between us. Jimmy O'Day had no weapon. If he had I would have taken it away from him.

I may be foolish but I wasn't stupid.

There was one more thing I had to do before we ventured out again. I keyed the mic for Sean's earpiece and told him what had happened between Castille and Ysabeau van Zant. I warned him, clear and concise, that he should keep his head down. I received a brief U. 2. by way of reply.

I had no intention of obeying that order.

The people who'd taken over the *Miss Francis* were professionals. I didn't believe that Jimmy O'Day had simply managed to free himself so easily and been left to his own devices. That didn't leave many choices, none of which I could voice in front of his father.

Castille's words kept coming back to me. The fact he'd been disappointed that Ysabeau van Zant had not tipped him off about the helicopter trip—that he'd been forced to get his information from another source. They couldn't have got aboard the boat without inside help, and Jimmy was at the top of my list. There was a chance, of course, that the hijackers had no idea who'd been helping them, but in that case why had they let him go with such apparent ease?

And now Sullivan was going to act as a human lie detector for me.

I didn't need him to speak. All I needed to do was see his face when presented with Jimmy O'Day, and see Jimmy's face when presented with Sullivan—especially with the message taped across Sullivan's chest. It had been intended for the hijackers. It would work just as well on Jimmy.

People have a tendency to believe things they see written down. It seems to carry more weight than a chance remark, as if nobody lies on paper.

As we tiptoed along the intervening decks I weighed the possible outcomes. They boiled down to Jimmy reacting to Sullivan as a known or an unknown. And Sullivan reacting to Jimmy as a known or an unknown. Any combination of those reactions would give me more info than I had already. Probably. I was reminded of some US politician who'd gone on about

213

known-knowns and known-unknowns until nobody had any idea what he was talking about.

As we reached the cabin door I paused, waiting for them to bunch up behind me. I had only one chance to catch that first unguarded impression and I needed to be in a position where I could easily see both Jimmy's face and that of the man we'd caught.

Jimmy's had to be the one I watched as I opened the door. He thought he was among friends and his face was exposed. Whatever emotions crossed Sullivan's features would be masked by the tape he still had across his mouth and the fear of not knowing who was coming in. His eyes might tell me something, but it would be momentary at best.

I opened the door, stepped sideways and put a hand on the small of Jimmy's back to usher him inside.

He stopped dead despite my urging. I saw his eyes widen, horrified.

That, I thought, told me all I needed to know.

Then I flicked my eyes to Sullivan and discovered that Jimmy's reaction told me nothing at all.

FIFTY-FOUR

Sullivan was dead.

Definitely, irrefutably, absolutely, dead. I didn't have to press two fingers into the empty pulse point at his throat to confirm it, which was a good thing.

His throat had been sliced wide open. Ear to ear. Plenty wide enough for his head to flop back rather than forwards, despite the overhang of chin and nose. The pose made the wound gape. It left all the muscle and tendons that normally held his head upright exposed and on show. In a brief glance I saw blood and froth and bisected trachea and ruin.

Whoever had killed him had taken full advantage of his immobility, like a staked goat. That one, I knew, was on me.

There might have been a touch of grandstanding going on. They might have grasped his hair and yanked his head up and back to tighten all the vessels and sinews. To make for an easier cut. Either way, he couldn't help but see it coming, poor bastard.

Or they might simply have propped him like that afterwards, on full gory display to put the fear of God into whoever found him.

From the way Jimmy O'Day lurched sideways, gurgling in this throat as the vomit rose, I'd say the tactic worked pretty well.

"Not over the side," I said sharply when he would have groped for the railing at the edge of the deck.

I hauled him back into the cabin instead. Maybe the few gulps of fresh air he'd managed to force down had fortified his stomach because he fought back the rising tide. But his whole body convulsed, one hand braced against the corner wall to support rubbery knees. Below him, seeping across the floor, Sullivan's blood swilled with the gentle lapping movement of the ship.

215

I remembered back to the first dead body I'd ever encountered. That had been cut up too—almost disembowelled—but unlike this one it had not been a fresh kill.

Jimmy O'Day's reaction, judged by my own experience, was entirely normal.

I glanced at Blake Dyer and Tom O'Day. Blake's complexion had taken on a greenish tinge but he was holding it together. Jimmy's father was coping better. He'd been shocked by the sight of Hobson's body but the man had been, if not a friend then at least a trusted employee. And Tom O'Day had seen service in the navy, under fire. I guessed when it came to mutilated corpses this was not his first time out.

After a few seconds O'Day said with quiet intensity, "Who did this?"

I shrugged. "We have a ship full of suspects. These are not exactly nice people we're dealing with."

"And we are?" Blake Dyer's face screwed up a little and his voice was hollow. "If they saw the note they might have thought he'd betrayed them."

I looked at him for a moment, reminded myself that strictly speaking I was no longer in his employ, with all the social niceties that entailed. "It's possible," I agreed.

His mouth tightened but he nodded as if thanking me for not soft-soaping him.

"What now?"

I didn't answer right away. Now we were in the light I could take a good look at Jimmy O'Day—what I could see of him with his back towards me. His hand where it leaned on the wall up by his shoulder was bloodied around the fingers but no more than that. He was wearing a dark dinner suit, so any dried spatter elsewhere might not show.

So far, so inconclusive.

But then I looked at Sullivan again. The hole in his throat was horrific. At first glance it looked as though the killing stroke had been delivered with brutal efficiency as well as effectiveness. It was hard to look closer. I edged in, as if the wound might really turn into the ragged mouth it resembled and snap at me.

I looked beyond the obvious and saw the less obvious.

I sidestepped Sullivan's body and reached for Jimmy O'Day's shoulder, spinning him away from the wall. There was spittle hanging from his lips, but despite the contortions he had not

216

actually thrown up. He wiped the back of his hand across his mouth slowly. His eyes flicked from me to his father, his godfather, and back again. Anywhere but at the corpse.

No point in pussyfooting around ...

"What did you do with the knife?" I demanded.

"No way," Jimmy said, not even troubling to sound surprised. "No way—it wasn't me. I didn't do this."

I got the feeling it was not me he was trying to convince.

I said nothing, just let go of him and turned away. By the faces of the two men opposite they were not entirely convinced by his performance either, but Tom O'Day put up a token protest. "You can't suspect Jimmy—not of something like this."

His son scowled as if to disabuse him, hearing the slur as well as the endorsement.

"Even amateurs can secure a prisoner so he can't get loose without a hell of a lot more signs of it," I said. "And these people are not amateurs."

Tom O'Day shrugged, irritation in his face. "Jimmy's just a kid," he said, sending an angry flush across his twenty-something son's face. "They knew he wasn't a threat to them. Besides, takes skill to cut a man's throat."

"There are hesitation marks," I said. "Whoever did this, he took a couple of runs at it. So he probably wasn't a professional."

Or not one who'd had cause to kill before, up close and very personal.

"Even so—" Tom O'Day began.

I held up a weary hand. "We'll deal with this later," I said. "Right now, we have other things to worry about." I took a last look at Sullivan, bled out in the chair we'd tied him to. The chair *I'd* tied him to. "Let's move."

FIFTY-FIVE

We moved back out onto the deck, pulling the door closed behind us. Once again I led the way with Tom O'Day right behind me. The layout of the boat was solidifying in my head now, but it was nice to have a second opinion.

Blake Dyer was bringing up the rear, with Jimmy in front of him. Tom O'Day might not believe his son was capable of murder, but I wanted the lad where at least one other person could keep an eye on him.

I kept telling myself that surely there had to be far easier and less elaborate circumstances around the home where Jimmy could have arranged a suitable "accident" for his father. Going to all this trouble seemed overkill. Unless there was some other game at play. A game I was unaware of.

And until I knew what that might be I was reluctant to risk my hand. Or the rest of us, either.

We reached the exterior staircase that led to the lower deck. Tom O'Day started to guide us down when I heard footsteps below and grabbed his arm. He scurried back up and the four of us crouched near the top, peering down.

Two of the hijackers appeared on the lower deck. Both were carrying nylon bags, the kind you'd use for a weekend trip. But whatever was in them looked heavier than just a change of clothes.

At that moment, the *Miss Francis* was jostled by a small wave or maybe we crossed over the wake of another vessel. Her bow dipped suddenly.

Jimmy, leaning over the top of the stairs, staggered and almost lost his balance. He reached for the railing in automatic response to prevent himself falling. As he did so the metal strap of his watch clinked audibly against it. A tiny noise, but the pitch

218

was higher than the natural sounds of the river and the boat, making it stand out.

I swore silently, glaring at Jimmy. He flushed.

Below us, one of the men stopped and turned, hand straying to the MP5 on the strap over his shoulder.

"What was that?"

"What?" asked his companion, further ahead. "You getting jumpy, man?"

"I heard something."

There was a short laugh. "You *is* getting jumpy," the second man said. "Case you hadn't noticed, bro, we're working to a schedule here."

The first man hesitated, almost turned away and then stopped again. "You go on ahead. I'll check it out."

I shuffled back from the head of the stairs as fast and quiet as I could manage, indicated to the others to do the same. I shot a hard stare in Jimmy's direction but he was avoiding my gaze.

"Restaurant," I whispered in Tom O'Day's ear. "I'll meet you there."

He nodded and the three of them scurried away along the side deck.

The man with the bag, meanwhile, had started to climb the staircase, his movements cautious. I edged back behind the nearest bulkhead, gripping the Maglite. If he turned in my direction once he got to the top of the stairs I'd risk tackling him. If not … well, I'd play that one by ear.

The man reached the top step, body tense. He paused there a moment, listening, but heard nothing that alarmed him.

Then from further forward there came the faint sound of a door closing. The man spun in that direction, the MP5 already off its shoulder strap and in his hand. I cursed under my breath. I just knew without being told that it was bloody Jimmy, being careless again.

Carefully, the hijacker put down the nylon bag and took a firmer grip on his gun. He started to move along the side deck away from me, focused on the sound that had alerted him. Unwilling to be weighed down in a possible fight, he left the bag where it was.

The temptation of that proved too much.

As soon as he was out of sight I slipped out from concealment, crossed the deck in a few quick strides and squatted by the bag.

All the time, I was checking that nobody was creeping up on me, or that the second man wasn't on his way up the stairs.

If there were spare weapons in the bag, it was a risk worth taking. I slid the zip open quietly, looked inside, and froze.

There were no guns. That would have been better.

Instead, the bag was packed with blocks of off-white material, soft and pliable, the consistency of modelling clay. The blocks were about the size of a house brick but half the thickness. I didn't need to pick them up to know what they were. I'd handled enough C-4 plastic explosive to recognise it instantly by sight.

And from my experience there was enough in that bag to send the *Miss Francis* and all aboard her straight to the bottom of the Mississippi without any trouble at all.

FIFTY-SIX

I reached into the bag and searched the dark corners, just in case the hijackers had been foolish enough to carry the detonators in there as well. Sadly, they were not.

Ah well, I can dream.

C-4 is relatively stable as far as explosive goes. You can't set it off by shooting at it or burning it—in fact I'd actually come across some squaddies who used it for instant campfire fuel. It was pretty effective provided you avoided inhaling the fumes while you cooked your food.

Footsteps sounded along the side deck, coming back in my direction. I grabbed the handles of the bag and rose, turning fast to build up momentum. Then I let go and sent the whole lot winging out into the gloom. I even thought I heard a distant splash as it landed in the river.

Let's just hope it sinks.

Still, even if they turned around now, the chances of locating a small black bag, floating somewhere in the night, were negligible.

I snatched up the Maglite and ran along the deck in the opposite direction. Almost as soon as I did so, I realised my mistake. This way led towards the stern. There were cabins I might be able to hide in, but nothing that offered an escape route to the rest of the boat. The other man was still on the deck below, so they'd know I hadn't gone that way.

It would not, I judged, take them long to find me.

Shit.

The footsteps reached the area at the top of the stairs and paused. It would only take him a moment to overcome his disbelief at the disappearance of the bag, another to act.

I glanced at the railing. The only way was over the side but I didn't fancy my chances in the river, not to mention leaving

Blake Dyer and the O'Days to their own devices. Still, there were times when you didn't have the luxury of choice.

I climbed up onto the railing, almost losing my grip because of the Maglite. I briefly considered stuffing it into my belt, but it had stretched too loose to hold the flashlight secure. I wavered for a second, then threw the Maglite after the bag of explosives.

Sorry, skipper.

With both hands free, I managed to reach the edge of the deck above. I got a firm grip on it and jumped, swinging my legs up and hooking one foot onto the deck as well. All the time I expected to hear a shout from beneath me. Or maybe he'd go straight for a shot.

Neither came—yet.

With a grunt of effort I heaved myself upwards. I got one hand onto the bottom railing, then another. The railings were damp with salt and hard to grip. My hand slipped, scraping my forearm raw on the edge of the deck. I gritted my teeth and stretched again. The assault courses I'd tackled regularly in the army seemed a long time ago.

I made a mental note—if I survived this I'd get back into practice.

Feet scrabbling, I got a toehold and used that to lever myself up further, pulled my body over the railing and almost slumped onto the upper deck, gasping for breath.

Come on, Fox, get up!

Now without any kind of a weapon, I sprinted lightly along the deck, heading forward. There were shouts below me now, raised voices, alarm. I passed the exterior stairwell, expecting pursuit at any moment. From the banging of doors on the lower deck, it seemed they'd assumed I'd taken the option to hide. Good thing I had not.

I dodged into the bar, through the service doors and forced myself to slow down so I could make it down the stairs there without too much noise. The loudest sound was my own breathing.

On the deck below, I paused by the service doors leading into the restaurant area, peering out of the glass panels. It all looked quiet.

Cautiously, I pushed the door open and crept out.

"Charlie!" came a loud whisper off to my right. I spun, caught a glimpse of Blake Dyer's face just peeping out from behind the small bar in the corner. Behind it, all three of them were crouched down.

It was cosy behind there with the four of us, but for the moment it was the best concealment we could find.

"You OK?" Dyer asked.

"I'll let you know that in about ten minutes—if they don't find us," I said.

Tom O'Day was eyeing me with concern. "You find out what was in the bag?"

In low tones, with one ear listening for intruders, I told them. Tom O'Day and Blake Dyer took the news in solemn silence. It was Jimmy, characteristically, who half rose in shock and had to be pulled back into cover by his father.

"We gotta find Autumn." Jimmy's voice was strained to cracking. "They took her away someplace the same time as me. I don't know where they took her, but if they're going to sink the ship—please ..."

For the first time he seemed genuinely scared.

"We don't know for sure that's what they're aiming to do, son," Tom O'Day said, casting dubious eyes in my direction. "Just because they brought explosives on board doesn't mean they're planning to scuttle us."

But I saw from his face that he couldn't think of many alternatives, even if he didn't want to say so.

I sat with my head rested back against the bar. My gaze went naturally upwards to the rows of bottles hanging above us.

"If it's a drink you're after, best make it a cola," Tom O'Day said casually, following my line of sight. "We need all our wits about us."

I'd already dismissed the idea of using the spirits as Molotov cocktails, but that didn't mean they wouldn't still make a good distraction.

"On the contrary, I think a bottle of strong drink would be a really good idea."

I rose, reached up and began to disconnect the nearest bottle from its optic.

"What the heck are you doing?" Tom O'Day demanded.

"You were a navy man," I told him. "I'm making depth charges."

His bushy eyebrows rose for a couple of seconds, then he got to his feet and began to dismantle the optic nearest to him.

223

Blake Dyer took a moment longer to catch on, but he was still looking shaky from tackling the man who'd gone into the water. I realised it was probably better that he had not been forced to look at the body afterwards. This way, he could kid himself that his victim might have survived.

If I could manage it I would not, I decided, put him in a position where he had to do the same again.

Then he pushed to his feet and began to help.

Still listening carefully I moved round to the front of the bar, lining up the spirit bottles as they were taken down—whiskey, brandy, vodka, gin, rum. There were eight in total. Not many but it would have to be enough. All I was looking for was enough of a diversion for me to get hold of a gun.

"What the hell are you planning to do with—?" Jimmy began.

A sudden noise just outside the double doors to the restaurant had me waving him to silence. A coverall gesture that I hoped he would realise meant for him to get out of sight, too. Jimmy froze like a startled deer. His godfather grabbed his collar and yanked him down into cover behind the bar.

There wasn't time for me to join them. I grabbed one of the bottles, which happened to be vodka, dived under the nearest table and willed myself into total stillness. The average human eye divines movement better than features or change in colour. Out on the deck before—when I'd watched Castille murder Ysabeau van Zant—this theory worked for me. I hoped the newcomers weren't the exceptions to prove the rule.

The bar doors open slowly and a shaft of light from outside blazed directly onto me. I almost shut my eyes, as if that was going to help.

The man whose bag I had flung overboard advanced carefully into the restaurant area, putting his feet down with almost no sound, sweeping left to right with the gun in his hands. His face was hidden under a balaclava but I didn't need to see his expression to read the anger in him.

From my hiding place I saw his head moving, saw him start to approach the bar itself. I gripped the neck of the vodka bottle tighter. If he reached the bar and looked over it, Blake Dyer and the O'Days would be trapped in a tiny kill zone. It would be impossible for the gunman to miss.

I knew if I tried to launch an attack, armed only with a bottle, I stood almost no chance of success. I'd been lucky to overpower

Sullivan, but this man was too tense, too alert. Nevertheless, I couldn't just let him slaughter the others without moving a muscle to help. However useless that attempt might be.

He was only a couple of steps away when the outside door shoved open. He whirled, only to find the other hijacker standing in the doorway. The other bag was still in his hand, I noted.

"Hey, bro, you need to come see this," the newcomer said, his voice betraying a trace of shock and anxiety.

"Can't it wait?"

"No."

The single word was urgent enough for his companion not to question it further. With a final glance at the bar he crossed quickly to the doorway and they both went out.

I let my breath out very slowly. The adrenaline was making my hands vibrate with unreleased tension. I crawled out from under the table and went over to the bar. As my head appeared over it, three pairs of eyes swivelled in my direction.

"It's OK," I said. "They've gone."

"Didn't you try to grab one of them?" Jimmy demanded. "We need to know what they're planning to do with the boat."

I didn't bother to argue with him. Another prisoner might have been useful but I didn't want to become one myself, never mind dead.

A clicking in my earpiece made me pause. It was the one I'd taken from Sullivan—on the hijackers' own network. I covered my ear to cut out background noise at my end. At the other end was a burst of accelerated static, then a cool male voice:

"We are one man down and one man missing. Repeat, one man down, one man MIA. Stay alert for intruders and switch to the alternate frequency."

There was a final click. I picked the earpiece out and dropped it into my pocket. They had clearly made a plan in case a comms unit fell into unfriendly hands. Without the back-up frequency there was no point in listening any longer.

"I think they just found Sullivan," I said. "And now they're going to be looking for us, so—"

This time it was my other earpiece that burst to life.

To preserve the battery life, Sean was not keeping the mic open when there was nothing happening I needed to hear. But he thought I needed to hear this.

"So tell us about your girlfriend?"

225

It was the man with the New Jersey accent who asked the question, loud enough that he must have been standing close to Sean.

"My girlfriend?"

"Yeah"—there was a rustle of pages, as if he was consulting a manifest—*"Charlie Fox. Remember her?"*

"She's a capable girl," Sean said easily.

"Yeah, so it seems. Capable of cutting a man's throat in cold blood?"

There was a pause. The old Sean would have denied it. The old Sean would not have believed me capable of murder. But the new Sean, it seemed, had no such doubts. *"I reckon so—if she had to."*

I would have told him I had nothing to do with it, but with his mic open I couldn't communicate from my end. The comms only allowed one mic to be keyed at once to avoid confusion on the net.

A muttered, *"Shit."* And an aside to someone probably behind him, from the way the volume dropped a little: *"Find them. Now. And if you get the chance, kill the—"*

I never got to hear exactly which of us the man from New Jersey wanted to see dead or by what means, because his voice cut off so abruptly that for a moment I thought Sean had let go of the mic key.

Tom O'Day demanded, "What's happened?"

"They think I killed their man."

"That's ridiculous," Blake Dyer said. "You haven't been out of our sight for a moment."

I raised a tired eyebrow. "Thanks for the vote of confidence, but I don't think—"

Noises came through my earpiece again, faint like scuffling, bootsteps on wooden planking, moving fast. I jerked my head up as if expecting to see men approaching our position but it was all coming down the wire.

"What?" Tom O'Day asked again.

I silenced him with a finger.

At the other end of the open channel, down in the casino, I heard a single set of footsteps, moving slow and precise and arrogant. There was a definite swagger. I recognised them.

Castille.

"Thank you, ladies and gentlemen, for being so ... patient in such difficult circumstances," Castille's voice said, further away

from Sean's hidden mic but still clearly audible. *"As you may have guessed, there has been a change of plan for this evening's entertainment. Another one. I will be your host for what remains of your ... celebration."*

Why did I get the distinct feeling that wasn't either what he meant or had been going to say. *The remains of your what? Lives?*

More footsteps, still slow and deliberate. Still swaggering. He was the star of the show and seemed determined to savour every moment. The footsteps halted.

"So, you are the famous Gabe Baptiste," Castille said. *"I have wanted to meet you for a long time."*

FIFTY-SEVEN

I repeated the gist of the conversation to the two men.

"Gabe Baptiste," Tom O'Day repeated slowly. He shook his head, mystified and more than a little angry. "Why go to all this damn trouble to grab a ball player?"

"A ball player who hasn't been back to New Orleans for years," I reminded him. I caught something through my earpiece, tilted my head as if that would help. "Shush."

"You some kind of deranged fan or something?" Baptiste said now. There was fear in his voice but bravado, too. He was too young or too foolish to realise how serious this man was.

If he'd appreciated that, he would have taken the first flight out after the helicopter crash—OK, maybe the first bus. Either way, he would not have hung around waiting for them to try again. Like I said—too young or too foolish.

Unless he was very lucky, he was going to die before he had a chance to outgrow either.

Castille laughed. It was a soft almost gentle laugh that contained no trace of humour.

"'Deranged?' Who knows," he said. *"But a fan? Of course. I have been following your career very carefully, cher. I know everything about you ... Everything."*

Baptiste said nothing.

"You should have given yourself up," Castille said. *"Instead, you have caused all this"*—I could imagine a negligent wave of a hand—*"unpleasantness."*

"Given myself up for what? What have I done?" Baptiste asked, sticking it out. I couldn't decide if that was purely stubbornness or the fact he had a captive audience, as it were. He sounded nervous, but that was nothing to go by. The guns were there even if I couldn't see them. In that kind of stressed-

228

out situation Mother Teresa would have sounded guilty of something.

"What have you done?" Castille repeated. His voice betrayed a hint of underlying steel, under tension like a suspension bridge wire beginning to vibrate in a high wind. *"Murder, cher. You murdered my little brother, Leon. And I have waited a very long time to make things ... right between us."*

"Wait a minute. 'Make things right'? How?"

Which was the wrong question, I thought. Dead wrong.

Unless he was guilty.

I remembered Parker's brief report on the murder of the dead drug dealer, Leon Castille. The guy everybody assumed Ysabeau van Zant had contracted a hit on. One in the back to put him down, then finished off with a second round to the base of the skull at close range.

It certainly sounded cold, calculating, professional.

It didn't sound like the work of an immature kid, which was all Gabe Baptiste had been at the time. It sounded more like ...

"It wasn't me!" Baptiste's voice was close to a yelp, distorted through guilt or fear or a combination of both. *"I didn't kill him. Shit, you got to believe me. You think I done that? No way—"*

"You were there," Castille said, cutting across his protests, icy. *"You were seen, just before. Your face was known, even then."*

"Yeah, I was there, so what? Doesn't mean I did it. Doesn't mean I killed him."

"So who did?"

"I–I—"

The man's voice grew almost soft, harder to hear. *"I would advise you to think very carefully before you lie to me, cher. After all, what good is a ball player without the use of his legs, hmm?"*

"It was the fucking bodyguard—him!" Baptiste shouted. *"Meyer. Sean Meyer. Your fucking brother tried to roll me—pulled a gun. And that's when my bodyguard arrived, all right? That's when Sean Meyer shot your brother."*

FIFTY-EIGHT

Y**ou** *don't deny it,"* Castille said, his voice louder again. He had closed on Sean, was asking him the question. *"So, is it true, what he says?"*

I held my breath. The O'Days and Blake Dyer were staring at me. I ignored them, willing Sean to give the right answer.

Not necessarily the true answer—just the one that wouldn't get him killed.

Because the truth was that Sean would have been more than capable of pulling the trigger if the circumstances had been as Baptiste had described. I thought back over his words. *"And that's when my bodyguard arrived ..."*

If that part was correct—if any of it was—then Sean had not been there from the outset. It sounded plausible. No way would Sean have gone with a principal to buy drugs. Nor would he have let him out on his own to do so.

But if Baptiste had lied to him about the destination, or the purpose, that would only have kept Sean out of the way for so long. Long enough for him to work it out and go charging in there.

Long enough for him to take down a possible threat.

"It might be," Sean said now. *"Might not be. I don't know."*

Not the answer I'd been hoping for.

"You don't know," Castille repeated flatly. *"Is that your best answer? Because, it is not only your life at stake here,* cher, *but the manner of your death."*

Sean's tone matched him. *"Dead is dead."*

"This is true, but not all roads that lead to death are the same. I could make yours long and ... torturous."

"You just said you didn't want lies," Sean said, brusque with tension. *"Now you're asking me to do just that."*

"How can you not know if you killed a man? Was this so easy for you to forget—shooting him in the back, severing his spine with your bullet, so all he could do was lie there, helpless, and watch you walk towards him with your gun?" I didn't need to see the man's face to feel his fire. *"Did his eyes call you for the coward that you were? Is that why you couldn't meet them when you finished him, hmm?"*

"How do you know that's how it happened?" Sean asked.

I knew he was hedging, but what else could he do?

Then I heard the sound of a blow landing. Not a fist, but something heavier, harder—the butt of a pistol maybe—smacking hard into flesh and muscle and bone. A grunt of pain.

"What do you hope to gain by lies except more pain?" Castille said now, something close to curiosity in his voice. *"Do you still think you have to protect him? Look at him—he is not worthy of your protection."*

I could guess that by *"him"* he meant Baptiste.

"He can't tell you what happened," Baptiste blurted out. *"He was in a coma. He can't remember anything. So, you're just gonna have to take my word on it."* He sounded almost triumphant.

There was a long pause, then Castille said, *"Is this true?"*

"Yes, it's true," Sean said tightly.

He sounded as if he'd rather keep taking hits than admit to such weakness in front of the assembled crowd. More to the point, in front of their close-protection people. There were bodyguards here from major agencies all over the country. And right now they had nothing else on which to focus their attention except the scene being played out in front of them.

Sean added grudgingly, *"I was shot in the head—doing my job."*

That much, at least, was common knowledge.

"Ah, like my brother. But unlike my brother you did not die," the man said. *"And now you are returned to full health, yes?"*

"Yes."

I heard just a touch of defiance.

"And yet you claim you do not know what happened to my brother." It was halfway between a statement and a question. *"Unless you are somehow ... brain damaged, cher, how can it be that you do not remember? Perhaps this is a convenient lapse of memory. A little too convenient, yes?"*

Sean said nothing. There was nothing he could say without damning himself before one audience or another.

If he admitted that his whole memory of guarding Baptiste years ago was missing, he might save his own skin right now, but he'd be hanging himself later. Not only that, but he'd be hanging Parker out to dry, too. The news that one of the partners in the prestigious Armstrong-Meyer had gone back out into the field with such huge gaps in his recall would go round the business like wildfire. It would cause a sensation.

And not in a good way.

But, if he hoped to come out of this alive how could Sean admit to being involved without contradicting Gabe Baptiste's own story?

Baptiste might be a coward—he might even be a murderer—but he had still been a client.

And close-protection operatives do not sacrifice clients—even former clients—to save themselves.

That would cause another sensation.

Again, not in a good way.

I closed my eyes, might even have let out a low groan.

"What the hell is going on down there?" Jimmy O'Day demanded.

I said nothing.

I felt his hand on my arm, a rough little shake.

I said, "Move it or lose it," without opening my eyes.

The hand went.

"Charlie—"

"Shush."

In my ear, Sean had started speaking again. *"You want to know what really happened?"* he asked. *"Then I'll tell you. But you're not going to like it."*

FIFTY-NINE

Y*es, I was with Baptiste that night,"* Sean said calmly. *"I didn't like it much, but it was my job to be there, right?"*

"Sean, what the hell are you doing?" I murmured uselessly. He couldn't hear me any more than he could remember anything about that night—could he?

Or could he?

He paused a moment and I cursed the fact I couldn't see Gabe Baptiste's face.

When Baptiste had first arrived and seen Sean in the lobby of the hotel, the ball player had been shit-scared. Here was someone who knew all his shameful little secrets.

And then he'd discovered that by some remarkable quirk of fate Sean could remember nothing at all about him. I remembered Baptiste's palpable relief, on the roof of the parking garage the morning of the helicopter crash, when the truth of it finally hit home.

Clearly Baptiste hadn't been able to believe his luck. At first he'd treated it as some kind of joke at his expense, and later as one that he could join in with impunity. He'd invited himself onto the same flight as Sean purely, I realised now, to do some private gloating at close range.

After all, here was someone who could probably sink Baptiste's precious career. A man he believed had kept silent only out of some old-fashioned sense of duty and honour that Baptiste could not understand. He must have wondered constantly if he could rely on it.

Was that why his manager had approached Armstrong-Meyer earlier in the year to deal with the stalking fan—just to see if his past crimes were going to be resurrected and held against him?

How heartened he must have been by Parker's polite but noncommittal response.

Now here was Sean about to spill the beans in front of everybody who was anybody in New Orleans. His home town.

And there was nothing he could do about it without making things ten times worse.

"No, I didn't know why Baptiste had gone there—he spun me a line about meeting with someone," Sean said easily. *"Some girl he'd met."*

From the way Baptiste had been all over Autumn Sinclair, that wasn't a stretch of imagination on Sean's part. Or anyone else's.

Baptiste, I noted, did not interrupt him.

"He told me to wait outside, so I stayed with the car. That kind of area, I wanted to make sure it still had all its wheels when he came out."

"You expect me to believe that you, his bodyguard, did not stay close to him?"

Sean gave a half-snort of mirthless laughter. *"Like I said, he told me he was meeting a girl and there are some things I really don't need to watch."*

There was a moment's silence. I held my breath. Jimmy O'Day shuffled from one foot to the other. I glared at him. He stopped shuffling.

"What changed your mind?"

"Now that I don't *know,"* Sean said. *"Instinct? Experience? Mainly, though, I think it was the smell."*

"What smell?"

"Something about the whole set-up stank." I almost heard Sean shrug. *"I decided to go in—quietly. If I was wrong and the kid was just getting his leg over, I'd back out and he'd never know I was there."*

"But he was not 'getting his leg over' as you put it."

"No," Sean agreed. *"He wasn't. Instead I found him facing off with another guy. The other guy had a gun on him. Baptiste was wailing and whining and saying how he was sorry. Whatever had gone on, he was offering the guy money to 'make things right', or something like that."*

I had no idea where this was coming from. I only had the information from Parker's report. In theory, the same information Sean had. So was he genuinely working from memory, or spinning a desperately well-played line?

234

Either way, he had Castille hooked hard enough not to call him a liar outright. Not yet anyway.

Even Baptiste wasn't voicing denials, so either Sean had it nailed or he had pretty good insight into Baptiste's character. Good enough to guess how he might have behaved.

"And how did you react to this ... situation?" Castille asked now, his voice almost a hiss.

"As I'm trained to," Sean said, matter-of-fact. *"I gave him a warning, then took him down."*

There was another pause, longer this time. *"You, cher, are a liar,"* Castille said. *"A good liar—but a liar, nevertheless."*

"That's how it happened," Sean said, and I heard the stubborn tilt of his chin. Now he was playing this hand, he was playing it to the end. What other choice did he have? *"Were you there? No. So how am I lying?"*

"It may have happened mostly as you say. An argument over money. A gun drawn. But there was no warning. You crept in like a coward and you shot my baby brother in the back without giving him a chance to ... consider his options. That *is what happened. Hmm?"*

Sean said nothing for maybe half a minute. An eternity. I could picture him standing there, face cold and blank while his mind whirled. At the other end of an open comms link, my own mind whirled in tandem. How the hell could he get out of that?

More to the point—would he even try?

"Admit it," the man said, closer now, in Sean's face. Close enough that I could hear his breath. *"You were too arrogant to think that anyone would grieve for him. That anyone would wish to avenge him. Too arrogant to care."*

"No," Sean said. *"Your brother was the arrogant one."*

Another stinging blow reverberated through my earpiece, less metallic this time. I imagined a back-handed slap. An insult, as it was intended to be.

"Don't speak of—"

"He was the arrogant one," Sean repeated, slow and precise as if speaking through stiffened lips. *"He saw I had the drop on him and he still thought he could beat me. He tried. He failed. One round centre body mass to put him down, one round to the head to make sure he wasn't getting up again. End of story."*

"And you expect me to believe this?"

"It's the truth. I told you you weren't going to like it."

"Maybe yes," Castille said. *"Maybe no."* His voice turned away from the mic again. *"So, is that how* you *say it happened?"* and I knew the question was directed at Baptiste.

"Pretty much."

But there was something in Gabe Baptiste's voice that hadn't been there before. Something I recognised as just a hint of relief.

Whatever had happened that night, I realised, Sean had come close to the truth without telling the whole story.

So what had he added? And what had he left out?

A sudden sharp sound made me jump. For a second my brain translated it into a gunshot, heart rate leaping into panic mode.

Then the sound came again. And again. I realised someone was clapping, loud and slow and mocking .

"An excellent story, my friend," Castille said, his voice deadly soft now. *"But just that—a story. A fabrication. You see, you are leaving out one small but very important fact in all this."*

"Which is?"

"That after you had shot my little brother in the back as you say, you did not immediately shoot him in the head, as you claim. You waited a few minutes. A few long minutes for him to bleed and to suffer, hmm?" The voice snapped from fake warm to instant freeze. Cold enough to burn. *"And then you picked up his own gun and you executed him. Like a dog in the street."*

Sean said nothing. There was nothing he could say.

Somewhere near him I heard Baptiste give a low moan, an almost unconscious expulsion of breath and hope.

Take them up," Castille said now, louder—an order. *"When they have bled—when they have suffered—then perhaps we will finally hear the truth before they die."*

SIXTY

The sudden silence in my ear was deafening. I took a second to react to it.

A whole wasted second.

Then I was moving towards the stairwell, pushing open the swing door just a fraction, listening.

I heard multiple bootsteps, not fast, not slow, but on the way up. I let go of the door and spun back to meet three pairs of bewildered eyes.

"Blake, Tom—either side of the door," I snapped. "Where are those clubs?

Dyer baulked. "Charlie, I can't—"

"Yes you bloody well can. Move!"

I grabbed Jimmy's arm, shoved him towards the bar. "Grab some of those bottles."

"W-what?"

"You heard." I picked up the nearest of the bottles we'd liberated from the optics behind the bar—a half-empty bourbon—and grasped it by the neck. It had an effective weight to it, just heavy enough to get some speed behind.

I had just a moment to rue abandoning the Maglite over the side. Instead I took out the pen I'd taken from the crewman's cabin, gripped it like a blade.

Not much of a weapon against armed opposition but it would have to do.

Across in the stairwell, the approaching men were nearly up to the level of the bar deck. If they kept going I was screwed—and so was Sean—but they had no reason to. If all they wanted was to be outside this was the quickest route.

I slipped behind the bar with Jimmy. He was half crouched, frozen, with a bottle in either hand like he was making the world's most bizarre cocktail.

The footsteps grew louder in the stairwell. I glanced across to the doorway, where Tom O'Day and Blake Dyer were in position. Both men had golf clubs readied in a classic driving grip. I mouthed, "Get ready," at them.

The only noise was the trembling throb of the *Miss Francis* engines somewhere beneath us.

The door from the stairwell pushed open. Two men came through holding Colt M16 submachine guns with the stocks retracted for close-quarter work.

Then came Gabe Baptiste and Sean.

Behind them were two more men. Prisoner escort. The door started to close behind them.

I shouted, "Now!" and lobbed the bourbon in an over-arm throw, smashing it down at the feet of the front pair. Snatched another off the bar and followed it up with a third as fast as I could throw them.

As the bottles smacked down onto the hard wooden deck the glass shattered into fragments, slopping the raw spirit everywhere.

Momentarily blinded by the spray of stinging alcohol, the foremost man reached automatically for his weapon. Too late. I was out from behind the bar and already on him.

He tried to bring the gun up but I swiped it aside and got in close. The pen was in my fist. I stabbed the tip of it into the side of his throat, ripped it free. He gave a roar but didn't drop. Without switching my grip I adjusted my aim and went for his right eye. He howled, out of the fight. I wrenched the gun from his hands and kicked his legs out from under him.

I targeted his knee with a brutal sideways stamp. Felt the joint let go with a graunching pop of cartilage and muscle under my heel. Knew he wasn't getting up again.

Dyer and O'Day had stepped out behind the rear guards but I saw Dyer hesitate at the last second, as if he couldn't bring himself to strike. Tom O'Day had no such qualms. He attacked like a man in a bad temper in the rough. His club arced through the air with a whistling zizz of sound, impacting knees and shins with devastating effect. Both men went down like they'd been axed. As Dyer stumbled back, O'Day waded in and kept hacking.

I spun for the second front man, but he was already down with Sean standing over his body. The man's M16 was in Sean's hands but there had been no shots fired. Instead, the dead man's neck was twisted at a wholly unnatural angle. I didn't need to ask what happened.

Sean himself was bloodied and torn. From the eavesdropping I'd been privy to, I'd expected that. What I hadn't expected was the wild eyes, the shock, as he surveyed the man he'd just killed. As if he couldn't quite believe what he'd just done.

"Sergeant!" I snapped. "You with me?"

He shook himself, beginning to surface. "Yeah, of course," he said, but his voice was not so sure. He extended the stock and settled the gun into his shoulder.

Tom O'Day stepped back, breathing hard, to reveal the two men who'd been at the back of the group. They lay groaning on the floor of the bar. If they moved at all, it was slowly and painfully. Tom O'Day had nudged their guns out of reach. Now, he laid aside his club and picked up one, handling it like a man putting on a half-forgotten piece of once-favoured clothing.

Blake Dyer stumbled back, his own club slack in his hands. I glanced at him, worried. He was a man teetering at the far reaches of shock.

Gabe Baptiste, meanwhile, had dropped into a defensive crouch the moment we'd launched our attack and was still curled on the floor, hands clamped tightly around the back of his head. When I tapped him on the shoulder he flinched, tried to squeeze his limbs together even more.

"Get a grip, Baptiste," I said roughly. "Come on, up!"

He uncoiled himself, his movements annoyingly sluggish. I saw his eyes were shut. The first thing he saw when he opened them was the man Sean had killed, lying maybe half a metre away and staring sightlessly right at him.

"Jesus Christ!" Baptiste yelped, scuttling backwards. That brought him into contact with another of his erstwhile captors. This one let out a moan at the contact. He was clutching a bloody shin.

I reached over, grabbed a handful of Baptiste's jacket and hauled him out of the way. He made an involuntary noise in his throat, almost a squeak.

I let go in disgust, rounded on Sean. "Where is he?"

"Who?"

"Castille," I said. "The man whose brother *one of you* is supposed to have killed."

Tom O'Day and Blake Dyer gaped at me. I had to remind myself they hadn't heard the rest of the conversation, didn't know what had just taken place down in the casino.

"I don't know," Sean said, shaking his head. "He was just—"

"—behind you," said a new voice.

SIXTY-ONE

The door from the stairwell pushed open wider and Castille revealed himself. He was not obviously armed, but he had the look of a man who did not need to be. The kind of power he wielded was present in his body, his voice, and especially in his eyes. Close to, I felt it even more strongly than out on the deck when I'd watched him kill Ysabeau van Zant with his bare hands.

Sean came together in a split second, crouching and turning all in the same move, bringing the M16 up to fire, sighting by muscle memory and reflex alone.

Castille let the door swing closed behind him and stopped, spreading his hands. He looked around very carefully. At his fallen men, at the blood on my hands, at O'Day and Dyer. At Jimmy O'Day half ducked behind the bar, and Baptiste still cowering. And finally at Sean. He ignored the weapon clasped in Sean's hands, looked at the man behind it instead as if seeing him for the first time.

Then he nodded, as if he'd played his hand and lost and he accepted that was the way the game went.

"So, will you tell me now what happened to my brother?" he asked. His voice was utterly calm. Only the stillness of his body gave away his intensity.

Sean didn't speak, just gave a fractional shake of his head.

"Why?" the man asked. "You have nothing to gain by silence, my friend. You think I will go to the police?"

Baptiste straightened. It finally seemed to dawn on him that the balance had shifted, that his life was no longer about to be snuffed out like a guttering flame. He stabbed a finger, keeping his distance. When he spoke his voice was harsh with tension and bravado. "No, you can go fuck yourself!"

I stepped closer to him. I knew now was not the time to ask questions.

But somehow I recognised there would also never be a better time.

"Tell him," I said.

Baptiste wheeled, disbelief in his face. "What? You gotta be shitting me."

"Tell him," I said again.

"No!" Baptiste said. "You gonna threaten me, too? Yeah, right. Besides, your guy already told him what happened."

I shook my head. "No, he didn't. He told a convincing story that fits the facts as he knows them. But you know as well as I do, Gabe, that Sean has no idea what went on that night." I paused, let it settle on him. "Only you know that. And—one way or another—you're going to tell us."

"Well, lady, that ain't gonna happen, so you can just go fuck yourself as well." He started to turn away, flapping a dismissive hand.

I caught the hand as he moved—his right hand—in a pinch grip, my fingers and thumb spanning the back of his knuckles. The grip was a good one. I squeezed the bones of his hand tight together.

"Hey!" He went rigid, then started to shift his body round as if to take a swing at me with his left. Instead of moving back out of the way I went closer, twisting his hand upwards as I did so. Compressing and rotating his arm as it folded, first at wrist and then at elbow.

By the time he realised the severity of the lock it was too late. I had him immobile, his whole arm under tension to the shoulder.

He froze again, but this time he didn't try another swing. He was a professional athlete, one who trained hard enough to recognise when muscles and sinews strained to danger point. He knew when things were about to get very painful. When recovery would be prolonged, and frustrating, and doubtful.

I waited until I saw the fear in his eyes and knew I had his absolute attention.

"You made the wrong threat before," I said over my shoulder.

For a moment Castille didn't respond. Then: "Please— enlighten me."

"My boss tells me I will never be accepted as a native in this country until I understand the national obsession with baseball, but it seems I understand the men who play it better than you," I said. "You threatened his legs, but Baptiste is a pitcher—with the potential to be one of the greats—isn't that right, Gabe? And great pitchers are not all about the legs."

I reached out with my free hand and pressed down on his levered elbow with one finger.

One finger, I knew, was all it would take to carry the lock to its final, bone-splintering conclusion. The torsional twist would fracture every major bone in Baptiste's right arm and it would take months of surgery and rehab and more surgery before he got the use back. Before he got enough use back to feed himself.

As for ever playing professional baseball again ...

"It's a combination of flex in the hips and stride length and suppleness in the torso. But all that is nothing without the arm. And you've got one of the best arms in the business, haven't you, Gabe? For now." I paused again. His eyes were pleading with me, silently begging. I leaned in closer, said quietly, "Who will they get to take your place on the team next season?"

"All right, all right," he said through lips clamped in pain. "I'll tell you! I'll tell you everything. Just get this crazy bitch off of me!"

I slackened my grip slightly but I didn't let go.

Baptiste made to snatch his arm away. I locked his joints up again. "Hey—"

"*When* you've told us the truth," I told him. "Until then ..."

He threw me a last frustrated glance and after that wouldn't meet my eyes. He stared at Sean instead, as if looking for signs of recognition for his story.

"He never went with me that night," Baptiste said, his voice low and sullen. "Wouldn't even consider it, but I *needed* to go, you know?"

Tom O'Day said, "You were a junkie," with austere disgust in his tone.

"No! I just needed a little something," Baptiste muttered. "To keep me sharp. To keep me calm. You don't know what it's like, old man, having that kind of pressure on you. Big decisions, big games. I was just a kid back then."

Tom O'Day said nothing. I wondered how old he'd been back when he'd served in Korea. Back when there was more than the outcome of a big game at stake.

"Meyer wouldn't take me where I needed to go, and he wouldn't go for me," Baptiste said. "So I told him I was turning in for the night, and went out the back way. I never thought he'd catch on so fast—never thought he'd follow me."

"Addicts are rarely as subtle as they think," Castille said dryly.

Baptiste flushed. "The dealer— um, your brother," he said, stumbling over the distinction. "He musta recognised me. He threatened to go to the press, the National League, unless I paid him. He was talking big bucks. I didn't have that kind of money."

Castille's face tightened more in sadness than in anger, as if he could entirely believe that his little brother's greed had got the better of him that one last time. "So that is when your bodyguard stepped in, hmm?"

Baptiste threw me a look that was half fear, half loathing, for dragging this out of him. "No," he said, and the bravado was back again. "I didn't need him to."

SIXTY-TWO

I had a gun," Baptiste said. "I saw my chance and I used it."

"You shot my brother in the back," Castille said. It was not a question. It was a judgement.

"It was him or me," Baptiste mumbled. "He had a gun, too. He'd been threatening me. I promised to pay him. Told him I still needed the stuff. He thought he had me beaten. He thought—"

Castille cut him off. "He thought your word was good—that he could trust you."

Baptiste said nothing.

Castille turned to Sean. "Is *that* how it happened, *cher?*"

Sean gave a slight "don't know" twitch of his shoulder. The man stared at him for a moment longer.

I tightened my grip on Baptiste's arm. He flinched, rose on his toes as if that might lessen the way his bones and tendons were being prised apart.

I said, "What then?"

"He was down but he wasn't dead. I thought he'd die, but he didn't—just lay there, looking at me. I ran. What else could I do? And then Meyer came in with his gun out. He'd heard the shot. He was gonna call the cops. I mean, Jesus! I shouted at him to kill the son of a— to kill the guy," Baptiste amended. "To put him out of his fucking misery. But he wouldn't do it." His voice turned plaintive. "He was supposed to protect me."

"He wasn't supposed to cover up your foul-ups," I said. "That's not part of the job description."

"Then he should have stopped me before I ever got there," Baptiste complained.

How could you let me make this mistake? I shook my head. We were guardians of their physical well-being but half the time a principal also expected us to be the keeper of their soul.

245

"So your bodyguard finished him off, is that what you are saying?" Castille demanded.

"He wanted it!" Baptiste said, almost a shout. It took me a moment to realise he was talking about the man's brother, not Sean. "He was crying and shit, begging for it."

"Wait a minute," I said, incredulous. "The guy you shot *asked* to die?"

Baptiste nodded, his own throat filled with tears—for his own loss, I suspected, not anyone else's. "He … he knew he was paralysed, couldn't move his arms and legs, could barely breathe. He said he couldn't live as a cripple. Said if I was a man I'd finish what I'd started. I–I couldn't do it."

"So your bodyguard did it for you," Castille said, and his tone was quieter now, subdued. "In the back of the head?"

"He didn't want to, but he did it. So's your brother could have an open casket," Baptiste muttered, shame flooding his face. "For his mother—"

Castille lifted an abrupt hand, silenced him. For a moment he said nothing, fighting for control. When he met Sean's eyes his voice was calm again, almost light. "Will you accord me the same honour?"

Sean rolled his shoulder a little into the stock of the gun, looked for all the world as if he was going to comply. Then he straightened slowly, let the muzzle drop.

"No," he said roughly. "I won't be your bloody executioner."

Castille looked downwards, pointedly, towards the man with the broken neck lying at Sean's feet. He raised an eyebrow. "You have grown soft, *cher.*"

I let go of Baptiste, gave him a shove. He staggered away clutching his wounded arm to his chest. I stepped forwards alongside Sean, a united front.

"If you don't get your thugs off this damn boat you'll find out just how soft we are."

The man's gaze lingered for a while on Sean, then switched to me. "You—you I think would kill me if you could," he said at last. "You have the eyes for it, *chérie.*"

"Try me."

The man glanced at Tom O'Day, still standing with another of the M16s in his hands. "What about you, old man?" he asked. "If I try to leave are you going to shoot me in the back, also, like my brother?"

O'Day shook his head. "Like Charlie said, all we want is for these people to be safe and you to be off this damn boat."

Castille inclined his head, gave a smile that I did not entirely trust. "Do not worry," he said, "as soon as—"

Gunfire cut his words short. A short staccato burst from somewhere below and aft of us. We all reacted instinctively, according to temperament and training.

Baptiste dived under a table, his arm miraculously forgotten. Jimmy disappeared back behind the bar. Sean and I both moved for the nearest main bulkhead, knowing it was made from steel plate.

Even as we did so I saw Castille twist lightly on the balls of his feet, heading back for the stairwell. Saw the way his hand slid under his jacket.

I shouted, "Gun!" even before he'd cleared the weapon. Before I saw that I was wrong.

In his hand was not the gun I'd been expecting. Instead he gripped a short narrow-bladed knife.

My warning should have made Tom O'Day and Blake Dyer head for cover. It should have made them leave him alone, think of their own safety and let him go.

It didn't.

Instead, buoyed by his earlier success, Tom O'Day moved to block the other man's escape. He started to bring the M16 up. I could tell he was tracking too slow to fire and stand a chance of hitting his target.

But Blake Dyer suddenly seemed to come out of stasis. He stepped in close to Castille, the golf club unwinding into a low blow aimed straight for the man's shins. Hard enough to put him on the ground and make sure the only way he was getting up again was to be lifted onto a stretcher.

It never landed.

Castille leapt to the side, lithe as a dancer. He elbowed Dyer aside with contemptuous ease and was through the doors and away before you could blink.

I glared at Sean. "What the hell—?"

"Charlie," he said, already letting the muzzle of the weapon drop and moving forwards fast.

I turned, just in time to see Blake Dyer let go of the golf club. It rolled out of his open fingers and dropped to the deck. He folded both hands very slowly and carefully against his abdomen.

Through his fingers, the blood welled out in a vivid, violent rush.

SIXTY-THREE

This is going to hurt."

Blake Dyer gave a breathless little laugh. "What do you mean, 'going to'?"

I'd eased the tails of his dress shirt out of his trousers. Underneath, just below the level of his belt, was a small slit in the wall of his abdomen. It was maybe two or three centimetres long, but the blood oozed from it as fast as I could wipe it away.

Not a good sign.

Neither was the colour of the blood—very dark, almost black. Nor the way his stomach had already begun to swell.

The blade of the knife had been long enough to reach deep into Dyer's body. From those two indicators it was almost a certainty that he had internal bleeding.

He needed a paramedic and a hospital—fast.

I doubted we could provide him with either in time.

So I improvised as best I could with what remained of the duct tape we'd used to bind Sullivan and serviettes from the dispensers on the tables. I wished I still had my evening bag, long since jettisoned in the casino. The tampons I'd put in it would have made ideal dressings shoved into the wound to stop the external bleeding at least.

Not much I could do about the rest of it.

I remembered a time when I'd watched my father, a surgeon of considerable skill, save a man's life by the side of the road using a pair of pliers from a vehicle tool kit to clamp off a severed artery.

What I wouldn't have given to have him here now.

We'd dealt with the fallen men—the survivors, anyway. They were all going to need their legs splinting before they could move, so the threat they presented was static at best. We still searched them, and roughly taped their hands. I made the guy

249

I'd dealt with improvised dressings for the wounds to his eye and throat. He didn't thank me for it.

Dyer shivered as the shock set in. Jimmy found some spare tablecloths folded behind the bar, brought a couple over and draped them around his godfather's shoulders. I gave him a brief nod. He looked as if he might speak but eventually just shook his head mutely and turned away.

He'd been about to ask a question he already knew the answer to.

"Bet you're glad you ... got that dismissal ... in writing, huh?" Dyer said now, struggling for breath. His abdominal cavity was slowly but steadily filling with blood from some punctured organ. It was compressing his lungs, suffocating him.

"I'm counting on you to rescind that," I said, trying to keep my voice neutral. "It will look bad on my record."

He gripped my sleeve, fingers suddenly strong, leaving greasy stains on the material.

"Tell my wife ... I love her. Tell her ... I'm sorry ... for being such a damn fool."

I should have said, "You can tell her yourself," but we both knew that wasn't going to happen. I said nothing. After a moment Dyer nodded as if thanking me for not continuing the lie.

"Tom ..." Dyer said. "My grandkid ... was going to ask you ... to be godfather."

"Of course—if you stop talking like a damn fool," O'Day said briskly, but his voice was filled with sorrow. He'd seen enough wounded to make his own judgement.

"Uncle Blake," Jimmy said. "I—"

It was as far as he got before his voice gave out.

Dyer gave him a lopsided smile. "Walk tall, Jimmy," he said. "Gotta come ... out of the shadows." He coughed, every breath a violent drag of air now. "Always thought I'd have ... more time with you."

Jimmy turned away, hands to his mouth as if to hold back the sobs.

I glanced at Sean still braced behind the M16. There was nothing in his face. Was that good or bad?

"Hey, people! We need to get off of this goddamn boat!" The words burst from Baptiste. I shot him a vicious glare. Baptiste swallowed but hardly missed a beat. "Um, 'cause we need to get Mr Dyer some help, yeah?"

Dyer gave a single shake of his head. "Go," he said. "Save the others."

I put a hand on his shoulder, squeezed. He gave a faint smile. I turned away from him, asked Sean, "How many left guarding the casino?"

"Two," he said. "We should clear the hostages before we take the bridge."

"Was anyone else separated out?"

"Apart from Mrs van Zant, just Miss Sinclair and Vic Morton—I don't know where they were taken." He glanced at Jimmy as if seeing him for the first time. "He should know."

I indicated Tom O'Day. "Tom suggested we try the meat locker in the galley."

Sean nodded. "Good idea," he said. His eyes shifted across Blake Dyer's figure. There was a hollow note to his voice I recognised as guilt—guilt that he hadn't killed Castille while he had the chance. "Someone should stay here."

Baptiste said quickly, "I'll stay."

"Someone Blake knows," I said, ignoring him.

Someone he loves—someone who loves him.

"I guess that would be either me or Jimmy," Tom O'Day said. He glanced at his son. "Jimmy, I think—"

Jimmy must have known what was coming. "*You* should stay with Uncle Blake," he interrupted, voice firm and calm. "I–I need to find Autumn—see that she's safe."

Tom O'Day rocked back a little. He nodded, swallowed as if unable to speak.

"OK, son," he said quietly. "If that's what you want."

He flicked the safety onto the M16 and handed it across. Jimmy took it gingerly. He rolled his shoulders and covertly copied Sean's stance.

I sighed, picked the gun out of his hands and held it so he could clearly see the fire selector. "Safe. Single shot. Full auto," I said. "Stick to single shot—one round at a time. Keep your finger off the trigger until you're ready to fire, and don't point it at anything you're not prepared to kill. OK?"

Jimmy glanced at Sean again, as if hoping for more advice.

Sean shook his head. "That about covers it," he said.

Most beginners, I remembered, fared better with a long gun than a pistol. I could only hope Jimmy fell into the majority. Probably best not to have him behind us, though. Just in case.

"What about me?" Baptiste demanded.

Sean checked over our captured weapons supply, gave one to me and left one on the deck next to Tom O'Day where he sat with his dying friend. He turned back to Baptiste and shook his head.

"No way," he said coldly. "The last time you had a gun in your hands, you shot a man in the back."

SIXTY-FOUR

In the end we gave Baptiste a couple of the unbroken bottles from the bar. After all, he'd proved numerous times on the baseball field that he could pitch a fast ball at close to a hundred miles an hour, and hit a target as small as a catcher's mitt more than sixty feet away. What better weapon to give him than something he could throw?

Sean led us down the service staircase towards the casino deck. Baptiste followed, then Jimmy, still nervously clutching the unfamiliar M16. I brought up the rear, checking up and back to make sure nobody came down on top of us.

The casino was on the lowest deck. We reached the bottom of the staircase unmolested. Sean made a closed-fist "hold" gesture as we gathered outside the double doors leading through into the bar area at the back of the casino floor. We waited, straining to hear what was going on inside. Noises, voices, confusion.

Sean indicated that Jimmy and Baptiste should wait. He signalled me low right while he would go high left. I swallowed, just once, then nodded.

I'd been through doors before with Sean but this time was different.

This time *he* was different.

I tried not to let that matter, moving at the same instant he did, diving through the door the second he pushed it aside. I hit the deck, rolled, landing on my belly with my elbows spread into a firing stance, anchored, tight.

Even as I went in, as fast and aggressive as Sean himself, my eyes were searching for the first target. The first man with a weapon in a room full of non-combatants. In a fraction of a second my eyes fed information and my brain processed it.

Two armed assailants, in two locations with hostages behind them.

253

I tracked the one on the right, knowing Sean would automatically target the other. The man half-turned and froze at our explosive entry, presenting me with a near perfect sight-picture. I would have normally aimed for low centre body mass, but I had a solid opportunity for a head shot with no clutter behind him. I let my body drop to raise my aim a fraction, took up pressure on the trigger.

The butt of the M16 kicked into my shoulder. I had time to see the hijacker jerk from the impact and start to fall. There was no need for a second round.

In my peripheral vision I saw the second gunman take a couple of solid hits to the body but he didn't go down. Some of the security guys had elected for body armour, I recalled. It was clear our assailants had done so as well.

I twisted onto my side, sweeping the gun round fast. The hijacker was already lining up on Sean, a snarl of pain and fury on his face. I knew there was no way Sean should have let him get that far.

Come on, for God's sake, take him!

Still he hesitated that vital split-second.

I couldn't afford to wait. I squeezed the trigger for another head shot, feeling nothing but frustration. The shot was clean, and all animation abruptly left him. Part of me knew I should have let Sean counter his own demons.

And part of me was afraid he wasn't going to.

The sound of gunfire inside the casino was raucous. Into the artificial silence that followed the sounds of the room returned slowly to my bruised ears. Muffled sobs and sounds of fright. As it equalised I saw one of the bodyguards rise. He'd thrown himself over an elderly man in a tuxedo as soon as the shooting started.

"Meyer?" he said in disbelief, coming up out of a crouch. "Hey, man, we thought you were fish food. How d'you pull that one off?"

Sean didn't say anything, just jerked his head sideways. The man followed his gaze across to me, lying behind the gun. After a moment, he nodded.

"Ah ... good work," he said, and if the praise was cool the fact it was offered at all meant more.

Then, with sudden force, the doors to the casino were shoved open. I rolled over onto my back, lifting the M16 up and ready.

Baptiste and Jimmy came in, hurrying. Behind them, as if using them as a shield, came another man with a gun.

I lined up on him instinctively, sights on his mouth where he would drop fast and clean. It was all smooth and automatic now, drilled in. I started to take up the trigger.

And realised the man behind the gun was Vic Morton.

I almost took the shot anyway.

Almost.

Then he swung the muzzle of the gun up and to the side, spread his arms in the universal gesture of, if not surrender then too much of a non-threat for me ever to justify.

Shit—too slow.

I let the muzzle of the gun drift down slowly.

Shaky from the adrenaline flooding my system, I got to my feet. "I thought they took you away," I said, aware of a slight note of disappointment in my voice. "How did you get loose?"

Morton held up his right arm. One bracelet of a set of handcuffs was still fastened around his wrist. The other was locked but hanging free. Now I checked him out, Morton had a narrow sliced cut through his eyebrow, the blood congealed around his eye. There was also a darkening bruise on his jaw.

"Guess the bit of this old tub they attached me to wasn't quite as structurally sound as they hoped," he said.

The realisation that they'd been rescued was gradually dawning on people. Their faces were shocked and greyed, but relief started to show through. Some had recovered enough to eye Baptiste with contempt. Whatever else they tried to forget about this night, they would not forget his confession—however it had been extracted. Watching Baptiste's face, I saw the moment that fact settled on him.

"If these people are safe, we need to secure the rest of the ship," I said. "Do we have any other casualties down here?"

The other bodyguard shook his head. "Just these two bad guys," he said.

"And another further aft," Morton said casually. When Sean glanced at him he shrugged. "I had to get a gun from somewhere, didn't I?"

The bodyguard raised his eyebrows, cracked a smile. "You Brits really don't mess around, huh?"

Morton grinned at Sean. "That's how I was trained," he said. He switched his gaze to me. "Eh, Fox?" And I realised he knew

255

without a doubt how close I'd been to killing him. The satisfaction at my own self-restraint was blunted only by his smug expression.

"Did you find Autumn?" Jimmy blurted.

"No," Morton said. "I thought they took the two of you off together."

"They kept us apart," Jimmy said, sounding desperate. "We *have* to find her."

He started for the door, still clutching his M16. I put my arm out to stop him.

"Nobody goes off anywhere until we have retaken control of this ship." And when he would have struggled to pull free I added, "You saw what happened up in the bar, Jimmy. Want that to be you?"

He stopped struggling.

"What happened?" Morton asked. "Mr O'Day—is he all right?"

I should have known he'd be worried about the guy who signed the cheques.

"He's fine," Sean said. "But Blake Dyer took a knife in the belly. If we don't get him some help soon ..." He didn't need to finish that sentence.

Morton let out a low whistle and fixed me with a crafty eye. "Bummer of a thing to have happen on your watch, Fox."

Bastard.

I had neither the time nor the inclination to start offering feeble excuses, knowing that's exactly how they would have come across.

"We need to move," Sean said shortly. "These guys obviously had an exit strategy. If we're going to stop them using it we need to act now."

"We should split up—cover more ground that way," Morton said. "I'll head for the bridge. See how fast the skipper can get this old crate dockside."

"See if he's got any kind of radio gear that isn't being jammed," Sean said. "We need some reinforcements—and a medevac."

Morton nodded, pulled the M16 up into his shoulder and went out.

"What about Autumn?" Jimmy demanded, his face flushed. "We can't just forget about her. Dad said we should try the meat locker—"

"We haven't forgotten," I said, although I got the feeling Sean did not have finding the missing woman high on the priority list. "I'll check out the galley."

I turned, would have followed Morton out through the doors to the service stairwell when Sean called me back.

"No, I want you with me, Charlie," he said. I would have argued, but something in his voice warned me it would not be a good idea. "Jimmy, stay here and help look after these people." He jerked his head to me and headed for the outer deck instead, without waiting to see if I was right behind him.

As soon as we were outside he paused.

I took a breath. "Sean—"

He whirled to face me. "No," he said again, more sharply this time. "You think I didn't see what happened back there? You think I don't know how close you were to slotting him?" He let his own breath out, fast and hard. "No, Charlie, I want you right where I can see you."

SIXTY-FIVE

Yes. He dropped into my sights and just for a second I was tempted," I said. "But do you honestly think I'd go after him in cold blood?"

Be very careful how you answer.

"I don't know." Sean made an impatient gesture, ended up rubbing his scar as if it itched in some kind of warning. He let out his breath. "OK, no. I just don't want to give you the opportunity—to let temptation get in the way. We've got enough on our plates."

"If I was planning to follow through on a vendetta," I said tightly, "I would have gone after Morton and his pals years ago."

He looked at me for a moment, then murmured, "Yeah, you would as well, wouldn't you?"

But as he turned away and we hurried along the side deck heading aft, I saw the doubt in his face.

Good thing he moved ahead and couldn't see the doubt in mine.

Sean feared I might shoot too easily. I remembered his hesitation and feared he might not shoot easily enough.

We progressed as fast as we dared while still remaining quiet, keeping as far apart as the side deck allowed to present a wider target spread. Sean stayed a little in front. I hung back, covering his rear and my own.

It was Sean, therefore, who caught first sight of the man's body.

He brought a hand up abruptly. I stilled, kept my eyes moving just in case this was a blind. Nothing popped.

I edged forwards. Just around the next corner a pair of legs had come into view. They were stretched out, one foot twitching slightly, almost a quiver. Sean nodded to me. I stepped out and went wide of the guy on the floor, circling fast so it must have seemed that we suddenly appeared on both sides of him. I kept the M16 up into my shoulder and ready all the way, slipping my trigger finger inside the guard. He didn't react.

The man was slumped against the side of the superstructure, hands clasped loosely to a wound in the side of his chest. He was wearing body armour but the wound was high, close to his armpit, circumventing the vest. Either an accurate strike or a lucky one. He'd pulled off his balaclava and was using it to staunch the blood. It was not proving effective.

I nudged his discarded MP5K further out of reach with my foot. The man's eyes flicked to the weapon as I did so, but he made no moves to reach for it. I guessed he didn't have the energy or knew he'd be wasting what little time he had left. Blood had seeped out onto the deck alongside him. It surrounded his mouth and nose as if he'd been eating raw flesh.

Sean went down on one knee alongside him, looked dispassionately at the wound.

"Knife," he said to me. "Must have nicked his lung, I think."

I remembered the deft way Castille had handled a blade, the speed with which he'd plunged it into Blake Dyer as he'd made his escape. At least he was leaving us a trail of bodies to follow, even if it did seem a brutal way to tidy away the possible loose ends.

The wounded man's eyes were on me, resigned and almost incurious.

"Well, Castille did say he had a plan of his own," I told him.

"You recognise him?" Sean asked.

I nodded. It was the fair-haired man with the New Jersey accent. The one who'd delivered Ysabeau van Zant to her execution. I watched his chest flutter with each flooded breath as the blood flowed into his damaged lung, constricting his chest and slowly suffocating him from the inside out. I thought of Blake Dyer and couldn't find much sympathy.

New Jersey's lips began to move, blood frothing into his mouth as he tried to speak. "Weren't expecting ... him to double-cross us," he said at last, little more than a whisper.

"His type always do," Sean said bluntly. "How does Castille plan to get away?"

New Jersey half shook his head, though I wasn't sure what he was trying to deny. Then his eyes flicked to the side, out towards the darkened waters of the Mississippi. I followed his gaze.

"By boat? What boat? How will he call it in?"

New Jersey was gasping now, his voice drowned by the river and the blood. "Signal."

"Signal?" I repeated, frustration leaching through. "What signal?"

"You'll know," New Jersey whispered. His eyelids had begun to droop, one slow blink after another, the gaps narrowing until his eyes were more shut than open.

"We're losing him," Sean muttered.

I thought of Blake Dyer again, my erstwhile principal, dying in the arms of his friend on the deck above. I thought, too, of the unlucky Sullivan, whose neck had been slashed wide open while he'd been tied to a chair in that tiny cabin.

I leaned in closer. "It wasn't me who cut Sullivan's throat," I said. "Are you going to let Castille get away with killing your own crew?"

New Jersey's eyes opened again, a monumental effort that clearly cost him to maintain. He gave another half shake of his head and just for a moment he looked as if he was about to say something important. Then he sighed, closed his eyes again, and died.

"So much for a bloody deathbed confession," I said, rising.

Sean shot me an almost reproachful glance as he got to his feet.

We were more or less at the centre section of the boat, where stairs led to the upper deck. Lots of possible escape routes.

Sean jerked his head, indicating I should take the starboard side while he went to port. Then he turned away without a word. I shrugged and followed his order. My eyes were not only on the deck now, but also ranging out across the dark, misty water.

I moved further aft, careful after the discovery of the man from New Jersey. The fact it was a knife wound disturbed me. I'd been cut before, still had the scars to prove it—it was not an experience I wanted to repeat. The noise level increased as I neared the huge wooden paddlewheel which threshed at the water behind us to propel the *Miss Francis* forwards into the night. The deck came to a dead-end.

I found nothing, retracing my steps. As I cleared the superstructure I saw a figure move into view from the direction Sean had taken. I brought the M16 up out of habit, relaxed a fraction when I recognised his familiar figure.

260

I opened my mouth to ask if he had found anything, then shut it again as I realised something was very wrong. Sean was moving too stiff, too upright. And he was no longer armed.

I tightened the gun into my shoulder, but knew I was too late. Another figure, a man, side-stepped quickly out from behind the superstructure and into line directly behind Sean, using him for cover.

I didn't need to see the gun to know he had one at Sean's back. Or a knife. No other way to keep him still. I kept the M16 up but had no clear shot.

Sean stared straight at me. I could read nothing in his eyes, nothing in his face. No hint of how he wanted me to react.

"Put down your weapon, *chérie*," Castille said. "If you want your friend to live."

SIXTY-SIX

That's not how it works," I said. "I put down my weapon and you'll kill the pair of us."

"Perhaps," he agreed. "But if you do not then he will die for sure. Are you willing to take that risk?"

I kept my eyes on Sean's. He stared back blankly. I tried to put all my emotion—everything I felt for him—into my face, knowing Castille could not see it, trying to keep it all away from my voice.

But I remembered Sean's doubt and prayed he'd realise I was bluffing. He must know I couldn't back down—for both our sakes.

But when I looked for trust I didn't find it. Only a coldness that reached right inside my chest and froze my heart.

I almost faltered, almost followed Castille's order just to take away the sudden shaft of pain.

Almost.

I tightened my grip on the M16, rolled my shoulders a little to try and take the tension out of my arms.

"Why should I trust someone who murders his allies as easily as his enemies?" I asked. I was aware I was playing for time in the hope Sean would make a move of his own. He did not.

"Those who are loyal to me have nothing to fear," Castille said.

"Ah, so what did the guy from New Jersey do to incur your wrath?" I demanded. "As far as I could tell he played his part. He delivered Ysabeau van Zant to you like a sacrificial lamb."

There was a pause. I knew Castille had heard the acid note in my voice, the bitterness, and I felt rather than saw him smile.

"Ah … you saw me deal with that woman and now you think I am a monster who kills for pleasure, with no reason?"

"There's no 'think' about it."

"*She* was the monster," he said. "She sold her soul and did not like it when the devil came to collect."

"You still murdered the pair of them."

Castille was stubborn, if nothing else. "If that is what you believe, so be it. But standing here arguing about what I did or did not do is not going to get us anywhere, *chérie*." His voice hardened. "Last chance. Put down the gun."

My eyes flicked to Sean's again, willing him to understand, to pick up a message that once he would have done without a flicker.

"I'm sorry," I said. "I—"

The burst of gunfire came suddenly enough to make me flinch. I leapt forwards, focus narrowing onto my target, aware of Sean falling away. And inside my head began a terrible screaming that went on and on until it became an all-encompassing howl of rage and despair.

My own finger tightened around the trigger, came within a fraction of firing.

Then I realised Sean had bucked out from Castille's grasp, not dropped lifelessly away. That even now he was rolling back to his feet, crouched and tense.

That it was Castille himself who had fallen back against the superstructure. As he slid slowly sideways and down he left a dirty red smear across the glossy paintwork.

I heard footsteps and spun, keeping the gun up. There was another man approaching cautiously along the far side of the deck. This time I had no problem recognising him.

Vic Morton. He held the M16 still at firing position as he came on. His eyes flicked from Castille's body across the pair of us. He stopped a couple of metres away and relaxed.

"Lucky I stopped by, eh?" he said cheerfully.

"Yeah," Sean said slowly, straightening. He barely glanced in my direction. "Thanks, Vic."

I leaned over Castille. Morton's burst had caught him in the side, spun him around and stitched across his chest, tearing up his heart and lungs. His eyes were already sightless and the blood flow had begun to dwindle. I'd been expecting to find him with a knife but saw instead a compact MP5K resting slackly in the man's hands. I picked it out and slung the strap over my shoulder.

"No sweat," Morton said. He grinned, buzzing—on a combat high. I'd seen it before and never liked it much. I trusted it even less.

"What are you doing here?" I asked, aware of a roughness in my voice.

"Saving your arse, Fox," he shot back. "Can't afford to hesitate in the field."

I clenched my teeth until the enamel crunched. "I didn't," I said. "I had no clear shot."

Morton didn't immediately reply to that one. The upward flicker of his eyebrow spoke volumes, though. His eyes went to Sean again, then he shrugged. "Well ... good job one of us had, eh?"

There was too much I wanted to say to that. Back when we'd been training together Morton's weapons skill had always been middle-ground—a solid performance rather than sparkling. I knew that was why he'd aimed for centre mass when only a head-shot would have guaranteed a clean kill. Besides anything else, if Castille had been wearing body armour all Morton would have done would be to piss him off.

And Sean would be the one lying there dead.

There was no point in arguing. Not now—probably not ever. I knew if I said anything Morton would point to the dead man's body as proof of an effective strategy. If Sean couldn't work it out for himself how close it had been, there was no point in me doing it for him.

"The skipper's OK—back in charge," Morton said. "He's heading back for the dock as fast as this old tub will motor."

Sean peered out into the darkness that surrounded us. The fog showed no signs of thinning but occasionally the glow of New Orleans lights gleamed through in patches, creating a spooky haze like distant fires. "Does he know where the hell we are?"

Morton shrugged again. "Probably," he said. "He just yelled at me to get off his bridge and let him navigate his own bloody ship—or words to that effect." This last was directed at me with a sly glance, as if my delicate female constitution wouldn't take the weight of heavier expletives.

"Did he at least give you an ETA?" I asked.

Morton shook his head. "And if you're prepared to go back up there and ask him yourself, you're a braver man than I am, Gunga Din."

264

Kipling actually wrote that it was "a *better* man" but I didn't bother to correct Morton's misquote. I turned away. "We need to keep moving," I said to Sean. "We don't know how many of these guys are left, or—"

I was about to mention that we also still didn't know how Castille had been intending to call in his extraction team. But at that moment there was a huge dull crack of sound from somewhere deep beneath us, following by a rumbling boom that echoed out across the water.

The *Miss Francis* gave a lurch as if she'd struck an underwater obstruction. We staggered to keep our footing, had to grab for the nearest fixed object. A giant shiver passed through the entire ship. She began to lean to starboard, slowly veering over to that side.

"Shit," I muttered. "The bastard blew the bottom out of her."

"Stay sharp," Sean said. "We may have company. Because if that wasn't a bloody big signal, I don't know what is."

SIXTY-SEVEN

The skipper abandoned all ideas of getting the *Miss Francis* back to her berth and drove her straight for the nearest piece of shoreline as fast as he could push the wounded hull. It seemed to be a hell of a long way in the dark and murky distance.

Castille's charges had been placed aft somewhere back near the engine room on the starboard side. The only good thing was that losing half his C-4 mean he hadn't been able to instantly sink her. So, although the *Miss Francis* was listing heavily and dragging her arse in the water like a giant drogue 'chute, the paddle steamer struggled on. The giant paddlewheel itself threshed the river behind us into froth with an out-of-balance, edgy vibration. I knew it was stupid to assign emotions to an object, but it almost felt like fury.

Maybe I was just projecting.

"We got company," Morton said.

Even as he spoke, I heard the rising buzz of an outboard motor. A Zodiac appeared, skimming fast over the slight chop with the vee of the rigid lower hull visible below the inflatable surround. There were three or four figures clinging on as they hammered towards us.

We dropped flat to the deck, suddenly aware of being on a brightly lit target, aiming out into the cover of semi-darkness. Another Z-boat came into view, heading wide. It held another three men.

Castille's extraction team.

We could not keep them off the ship indefinitely, I realised with a hollow feeling up under my ribcage. They would be heavily armed—maybe even with another of the RPGs that they'd used to such devastating effect on the Bell. We had too many civilians on board and no time to prepare a plan. We would just have to hope that these men were not prepared to fight to the death for a man already dead.

Already dead ...

"Let them close in," I said.

It was Sean who objected. "We should take them out now."

"For once, I agree with Fox," Morton said, then added, "Better to pick 'em off at closer range."

I bit back a comment about him knowing his own shooting abilities. "Who said anything about picking them off?" I asked. "It might not come to that."

"What?"

I scrambled to my feet, leaving the M16 lying on the deck and ran back to where Castille had fallen.

The Z-boat jinked almost immediately, carved a swathing turn that allowed the occupants all to bring weapons to bear. I could feel them tracking me as I moved, but for the moment they held their fire.

I could only hope Sean—and Morton—would do the same.

I reached Castille, grabbed the shoulders of his suit and dragged him away from the superstructure, turning him so he was facing the incoming Z-boats. The body was still loose, slightly warm to the touch, but awkward and heavy to manipulate. His torso was slick and sticky. I managed to heave him into a sitting position with my knee jammed into his back to stop his corpse flopping down again.

I heard the outboard of the nearest Z-boat die back as the helmsman rolled off the throttle. They were staring right at me, and the man slumped in my arms. I pulled Castille's head back by the hair, letting them get a good look at his features.

The second boat swung in just beyond the first. The men on board also stared. I read nothing in their faces. I raised one hand—the hand that had been clasped around Castille's chest— so that they saw the blood.

Shit. This isn't going to work.

Then the man furthest forward in the lead boat jerked his head to the helmsman. The outboard screamed as the throttle was jammed wide open again. Both Z-boats surged away and disappeared into the night.

I shifted out from behind Castille's body and let him thump back down onto the deck. When I rose I found my legs would hardly support me.

"Jee-*sus!*" Morton said, getting slowly to his feet. He looked at me, at Castille's body, and shook his head. "I take it back, Fox. You have got some serious balls."

Sean stood motionless, still watching the gloom that had enveloped the two Z-boats. Then his eyes flicked back to me. "How did you know they'd go for it?" he demanded quietly. "How did you know they'd back off rather than try to avenge him?"

I remembered the way Castille's men had avoided meeting each other's eyes when he had strangled Ysabeau van Zant. "Just because they obeyed his orders doesn't mean they liked the bastard," I said. "Not enough to risk their lives for him when he was already dead."

Sean looked about to say more, but the clatter of feet on the deck had us all turning.

Jimmy O'Day appeared at a run, cautious on the slanting surface. When he saw Castille lying dead at my feet, the blood on my hands, he faltered.

"What do you want, Jimmy?" Morton asked, snapping his attention back.

"We're, um, taking on water pretty fast down there," Jimmy said. "People are starting to panic. And Autumn's still missing ..." His voice trailed off.

"We'll find her," Sean told him. He turned to me. "Charlie—"

"No," Morton said. The abrupt note in his voice stilled all of us. Morton acknowledged this with a wry smile, touched a finger to his bruised face. "I feel guilty I let them take her away," he said. "I'd kind of like to be the one who gets her back."

Sean paused a moment, then nodded. "Good luck," he said. "Oh, and Vic—thanks again."

Morton grinned at him. "No sweat, mate. Old comrades have to stick together, eh?"

The flash of rage, a swift railing at ingratitude and circumstance, roared over me hot, fierce and deadly, like opening the door to a blast furnace. I'd been a comrade, too, and look where it had got me. Beating back that fire took a moment of inner struggle I hoped neither man could see.

"I'll help," Jimmy said immediately.

Morton's face twitched. "No offence, kid, but you'll just slow me down," he said, although not unkindly. "You need to help get everyone topside." He jerked his head upwards, indicating the wheelhouse. "Looks like the skipper's planning to hit the dock at ramming speed."

"You don't understand," Jimmy protested, sweat and desperation in his voice. "You've *got* to find her. She's pregnant."

SIXTY-EIGHT

We helped the shaken guests up from the casino to the forward deck and handed out life jackets. There were not enough to go around, but the bodyguards were largely happy to go without. As long as the principal was safe, anything else was secondary.

I noticed Gabe Baptiste huddled inside his life jacket. For once he looked as though he'd do anything to avoid being noticed.

Five of the hijackers were kneeling with their hands bound behind their backs, Sean and I keeping a close eye on them. For the most part they were dazed and sullen, as if they couldn't quite work out where things had all gone wrong for them.

There were those who wanted to leave the wounded hijackers where they'd fallen. Humanity prevailed and instead they were brought up and laid on the deck. I daresay the bodyguards who carried them were not as careful of their injuries as they might have been.

It contrasted starkly with the gentle way they handled Blake Dyer as they brought him down from the restaurant with Tom O'Day walking slowly by his side.

I took in Dyer's closed eyelids, the waxy tint to his skin, and could not bring myself to go to his side. It seemed a vicious reminder of my own failure. Dyer's hastily written note dismissing me from his service burned hot in my pocket. Without it, I would be damned, but the prospect of showing it to anyone felt like condemning myself.

Jimmy O'Day was helping people into life jackets, flitting between them. His manner was nervous, twitchy, and did not exactly inspire confidence. Every time he caught sight of movement along the decks he froze. Every time it wasn't Autumn, a little more life went out of him.

He also threw worried glances towards his father, who was staring down at Blake Dyer as if he could will the life back into him. Eventually, Jimmy moved across, tentatively touched his father's shoulder.

"Dad, come on, these people need you."

Tom O'Day did not look up. "My friend needs me."

"Yes, I know, but—"

"Leave me alone, Jimmy."

Jimmy lifted his hand away in conditioned response, then stilled, muttered something under his breath.

Tom O'Day looked up, eyes narrowed. "What was that?"

"I said 'suck it up', Dad," Jimmy said, louder. His head came up. "You need to suck it up." His eyes stayed on his godfather. "Yeah, this is awful, but sitting there doing nothing to stop it getting ten times worse is no way to honour him."

O'Day flinched. "He's not dead yet."

"So why are you behaving like it's all over?"

"Look around you, son. It *is* all over."

"Only if you stop fighting and give up on it," Jimmy said, his voice low but fierce. "Are you going to throw away everything you've worked towards here? That's not the man I know."

O'Day gave a flick of impatience. "You have no idea what I feel right now, Jimmy."

"Don't I? You forget, Dad, I've spent a long time in your shadow, watching how you work. The tougher things get, the better you like it."

"This is not just some business deal," O'Day said. He lowered his voice, aware of an audience. "Blake might die. So might—"

"Autumn's pregnant, Dad," Jimmy said flatly, cutting across his father's words.

That finally seemed to penetrate through the layers to register in Tom O'Day's grief-struck mind. His mouth opened but no sound came out. He swallowed, then said, "Who ...?"

"Who do you think?" Jimmy said, flushed with anger now. "So, if not for me, do it for her. She needs you. We *all* need you. So, like I said—suck it up and get *out* there."

Tom O'Day did not move. For a while I thought he wasn't going to. Jimmy stood over him, hands clenched into white fists at his sides until eventually he let out a ragged breath, started to turn away. But as he did so, O'Day reached out and caught his

271

arm, used it to pull himself to his feet. He patted Jimmy's shoulder without a word and walked forward.

I watched the change come over him as he neared the huddled crowd in the bow. The movement of the deck had become more erratic as the stern of the *Miss Francis* dug deeper into the water and she listed further over. But Tom O'Day's step acquired bounce and confidence.

"Thank you for staying calm, folks," he said. "Our skipper is doing his best to bring us as close in to shore as he can, but it looks like we're gonna make landfall with a bit of a bump, so you might want to hold on to something solid." He paused, gave them a slow smile. "Maybe not quite how we planned this evening to go, but a hell of a thing to tell your grandkids, huh?"

It didn't raise a laugh. But, as people reached for the nearest immovable object and clung to it, maybe just a little of the gathered tension had gone.

Jimmy picked his way aft to us. His face was twisted with anxiety.

"Anything from Vic—has he found her?" he asked without much hope.

Sean shook his head. Jimmy looked about to cry.

"Keep your eye on this lot and I'll go look," I said, nodding to our captives. "Once we hit the shore things are going to get chaotic."

I handed the M16 to Jimmy and unshouldered the MP5K I'd taken away from Castille. The shorter weapon was easier to use for close-quarter work. We couldn't be sure all the hijackers were accounted for. Without knowing their original number it was better to be safe than sorry.

Maybe we shouldn't have let Morton go below decks alone ...

"I'll come with you," Sean said. And when I glanced at him he added, "Someone to watch your back."

I nodded, took in Jimmy's wretched expression.

"Is your father ... the father?" I asked, feeling awkward about it.

"What? God, no." Jimmy's eyes flashed. "It's mine," he said, defiant. "We've been seeing each other for a year. Who do you think put her name forwards for the PR job?"

"Did your father know?"

"Of course not. We were going to tell him tonight—at the party—that we're going to get married." The fire seemed to go

272

out of him, his voice turning forlorn. "He likes her—admires her. I thought maybe I'd finally be doing something he'd be proud of."

I didn't point out that parental approval was a terrible reason to get married. "We'll find her," I said.

I turned, found Sean waiting for me. We stumbled back along the sloping deck and ducked into the lower bar area. Anything that wasn't bolted down had slid to the lower side of the room.

I pushed through the service doors into the stairwell. The increasing angle gave the space a surreal quality. Going lower went against every instinct for survival. We descended anyway.

I glanced back at Sean, following me down. There was an unreadable expression on his face and he was watching me.

"You OK?" I asked. Better than silence, but still a stupid question. He had not been OK for a long time.

Sean stopped. His head gave a little jerk, not quite a nod, not quite a shake either.

"Something Jimmy said—about Autumn being pregnant." His eyes flicked over me and he was frowning. "There's something ... I can't put my finger on it," he said at last, frustrated. "Something about that. All I get are fragments. It means something I feel I should know."

My heart rate accelerated. "Oh?"

He pinned me with an ice black gaze. "*Is* there something I should know?"

Shit. How do I answer that, Sean? Do you really want the truth?

"I was told not to force memories on you," I said. "To let whatever was going to come back do so in its own time." And to leave whatever was never coming back well alone.

He turned into me, crowding me, close enough for him to hear the hitch in my breath, the lurch in my pulse.

"I remember a child," he said suddenly, intense. "A little girl ... Emily, or Emma ..."

The blood was thundering in my ears. "Her name was Ella," I said. "She was the daughter of a principal—someone I was protecting. Apart from that she was nothing to do with me."

She wasn't ours.

He stepped back. I was unsure whether to be relieved or disappointed—either at the action or the line of questioning. I felt my shoulders sag.

273

"But you *were* pregnant, weren't you Charlie?" he asked, sudden as a blow to the chest.

"I—" My first instinct was denial, but I knew he'd seen the truth in my face, my eyes. "Yes," I said finally, my tone flat.

He nodded as if I'd confirmed some vague idea rather than anything more certain. "What happened?"

I took a breath, used it to keep the emotion out of my voice. "I … lost the baby." Such a little sentence to describe all the heartache and confusion.

He still flinched as if I'd slapped him. I put a hand on his arm, wanting to give comfort as much as I needed to take it myself. Perhaps, finally, here was something we could face together.

Sean pulled away from me, then stiffened. "What was that?"

I froze, listening intently, and heard a regular noise like slow uneven knocking.

We dropped lower, moving faster now, and found the galley area. In the rear half of the long narrow compartment dirty water had started to slosh up to ankle level. The surface was rainbowed with oil, sheening in the overhead lights.

The two meat lockers were positioned halfway along. The door to one swung open, clattering back against the bulkhead with every lurch of the ship.

We reached the aperture and I peered inside, a fast look. It was enough to tell me the locker was empty apart from two swinging sides of meat and racks filled with plastic containers. I gave it a longer inspection.

"Someone was here," I said. On the floor was a large plastic zip-tie, cut through and discarded. Even so, it wasn't hard to tell it had been big enough to be fastened around a pair of wrists.

Sean stepped sideways, grabbed hold of the handle to the other meat locker. I nodded and he yanked the door open.

A body lay crumpled in the far corner, face down. It was clearly a man, dressed in black like the hijackers, but it gave me a momentary jolt even so.

"Admiring my handiwork?" asked a voice from the galley doorway.

This time it was Sean who swung round fast, M16 at the ready. Morton just grinned at him. He had picked up a flashlight from somewhere and was wet to mid-thigh.

I glanced back at the dead man in the meat locker. The blood pooling around the body had congealed in the chill.

"Took him out when I got loose," Morton said.

If he was looking for praise, I wasn't about to give it to him. "No sign of Autumn?"

Morton shook his head. "I've been all over this tub," he said. "I don't know how they did it, but I reckon somehow they got her away."

I remembered the Z-boats that had delivered Castille. I hadn't seen them put anybody aboard before they pulled away, but that didn't mean it hadn't happened.

Damn.

"OK, let's—"

The overhead lights flickered a couple of times and went out, plunging the galley into total darkness. It took Morton a couple of seconds to fumble the flashlight on. As he did so, we heard the ragged rumble of the engines finally die away as the water finally flooded the rear part of the hull.

"I don't want to sound like a big girl's blouse," Morton said, "but if we're going to the bottom of the Mississippi I'd rather be topside, if you don't mind."

For once I didn't argue. We stumbled our way back up the stairwell, through the bar and out onto the sidedeck. The lights of the shoreline were suddenly bright and brash ahead of us.

"We're coming in hard!" shouted Tom O'Day from the bow. "Brace yourselves, everyone!"

As I moved forward, Sean put his hand on my arm. I looked at him, surprised.

"I'm sorry, Charlie—about the baby," he muttered stiffly, but they were the toneless words you'd offer to a stranger.

SIXTY-NINE

The *Miss Francis* came ashore like she meant it.

Even with the engines dead, the boat's forward momentum was enough to drive the bulk of her up onto the steep rocky embankment that marked the edge of the Mississippi. The shallow-draught steel hull grated as it rode out of the water, buckling with a drawn-out screech of protest. As the current caught the stern the boat slewed sideways, threatening to topple us over into the river. Out on the decks, we clung to railings and stanchions and willed her not to capsize.

It seemed to take her a hell of a long time to make up her mind about that.

Finally, the *Miss Francis* came to rest at a steep angle, leaning away from the bank. I staggered to my feet. It still felt like she would roll over and slide beneath the water at any moment. I was only too aware that we needed to abandon ship and we needed to do it fast.

I managed to climb uphill to the landward railing and looked out. To my amazement, I recognised the three white spires of St Louis Cathedral almost dead ahead, lit stark against the night sky. We were smack bang in the middle of the French Quarter, maybe half a mile from our original start point.

If Tom O'Day had hoped to keep *this* under wraps, I reflected, he was out of luck.

Behind me, a voice shouted, "We need to get a line ashore!"

I turned. Jimmy O'Day was dragging one of the *Miss Francis*'s mooring ropes towards the side. He started tying one end to the railing.

"Hang on a minute—that won't hold us," I said, untying it again. I passed the rope under the railing and took it back to a more substantial-looking bollard further inboard, trying to remember a decent knot.

I looked over the side. The bow was over land but substantially further out of the water, making for a longer drop onto the rough ground. Further aft the drop was less, but chances were you'd land in the edge of the river and have to wade through the shallows. "You better let me do it."

Jimmy flushed, almost snatching the rope out of my hands. "I can manage."

I shrugged. "Just be careful how you get down there," I said, nodding to the jumble of rocks beneath us. "If you jump from here you'll break your legs."

He looked about to argue, but realised I was probably right. He moved further back along the railing, peering down nervously every metre or so until the drop lessened. He seemed to feel that getting his feet wet was a less scary option. I would rather see what I was about to hit.

"We'll lower you down," Sean suggested, but Jimmy didn't like that idea either. Really, he would have liked to vault over the side with the rope in his teeth, if he'd had the guts for it. The fact that he did not clearly irritated him.

"I can manage," he snapped again.

Eventually he climbed cautiously over the railing and dangled himself down as far as he could.

"Don't dither," I muttered under my breath.

At that moment, the ship gave a judder and slipped backwards abruptly, her stern settling further into the river. The gap between hull and rocks widened as she rolled.

Jimmy let go.

He dropped straight down into the water, stumbled and fell. He slid under, thrashing. The boat started to recover, started to roll upright again.

"Get up!" I shouted, reaching for the railing myself. "Jimmy!"

But Sean was over the side in an instant. He half jumped, half abseiled, using the rope to slow his descent. He still ended up in the water to his waist, grabbing Jimmy and hauling him out from under the ship as she settled onto the rocks again.

He dragged Jimmy clear and left him gasping up throatfuls of dirty water while Sean dragged the rope up the embankment. There were now many hands reaching out to take it.

I hesitate to call the grounding of the *Miss Francis* a shipwreck—it was more of a waterborne car crash. The noise of our arrival had brought people running. Plenty of them. It was close to midnight on a Saturday—a time when the nearby bars and clubs were crammed with revellers. They appeared across a parking area, stepping carefully over the railway tracks that followed the line of the river. First a trickle, then a crowd began to form.

The first people who arrived treated is as some kind of joke, a careless mistake by some pleasure boat skipper that was providing some new form of outdoor entertainment. It only took a few minutes for them to realise it was a disaster in the making.

The mood changed. Almost out of nowhere they produced ladders to lean against the hull. As more of the shocked and frightened hostages staggered ashore, people arrived with chairs, blankets, hot drinks, and sympathy.

Every man and his dog, it seemed, was videoing the wreck of the *Miss Francis* on their cellphone. I wondered briefly how fast this was going to feed out to the late-night news networks and found I didn't care.

We did what we could. Then the police and the paramedics arrived and things were taken out of our hands—firearms, mainly. At least they didn't arrest us all in the process.

It was fortunate we had liaised with local law enforcement in one form or another during our pre-event prep. The prior contact meant they had already vetted us, had a record of who we were and what we were doing. Now, they checked our IDs and seemed prepared to listen to us long enough to keep the hijackers we'd captured contained—temporarily, at least.

At this stage it was the best we could hope for.

And there the good news ended.

Blake Dyer was strapped onto a stretcher and brought ashore as carefully as they could manage. It was still not a smooth journey but he made no sounds of protest. I would have been more encouraged if he had.

The paramedics took him only as far as the nearest piece of flat ground before they began working on him. They slipped a CPR mask over his face and began pumping air into his lungs. I recognised the haste in their smooth, practised movements, and something contracted hard inside my chest.

I sat down on the rocks, tired to the point of numbness, cold despite the muggy heat still retained in the air.

Somebody dropped a blanket around my shoulders. I looked up, found Sean standing over me. He was wrapped in a blanket of his own. His clothing was still dripping.

I nodded my thanks. "Nice save, by the way."

"I would have preferred to manage it without going swimming," Sean said. He reached into a back pocket, brought out a soggy wallet. "One thing to tell Parker about this state-of-the-art new comms system," he added, sliding out the slim-line transceiver. "It's not waterproof."

"Ah, I'll let you tell him."

I peeled out the tiny earpiece. With Sean's unit dead there was nobody to hear.

I realised suddenly that my pocket was vibrating against my side. I reached into it, picked out my cellphone. I was almost surprised to find it lit up and buzzing but I had no difficulty recognising the number.

"You might get that opportunity a bit sooner than you were expecting," I murmured, taking the call.

"Charlie! What the hell is going on down there? I've been trying to get through to you for hours!" Parker's voice was clipped enough to betray him. His anxiety came across clearly when my boss was usually one of the calmest men I knew. In a crisis he was so cool I swear his core temperature actually dropped.

Was this near-panic caused by uncertainty about Sean's ability to perform? Or did it have more to do with far more personal concerns for me?

Either way, not good.

"Yeah, sorry about that," I said, adding blandly, "but the hijackers were jamming us until the boat started to sink." I heard his sharply indrawn breath and gave him the bare essentials, managing to keep it voice flat and neutral.

Right up until I glanced across and saw the paramedics tending Blake Dyer lose their sense of urgency. They sat back with a resigned air, defeated. One checked his watch and pulled the blanket up over Dyer's face. I looked away, my throat burning.

I swallowed. "Parker, I ... I lost Dyer," I said into the phone, interrupting him.

There was momentary silence at the other end of the line. Then I heard him let out a long slow breath. "That's ... not good,"

279

he said at last, unconsciously echoing my earlier sentiment. Parker always was the master of understatement.

I said nothing. There was nothing to say. The weight of my own shame kept me from launching into any explanations. Anything I might have said in my own defence sounded nothing more than a weak excuse in my own mind.

Suddenly, Sean peeled the phone out of my hands. "It wasn't Charlie's fault," he said into it, his tone abrupt. "Dyer was set on playing the hero."

He was holding the phone tight to his ear so I didn't hear whatever response Parker made to that statement. I could guess, though. Something along the lines of it being my job to disabuse a principal of any heroic notions. It's what I would have said, in his position.

After a few moments Sean handed the phone back to me. I eyed him warily as I took it.

"Yeah?"

"You asked about this guy working for the O'Days—Vic Morton," Parker said. I was not reassured by his change of subject. "We've been doing some digging. Is that still relevant, bearing in mind the current situation?"

I paused. Morton had shot Castille. He had undoubtedly saved Sean's life in the process. Was that enough to cancel out other debts?

I said, "What do you have?"

"Well, we didn't turn up anything on the guy himself," Parker said. "He's been keeping a low profile since he got the job."

"Oh." I was aware of an intense disappointment. "Thanks for looking anyway," I added.

"No problem," Parker said. "There was one other thing, though—I'm not even sure if it's worth mentioning. The guy himself has done nothing to set any alarms ringing, but his employers are a whole different ball game."

I remembered my suspicions about Jimmy when we'd found him loose aboard the *Miss Francis*. An image of the hapless Sullivan, tied to a chair with his throat sliced open, flashed into my head.

"What gives?"

"A month ago a considerable sum of money was transferred to an account in the Caymans."

"When you say 'considerable' how much are we talking?"

"Close to a half-million dollars,"

I let out a low whistle. "Yeah, that's not to be sniffed at. But the O'Days are rich people," I said. "Surely they transfer money around to banking safe havens all the time?"

"Not at short notice, when it incurs penalties. Rich people don't stay rich by being careless with their money."

I frowned. "And he might be the son and heir, but I didn't get the impression that Jimmy had much personal money of his own."

"Who said anything about Jimmy?" Parker said. "Morton works for Marie O'Day."

SEVENTY

I can't believe Marie has anything to do with … all this," Tom O'Day said. "It's ridiculous."

"Can't believe", I noted, not "don't believe".

"Why would she move that kind of money around in a hurry?" Sean asked.

"I don't know—some piece of art she wanted to buy? If it came onto the market unexpectedly maybe," O'Day said, but even he didn't sound convinced.

Sean and I said nothing. The silence worked at O'Day better than any arguments would have done. He stared with unseeing eyes at the milling rescue workers, the medics and police. The fire department had been called in to secure the *Miss Francis* until some kind of marine salvage operation could be organised. She sat at an angle on the shore with her bow pointing defiantly upwards, almost jaunty.

They'd sent bomb disposal experts on board to check for more explosives, but with half the hull under water there was only so much they could do. We'd all been moved back to the far side of the parking area, just in case. The waft of fresh coffee from the nearby Café du Monde was almost enough to take the scent of death out of my nostrils.

The body of the man from New Jersey had been recovered from the deck, but Castille's had not. I could only assume he'd been swept into the river as the *Miss Francis* started to slide under. I was glad I'd had the opportunity to check that he was really dead.

"Morton would know," O'Day said suddenly. "Until Jimmy's guy got sick, Morton was with Marie full time. Went everywhere with her."

"So why didn't he say anything?" I demanded. *Unless he's in on it …?*

282

"I don't know," O'Day said again. He sounded tired. "I guess that's a question you'd have to ask him."

Oh, I intend to.

I whirled away, started moving through the crowd looking for Morton. I'd last seen him industriously helping bring people down off the *Miss Francis*, wrapped in blankets. Playing the bloody hero. How ironic was that?

Sean caught up with me inside half a dozen strides, snagged my arm. "Aren't you overlooking something?" he said tightly. "What about Autumn Sinclair?"

"She's still missing."

"Is she?" Sean asked. "Or does she simply not want to be found?"

I felt a flush of anger—or was it fear? "What would she have to gain?"

He shrugged. "Power?" he suggested. "With Tom out of the picture and her claws already into Jimmy, she's suddenly in a pretty strong position." He paused, added, "And what proof does Jimmy have that she's actually pregnant?"

"That's enough," I said, surprised by the snap in my own voice. "*You've* no proof she's lying about that. You've no proof she's involved at all—"

"And you've no proof she isn't," Sean fired back. "She disappeared off the boat in the middle of a hijack. What is it about this woman that you're defending her? If it was anyone else you'd be suspicious. Instead, you're determined to put the blame onto Vic Morton."

I pulled away from him. "People don't change their basic nature," I said. "Not that fundamentally."

"So where does that leave us?" Sean asked. He stared at me for a moment, shook his head in frustration. "You *have* changed, Charlie. You're not the girl I remember. The way you threatened to take out Baptiste's arm ... You're harder, more ruthless."

My instinct was to get in a fast verbal blow—that if I'd changed then it was because he'd shaped me, coached me, to let go of my hesitations and regrets. To act decisively in high-threat situations.

To kill when it was called for.

And maybe when it was not.

I didn't want to go there. Deliberately, I latched onto the reference to Baptiste, believing it was safer.

"If I hadn't threatened Baptiste, do you think we would have got the truth out of him?"

"Torture rarely produces the truth—only a version of it. The version they think you want to hear."

He sounded so certain, so sure.

A flutter of images passed my eyes like a film projector running at half speed. Of Sean threatening to torture a man who held my mother's life in his hands. Threats are nothing without intent. Had our victim not believed absolutely that those threats would have been carried through, they would have been useless.

As it turned out, they had not been useless. At the time even *I* had believed Sean would not falter.

But now?

I realised that I'd been wrong when I said that people don't change on a fundamental level. Sean had changed. Not just his recollections of me, or even his emotions, but his character.

I'd spent the last few years of my professional life trying to be more like him. And just when I thought I'd finally succeeded, I discovered the Sean I'd known was gone.

As you said, Sean, where does that leave us? Where does it leave me?

I shivered despite the balmy night. "Sean, I—"

"Hey, Sean! Charlie!"

We turned together, found Jimmy O'Day hurrying towards us.

"Have you seen Morton?" I asked.

"What? No," he said. "He's about here someplace." He looked round, distracted. "Dad needs you."

We followed him back to Tom O'Day, now clutching a cup of coffee with both hands, as if he too were feeling the cold. He looked up as we approached. I saw the worry in his face.

"I can't raise Marie," he said. "She's supposed to be back at the hotel. I wanted to ask her ... I know she has nothing to do with this, but I need to know that she's safe. Will you ... bring her here?"

I heard the contradictions beneath the words, the uncertainties and the pain.

"Why us?" Sean asked.

O'Day shrugged. "My own guy is dead," he said flatly. "Morton's place is with Jimmy." I flicked my eyes to Jimmy, standing alone, but nobody mentioned the fact that Morton seemed to be neglecting his duty in favour of personal glory. "Just bring her here—that's all I ask."

"What if she doesn't want to come?" My question was double-edged.

Tom O'Day met my gaze with more bravado than confidence. "She'll come."

SEVENTY-ONE

Sean and I took a cab back to the hotel. Tom O'Day had given us his key card, but we knew we couldn't verify his wife's presence from the front desk. The system in place dictated that any enquiries about guests would be passed on to their security staff immediately, no exceptions. I couldn't complain too much about that, though. After all, we were the ones who'd insisted on it.

We split up in the lobby. Sean needed to go back to his room to change out of still-damp clothes. He headed for the elevators. I decided to take the stairs up to Marie's suite on the sixth floor. There was a feeling of urgency niggling away at the back of my mind that wouldn't let go.

I pushed my tiredness aside as I jogged up the first flight. I knew I was the only one who suspected that Vic Morton might be wrapped up in this. And being totally honest with myself, I didn't know if the reason behind it was my own bitter experience with the man. Had he changed?

OK, so he was dismissive of his client and still seemed on the cocky side, but he'd certainly stepped up when it mattered.

On this occasion.

I remembered again the way Castille had gone down, when just for that split second I'd thought it was Sean who'd taken the hit. Morton could easily have let Castille shoot the pair of us if he'd wanted to. Could have waited until a fraction afterwards to kill Castille, and still made himself out to be the hero.

He could have done.

But he didn't.

Why?

I kept heading upwards. The stairs were formed concrete covered in thin corded industrial carpet. No frills. My feet were almost silent as I moved.

Unfortunately, so were his.

I don't know what warned me—a change in the air pressure, maybe even a faint scent of something. I'd reached the fourth floor, started to turn up onto the flight leading to the fifth. I was almost to the half landing when my stride faltered.

Vic Morton stepped into view above me. I don't know which of us was more startled. Just for a second his face betrayed him. His expression cracked and I saw not just loathing but fear, too. It was not a pretty combination.

"Fox!" he said, forcing a rueful smile. "Can't believe I ever thought I'd say this, but am I glad to see you." His eyes went to the stairwell behind me. "Meyer not with you?"

I eyed him warily. I was in a poor defensive position and didn't like it much. I moved up onto the landing so we were on a level, put the wall at my back.

"No," I said, not inclined to explain where Sean had gone. "What are you doing here?"

The smile faded. "I spotted the blonde sneaking off the boat. Can you believe it? Definitely something dodgy going on. I thought I'd follow her—see what her game was."

"Autumn?" I said blankly. *Autumn Sinclair.* I didn't want to believe she had a game at all. "Everyone in their right mind was getting off the boat—what's dodgy about that? And I thought you couldn't find her."

"I couldn't," he said. "Which means she had to be hiding, right?"

Or you're just not very good at searching.

"So you walked away from your principal without a word, leaving him unprotected in a crowd of strangers, while you went swanning off to play detective?"

He flushed, moved in closer, sneered, "I don't think you have any room to lecture me about how to protect a principal, Fox, do you?"

My hands ached to act, to strike. I ignored the temptation presented by the vulnerable sweet spots of the point of his chin, the side of his jaw, his nose, eyes, temples, ears. Instead I took a breath and said, "You didn't answer my question."

He shrugged, recognising the avoidance mostly for what it was. "This is where she came," he said. "Went straight up to O'Day's suite."

287

Which might or might not be true. *Nothing to be gained by arguing at this point.*

"OK." I glanced around, stabbed a finger towards my feet. "But what are you doing *right here?*"

His jaw tightened. "On my way to call in reinforcements," he said. "After everything that's gone on tonight, you never know what that bitch is planning next, eh?" He tried another smile, seemed disappointed when that didn't work any better than the first. "Besides, Mrs O'Day's got Thad with her—Jimmy's usual guy. He's not bad, providing nobody feeds him anything with nuts in it."

Jimmy's official bodyguard had fallen sick just before this trip, I remembered—conveniently sick—and Morton had stepped in as a last-minute replacement. The cynic in me wondered how much he'd had to do with that.

But ...

He could have let Castille kill you, I reminded myself again. *He didn't.*

"OK," I said at last, my tone still cautious. "Let's go and see what she has to say for herself, shall we?"

He stepped back with a mocking half bow, gestured to the stairs leading upwards. "After you."

I made no moves to go first, just gave him a level gaze. He pulled an apologetic face. "Yeah, well can't blame you for that, I suppose," he said over his shoulder as he started to climb. "I'll tell you one thing, though."

I started up after him, still wary. "What's that?"

Morton put both hands on the railing and jacked his lower body up, punching down and back with both feet, aiming for my head and upper body.

I ducked instinctively. My change in pace threw off his aim. The heel of his shoe caught my cheekbone, scuffed past my ear. The other foot hit me square in the chest. My ribs imploded as the air blasted from my lungs and I went down in a twisting tumble of limbs.

I tried to go loose, to remember all those break-falls from the martial arts and self-defence training I'd done.

The corded carpet was still thin and the concrete steps underneath it were still bloody hard. I smacked down brutally on elbows, hips and knees, bounced into a heap and lay there for a moment. My back was wedged painfully against the corner of the wall by the exit to the fourth floor. I fought to catch my breath.

Morton jumped the last few steps and booted me almost casually in the ribs as he landed. The jolt of pain was electric. I fell back, gasping.

"Yeah," he said cheerfully, nodding down at me. "I think that about covers it."

SEVENTY-TWO

I said nothing. I didn't have the breath to speak.

Being taken by surprise was different to being surprised. In truth I realised I'd been expecting this moment—something very like it—since the first time I'd laid eyes on Vic Morton again at Ysabeau van Zant's mansion.

A painful image of him shaking hands with Sean just before we'd left the reception flashed into my mind. So that was something else Sean seemed to have lost along with chunks of his memory—his judgement of character.

I managed to get one hand underneath me, started to push myself off the floor. Morton waited until I was nearly there, then kicked at my elbow. I saw it coming just early enough to let the joint fold before he struck. My face hit the floor, but at least he hadn't succeeded in breaking my arm.

I turned my head, scraping my already grazed cheek against the rough carpet, and looked up at him. He was not close enough for me to do anything about, but too close for comfort. He was breathing fast through his nose and his hands were clenched rage-tight.

"Going to finish what you started?" I asked, my voice still wheezy.

We both knew I wasn't talking about now.

"Oh, don't tempt me," he muttered. "I've dreamed about doing this ever since I saw your name on the list for this thing. That was weird—actually seeing it there in black and white because you've been fucking haunting me for years."

Whose fault is that?

A bubble of laughter forced its way out of my mouth bringing blood with it. I'd bitten my tongue but let him think it might be something worse.

"Finally growing a conscience, Vic?"

290

He ignored the question. "If there's one thing I regret it's that we didn't kill you when we had the chance and put you in the ground somewhere out on Pen-Y-Fan where you would never have been found," he said calmly. "If I'd known the stink was going to follow me around for years afterwards ..."

No words of regret for the rape itself, I noted bitterly. Or for what effect it might have had on me, either at the time or in the intervening years.

The pain had settled back from piercing to dull. I took a shallow breath and sat up in one movement, not letting him get the boot in again.

Morton stood over me, almost casually, balanced on the balls of his feet waiting to strike again. I knew I shouldn't do anything to antagonise him while I was at such a tactical disadvantage.

Sod that.

"I was the one who was court-martialled," I pointed out. "I was the one thrown out in disgrace."

"And yet here you are now, working for one of the best outfits in the country. Do you know what it's cost me to have my record cleaned up so I can get *any* kind of a job in this industry?" he demanded. "And sod's law says when I do—just when I think I've got it made—I run across someone who was around at the time, or heard about it from a mate of a mate, and then I'm being shown the fucking door again. All down to you."

I took in his words in silence for a moment, realisation settling over me. Then I shook my head, managed a small bitter laugh. "Bollocks," I said. "That's utter bollocks and you know it, Vic. The reason you keep getting shown the door is because you talk big but when it comes down to it you're just not good enough, and you won't admit it."

He took a step in closer. "You're in no position to get smart with me, you little bitch."

I watched him without fear, bolstered by the knowledge that I was right. I'd been a better soldier and now I was a better bodyguard, and the fact burned him until I'd become his personal nemesis—the reason for all his faults and failings.

I made a limp gesture with one hand. "And how is ... *this* going to help you?"

He blew out a frustrated angry breath. "You think I don't know you'll have put the word out? That I won't be out on my ear again by Monday morning? By which time you'll be back in New

York or wherever—all nice and cosy and out of reach. I reckoned this was my last chance to give you a kicking."

I thought of my conversation with Parker. He'd offered to do exactly what Morton feared—to have him blacklisted. I'd settled for a quiet word in O'Day's ear, but the effect would have been the same. Morton would indeed have been sent packing.

So, was this little more than straightforward revenge? Do unto others before they do unto you. Was that it?

No, I realised. That was never going to be it.

"How much did Castille pay you?" I asked instead. "To tip him off which flight Baptiste was on."

Morton stared down at me for a moment. He was trying to keep nothing in his face and not managing it well. I caught glimpses of nervy surprise, fear and a kind of weary resignation.

"How do you work that out?" he asked, a challenge more than a question.

"Because I saw Castille kill Ysabeau van Zant, and I know she was the one who got him onto the boat. But somebody else tipped him off about the helo flight. And that someone had to be you."

He shrugged. "Plenty of people on that rooftop. Could have been any of them."

"But you've got a rep, Morton, for being able to supply whatever a client wants. In this little corner of the world, Castille seems to have been the go-to guy. That means you had to know him. And he knew you—that you had a price. He missed Baptiste in the parking garage, didn't he? So he wanted a second bite."

Morton smiled, little more than a bitter twist of his lips, but instead of the denial I'd been expecting he said, "Ah well, it's not easy saying no to a guy like Castille. He's had a hard-on for the kid since the whispers first got out that Baptiste might have been around when his brother bought it."

"So you sold him out," I said. "What about John Franks? What about the other people on that helo?"

If anything, the smile widened and I knew he was thinking of the fact that I'd been one of those extra passengers. A bonus, clearly.

"Franks was a pro—he knew the risks." He shrugged again. "And everyone has a price, Charlie. Even you."

292

I shook my head. A mistake. It made the world tilt and waver slightly. I waited for it to level out, said tightly, "I don't think so."

He laughed out loud then. "Course you do. Only with you it's more of a weak spot rather than a price, isn't it? Sean Meyer."

My heart rate jolted. I didn't answer. That was an answer in itself and both of us knew it.

Morton nodded as if I'd spoken. "Only trouble is he doesn't remember you, does he? If he did, he wouldn't have let me get away with saying a word against you. Don't take it personally, though—he can't really remember me, either, can he? Not *really* remember. Or Gabe Baptiste for that matter. Tell me, Charlie—does it eat you up inside that you only got half of him back?"

"I don't know, Vic," I said, putting everything I had into keeping my voice level. "Does it eat *you* up inside that he's still twice the man you'll ever be?"

His face pinched. He hooked his free hand under my good arm and wrenched me to my feet. I allowed him to yank me upright and deliberately overbalanced into him, stumbling against his legs.

His hands dropped automatically to block me, just in case I was about to bring a knee up into his groin. Instead, I reached over the top of his guard and chopped the straight edges of my hands into the sides of his neck.

A relatively light blow to the vagus nerves and the main arterial blood supply to the brain is enough to disorientate an opponent. I'd given it just about all I'd got and was mildly disappointed that Morton had stayed on his feet, albeit semi-conscious.

The shocked eyes and unfocused stare told me he was out of it. Even if he hadn't quite realised it yet. I opened his jacket and patted him down. He made a half-hearted attempt to bat my hands away. I found a folding pocket knife in his trouser pocket, and a Glock 9mm in his jacket.

I dropped the knife inside my own jacket, stepped back and slid the magazine out of the Glock. It had one in the chamber and a full load. Something about the gun bothered me, but I couldn't put my finger on it. I shook my head, slotted the mag back into the pistol grip.

Morton, meanwhile, had slumped back against the stairwell railing, legs beginning to fold.

We were four floors up. Behind him, the drop was around twelve metres—forty feet—straight down onto the bare concrete floor at ground level. The stairwell was deserted and not covered by security cameras—no doubt part of the reason Morton had felt free to attack me there in the first place. I had the bruises to prove it.

Do it. Do it quickly. Do it now.

I got as far as putting my forearm across his throat, starting to arch him backwards over the railing. I looked straight into his eyes as I did so. He returned the stare glassily, barely comprehending.

Who would know?

Very slowly, I relaxed upright, let Morton straighten. He did so gasping, bending forwards to catch his breath, trying to lessen the buzzing in his ears, the haziness in his brain. I was pretty sure he had no idea how close he'd just been to dying.

And still the words echoed bitterly inside my head.

Who would have known?

I would.

SEVENTY-THREE

Morton was still shaky as I prodded him along the fifth floor corridor towards the O'Days' suite. Just before we reached the doorway, I halted, forcing him to halt with me.

"So why *didn't* you let Castille kill the pair of us—back there on the boat?"

He glanced at me and laughed softly. "Never had anything personal against Meyer," he said. "And I needed someone alive to tell the world what a fucking hero I was. In fact, I'm kinda hoping he might offer me a job. Seeing as how I was the one who saved his life when you didn't have the nous to take the shot."

I didn't bother to repeat there was no clear shot to be taken. We both knew that already. "And you expect he might—even after all this?"

"Why not?" he demanded. "Better than having me running round loose, telling the world how your lover boy is so brain-damaged he can't even remember who he's killed."

There had been enough rumours about Sean's state of health already, and the close-protection industry thrived on gossip. Could Sean survive this?

Would he want to?

Even so, sheer bravado made me ask, "What makes you think anyone would believe you?"

He shrugged, apparently unconcerned. "Why not? Meyer came over here and walked straight into partnership with Armstrong when there was plenty of home-grown talent who thought they should have been in with a shout. Put a lot of noses out of joint. They can't wait to see him fall." His eyes flicked over me. "And if he goes, so do you."

I didn't point out that he had so nearly been the one who'd fallen—four storeys straight down onto concrete.

I hoped my regret would fade over time.

"I earned my place with Parker's organisation," I said, "and I keep it on merit, not sentimentality."

"Shagging him as well, are you?"

I sighed. "Just open the bloody door."

His tone was mocking. "What makes *you* think I have a key?"

I shoved the business end of the Glock into his groin, not gently. "As a member of the O'Days' security staff you have a key to all their rooms," I said. "Don't make me ask again."

I left the Glock where it was while he reached into his jacket pocket. He moved slow and careful.

I took the card he offered and slid it into the electronic lock, waited for the green light to blink and pressed the handle down. The door swung open soundlessly. I nudged Morton through the gap ahead of me.

Inside, the first thing I saw was the body of a man lying face up in the hallway. He was so close to the entrance to the suite that the door bumped his foot.

The dead man was young, muscular, dressed in a suit with the jacket flipped open to reveal a white shirt and sober tie. He wore a paddle-rig holster on his right hip. It was empty. The gunshot that had killed him had been fired into his chest at very close range. His white shirt was stippled with powder burns. There was very little blood. His expression was one of frozen open-eyed surprise.

Through it I recognised him as the guy who'd accompanied Marie O'Day to Blake Dyer's suite after the Bell crash. Thad. I guessed nut allergies were no longer a worry for him.

Rule one, page one—first kill the bodyguard.

"Shit," I heard Morton mutter. "That *bitch* ..."

My mind still flinched away from the possibility that Autumn was behind all this. She'd been the last person I'd suspected. She already had it all—why kill for more?

Because no matter how much some people have, it's never enough.

I pushed Morton forwards roughly. We stepped over the unlucky Thad's legs and ventured further into the suite. I tried to keep my spatial awareness broad, not let the tension narrow my focus.

Sean was sitting on one of the upright chairs at the small dining table. He was very still, with both hands on the tablecloth in front of him, fingers spread. His eyes tracked us as we came into view, flicked sideways towards the bedroom doorway to his right. Apart from that he didn't move. I could read nothing on his face.

I didn't ask what was going on. I didn't need to. A woman appeared at once from the bedroom. She was wearing one of the thick white towelling robes the hotel provided. It contrasted strongly with the ratty straggle of her hair, her dirty face and bare legs—completely at odds with her usual effortless style.

Also not her usual style was the fact she was holding a hammerless compact-frame Smith & Wesson revolver in both hands. It was pointing firmly at the back of Sean's head.

"Hello, Autumn," I said, keeping my voice conversational. "Want to tell me what the fuck is going on?"

"I could ask you the same thing," she said with surprising composure.

"What happened?" I asked. "How did you get off the boat?"

"I have no idea," she said. "One minute I was being hustled out of the casino and shoved into some kind of a storage locker on the *Miss Francis*, and the next I woke up here, bound with tape." She lifted a shoulder. "I guess they must have given me something."

"Nice story," Sean said through his teeth. "But I arrived to find you standing over a dead body with a gun in your hand."

"Believe what you want," she snapped. "When I got loose Thad was already lying there dead. He was wearing this in an ankle holster." She nodded to the revolver she was holding, still pointing at Sean. "You really think I could have taken a gun away from a professional bodyguard if he'd still been alive?"

"Why not?" Morton said casually. "Thad was Jimmy's guy. You knew him pretty well—must have been well enough for him to let you get too close."

There was something sly in his voice I didn't like. Autumn liked it even less.

"You always were a slimy little bastard—"

"How *did* you get loose?" Sean interrupted.

She switched the gun into her right hand and held up her left, back towards him, fingers straight. On two, the nails were raggedly broken off, but on the others she had a set of talons like a wolverine. Duct tape has plenty of tensile strength, but slice it and it's easy enough to tear.

So it was possible she'd escaped by herself, yes.

But likely ...?

"Where's the knife?" Sean asked. His voice was harsh and cold. It set the hairs riffling along the tops of my arms, the back of my neck. I glanced at him, wary. His jaw was set rigid, eyes narrowed.

"Sean, we don't know that—"

"Shut up," he said.

And suddenly I was back at the Stress Under Fire course we'd taken only a few weeks before. He'd said the same words to me in much the same way. Morton had been right—there were times when Sean didn't remember me at all. Or—worse still –he remembered me only with contempt.

I swallowed, picking my next words with care.

"We need to know where Marie O'Day is," I said, keeping my voice neutral. "Tom sent us to find her—remember? To make sure she's OK."

"Why—you think I killed her too?" Autumn laughed, short and sharp with an edge of hysteria to it. "Jesus, Charlie. I thought, of all people, I could rely on you."

She ducked sideways, shifted her aim so now she had both Sean and me covered with the revolver. Her grip had a practised look to it and her aim was steady. I watched the tendons in the backs of her hands begin to stand out as her muscles tightened.

"You *can* rely on me," I said quickly, trying for calm and hearing only a quiet desperation in my own voice. "But not like this. Please, where's Marie?"

"She's safe."

"You're covering for her," Sean said with quiet vehemence. "Marie O'Day arranged the hijacking as a cover to have her husband killed and you're covering for her."

"What? No!" The revolver jerked dangerously in Autumn's hands. Her voice was low and shaken. "Marie would never do something like that."

"So why has she been transferring money to the Caymans unless it was for the payoff?"

Autumn's surprise was evident. Her arms started to drop, letting the gun slide off target.

Sean shoved his chair back and came to his feet abruptly. My heart bounced into my throat, half expecting Autumn to squeeze the trigger in nothing more than involuntary reaction. I brought the Glock up fast. She caught the movement, her attention split between us.

Sean dived for the gun in Autumn's hands, wrapping himself into her body and bringing his elbow back hard into her sternum. Her grip released instantly. She fell back, gulping for breath.

"Sean, for God's sake—she's pregnant!"

"We only have her word for that," Sean said. "Easy to say—harder to prove." And I knew he wasn't just talking about Autumn now.

"I'm sure we can arrange medical reports if you need to see them," I said icily, and I wasn't talking about Autumn either.

I helped her to stand. There was a low sofa just behind her and I manoeuvred her onto it without meeting resistance. The fight seemed to have gone out of her along with the breath.

Behind me, Morton said, "So, what kind of a deal have you two ladies come to, that she thought she 'could rely on you', Charlie?"

I turned, ready to give him a mouthful. Only to find that Sean had moved across to stand beside Morton, and was now pointing the revolver at me.

SEVENTY-FOUR

I straightened, taking my time about it. The Glock was still in my hand, but gripped loosely by my side. For all his problems there was nothing wrong with Sean's reflexes. If anything he was more tightly wound now than he'd ever been. I knew if I made any attempt to bring the gun up he'd react solely on instinct. I would become a viable threat to be eliminated.

Again I wasn't sure if he really knew who I was.

Or what difference it would make if he did.

By his side, Morton's eyes flicked between us, gleeful and predatory.

"Can't trust 'em, mate," he murmured. "They scheme behind your back and the next thing you know, you're out in the cold. Happened to me, happened to you. Going to happen again ... if you let her get away with it."

"Get away with what, Morton?" I demanded.

"Obvious, isn't it?" he said, his eyes still on Sean. "The blonde tries to get rid of O'Day, has her claws into the son and heir, and suddenly she's in control of a multimillion-dollar enterprise. And when it all goes wrong she hightails it back here to disappear Mrs O'Day as a convenient scapegoat."

"You're mad," Autumn said faintly. "I love Jimmy. And I told you—Marie's safe."

"Maybe the wife's in on it too," Morton said. "Wanted rid of the old man and knew she'd get bugger all if she went for a divorce." He allowed his gaze to trail over me briefly. I had the urge to scrub where it had passed. "Made you a nice fat offer, did she, Charlie? You going to be her new head of security? Convenient, good old Rick Hobson getting his head stove in, now wasn't it?"

300

"But Tom O'Day isn't dead," I pointed out. "Because *I* got him out of there. Why would I do that if I was playing any part in this?"

Being goaded into defending myself was a mistake. I realised that as soon as I saw the gleam of triumph in Morton's eye. By then it was too late to call it back.

"Didn't say you were in on it from the start, but you were never slow on the uptake, were you? Always had an eye to the main chance. Hooked into Sergeant Meyer here fast enough back when we were training. Needed him on your side if you were going to make it. Dropped him like a hot brick when the shit hit the fan though."

"That's not how it happened and you bloody well know it," I said. A trace of anguished frustration had slithered into my voice. It made me sound desperate, maybe even a little guilty. I didn't like it but there wasn't much I could do.

Morton was spouting lies with a straight face and an earnest tone, just like he'd done at my court-martial, and later at the equally disastrous civil trial I'd allowed myself to be talked into. Why hadn't I remembered what a good liar he was?

Sean was showing me nothing except the muzzle of a loaded gun. I tried to ignore it. My fingers tightened slightly around the pistol grip of the Glock. My only hope, I reasoned, was to give Morton enough rope and pray he'd hang himself.

"Come on then, Vic, let's hear your theory on what's going on."

He grinned as if I'd just played into his hands. "Bluffing right to the end, eh, Fox?" he said. "Got to admire your nerve if nothing else."

"Why not start with how you tipped off Castille about the helo trip so he could bring it down?"

"Nice try, but that must have been that tart van Zant," Morton said without a flicker. "Castille's been blackmailing her for years—ever since he was funding her run for office years ago. Why else would she give up her seat as soon as Baptiste got on board if she didn't know it was all going to kick off?"

His confession in the stairwell, it seemed, was for my ears only. I stared at him, saw the momentary satisfaction and realised he'd done it deliberately, to make me suffer more.

"But—"

"Looks like this is an all-girl conspiracy," he said to Sean. "Mrs O'Day provides the funding to get rid of her husband

301

because of the punitive pre-nup. Autumn there arranges the hijack. And Charlie comes on board, as it were, at the clean-up stage."

"You're Mrs O'Day's bodyguard," I pointed out. "Surely if she was arranging to have her husband killed, you'd know all about it?"

For a moment I thought I saw a flicker of annoyance, of conflict, pass across Morton's face. Admitting he'd missed something and done a slipshod job did not sit well with him.

"Hey, when she's at home I don't follow her round the house like a bloody lap dog," he said.

"And how the hell would I arrange something like a hijack?" Autumn burst out. "I work in PR, for God's sake."

Morton shrugged. "Maybe you recruited poor old Hobson. Fluttered those pretty baby blues at him, got him to find you some manpower willing to do the job. Just your bad luck he used local muscle and Castille decided to screw the pooch."

"So who killed Hobson then?" I asked. I fought to keep my voice reasonable. "He'd been with Tom O'Day for ten years. You really think he'd betray his principal so easily?"

"Who knows? Maybe he was just in the way, or had an attack of conscience and had to be got rid of? Even a woman could have done it—if they'd blindsided him."

"You are so full of shit, Morton, I'm amazed your teeth aren't floating."

The grin widened. "Who was it said that insults are the last resort of someone who knows they're fighting an argument they can't win?"

"How is Charlie mixed up in it?" Sean asked suddenly. I barely recognised his voice. The emotionless tone of it sent my stomach plummeting.

"Sean, I'm not," I said quickly. "I swear to you, I'm not."

"She was going to let Castille kill you," Morton said softly. "You were *there*, mate. You saw it. She wasn't going to back down. If I hadn't stepped in and saved your bacon, she would have gone through you to get to him. What kind of cold-blooded bitch does that?"

"It's how she was trained," Sean said. He frowned, as if his own words surprised him. "Charlie always was ... determined."

302

"Determined to save her own skin, more like," Morton scoffed. "I thought you and she were supposed to have a thing going. Well, back there you could have fooled me."

Sean's head lifted a fraction. It was the first sign of a mistake on Morton's part, a misjudgement. The tension was closing up my throat. I had to swallow before I could speak.

"If I'd put down my weapon, you know as well as I do that Castille would have killed the pair of us before we'd drawn another breath," I said carefully. I kept my eyes on Sean, willing him to believe me, to believe *in* me. "Not giving up is how *you* trained me. How you've always trained me."

"Is that why you're still fighting now—even after the battle's lost?" Morton asked. "Face it, sweetheart, you sold out. Maybe you reckoned that getting rid of Meyer would clear the way for you and your boss to get it together, eh?"

My head snapped towards him. Part of me knew it was just a follow-on from his previous jibe, out in the corridor, but my reaction was betraying, even so. I saw it register in Sean's face, his eyes. He'd walked into the apartment back in New York that day and seen me with Parker and he'd known then on some subconscious level that our relationship had changed.

Parker and I had grown closer over the months of Sean's coma. Apart from a fleeting kiss things had gone no further. And yet I'd always feared that if—*when*—Sean woke he would sense the change in us. It had both relieved and saddened me beyond measure when he did not.

Until now.

Morton watched the minute effects of his throwaway line on Sean and played his next card with casual skill.

"What will you do with Armstrong when you're done with him—roll him up and throw him away?" He paused, deliberate. "Or take a blade to him?"

The calculating way he spoke had me drawing in a sharp, audible breath.

There was no way Vic Morton could know how close I'd come to having my throat cut—unless Sean had told him. It happened long after my army career had come to its wretched end, and well before my close-protection career began. So why had he mentioned a blade with that particular emphasis, that particular tone?

I remembered Sullivan, sitting tied to his chair with his throat opened up wide. The man from New Jersey, drowning in his own blood.

And I remembered …

No…

"Maybe we should search her," Morton said.

"You just try it, sunshine," I warned, my voice low.

He threw Sean a brief smile, as though I'd just confirmed his suspicions.

Morton nodded to Autumn. "The blonde can do it—empty out her pockets. See what she's hiding."

"Sean—"

"Do it," Sean told Autumn, cutting off my protest.

She approached me warily. I didn't shift my gaze from Sean's, even as I felt the pull of my jacket, her hand dipping into the outside pockets. She retrieved my hotel key cards, the comms earpiece and the slim wireless transmitter that went with it, earning a narrow-eyed look from Morton.

She put the items on the table and stepped back. "That's it."

"The jacket has an inside pocket," Sean said.

Oh shit …

Autumn pulled back my lapel and reached inside. Her fingers stilled as they bumped against steel, her eyes flying to mine.

Then she withdrew her hand, turned and laid the folded lock-knife on the table with the rest.

Morton moved forwards, picked up the knife and flicked the blade open. It had been wiped but there were clearly still traces of blood on it. He showed the evidence to Sean, eyebrows raised.

The silence that followed was thick and deafening.

"You know damned well that I just took that away from you in the stairwell, before we came in here," I said. I moved my right hand slightly, a twitch rather than anything that could be misinterpreted, just enough to draw attention to the Glock. "The same time I took away your gun."

Morton put the knife back on the table and shook his head, his expression almost one of pity. "Not my gun—when I'm armed I carry a Beretta." He pursed his lips, added quietly, "Thad always carried a Glock, though."

And there it was. I heard the last piece of his double-cross slip into place and lock there with a noise like a coffin lid being nailed down.

I murmured, "You bastard," and brought the gun up fast and smooth. I sighted automatically on the centre of Morton's face, where the round would enter through his upper lip and take out his brain stem on the way through. It was better than he deserved.

All the time, I expected the monstrous report of the revolver in Sean's hands, the impact of the bullet ploughing into me.

He'd always been good. If I was lucky I'd know nothing about it.

SEVENTY-FIVE

The shot never came.

I risked a quick look. Sean was still on target, the muzzle of the revolver pointing straight and level at my head. I could see his finger inside the guard, the whiteness around his knuckle as he held the pressure on the trigger. He was a hairsbreadth from firing.

But he did not fire.

It was more of a second chance than I thought I'd get.

So don't waste it then.

"Morton got most of it just about spot on—with one very big difference," I said. "He was talking about himself, not me. Isn't that the secret of the believable lie, Vic? Stick as close to the truth as you can?"

Morton stood apparently relaxed inside the confines of my sights. He looked supremely confident. To me, it only confirmed his guilt. An innocent man should have been more worried about having a loaded gun pointed at him by someone he claimed was guilty of multiple murder.

Instead, he knew I hadn't done it. Maybe didn't even think I was capable of it.

Should have pushed him over that bloody stairwell when I had the chance.

I kept my eyes on Morton, but when I spoke it was directly to Sean.

"Back on the boat, when we found the guy from New Jersey— you remember what he said?" I asked. "He said, 'I never expected *him* to double-cross us.' Remember?"

"Castille," Sean said.

I gave a fractional shake of my head, not willing to lose my aim. "I don't think so. As soon as Castille came aboard New Jersey must have expected him to do the dirty on them. It wasn't

306

part of the plan. And once it all started to go bad, he never would have let Castille get close enough."

"Castille was fast with a blade," Sean said grimly, "as Blake Dyer found out to his cost."

I felt his accusation like a punch in the chest. "Blake Dyer was a civilian," I said. "New Jersey was a pro. With Castille he would have been on his guard. But even he didn't expect a double-cross from his own inside man."

Morton smiled. "Nice try, aren't you forgetting one thing? When they dragged Jimmy out of there I was the one tried to stop them and took a hammering for it. Why would they do that to their own *inside man*?"

"To make it look good," I said. "And for someone who's had such a hammering, you seem to me to be moving pretty freely."

Sean said nothing. I couldn't tell from a quick sideways glance if he was convinced or not.

I was suddenly overcome with weariness, sapped by his ambivalence into a reckless bravado.

"Morton is the one with previous ties to Castille," I said. "And I'll bet when Parker starts digging he'll find connections between Morton and the New Jersey guy, too."

I let the Glock come up off target, uncurled my finger from the trigger and leaned forwards to set the gun down very precisely in the centre of the table, spinning it so the pistol grip was away from me. I was looking straight at Sean while I did it.

I heard Autumn let out a low groan at my surrender. I'd almost forgotten she was there.

"I did not do this, Sean," I said simply. "And if you don't *know* that—can't bring yourself to trust me enough to believe that—then you may as well shoot me now in cold blood. I'm not going to provide you with the excuse to do it any other way."

Just for a second he tensed. I saw the intention spread from his shoulders, down his arms towards his hands. I almost shut my eyes, forced myself to keep them open. If this was the end I wanted to see it coming.

And then, right at the last moment, Sean hesitated.

Morton had been watching his every move with a triumph he barely managed to conceal. Now the frustration that passed across his face was fast but deep.

"Just shoot her, for fuck's sake! Finish it, soldier!"

But if he'd been expecting Sean's military background to make him follow orders without question, he was disappointed. Somewhere within Sean's fractured memory that automatic obedience had been long since broken. And instead a certain independent stubbornness had taken its place, as I'd found out for myself.

Slowly, Sean lowered the revolver, turned his head and pinned Morton with a cool dark gaze.

"Finish what, Vic?"

"This! All of it." He waved a hand towards the gun and the knife on the table. "Come on, mate. I thought you had more bottle than this. She ruined your army career."

"No, I don't think she did." Sean's eyes flicked back to mine and for the first time I saw something recognisable within their depths. "If anything, Charlie ... saved me from it."

I'd managed to keep it together right up until that point. Those words were nearly my undoing.

Morton turned away from him, letting out a long breath of disgust. "Well, if that's the way you feel about it, there's nothing else I can say except—"

Abruptly, in mid-sentence, he whirled for the table, reaching for the Glock. He snatched up the gun, swung it towards Sean in a smooth arc as his finger looped around the trigger.

I froze, unable to move or shout. There was nothing I could do. I saw it all happen in slow-motion and my imagination immediately turned it into a terrible replay of the shooting that had so nearly ended Sean's life back in California. A random, snapped-off shot, taken in haste and desperation. The endless possible repercussions streaked away into the distance like missile trails.

Two shots cracked out, so close together they might have been one. The noise of them was devastating in the interior of the room. Autumn screamed and flinched back, hands covering her assaulted eardrums.

Morton fell, twisting. At the same instant, Sean dropped back and disappeared from view behind the table.

No!

I leapt for Morton, kicking the Glock out of his grasp as he tried to raise it again. My foot connected hard with his wrist. I heard the bones snap and was fiercely glad. His other hand was clamped to his chest. The blood was already beginning to leach out past his fingers.

I looked for Sean, hoping for the best but fearing the worst.

He was on the ground, feet braced, leaning back, with the revolver still gripped in his hands. It was pointing unwaveringly at Morton. Sean looked dazed, as if he couldn't quite work out what had just happened.

But whole.

I took in the unfocused eyes, the sudden tremble in his hands, and approached with caution. "Are you OK?"

He didn't answer for a moment, then he sat up, gave me a brief shaky nod without meeting my eyes. "He missed," he said. "What about—?"

"Don't worry—you didn't miss."

Morton had subsided slowly backwards, rolling a little as he attempted to escape the pain. If his gasps were anything to go by it wasn't working well for him. He was cradling his broken wrist with his good hand and pressing both arms tight against the wound to stem the bleeding. I noted with a certain dark satisfaction *that* didn't seem to be working brilliantly for him either.

I bent over him, pushed his hands aside. It had been a close-range shot, but both targets had been moving fast. Sean had aimed for centre body mass, textbook style. The round had entered Morton's chest high on the left-hand side and must have missed his heart by fractions.

The similarities with the stab wound Morton had inflicted on the man from New Jersey were not lost on me. Without medical intervention the lung would soon collapse. He was already gasping for breath and would continue to struggle, slowly and painfully, until he physically couldn't take in enough air and he suffocated. It would not, I realised cheerfully, be a pleasant experience.

I'd almost found out that for myself, first hand.

"He might live, he might not," I said, my voice dispassionate. "Depends on whether he gets treatment."

Autumn was rubbing her hands along her upper arms as if she was cold. "We should leave him," she said abruptly. "Louisiana still has the death penalty anyway. Why make the state pay the cost of a trial?"

"If he ever gets to trial," I said, thinking of the man who had so nearly killed Sean. He'd squirmed away from justice by making promises to Homeland Security he'd never intended to keep. "And if he doesn't lie his way out of it."

Again.

"If he survives, he *will* come to trial," Autumn said. "You think Tom O'Day would let him get away with this?"

"I don't know," I said. "There's going to be an awful lot of dirty washing on public view. As his head of PR, is that what you'd advise?"

"Probably not," she said. "But as his friend? Yes I would."

"You've no proof," Morton managed, starting to struggle to draw breath. "No witnesses ... You got nothing."

"Do you honestly think modern forensics won't find any links between you and the victims?" I said. "And everyone in the crowd was videoing the wreck of the *Miss Francis* on their cellphones. Do you think you managed to get Autumn off the boat and back here completely unseen?"

Morton's eyes closed briefly, as if he were praying, and he mumbled, "No proof."

"If he cut them, his DNA will be on the knife," Sean said.

Morton's eyes opened again. Every breath was making him shudder with the effort, achieving less effect. "Course ... just picked the fucker up."

I shook my head. "Cutting people is a messy business," I said. "You made a mess of Sullivan, didn't you?" I murmured, thinking of the hesitation marks on the man's neck. I'd assumed they were the result of someone who was not a pro. Instead, they were the work of someone without the courage of his convictions.

"There's always transfer," I said. "Just picking up the knife in here wouldn't account for any other blood evidence they find— and you can bet they'll fly in the best forensics experts in the business for this one." I paused, kept my voice level, trying not to let the satisfaction, the vindication, show. "Face it, sunshine— you're fucked."

I leaned in close, lowered my voice so it reached his ears only. "And you're going to find out all about gang rape in prison, Vic. But somehow I don't think you'll enjoy it quite so much when you're on the receiving end ..."

I was rewarded with a flare of genuine emotion in his eyes. Fear. I straightened up, retrieved the Glock from across the room where it had come to rest when I'd kicked it from his hand.

"Stay or go—we need to make a decision," I said, terse. "I'm amazed the police aren't here already."

Sean nodded. "If there's anything you need to take with you," he told Autumn, "you'd best get it now."

"There's just one thing," she said. She moved past him into the bedroom, rapped loudly on the door to the bathroom. "Marie," she called. "It's OK. You can come out now. It's safe, I promise."

After only a moment's hesitation we heard the door unlock and Marie O'Day ventured out into the room. She was in her nightclothes. There were remnants of duct tape still attached to her wrists and she looked frightened but lucid.

She came out cautiously into the living area of the suite, stopped when she saw Vic Morton lying bleeding on the floor. For a moment her expression was stricken, then it hardened.

"Oh, Vic," she said softly. "Why?"

Morton gave her a derisory stare. There was blood in his mouth now, on his lips and staining his teeth. He spat out a gob of it before he could speak. "You were going to … get rid of me," he said. "Heard you talking about the … new Mrs O'Day." His eyes shifted to Autumn. "Her."

"Of course," Marie said sedately. "She's going to marry Jimmy."

Autumn gaped at her. "How did you—?"

Marie smiled. "A mother always knows," she said.

Autumn smiled. "I do love him," she said sincerely.

"I know you do, my dear, however well hidden the both of you thought you had it."

"What about the money?" I asked. "The half a million you moved to the Caymans."

She looked at Morton again. "Why do you think I came down here?" she murmured. "I trusted him too much."

"You lent him the money?"

"No," she said, looking embarrassed. "I can never remember passwords or account numbers at the best of times. While I was ill, the medications made me more confused. Vic became as much a personal secretary as bodyguard. I–I trusted him a little too much," she admitted candidly. "I never thought to question how *helpful* he'd become—until I got a phone call from my bankers."

"Theft on a grand scale as well—this just keeps getting better and better," I said. "OK, let's get him a doctor."

"No."

I turned, looked back at Morton. "No?" I repeated.

His gaze was fixed on Sean. "No medic," he said. "Just ... finish it. Please, mate ..." He lifted his hands away from the wound. A fresh welter of blood bubbled out and slid across his shirt. He was down to a breathy whisper now. "I'm halfway there ... Get it done."

Sean got to his feet slowly. He glanced almost numbly at the revolver in his right hand as if he'd forgotten it was there, forgotten what it was for.

I remembered Castille's brother, Leon, and the confession I'd forced out of Gabe Baptiste back on the *Miss Francis.* I wondered if Leon had used the same words, the same plea, when he'd demanded that Sean save him from a lifetime of paralysis, dependency, and frustration. A coward's way out, making a mockery of all those who endured and overcame.

Autumn looked at each of us. "Surely you're not going to—?"

"You wanted to leave him to die," I pointed out. "What's the difference?"

Before she could answer, Sean shook his head. "If he wants to die, he can damn well do it himself."

He thumbed out the cylinder and emptied all the rounds into his hand, then reinserted one only, pocketing the rest. He closed the cylinder, rotating it so the live round was uppermost. "Gather your stuff," he said to me.

"Charlie," Autumn protested. "You can't let him do this."

"Why?" I said. "Yes, Morton should stand trial and go to Death Row for what he's done, but you know as well as I do that could take years. This is justice, of a sort."

It's closure. And I've already waited a long time for it.

Autumn turned to Marie, as if expecting her to plead for reason. "Marie?"

"He's a thief and a liar and a cheat," she said, her voice calm. "But he was also a soldier, and I can understand him wanting to die like one."

And without revealing your foolishness in public, I considered, but didn't say so out loud.

I shoved the comms gear and key cards back into my pocket, leaving the knife on the table. Sean put down the Smith &

Wesson revolver, with its single loaded round, about a metre from where Morton lay. For a moment Sean looked at him without speaking, then turned away.

I paused. "Any last words, Vic?"

"Fuck you," he said.

"No thanks," I said, cold and clear. "Been there, done that. Didn't think much of it."

We stepped around Thad's body, unlocked the door of the suite and went out into the corridor. The door clicked shut behind us.

We were halfway to the stairwell when we heard the gunshot.

EPILOGUE

The hijacking of the *Miss Francis* and all that entailed was still a hot story when Sean and I returned to Manhattan.

I don't think New Orleans had been in the headlines as much since Katrina itself.

The news channels constantly played the shaky hand-held footage, shot in the dark, showing the stricken paddlewheel boat sitting at an awkward angle, bows-up on the shoreline like she'd hit the French Quarter at ramming speed. People poured over the side like refugees, clambering to solid ground and being gathered up to safety by the waiting crowd. The reports were cleverly intercut to show the wealthy in their bedraggled finery, with their shocked and frightened faces, being comforted by the local population.

It was powerfully emotive stuff.

The donations had been flooding in to the After Katrina Foundation ever since the story broke. Tom O'Day's delight was only tempered by the loss of his long-term bodyguard, and of his friend.

Blake Dyer's widow had threatened to sue us, and I couldn't say I blamed her for that. Tom O'Day flew down to Miami to speak to her personally. I don't know what he said but after that all mention of a lawsuit was dropped.

It wasn't much of a consolation—for anyone involved.

Sean and I had spent the next week still in Louisiana, kept apart while we underwent countless interviews—bordering on interrogation—by local and federal law enforcement agencies. By the end of it they'd pretty much accepted our assertion that Vic Morton had planned the hijack and recruited the man from New Jersey and his crew. It would seem he'd intended not only to pocket the haul from robbing the guests, but also to lay in enough of a trail leading back to Marie O'Day over the death of

314

her husband that she'd be wide open to blackmail afterwards. He'd made the unauthorised transfer of money from her account to the Caymans with that in mind.

But whatever his ultimate plan, he wasn't around to ask.

The feds were not happy about that, but we told them blandly the Smith & Wesson must have been dropped and forgotten in the confusion, that our first priority had been to get the two civilians, Marie O'Day and Autumn Sinclair, out of the way and to safety. They didn't like it, but there was no question Morton pulled the trigger of his own volition, so no charges were brought against us.

Gabe Baptiste claimed his very public "confession" had been made under duress and was pure fabrication, told in an attempt to save his own skin. It did not do his sporting hero status any good, but it probably saved him facing a murder rap. He didn't mention the fact I'd threatened to finish his career by splintering his throwing arm, though, so I assumed what he'd told us then was the truth. I asked Parker to keep him blacklisted.

The flight back to New York was crowded, affording no privacy and little time for Sean and me to talk. We both slept for most of it anyway. I felt like I could sleep for a month.

It was only the following morning, over early coffee in the apartment, that we had sat down and finally talked to each other. Really talked, probably for the first time since he'd come out of his coma. We were on opposite sides of the breakfast bar in the kitchenette off the living room. We'd sat like that many times in the past, preferring it to the more formal dining area. Now the positioning felt both claustrophobic and adversarial.

"I'm sorry—for not trusting you," Sean said out of nowhere as I handed him a cup of fresh Jamaican Blue Mountain. I'd acquired an expensive coffee habit from Parker.

"You don't really know me," I said. "How could you trust me?"

He put the coffee down on the countertop in front of him and linked his fingers together. "I'm ... confused. No—I find a lot of things confusing—not quite the same thing." He stopped, took a breath. "It's like I can't trust myself to know what's right any more."

"You could have killed Morton and you didn't," I pointed out. I didn't express an opinion on whether that was right or wrong. I still couldn't work out if I was glad the man was dead or disappointed that I hadn't been the one to finish him.

315

"I found I ... couldn't do it—take a life in cold blood." Sean stilled, looked straight into my eyes. "However much I felt I should."

Both of us knew he wasn't only talking about Morton and a tiny shiver rippled along my spine. "In that case, perhaps I should be thankful for small mercies."

"He was convincing," Sean admitted. "And it didn't help that all I remembered about you was an overwhelming sense of betrayal. It still ... lingers."

I sipped my coffee and said nothing. We sat in silence for a time. Outside the windows of the apartment, down in the streets below, came the usual sounds of traffic threaded with the occasional wailing siren like an urban lullaby.

"It scares me, Charlie," he said at last. "This job, this life, it needs a ruthlessness that I don't seem to have any more. Did I ever really have it?"

"Yes, you did."

He nodded, his lips twisting. "It must have made me a right bastard to live with."

"You had your moments," I agreed sedately. "But it was a part of who you were, Sean. I knew that and accepted it."

He nodded again, more uncertainly this time. He was frowning. "But ... I loved you?" It was a question not a statement. The past tense made my heart contract into a hard, brittle knot inside my chest. "I was capable of that?"

"You were."

Silence overtook us again. There was so much I wanted to say but the words wouldn't come, wouldn't form. I leaned on my elbows and sipped more of my coffee, both hands clasped around the mug as if trying to pull strength from it.

"I need time, Charlie," Sean said. "Ever since I came back I've felt under pressure to fulfil a role that feels completely alien to me. I see the constant anxiety in your eyes, in Parker's. Like you're willing me to somehow just ... snap out of it."

"Sean, I—"

"I'm not saying you're doing it deliberately. But I still don't know how much is left of the person I was before—there might be nothing at all. But the snatches I get ... to be honest with you, I'm not sure how much I *want* there to be."

The irony of that was not lost on me.

Just when finally I become more like you, you become less like yourself.

"There was nothing wrong with the way you were," I said, gently.

"If Baptiste is to be half believed, I killed a wounded man without a second thought."

I took a breath. "Where does that leave …?"

"Us?"

"Everything." The single word seemed stark against the high ceiling of the apartment. I gave a helpless shrug in an attempt to soften the effect. "Life, work, us. All of it."

"I don't know," he said, his gaze level. "I think that's more up to you."

I didn't understand but I nodded anyway, trying not to let the bewilderment show. "In what way?"

"You rang Parker from New Orleans and asked him to recall me," he said. "Told him I wasn't right—wasn't ready."

"I had … concerns," I admitted. "Parker told me to sort them out on the ground."

"Yeah." His voice was dry. "And look how well that worked out."

"It wasn't your fault, Sean. If you want to blame anyone, blame that tosser Vic Morton. He set the whole bloody mess in motion."

"We're paid to anticipate trouble and to prevent it," Sean said. "Aren't we? But in that case I failed on both counts."

There was a stubborn set to his jaw I recognised of old. It troubled and infuriated me in equal measure, made my voice snappier than it should have been.

"What are you saying—that you want me to tell Parker you're not up to the job and save you having to make your own decision?"

"That's something only you can decide, Charlie. But I don't want another dead principal on my hands—or my conscience." He paused. "Do you?"

Inside my head I saw again the paramedics pulling a sheet over Blake Dyer's body, the weary defeat in their eyes. Another battle lost.

I pushed up from the breakfast bar and put my empty coffee cup in the dishwasher, using the excuse of tidying away to give myself time to think. No useful thoughts came.

317

When I straightened I found Sean watching me. "Losing someone always hurts—it's supposed to," I said. "As for what I'm going to tell Parker, well, until he asks the question ... I don't know what my answer will be."

I found out later the same morning. We weren't due into the office for our official debrief until the afternoon. Sean had gone out for a run, leaving me alone with my troubled thoughts.

When the buzzer at the apartment door sounded, I knew before I glanced through the Judas glass that it was going to be Parker. Only he had a key to get past the ground-floor security.

I tried to suppress my dismay, took a deep breath and opened the door.

Parker's face broke into a genuine smile at the sight of me. "Charlie," he said. "You're looking good."

"Thank you," I said. I stepped back before he could close in on me, aware from the flicker in his face that he'd registered it. There was very little Parker missed. I kept my voice pleasant, light. "Come on in. I'm afraid Sean's not here at the moment."

He moved past me into the living area, looking around. "I had a feeling he might not be," he said candidly, turning to face me. "I confess I was hoping I'd catch you alone."

"What's on your mind?"

He studied me for a moment, eyes shrewd as he took in my businesslike tone. I watched him mentally readjust, and somewhere inside my head I heard a door closing very softly.

"I'm sorry to disturb you at home," he said, more formally, "but we need to discuss Sean—his performance. I wanted to do that outside the office."

"Of course," I said. "How have things been affected there?"

He shrugged. "Purely from the agency's point of view things are not as bad as they might be," he said, matter-of-fact. "O'Day's PR people seem to be giving us an easy ride." He allowed himself an austere smile. "Maybe the fact you saved Ms Sinclair's life has something to do with that."

"I should have let you put the word out about Morton earlier," I said. "We might have managed to cut him off at the knees before he could do so much damage."

"I think this game was already in play well before anybody got to New Orleans," Parker said. "And Sean seemed to think he was OK."

318

I realised for the first time that Parker had been in contact with Sean while we'd been away as much as he'd been in contact with me.

Should have expected that.

"It was a difficult situation for Sean," I said. "His memory of Morton is far different now to what it was before. He only remembered him as an OK kind of guy. And don't forget that Morton was going out of his way to reingratiate himself."

"Nevertheless—"

"In the end, Sean came down on the right side."

Parker frowned. "But just how much of a close call was it?" he asked softly.

My brain was revving in time with my pulse.

"Until he asks the question ... I don't know what my answer will be."

I moved across to the wall near the window, leaned my shoulder against it and folded my arms as I regarded him. "It was close," I admitted. I lifted my chin, looked my boss, my friend, straight in the eye and ignored the stab in my heart. "Sean's undergone a change in mindset, certainly, but his reactions are still fast and his instincts are sound."

Parker continued to frown. Then he nodded, a little sadly. "That's ... good," he said. "I'm happy for him."

Parker knew, I realised. I wanted to go to him, but how did I explain the unexplainable? That—as Morton had pointed out—I may have got only half of Sean back, but he still had all of me.

And somehow it seemed like he needed me now more than ever before. Even if he didn't really know it.

"I'm sorry," I said at last. The words seemed hopelessly inadequate.

Parker, to his credit, managed to raise something that resembled a smile. "Don't be," he said. "I'm happy for you both."

By supporting Sean, I realised, I had almost certainly burned my bridges with Parker. I remembered Autumn Sinclair's offer, if I ever decided to go out on my own. I never expected to be giving it serious consideration.

At that moment I heard Sean's key in the front door. He appeared in the hallway, still breathing hard and sheened with sweat from the exercise. He looked as though he'd pushed himself to a punishing pace.

"Hi, Sean," Parker said. "I just called by to check you guys made it home OK. But I won't cut into your personal time any longer." His glance took in both of us. "I'll see you in the office later."

"No, I'm glad you're here," Sean said. "I guess you two have been talking about me."

Parker said nothing, which in itself was a confirmation.

Sean nodded as if he'd spoken. "I've been doing some heavy thinking," he said. His eyes met mine and I was surprised to see a lack of conflict there. The dark depths were almost tranquil.

"Sean—"

"I don't know what Charlie's said about the way things went down," he said. "But I really don't think I'm cut out for this job any more ..."

ACKNOWLEDGEMENTS

As always, although writing may seem like a solitary occupation, it could not be done without the help and support of other people.

In no particular order, therefore, I would like to thank fellow author and firearms expert, Tony Walker, for providing valuable information about Stress Under Fire courses; SWAT team leader Luke Causey for great insights into SWAT training; fellow author Kate Kinchen, and her husband Ben, for letting me into the Secret Ways of Ninjitsu; fellow author John Billheimer for sharing his knowledge of baseball; Phil Shuter for letting me know which golf clubs make the best real clubs; Murderato Allison Davis for New Orleans and legal info; Jane Hudson at NuDesign for the brilliant eBook cover; and to the wonderful Toni McGee Causey and her husband Carl for giving me the guided tour of the bits of New Orleans *not* usually seen on the tourist trail. Oh, and the crawfish!

Retired pilot Andrew Neal provided such terrific detail on how to crash a helicopter—most of which he knows from personal experience—that the least I could do was allow him to fly my fictional helo in this book.

My test-readers worked tirelessly, as always, to dig up the plot-holes. I am forever indebted to Peter Doleman, Claire Duplock, Derek Harrison, Sarah Harrison, Kate Kinchen, P.D. Martin, Caroline Moir, and Tim Winfield for reading through the first draft with such care and attention. And also all the members of the Brewhouse Writers Group in Kendal, who gave their input as I went along. A special thank you to eagle-eyed John Dowling, who set me straight.

My US publishers, Pegasus have been unfailingly enthusiastic in their support. I would very much like to thank Claiborne Hancock—the only person I know in the publishing industry who replies to email at weekends—as well as Jessica Case, and my careful and attentive editors, Maia Larson, Pat Sims and Liz Hatherell, who have undoubtedly worked towards making this a far better book than it might otherwise have been. Dosier Hammond, Director of Library Sales and Marketing at distributor WW Norton also deserves special mention. Thank you all.

And finally, I was honoured and delighted to be able to include Tom and Marie O'Day as characters in this novel. Tom made the winning bid at the charity auction held at Left Coast Crime in Santa Fe, New Mexico in March 2011. The auction benefits ReadWest Inc, a non-profit literacy agency.

Zoë Sharp opted out of mainstream education at the age of twelve and wrote her first novel at fifteen. She became a freelance photojournalist in 1988 and wrote the first of her highly acclaimed Charlie Fox crime thrillers after receiving death-threat letters in the course of her work. She has been nominated for Edgar, Anthony, Barry, Benjamin Franklin, and Macavity Awards in the United States, as well as the CWA Short Story Dagger. The Charlie Fox series was optioned for TV by Twentieth Century Fox. Zoë blogs regularly on her own website, www.ZoeSharp.com, on the acclaimed group blog, www.Murderati.com, as well as wittering on Twitter (@AuthorZoeSharp) and fooling about on www.Facebook.com.

If you've enjoyed DIE EASY, why not try this brand new standalone crime thriller from the highly acclaimed author of the bestselling Charlie Fox series?

THE BLOOD WHISPERER — winter 2012
by Zoë Sharp

They took everything she had, but not everything she was ...

Six years ago, London crime-scene investigator Kelly Jacks woke next to the butchered body of a man with the knife in her hands and no memory of what happened.

She trusted the evidence to prove her innocent.

It didn't.

Now released after serving five years for involuntary manslaughter, Kelly must try to piece her life back together. Shunned by former colleagues and friends, the only work she can get is with the crime-scene cleaning firm run by her old mentor.

But old habits die hard.

Sent to eradicate all trace of the apparent suicide of Matthew Lytton's wife at their country home, she draws unwelcome parallels with the past. The police are satisfied, but Kelly isn't so sure. She wants to trust Matthew, but is he out to find the truth or to silence the one person who can expose a more deadly plan?

Kelly quickly finds herself plunged into the nightmare of being branded a killer once again. On the run from police, Russian thugs and local gangsters, she is fast running out of options.

But Kelly acquired a whole set of new survival skills on the inside. Now she must use everything she knows to evade capture and stay alive long enough to clear her name.

"Zoë Sharp is at the top of her game"
New York Times bestselling author Harlan Coben

Lightning Source UK Ltd.
Milton Keynes UK
UKOW031438040613

211746UK00007B/33/P